Second Edition

Published June, 2012.

ISBN: 978-0-9881090-1-8

Printed in the United States of America.

thank you
谢谢

musicians & writers & artists around the world

mom & dad, for writing genes

jess & alicia & ken & danny,
for the skinnies

the zurevinskis

saskatoon & changchun & zhuhai friends,
for all the things you've helped me see & learn & feel

joy, 我想你

kristen,
for your heart

I

After high school I tried to get a job. So did Tiff. We spent the summer applying at places like Aunt Mandy's Dry Cleaning and Chuck's Diner at the motel near my place on the outskirts of Sloam. I didn't care where I worked as long as I wasn't pumping gas at Enginergy. Because of my flimsy resume, most of them didn't call me. Because I wore my best friend's sister's Nikes, some of them did.

Tiff got lucky midway through August; this ritzy new coffee shop in Elmview, just past Oakwood Heights, hired her on the spot. I was in the bathroom at the time, dabbing my sweat mustache and pinning my hair back. When I came out and begged to be a part of Team Bean, the manager with her bouncy brown ponytail and polyester apron said they'd only had one position available. Tiff got a tour and met her new coworkers while I caught the next bus and listened to Alexisonfire at full volume, picking at the fraying brown leather bus seat and trying not to think about punching fellow passengers.

A few months later, I was on my way home from a job interview at the downtown One Buck Store--the third interview I'd ever scored in my seventeen years of life. Down the sidewalk I went, kicking the few leaves the trees had lost. The manager was a frail blond lady who wore a pastel-blue windbreaker and called me Hon. She shooed me out after five minutes.

You'll hear from us later this week, Hon.

I wondered what she meant by 'us' and if it really took more than one person to run a store that sold stationery and hair-ties.

I took off to the main bus terminal downtown, where graffiti on the schedule for Route 84 prevented me from reading it. Some genius had scrawled Life blows in a black Sharpie. October brought more cold than it should have, sucking the patience out of me. I didn't have a jacket. Hopping on the spot didn't help, because all I could think over and over was This little piggy went to the market; this little piggy stayed home. At the time I had a blister between my second and third smallest toes, the one that had roast beef and the one that didn't. When I put pressure on my foot it stung, so I gave up hopping and ducked into the drug store on the corner.

Fluorescent lights welcomed me, humming and blaring. I spent the next three minutes pretending to look for the ideal shade of nail polish. I had no money and definitely no interest in buying makeup. I glanced out the window every few seconds, all the way down Main Street, the direction my bus would come from. I couldn't wait to go home and invite Tiff over to curl up on my basement sofa and watch movies.

Then Raizel happened, that dismal autumn day when even the sun wouldn't happen. I had become bored of the cosmetics aisle and the old guy at the cash register who peered over like a dare to steal. I couldn't blame him, me in my faded Nirvana sweater, baggy jeans all soggy at the bottom, and Nikes too clean for the rest of the ensemble. The worst part was my backpack--entering a store wearing a backpack was like wearing a sign.

I'M A THIEF

I shuffled away from him and his stare, down the fourth aisle where I could pretend to be interested in cough drops and laxatives. Another employee was stationed there, putting items from a cart in their according spots on the shelves.

I gave her a double-take, looking, and then looking away, and something about the image compelling me to look again. Closer. And closer. My cheeks felt hot. Her back was turned and she didn't notice me. I took the opportunity to stare at her hair. She had the blondest locks I'd ever seen, wavy and elegant and just long enough to brush her shoulders, an electric blond halo that made me think of those snowflake decorations people dangled from their light fixtures at Christmastime. I didn't know hair could look so good under fluorescent lights. I dragged my feet down the aisle. I tore my eyes off the back of her head, fixating instead on the rows of boxes and bottles of pills and syrups, playing with my backpack straps.

In my peripheral she turned toward me. Tiny parts of my body and face became warm as she looked, although I couldn't discern whether she was looking or her eyes were just passing over. She didn't return the double-take, assumedly because I was extremely regular--slightly heavy, slightly gapped two front teeth, a sheet of scraggly brown hair, gray eyes. If I had stayed in the cosmetics section I'd probably have found that the cover-up matching my skin was labeled Coffee Stain. But not as rich as coffee; my skin was like the kind of stain that's been spat on and wiped at. My cover-up would probably actually be called Skid Mark.

The hair dye was an even funnier story, Midnight Kiss, A Taste of Cocoa, Sunshine Blond. In grade ten I had messed up my hair with bleach and had subsequently dyed it black. Blackest Black, back then that's what the names on dye boxes were, no beating around the bush. I'd inherited my natural mushroom-brown hair color from my mother--more the color of mushroom mushrooms than grocery store mushrooms. The difference between grocery store mushrooms and mushroom mushrooms was that mushroom mushrooms cost a whole lot more and made regular things seem terrific.

Unfortunately, they weren't really a terrific color. My natural hair color made people yawn. I'd originally wanted to be blond, but when I couldn't have that I'd settled for black. As everything did, my hair had faded. Mushroom brown was my apparent fate.

While pretending to read the instructions on a pack of Gravol, I peeked out of the corner of my eye. The girl with the hair was facing me. Curiosity made me look over and scan her from head to toe. Scratch that--toe to head. She wore something most people wouldn't dare to wear, 'most people' meaning anyone with a touch of self-consciousness. She had on tall, bright red Doc Martens, tights, a beige cardigan. Under the cardigan, a pearl necklace dangled down the front of her blue Main Street Pharmacy smock. The tights were the best part, these sheer black things that clung to her slender legs, speckled with cupcakes like a pair I'd worn as a little girl.

I was taken aback by the fair skin stretching across her collarbone and up her neck. Everything about her was so *light*.

I imagined her saying, Take a picture, it'll last longer, and I'd miraculously take some high-tech camera out of my backpack to photograph her eyes facing sunlight, luminescent. They were deep, the color indistinguishable at a glance, framed by dark lashes. And they were definitely pointed my way

Did you know you can get high off those?

I thought she was talking about her eyes, and I nodded. My nod felt dense; my head bobbed without thought. Then it occurred to me that she was talking about the Gravol in my hand. I switched things up and started shaking my head.

For real?

I knew Gravol had something to do with nausea, because my mother kept some in the cupboard. I flipped the pink and white package over in my hand, scanning the back.

Yeah.

Her Doc Martens brought her over a pile of Benodryl to stand beside me. Take ten, and you're good to go. She toyed with her pearls, adjusting them around the back of her neck.

How do you know?

I felt like I had no choice but to look at her face. I noticed a labret piercing, a small silver ball under her bottom lip. She was shorter than me, and petite, but her voice exuded unusual sureness. She looked like one of those girls strangers approached to ask if they'd ever tried modeling. She was so unbelievable, in fact and opinion alike, that if a unicorn was to transform into a person it would look exactly like her. I wondered why she would talk to *me*.

Trust me; it's wicked. Hallucinations and shit.

At that moment I looked past her head at the rack of handheld mirrors and saw dozens of reflections of the street and its mess of traffic, SUVs and trucks and buses. I squinted into a small round Goody mirror and saw a city bus plowing down Main Street. I whipped around and saw the Route 84 bus.

Shit. I gotta go.

The girl had turned away to continue shelving, and merely waved her hand when I spoke. I felt myself blush for the second time and I fled down the aisle and out the door, the nosey cashier's eyes drilling holes through my pockets.

When I got on the bus I didn't care that it was packed. I had to sit beside an old man whose lips squished together like oatmeal when he smiled at me. Throughout the twenty-minute ride, my mind replayed two words like a scratched CD.

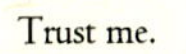

Trust me.

2

Tiff came over at seven that evening, toting with her a backpack of hang-out stuff, a box of Pizza Pops, a bottle of apricot lotion so we could rub each other's feet, and slippers for afterwards because I didn't have any. We lugged the stuff downstairs.

My basement lair: wooden stairs with spaces between where toys had been lost countless times while my brother Dana and I were growing up. A baseball-sized hole in the wall had been particularly fond of our belongings. When I was little my friend put my only Barbie doll in there, Hollywood Hair, feet first so all we could see was the head when we shone a flashlight in. That was the beginning of my resentment for Cecile Grey. By the time my fingers had grown long enough to reach in and pull on a strand of polyester doll hair, I was too old to play with Barbies. I'd taken her out and put her back in like I did bruised apples from the bottom crisper of our fridge.

A left turn off the bottom stair led onto the orange and brown checkered carpet so thin I could feel the cold of the cement below. I had long since blamed that carpet for the persistent smell of Old and for attracting ants in the summer. Random shit was framed and hung up on the off-white walls, an old Guinness advertisement, a painting of a duck, and a map of Europe, as if anyone in my immediate family had ever made it that far. Against one wall was a red couch with drooping arms and sunken cushions, beside that a brown armchair that rocked if you swung your weight the right way, a little window up near the ceiling, and under that the computer and the television with its wood-paneling and obnoxious metal dials.

Through the doorway with a Mexican bead drapery and down the short corridor there was half a bathroom, just a toilet and sink and a mirror with a little cabinet. The last time we'd had a towel in there for drying hands, when the tiles were a clean peach hue devoid of water stains, was before my mother had become so busy with work. At the end of the hall was a little room with a washer and drier and a closet full of things like Twister and VHS Disney Movies and boxes of Goosebumps books, and hangers upon hangers of floral-patterned dresses with shiny buttons in rows down the back and collars that looked like doilies. They had belonged to my grandmother on my mother's side.

Tiff and I sat on the couch the way we always did, legs crisscrossing so the quilt would cover us both. I raised my eyebrows when she pulled from her bag a couple of cranberry Bacardi Breezers, incessantly reminding me of the summer.

On a hot June day, my best friend and I and three hundred other kids are at our high school graduation ceremony. Not kids, young adults, as the principal refers to us in her speech. Students cling to their friends and shake hands with their acquaintances. Parents weep unabashedly. For me, the importance of the whole thing is that I'm finally getting away from a big bunch of imbeciles, teachers and students alike.

My mother attends the grad ceremony, sitting in one of the higher balconies in the theater. All of us students have to sit in the long rows directly in the front of the stage. I wonder if my mom's crying up there, weeping on another kid's father's shoulder about her baby growing up. We each have to walk across the stage while the parents snap a thousand pictures to choose from for their fireplace mantels, perhaps next to a portrait of Aunt Lucy or Max the Dalmatian. Our house doesn't have a fireplace or mantel.

Tiff takes a couple of pictures, but her last name is Abraham and that lands her a front row seat. Photographs from that angle make me look more double-chinned than usual. I end up thankful that there's no mantel on which to place those pictures.

Tiff and I have both chosen not to attend the grad supper or the grad dance. I turned it down the minute the notice appeared in our classrooms back in February, and when I informed Tiff of my choice, she decided she also couldn't go. She didn't admit she was afraid she would have no one to talk to if I didn't go. People tend not to pay attention to girls like Tiff--by which I mean girls who can't work up the courage to say anything when spoken to; plus, her facial expressions sometimes make her come off to others as a bitch. Tiff has complained to me about it more times than pictures I have taken, which says a lot. Her behavior bugs her, but apparently she can't do anything about it, so I've diagnosed her with terminal shyness. I'm one of the few people she'll talk to, which she only ever does because we were designated art class partners on the first day of grade ten. She once told me that when she's at work she just turns off the shyness, like a button on a radio, and forces herself to talk to customers.

The teacher draws names for pairs and I swivel in my chair to get a look at my partner. She makes no effort to come my way. She wears a black sweater zipped up to her chin, apparently trying to look dark despite her flowing, flaming hair and the brightly paint-splattered walls surrounding her. I trek to the back of the class where she's hunched over on a stool.

Hi. I'm Venice.

She rests her chin on the table and peers at me over a pair of square gold-rimmed glasses too large for her face. Her eyes are green apples and her mouth is small, closed.

Are you Tiffany? I think we're partners.

Still, she stares. I shift my butt on my seat and turned my stool so I can face the front of the room again. Oh, Mr. Marshal. Why have you paired me with someone who thinks she's King Shit? She's very small and her cheeks look as though she's sucking in, but not in an I-need-to-eat way. After receiving the assignment, I turn to Tiffany again. We are each supposed to paint a picture that we think reflects one another, according to the first things we say about ourselves.

I clear my throat. When her eyes fall to the floor, she doesn't look so freaky. Cute, even. I find it easier to speak.

We have to tell each other some stuff. Want me to go first?

She nods, for unknown reasons refraining from looking at me. I can only see the tops of her faint red eyelashes.

K. I live with my mother Kathy and my brother Dana. I watch her intently. People usually scoff at my brother's girl name, but nothing happens on Tiffany's stone face. And you?

Um. At my house it's just my mom and sister and me.

Oh, great! Something we have in common, I nearly shout, compensating for her lack of enthusiasm. Where do you live?

Oakwood.

Really? I raise my eyebrows. Me, too. Heights or Terrace?

Somewhere in between.

Oh, I see. I'm from those duplexes on Oakwood Terrace. Near that field with the bushes.

She tilts her head to eye me, trying to laser beam me off my stool. I've never seen you before.

I went to St. Timothy's last year. I glance around us at students chatting happily. Anyway, I like photography. I don't even know what I'm doing in this class. My favorite past-time is people-watching.

Tiffany seems to relax then, sitting back as I head to the center of the room to a table loaded with paints and tools and big, white sheets of paper. I grab a few things and return to my stool. Tiffany leans over and pulls some paintbrushes out of her backpack--Chinese Paint Tools, the package reads, definitely new.

Nice brushes! I exclaim, trying to provoke something from the quiet redhead.

Thanks. They were super cheap. She flips the package over and touches the label. You can get them at that Chinese store near the Sev.

I watch her dab one of the bigger brushed in red and bring it to her paper, starting the assignment.

Mr. Marshal hasn't specified whether the paintings should be a surprise for one another, but I try not to look at what my partner is doing. *Still...red? I strike her as red?* I take a deep breath and make a long streak of blue across the blank white page. Deciding the blue is too bold, I blur the edges with orange. The result is disorganized, a brown smear.

Shit. I wanted purple.

Purple? I strike you as purple? Tiff blurts, before continuing. And can I ask you something? Did you get expelled from St. Timothy's or something?

No, I say firmly, covering my paper with my right arm. Why don't *you* go there if you live so close?

My mom said it's for kids who are naïve, over-privileged, and burdened by their own wealth.

She covers her painting with her left arm, shutting me up.

I scrunch up my face and consider being jealous of the students around us with nice, respectful partners. I soon allow my mind to wander. I daydream about fourth-period photography class, about holding a real camera instead of the disposable ones I've resorted to since forever. I think about digi-cams and manipulating everything with a computer or using real film and chemicals and a black room and everything I've heard of people doing. I think about capturing the light cascading over things like two-seater bicycles and peoples' eyelashes and worms in the early-autumn puddles streaking the roads.

Time's up, Mr. Marshal announces, five minutes before the end of class. He tells us where to find supplies for cleaning our desks and brushes. Tiff and I finish cleaning and prepared to exchange illustrations of each other. We each hold them with the painted sides facing our chests.

You first, I confidently order.

The paper drops from her hands onto the desk before me. I gasp at the sight, a navy-blue night sky barely illuminated by an orange dot that may or may not be the moon. Far away on the horizon stand four tiny red people, not touching each other but coming close. Each person appears to be sprouting like a tree from an arrangement of roots deep in the ground.

Wow. Oh, wow, Tiffany. Thank you.

It's a fluke.

It's *so* good.

A small smile appears on her face then, and I place my painting on the desk in front of her. My creation is mostly brown with a splotch of purple in the top right corner, where I finally figured out an appropriate combination of colors. The part meaning to tie everything together is three large blue female symbols I've painted over the other crap--three identical circles with three identical crosses below them. They scream, WOMAN!!!

Soon our giggles are tripping over one another's and the hideous painting. My partner clutches her belly beneath her roomy sweater, her smile widening as chuckles leak out, and soon we're outright cackling. When the bell rings and Mr. Marshal dismisses everyone, I open my mouth.

It's nice to meet you, Tiffany.

Call me Tiff.

She stands up and gathers her backpack and Chinese Paint Tools, bee-lining for the classroom door.

After our grad ceremony I see my mother briefly in the throng of people leaving the auditorium. She stands there looking around, gray windbreaker looking dustier than usual next to the building's white pillars. When we make eye contact, I wave at her, and she waves back, mouthing, I have to go, pointing at the exit like there's a fire.

Just go, I mouth back, smiling for the sole purpose of ensuring her I'm alright.

I turn and watch everyone else. Cameras flash constantly. I see six embraces in one second. Tiff is swarmed by her mother and her older sister Sophie and her Aunt Wendy and her cousin Amanda. I wander over to them, curling and uncurling my grad certificate, enjoying the cracks I make in the italicized golden writing. My friend is buried in her family like a nut in a shell. I want to photograph Tiff's ear against Sophie's bosom, Amanda's grinning face against Tiff's back and their mothers' arms encasing them. Red hair is everywhere. Pam, Tiff's mom, notices me then as I stare with blatant desire for co-possession of their feelings. She pulls herself from Team Tiff, faces me, and puts her enthusiastically manicured hands on my shoulders. She's a big woman, a little overweight, but you'd never notice because she dresses so well. She's wearing gold thong sandals and a flowing summer skirt and a light green blouse on which her auburn mane rests.

Where's your mom, dear?

She was here, but she had to go to work. They're *so* busy these days, with the location change and everything.

I catch the others' swift exchange of glances before they embrace me in obligatory congratulations, telling tales of my alleged beauty as I'd wandered across the stage. If you can foresee anything about a person's life by the way they cross that stage, I'd ambled, with a ridiculous blue gown threatening to trip me, into my future.

Tiff's family is hot on our heels as we return our gowns and receive exaggerated winks from the handsome photography teacher, who presumably does so to congratulate us. I turn my back to him as we reveal our everyday clothes, black high-tops and ripped jean shorts and a black muscle shirt, Tiff in black sandals and a black spaghetti-strap dress.

I'd become interested in black clothing upon meeting Tiff. I still enjoy how it disagrees with her translucent skin and turns her hair into a pile of glowing coals. I never could achieve the skin thing, or the hair, but I come as close as I can on the inside. I appreciate black for letting me be as No One as possible at times when I want pictures of Someone. Everyone. When asked, I can say, Black slims me down, and when not asked, I can relish in the fact that black actually slims me down. Black also has the sly ability to distinguish us as artists.

Our classmates pay no heed as we go out the doors to the parking lot where Tiff's Aunt Wendy's minivan awaits us. We get a private room at a Japanese restaurant and kneel on cushions around a stout table and try to eat with chopsticks. When they give me a fork I stuff myself with noodles and seaweed and little rice-paper rolls with bean sprouts and carrots. We all drink Sake, despite Tiff and I being seventeen and Amanda being sixteen and the law saying we have to be nineteen to consume alcohol. Wendy is driving, not drinking, but she shouts, Cheers! and lifts her green tea nine times in the first hour. Pam strikes up a conversation about Garth Brooks and we go along with it. The six of us giggle incessantly.

The evening summer zephyr refreshes us when we leave the restaurant. The six p.m. sun dares to set as we drive to the liquor store. Pam won't let us come in with her, but she buys girly drinks, cranberry Bacardi Breezers, and a six-pack of Kokanee in case we have boys over. When we arrive at Tiff's place, Amanda throws up in the neighbor's shrubs and Aunt Wendy has to take her home. She kisses all of us on the foreheads and then waves as she speeds away, tending to her drunken daughter. The phone rings and pulls Pam into the house while Sophie and Tiff and I keep the party going. We summon up a fire in the backyard brick pit their father built before The Divorce.

Sophie and I have never hung out before, but the Sake in our bellies melts the boundaries between best-friend's-older-sister and little-sister's-best-friend. Words come easily as we watch Tiff set up the yard--a table with an ice cooler and liquor and a bowl of chips and a bag of marshmallows, six more canvas lawn chairs and a stereo with a pile of CDs. We laugh at her when she complains of our laze.

Sophie tells me about her job at Wal-mart and how she sometimes gets to work in the photo center, of which I'm envious. She asks about my brother Dana because they once had a class together in high school. At first I think she's asking out of interest, but realize she's probably just being nice.

How's he doing? Where's he working?

I give her credit for not once mentioning the topic people bring up on the day of one's graduation: the graduate's future, allegedly pre-determined by the graduate some time before such moments of interrogation. I've come to know that the people who ask are those in denial and inexplicably in fear of the impossibility to decide how the future will be.

When Pam is off the phone she brings the cordless out, telling me to call my mother when I got a chance. Then she prompts Tiff.

What are you waiting for? Call everyone over.

Tiff sinks into one of the lawn chairs and picks at the long grass by her feet. She flips the cordless over in her hand and gives Pam a Look. I can't count the amount of times I have witnessed arguments between Tiff and her mother, but I know why it happens. Closeness--Noun. Living with someone and being so close to them that they mean the world to you at the same time as being your biggest annoyance. Shameless, indiscreet, and regular to a point at which those around can feel the storm brewing. The Look begins with a squint of Tiff's eyes.

Here, I'll do it.

My arm hangs limp until Tiff puts the phone in my hand. Pam sighs and treks back across the yard, her big hips swaying and landing with a bounce every time. I feel two things--immediate pity because of how her daughter has just behaved, and something else. Something else, like grade three when Cecile Grey's cat had a litter and I got to play with the tri-colored one. I let Ralph lick my hand even though his tongue was rough and his fur flew into my nostrils when we cuddled. Maybe it was love.

First I dial my home phone number.

Hello? My mother says into the phone, breathless. I've probably interrupted her smoking time.

Who is it? Tiff whispers.

Hi, Mom. I stick my tongue out at Tiff and she settles back into her chair.

Hi, my peach. What are you doing?

We're using Tiff's fire pit.

That sounds fun. What are you drinking?

Cranberry Breezers. They're pretty good.

I see. How many?

Two. She doesn't have to know about the Sake at the restaurant. Or the cooler full of icy beverages three feet away from me.

And are you staying there all night?

Uh, yeah. Probably. We might go clubbing later, if we can get in--

No, my mother interrupts. Don't go to bed too late. You have a big day tomorrow.

I know. I picture the university application forms on the kitchen table at home, probably already dotted with coffee and bits of strawberry jam.

After hanging up with my mother, I dig through my backpack to find my address book. I choose a number and punch it into the phone, wishing there was a cord to twirl in my finger while I wait.

Hello?

It's a boy. Tiff's whispering. Who's it now?

I watch Sophie dig a stick into the fire and flip one of the logs over.

Oliver? It's Venice.

Tiff squeals, skinny knees bumping up and down.

Oh, hey, what's up?

Nothing, really. Having a fire at Tiff's. Do you wanna come?

Breathe in. Breathe out.

Tell him we have booze, Tiff hiss-whispers.

Sure. Oliver answers me before I can say anything. Can I bring someone?

Of course.

Let me get a pen. Okay. What's Tiff's address?

Here, she'll tell you. I give the phone to my friend.

She mouths at me, What. Does. He. Want?????

Give him your addy.

Sophie and I go back to chatting. When Tiff's off the phone the three of us play a game--Never Have I Ever. We pop open new drinks. Sophie has beer, even though she's a girl, while Tiff and I suck back Breezers. I start the game by saying something I've never done.

Never have I ever eaten a dog biscuit. I say it because I saw Tiff eat a dog biscuit once.

Damnit, you knew that. Tiff takes a swig of her drink.

Sick. Sophie's face scrunches up. Why the hell would you eat dog food?

We were playing truth or dare. Tiff shrugs at her sister. It's your turn.

Never have I ever kissed a boy.

Tiff and I make eye contact before sipping our drinks and concealing laughter.

Who did you kiss?? Sophie hardens her eyebrows.

I'm seventeen. Tiff shrugs again. You're twenty. I can't believe you've never been kissed.

I didn't say anything about girls. Sophie smiles.

I look down at my fingers, peeling the edge of my drink's label. When I looked up, Tiff's mouth is hanging open.

Are you a dyke?

Hey! I punch Tiff's shoulder. Don't be a bitch.

No. Sophie's toe plays with the sand around the pit.

Who did you kiss? Tiff rubs her shoulder where I've just punched her.

Have YOU ever kissed a chick? I challenge my friend.

No. Tiff turn to me. Have you?

All I'm saying is don't knock it 'til you try it. By the way, you have to drink.

Tiff's head tilted back and she drinks, rolling her eyes at the sky. Sophie sends me a little smile before she looks back down at the sand.

I forgot to tell you guys that he's bringing a friend, Oliver is. I take a swig of my cranberrylicious drink.

When I stand to go into the house the grass dares to tilt beneath my eyes. The sky has darkened into a strip of navy across the roof of the house next door. When I walk through the kitchen Pam smiles at me from her spot at the table, where she sits piecing a puzzle together. I could never imagine my own mother doing such a thing.

You girls behave out there.

When I return, the boys still haven't arrived.

They're not coming. Tiff sighs, blowing up at her bangs although she has none.

Relax. I pat her arm. It's not even nine yet.

Really? It feels like midnight.

We started drinking, like, five hours ago. I look at my wrist, as if I have a watch.

Well, I'm not about to pull an Amanda. Tiff grins.

Sophie laughs heartily and leans forward in her chair, letting her bottle clink with her sister's.

Cheers.

I feel the tension slip away like a buttery egg off a frying pan.

3

How was your job interview?

Tiff rubbed my heel with the apricot lotion, our butts sunk deep in my basement sofa. I'd cracked open a Breezer for each of us.

Kind of shitty, I think. I had to wipe my nose the whole time because it was so cold out.

Do you think you got it?

I dunno. She didn't say. How was your day?

Work was okay. Monica brought her baby in. He's super cute.

Probably. Since *she's* so cute. Does he have her mole?

Be nice! Tiff dug her knuckle into the bridge of my foot.

Ow.

And guess what, I'm pretty sure I'm gonna get the Honorable Staff Member award in November.

What did you do? Clean the coffee pots just right?

I just think Monica's really starting to like me. Hey, guess what else.

Huh.

I decided I'm going to apply to art school.

Art school? I raised an eyebrow.

Yeah. There's a course at the university.

Oh. Why?

So I can learn more?

But you're already really good. I guess I just don't see a point.

Why're you being like that?

I just said. I don't see a point to going to school when you're already a fabulous artist. If you're worried about not getting in, don't be.

You think so? She smiled.

Yeah, man. They accept everyone.

She stuck her tongue out at me.

For real, what do you think?

Go for it. You know you're a shoo-in.

I need to get a student loan from the bank. Maybe I could talk to your mom about it?

I wanted to spit my drink across the rug, not that it would have done anything but add to pre-existing stains.

She's *way* too busy. They're moving to that new bank in East Bay.

Sorry, I forgot. Well at least Easy Bay's a really nice area. We should go down there sometime soon.

What, when the water's frozen? Great idea.

The bridge of Tiff's nose scrunched up.

It's probably not frozen yet. There's not even snow outside. Hey, maybe you could apply for a photography course or something.

Why would you even say that? You know I failed photography in high school.

And *you* know you're freaking talented and Mr. Shepherd's a stupid fag!

He's gay now, is he?

You know what I mean! Anyway, whatever. Let's watch Planet Earth.

The deal with Tiff supplying the goodies was that I'd supply the movies. I rented them from the library and ripped them onto my computer and then burned them onto blank DVDs. We had a mighty pile to choose from, psychological thrillers, romances, comedies, kung fus, all for free. I grinned. She rarely suggested movies I liked. I found the DVD in my massive disc book and slipped it into the player, ready for a few hours of oceanic wonderment.

I couldn't take my eyes off the opening scene, slick dolphins surfacing and jumping and diving through the seawater. I wondered what went through their minds.

After the movie Tiff had her jacket on and was half-way out the front door when she looked over her shoulder.

I almost forgot. Ringette season is starting. You wanna come to the rink tomorrow?

What time?

The afternoon sometime. I'll call you.

I cleaned the basement, filled a glass with tap water, and quietly retreated to my room on the main floor. The pills lay in a line on my dresser like children waiting to leave the classroom at the end of the day. I'd done some research online and decided that ten, as the drug store girl had suggested, would be too intense. I swallowed one, then a second and a third. They went down easily, though my belly was flipping nervously.

Flip flip flip.

I was stepping into a dark room without knowing what lurked in the shadows. Within two minutes I had willed myself to swallow eight of my mother's Gravol pills.

The wait was tremendous. I wondered if the rum would affect my high, but I hadn't drunk much. I turned on Alexisonfire and sat on my bed and played with the edge of the thin cotton sheet. I expected really far-out things to happen, like a genie to float out of my lamp and offer me wishes, a leprechaun to peek out of my closet and offer me good luck, the moon to come knocking at my window, and when I pressed myself against the wall and looked outside the stars would be dancing marionettes.

After deciding they were fucking wicked, Dana and I had claimed two Andy Warhol prints from our random basement wall art collection. By rule of Rock Paper Scissors, he'd gotten the one I *really* wanted, with red and yellow bananas, while I'd settled for the one with guns. Influenced by Gravol, I expected real bullets to come blasting out of the white and red and black pistols.

Despite numerous offers since my childhood had ended and adolescence had begun, I'd never done drugs before. I wondered how I'd know when I was tripping.

Dana entered the room with one of my art projects from grade five, a pink pillow with a one-legged monkey embroidered on it.

Can I get rid of this? He squeezed the pillow against his slight beer belly. I'm cleaning the attic.

Why?

Why get rid of it, or why am I cleaning the attic?

I don't know, you tell me. I went back to what I was doing. What was I doing?

What are you doing?

Waiting.

Okay. Weirdo. Wanna come to Chester's?

No. I couldn't imagine being around the leaves as they slipped beneath my feet and snickered and licked me with ice-frosted tongues. I couldn't imagine the cars with their endlessly interrogative beams when we'd turn onto the busy road where Chester's Pizza Parlor sat squished in a strip mall between the Pet Den and 7-11. I couldn't imagine waiting while the prepubescent boy behind the counter took one of the Hot to Go pizzas from its warming case and traded it with Dana for a five-dollar bill he'd earned at Phantom Cinema.

I heard him thump down the hall to his room. I pictured him grabbing his old Sex Pistols sweater, walking back to the front door, and putting on his ratty running shoes. The squeak and soft thud must have been the door as it opened and closed.

I stood up and poked my head into the hall. The house was silent. My mother's door, across from mine, was closed. I pictured her sitting cross-legged on her heavily quilted bed meant for two, wishing photos were spread around her like the cards in a messy round of Go Fish instead of random papers from her job at the bank. The one thing we had in common was our natural mushroom-brown hair color, and a love for photography, but that's not saying much. Probably half the world also loved photography, and another great portion had mushroom-colored hair. I wondered if she ever pretended her mother was pacing the room, giving her advice and picking up after her instead of squatting on the windowsill, ashes in a coffee-can urn. I smelled the second-last cigarette in a pack my mother had bought at seven forty-five a.m. on the way to work.

I used to wish she was addicted to alcohol instead of cigarettes. The thing about being an alcoholic is that when you have a drink it doesn't affect the people around you in the same way. They don't feel it in their lungs, smell it on their clothes, or have black snot from your habit. They just watch you get drunk and turn you on your side so you don't swallow your tongue. Tiff and I saw that reality show, Intervention, once. Then I just wished my mother wasn't addicted to anything.

I started blinking differently; my eyelids dropped and hesitated to open again and my heart hovered high above my chest. I pushed myself back into my room and sunk into the chair at my desk and watched my hand twirl and morph into different things, a Smurf and a strawberry and a tiger and someone was sitting on my bed so I started talking about what I liked and didn't like about life and when I turned around I could squint through murky patterns of gray and brown and see that no one was actually there, but I spoke anyway. I couldn't decide whether I loved or hated how I felt. The drug store girl popped into my head and her bright-as-hell shoes. Or were they boots? Shoeboots.

I knew Dana had returned to the house when I heard whistling outside my room. I squiggled across the hard carpet and opened my bedroom door. I lay thumping my arm against the wall and talking. I was like the lady at the mall who thought the garbage can was a person. When my brother leaned over me his gray eyes were quizzical, perturbed. He became bigger and I became smaller, a piece of lint that would have wavered in the non-existent breeze.

Are you drunk?

No, are you? I laughed.

You seem fucked. His eyebrow pushed up into his forehead.

How does it do that?

Do what?

Holy crap. He can read my mind.

You said that out loud.

I laughed and clutched my belly.

Question of the day. Is hot mustard hot enough to melt chocolate chips?

Oh my god, you're wasted. Dana allowed his face to crumple into a grin. What are you on?

The floor. Hahahahaha.

Want some pizza?

Only if it tastes like a rhinoceros. I tried to grab a piece of air floating two feet from my face, but my hand came back to me, empty.

You're being so weird. Come up to the attic.

The invites were unusual, like he wanted to make peace over a fight we'd never had. He let me know it--I was tripping. I was definitely tripping. He helped me to my feet and pulled the stairs down from our attic. I made him go first into the blackness above us and he made me swear I could climb without falling.

I hadn't been up there since the last time I'd played Hide-and-Go-Seek. The attic had always been the best hiding spot, even though I could feel the dust immediately on my skin and in my ears and nose. Through the dolphins swimming behind my eyelids, I couldn't see much but the light bulb dangling from the attic ceiling and the edges of cardboard boxes. Dana told me to watch my step, because he had opened a box of Christmas decorations and they were scattered on the floor. He had strung tree lights around the ceiling's wooden support boards. I stationed myself on our old trunk of dress-up clothes near the window, where I could see the street. I felt like a lifeguard, supervising everything from one of those ridiculously high chairs I'd only seen in Archie comics. Every time I looked up I felt like I was floating, up up up, and felt the overwhelming need to catch myself and sit back down on the trunk, where I had to remind myself I'd been sitting the whole time.

What do you think? Dana asked me, waving his arm around the room. We could clean it up real nice and make it a hangout or something.

A hangout? For us?

Sure. We could get a little couch. Maybe a TV.

I have no money.

That's what Value Village is for.

While I talked to him about the moon, Dana handed me random things. He gave me binoculars. He gave me a candle that smelled like the ocean, it really did, even though I had never been to the ocean and wouldn't know saltwater if it crept up behind me Tsunami-style. He gave me a brown fedora with a feather on the side and when I wondered about the feather's bird it appeared before me, flapping it wings and snapping its beak and I must have screamed because Dana shushed me and handed me a teddy bear with fourteen eyes and I must have laughed because he shushed me.

Shut up, man. Do you want Mom to know you're on drugs?

On drugs, the words didn't weigh me down the way I'd imagined they would. They floated effortlessly in my mind and became something fabulous and pink and lively.

My brother handed me an envelope, brittle in my fingers because it was old and on the road to becoming nothing. I watched it like a confusing movie.

Just open it, Dana told me, and when I did so I had to yank on its innards for them to come out. I held a photo with Kodak's logo all over the back, and in the top left corner something I couldn't focus my crazed eyes on.

Lod. And a shitload of numbers.

Todd. Dana corrected. And probably the date.

Nineteen ninety-two.

I turned it over and gazed at his face, dark under the shade of an oak. Was I tripping, or was his smile really that wonderful? When I kissed the photo I tried to smell something--aftershave, the burnt edges of blueberry pancakes, the sweat of a hardworking man, evening beer breath, carwash soap, Rolex wristwatch, Christmas oranges, Cuban cigars, something other than dust. I knew my brother had pulled it out of the smallest drawer in the old oak desk; it was the photo we'd secretly assumed was of our father since finding it years earlier.

Snap, it was quick, bursting across my mind like the flash of a camera. Dana was trying to make peace over a real fight we'd had.

We're on a playground.

I'm the King of the Castle!

He calls this after climbing to the top of the jungle gym. I tend to take everything personally. The salt gathers tightly behind my eyes and I bite my cheek to prevent tears from spilling over my bottom lashes. I'm not a baby. I'm six. I've just finished kindergarten and I'm entering grade *one* in the fall.

School has let out for summer and we enrolled in some old lady's daycare program while my mom's at work. The other kids at daycare fight about everything--who gets the ketchup first at lunchtime, who gets the front seat in the daycare van, who gets the good Barbie. Fighting isn't for me and Dana, unless it's about something *really* serious. When I cry at home he shares his Hot Wheels with me, or imitates rickety old Mrs. Lewis from our elementary school, or the grumpy janitor. One time he gave me the fastest piggyback ride in the world; I know, because when he ran down our road my hair whipped my face so hard it hurt. I swore it left a red mark on my cheek. I've never laughed harder than that, ever.

This particular July day, Dana and I hop the fence of the daycare backyard into the park behind the house. The other kids go on screaming in the mist of sprinklers. The old lady's probably still lying in a patio lounge chair, sneaking puffs of Marlboros and pretending she's not sleeping under her sunglasses.

Then Dana becomes the King of the Castle. When I start crying he kneels before me and looks into my eyes.

Don't cry. I'll be the king and you can be my daughter, the princess.

Fuck off. I glare up at his fat, dark face. You're not my dad.

Dana just blinks, even when I spit on his shoe. He just looks down and blinks. He doesn't follow me home even though I'm not sure I know the way and it's not safe for little girls to wander around our scumbag neighborhood. I go home and lie on the front lawn, because I don't have a house key. The sun is so hot and the sky is so bright. So blue. I make up a word--'bluedom', the kingdom in the sky. It's not about God or Jesus or the other people the old daycare lady makes us pray to before we eat anything. It's about me being the king of something. I feel my heart calming, settling into the ground and the grass around me.

Some time later the daycare van appears on the road before our duplex. The old lady doesn't even get out to rescue me, just lays her wrinkly paw on the horn and honks through my dreams, straight through my ears and my eyes. I scurry into the backseat of the van, even though no one's in the passenger seat up front. The sun has burnt my face so hard that I can't frown. I can't smile. I just stare out the window.

I gazed back down at the photo. My maybe-father's hairline receded specifically to reveal nice features on a canvas of tanned skin. Gray eyes, the same as mine, but better on him, and I could only look at them for a second before mine had to flit away. I wondered if my father drank, like me. The background was faint, but somewhere green, perhaps a garden. Something was incredible about the picture, something that glowed on his face and tried to pull me into that moment with him. I'd seen the photo before, but couldn't bear it in my state of mind, terrified of erupting memories. I returned it to the envelope and threw it on the floor.

Some hangout.

4

My eyes opened, slits. I lay on my back, stucco ceiling above me. The sun came in through the thin curtains and covered everything. Something was off. I wiggled my toes and realized they were elevated on my pillow and my head was at the wrong end of the bed. My legs ached. I pushed my hands into the bed and forced myself up, feeling my neck strain the way runway models' looked. My bedside table clock read 12:03 p.m.

Twelve-o-three in the afternoon. I paused quizzically, propped on my hands, and looked around. Everything seemed fine. I had on my usual baggy jeans and black t-shirt and thick socks because of the poor heating in our duplex. My head hurt slightly, near my temples. My stomach rotated inside of me and emitted a groan.

When I lay my head back down I tried to think about the night before. Parts were clear and others were gone, completely absent. I couldn't figure out how the night had unfolded, when I'd been in the attic, or what time I'd gone to sleep. Or how I'd even gotten down from the attic. I remembered standing and staring at the dishes in the kitchen, and looking in the fridge. I faintly recalled pressing buttons on my CD player and letting Alexisonfire scream me to sleep, my face on a soft surface and my legs dancing. When people are so drunk they pass out, they're not really allowed to consider it sleeping. I wondered if it was the same for people who go to bed on drugs.

My shoulders began itching and I could barely lie still, rubbing them with my stubby nails. I wondered if this was some after-effect I hadn't known about, or a horrible allergic reaction that would spread all over and invade the cracks between my toes. Punishment for getting high, or getting low, whatever it was I had done. I grabbed a fork from the kitchen, went downstairs to our only bathroom with a lock on the door, and took my shirt off to have a good scratch. I turned to look at my skin in the mirror and that was when I saw it. I couldn't hold it. The fork clattered into the sink below me and I pissed, I really did. My nose caught the hot liquid's stench as it ran down my sweats. My cheeks reddened, embarrassed although I was alone.

My jaw hung slack, my fingers now clung to my face and my protruding ears and the horrible haircut I'd somehow received with no second thought. Or a first thought. Some strands were long and some were as short as an inch from my scalp. I wondered who the fuck had done that to me, chopped up my locks, my own personal curtain, and turned me into something even more freakish than my natural self. I took the rest of my clothes off and examined my body, frantic for clues. I wondered if it had been Dana, or my mother, or the worst culprit I could conjure up. When people are drunk they do things they don't want to. I was pretty sure it was the same for people on drugs.

My tears were angry with me for calling them on. I used my shirt to swat the tiny pieces of cut hair, the itch, off my skin. My legs were cold and wet. I pulled off my sweats and mopped the dirty linoleum with the dry parts before fleeing to my room.

I calmed down as much as I could, took an aspirin for my head, and got on the bus only with one comfort hovering in my mind: I could get off and walk home if I chickened out. I splayed across two seats with my legs up, the only reason I'd ever been thankful to come from Oakwood--I lived at the edge of the city and was therefore one of the bus's first stops. My head pounded with every threatening lurch of the vehicle.

By the time we arrived downtown, the bus was teeming with customers. Halfway there, I'd been forced to sacrifice my extra seat for an extremely pregnant fourteen-year-old. The driver parked at the terminal and stood up, stretching his arms and yawning. If I drove a screeching bus all day, I'd probably phone Tiff on my break and beg her to come over later and give me a neck rub. She would ask why I was so tired and I would ask if she'd ever been a bus driver. I would bribe her with a copied disc of The Sopranos and a bowl of spaghetti noodles with parmesan cheese, if my mother had gotten groceries.

I wondered if the driver would go outside for a cigarette. I wanted more time to devise a plan--what I would say and how I would explain myself without sounding completely accusing. I raised my hand to touch the place where my hairline met the old beige toque I'd covered my head with.

The driver glanced in his rearview at my staring face. He looked at his watch and retreated to his chair, preparing to take off again. The customers had unloaded and a new round had boarded, nothing left to help me stall. I jumped up from my seat and rushed to the door, landing on the pavement with a hard thump, backpack bouncing against my shoulders.

I breathed deeply when I made it outside, thankful for the bright day, crisp but not cold. In reality, adrenaline fooled me. Something about that day didn't feel real, stopped it from being classified as reality. I stiffly began walking to the corner, to the drug store, yanked the door open, and entered. I had no control over my walk changing to a saunter.

No one was at the till that time to watch me, the strange person in the weird hat. If someone had been peering at me again I probably would have pivoted on the spot and left. My nails pressed into my palms. I couldn't see any other customers, but heard a low murmur from the back of the store. I warily sought out the noise like a fish succumbing to the lethal combo of hook and bait. I walked down one aisle, the sound strengthening, and discovered a male voice. I stopped to pick up a box of tampons and read the instructions. Spread your legs so that you are comfortable. Try propping one up on the toilet seat.

Fuck, I'm tired, the guy said. He was in the next aisle. I listened keenly for a girl's voice to respond, *her* voice.

Unwrap the tampon. Never use a tampon with a punctured wrapper. I mulled over the idea of having officially received more womanly advice from a tampon box than from my mother.

Yeah? What did you get up to last night? Still a boy's voice.

Pause. I could smell smoke and hear a Bic lighter as a thumb pressed and rolled.

I went to a party at Morgan's. Have you seen the renovations? She charged people three fuckin' dollars for a Jell-o shooter, the boy added, laughing.

I heard the lighter again and a throat's faint inhalation. I became aware that someone was smoking something other than cigarettes.

I'm in the tenth grade the first I smell pot. Dana has made a friend from one of the duplexes down and across; his name is Randy and he only comes up to my brother's shoulder, with hair slicked down to trick people into thinking he's washed and gelled it. He has given true meaning to the term 'dirty blond'. School has finished for the day, my mother's at the bank, and I'm in the process of finding an outfit to wear to *The Wizard of Oz* at the public auditorium. I'm going that night with Tiff's family, to meet them for the first time. My jean skirt has a ketchup stain and I can't find a shirt that doesn't make me look lonely, or isn't black or ripped.

Dana knocks on my door, opening it a second later. Randy, on his heels, peers in at the mess of my girl-room. I watch his eyes traveling down my jeans and up to the yellow tank top that's too tight on my breasts and too bright for my tanned skin. Maybe he, too, feels visually raped as my eyes tear into his teenaged mustache and singularly pierced ear. I don't want him or my brother to see me in my nice-girl getup.

What. I say this as monotonously as possible.

You got a pop can? Dana asks, prompt and confident.

What? Why?

Nothing. Just give it to me.

Who's your friend?

Randy scowls and backs off into the hall.

None of your business.

Fine. I take the empty ginger ale can off my desk and hold it out. Here. Enjoy.

Why are you being so bitchy? Fuck. Dana snatches the can and slams my bedroom door behind him. I wondered how impressed Randy is on a scale of one to ten.

When I look in the mirror my eyes immediately fall on the puffy fat at the waist of my jeans. I grab my ponytail and break the elastic in a swift yank. My hair falls angrily to my shoulders. I pulled my jeans off and breathe out quickly, heavily. I lift the ugly tank top and gaze at my imperfect figure. I raise my arms and suck in and watch as my hip bone emerges. I exhale and watch it retreat. I pull the shirt off and throw aimlessly, letting it drape like an ugly flag over my CD collection. I crawl into bed and hide my stomach under my three heavy blankets. I disregard the amazing heat. I put my hand on my pounding heart in an effort to slow my breathing.

I inhale deeply, suddenly noticing the scent of a skunk. I've somehow messed with my karma--a skunk has chosen *my* backyard to crawl into and spray. I groan and glance up at my bedroom window, ajar and welcoming to the wondrous scents of nature. The wondrous sounds, too, the birds and the traffic and the coughing boy.

I throw the blanket off and cross my arms over my bra. I crouch beneath the window and rise slowly, peeking down at the tops of two heads, Dana's ball cap and Randy's greasy 'do glistening in the four p.m. sunlight. Randy holds a dented ginger ale can and a lighter. His suspicious lips meet the can's opening as he lights up and inhales deeply.

When Dana takes the can from Randy I think of the way I took the microphone from Cecile Grey's hand when she received a karaoke machine for her birthday in the fourth grade. Fear can freeze a person in the same way it can push a person to do something he or she obviously isn't meant to do. Dana watches his new chum as he blazes the aluminum and the lump of drugs on top. His turn ends quickly as he coughs and staggers and presses his hand against the old fence of our yard. Randy chuckles and pats his back like they're thirty-year-olds reliving college jokes.

5

In the pharmacy, I turned the corner at the end of the aisle and happened upon a young guy sitting on a stack of milk crates with his legs splayed lankily before him, a cell phone glued to his ear. When he noticed me through the curtain of black hair hanging in his face, we froze and watched each other. For too many seconds there was no sound but the puff of the joint at his lips.

Hi, I said, feeling one side of my mouth curl up into a smile. I felt like turning to the side and putting one foot back for a quick getaway from impending embarrassment. I hoped he wouldn't offer me a drag.

I gotta go, he hurriedly told the person on the phone before flipping it shut and dropping it in his blue smock pocket. He gazed up at me and I noted how well stoned pinkness matched his baby blues. When I saw his eyes I thought of one of my top five favorite National Geographic pictures, a lone Huskie surrounded by snow, icy blue irises trained not on the photographer but on something over the photographer's shoulder.

What's up? The boy tossed his head to one side to get the right effect with his shaggy black bangs. My eyes flitted around his outfit, a silver nostril hoop, black studded bracelet, and tight purple jeans. I decided that he was the kind of guy I would have liked to follow around in high school. I would have found out when his birthday was and put black balloons on his locker.

I'm looking for a girl. She works here. At least, she did last week. I saw her here.

What's her name?

No idea. She's pretty and has cool hair...

Cool hair, or fucking wicked hair? He smiled with quirkily crooked teeth as he stubbed the joint on edge of his milk crate throne. Of course he wouldn't offer me any of it; I was the strange girl creeping on his co-worker and, most likely, friend.

The latter.

He stared at me, smile evaporating.

I mean, fucking wicked hair.

He laughed and clapped his hands together like I was hired entertainment. You're cute. Is it Raizel, maybe? Ye tall, he stood up and held his hand out, slightly lower than my head, barely reaching his shoulder.

I nodded up at him, craning my neck. He towered over me and almost everything else in the store. Raizel? Raizel, like a hazel raisin.

You're damn right it is. There's only one chick working here, he laughed again. She's on her lunch break, back at one.

I broke eye contact, glancing around. A clock on the office wall read twelve forty-eight.

Okay. Thanks.

You can chill here.

He flicked his bangs out of his face again and bent to divide his milk crate chair into two shorter ones. His smock rode up slightly at the back and revealed the elastic waistband of pink briefs under his jeans. I giggled, believing that because I'd secretly seen his underwear I had nothing to fear.

Have a seat. I don't do this for everyone.

I sat, not caring as the plastic dug through my jeans into my butt cheeks. I imagined how waffle-like my ass would look.

I'm gonna go grab some air freshener.

He wandered away until all I could see was his dark hair bobbing down the aisles. I leaned my back against the wall, crossed my ankles, and waited. He returned shortly with a bottle of Hawaiian Ginger perfume, spraying generously in all directions.

So what's your name? I'm Liam.

I'm Venice. You ever get caught smoking in here?

Caught? Nah. We do whatever we want. To prove it, he grabbed a bag of Doritos off the hanging rack beside him. The skunk-like odor diminished with the perfume. We relaxed, sharing the chips, the first thing I'd eaten that day. He probably thought I was a crazy fatso, gobbling them down. I wondered if he was still in high school.

How old are you?

Eighteen. I just graduated.

Me too. I mean, I just graduated, but I'm only seventeen.

You're just a baby. He licked his orange fingertips. Nice hat, by the way.

I put my hand on my head. I had nearly forgotten about my problem. The toque was ancient, its wool thin and pilled, some piece of crap that smelled like our front hallway cupboard.

Yeah, I have a bad haircut. This thing is just to save face. Or should I say hair?

Liam chuckled, scarfing down the remainders of the bag.

No, really, it's a sweet hat. Let me see it. He ripped the toque off my head before I could react, pulling it down over his own hair. This would match my new scarf.

My cheeks became hot and I dug my nails into my palms, mortified. Sweat instantly collected on my upper lip and my hands flew to the scraps of hair I was sure hung dully off my head. I tried to reach his head, which seemed miles higher than mine.

A bell jangled then and the glass door opened at the front of the store.

Blah, customer. Liam turned lazily toward the door, my hat positioned precariously on his head.

It's just me!

Her voice, cinnamon music. I groaned and put my head in my arms. I stayed that way and listened as the voice neared us.

Nice hat. Who's that?

She was probably pointing at me like I was a dead mouse the cat had dragged in.

It's Venice. Liam sat back down on his crate. Don't you know her? She came here for you.

Huh.

I could feel her squeeze in between Liam and I on the milk crates. I saw her blood-red Doc Marten shoeboots and moved my arm to peer up, a one-eyed ogre, at her rosy lips. She knit her eyebrows confusedly, jogging her mind for remembrance.

I've definitely *seen* you before, she said, stroking her chin like an old man does his beard of wisdom. Were you at Morgan's last night?

I shook my head.

Wait, aren't you a customer? Her eyes suddenly brightened. She snapped her fingers, leather bracelets shimmying up her arm. I remember talking to you the other day.

Yeah.

I kept my face in my arms. She remembered me.

Hey, did you get a haircut?

My eyes welled up. I bit my arm and prayed the tears wouldn't spill over. She took her hand off her chin and perused my hair as though it was the best shelf at the library.

I took some Gravol and woke up like this.

Her eyes widened. She bit the tip of her thumb as if to punish herself.

Wow, that's fucked. Um. Don't worry. We'll fix it.

She ordered Liam to give my toque back, which he did immediately. She pinned on her nametag and waved her hand for me to follow her down the aisle. I kept my eyes on her tough-girl boots and her tights, which she'd changed from cupcakes to hearts. I wondered if she had a pink car with Hello Kitty seat covers.

My name's Venice. I overcame the lump in my throat to exercise common manners. Nice to meet you.

That was the moment I discovered the color of her eyes. They were golden brown in the center, like the shiny fur of a golden retriever. Around the edges was a dark green--rich, salty, seaweed floating in a provincial lake on the longest, hottest day of the year. She looked at me for a few seconds before her face gave way to a grin.

Yeah, right! Your name's Venice? That's *so* dope.

She made no offer of her hand for a shake, so I decided I shouldn't, either.

So…how can you help me? I mean, with my hair?

I'm going to fix you up. She examined a pair of scissors hanging off the wall on a metal hanger. Trust me.

I thought about those two words and was unable to stop myself.

Been there, done that.

She hardened her eyebrows.

I'm just trying to help you.

Something immediately stung inside of me.

I know. Sorry.

Besides, you *should* trust me. I'm gonna be Gwen Stefani's hair dresser one day. She pointed at my backpack. Can you put this in there? And meet me back here at two-thirty?

Okay, I complied dazedly. I put the scissors in my backpack alongside my sweater and wallet, zipped it up, and slung everything over my shoulder. I watched Raizel disappear into the back office before I headed to the front of the store.

Liam lifted his pinkish blue eyes from the lottery ticket he was scratching with cheesy chip fingers.

Win anything? I put my hand on the door.

Two bucks. You want it?

No, thanks. See ya later. I smiled.

Peace.

I pushed the door open and stood in the cool air. My backpack hung against my back slightly heavier than I had before. I wandered down the street to a shopping mall and sat in the food court, wishing I had a camera. The mall was next-to-empty, but those days I believed a camera lens could beautify anything. As I drew a picture of the custodian's wrinkled face, my head bobbed sleepily toward the table. I regretted not taking that Liam guy's two bucks. I could have had a fountain pop from Arby's, something caffeinated to perk me up. I found a quarter in the depths of my jeans pocket and considered buying a fortune cookie from Ming's Kitchen.

Guilt is a sudden, intangible enemy. Standing there, with my money in my palm and my fingers on the lid of the cookie jar, the feeling warmed my belly and traveled up. Tiff's sister Sophie's ringette tournament was that afternoon. As we'd done throughout the previous year's ringette season, Tiff would bring the cookies and hot chocolate thermos, I would bring the blanket, and we would yell, Go Sophie! as though it was the only thing that would make Sophie go.

I removed my hand from the fortune cookie jar and apologized to a stout Chinese woman who was frantically trying to up-sell to me Combo # 5: The Rice and Veggie Extravaganza. I retreated from her incessant plead and found myself dialing Tiff's home number from a dirty payphone. Ring. Ring. Ring. Ring. Ring. Ring. Her answering machine always kicked in on the seventh ring. I hung up before it stole my quarter. I dialed her cell phone number. Ring. Ring. Ring. Ring. Ring. Ring. I replaced the receiver and looked at the phone's digital clock. Ten minutes 'til Raizel Time.

6

Raizel, Liam, and a middle-aged man with a beer belly stood in a circle in front of the aisles, discussing something. I pulled nervously at my backpack straps, watching the white-blond back of her head. The man was tall and wore a white button-up shirt. I immediately thought someone was getting in shit for stolen chips, or stolen scissors, or the scent of marijuana lingering through a curtain of stolen perfume, but soon they all shared a laugh.

Ok, guys, I'm off. See ya tomorrow. Raizel threw on a long gray pea coat that fought magnificently with the ketchupy hue of her shoeboots. For the fifth time in the three times we'd met, I admired her fashion sense. She pulled keys from the pocket of her fabulous coat and looked up at me.

Hey, you. Ready to go?

Raizel bounced down the street to lead me to her car. The parking spot was prime, three pay-meters from the store.

This is my hunk of burnin' love. She patted the hood of a burnt orange Camaro. I only knew it was a Camaro because of my brother's fascination with cars. If possible, I would have shaken hands with the vehicle, relieved that it wasn't new, wasn't decorated in Hello Kitty, and there were no Roxy window stickers in sight. She unlocked the driver's door, leaned across the seat, and pushed the passenger door open for me. Come on in!

I smiled and slid into the seat, oddly low, my hand on my toque to keep it from jostling off. The black leather was cold through my jeans, though surprisingly soft.

What a great car.

Thanks, man. Do you have a hunk of burnin' love? She twisted the keys and revved the engine. She grinned.

Nah. I don't have a license.

No way! How do you get around?

Bus, mostly. This Oliver guy gave me his university bus pass 'cause he has a car.

I could never do it. I love driving too much. Have you ever driven stick?

I ran my fingers up and down the strap of my backpack.

Oh, hey, you can throw that in the back if you want.

I smiled and pulled the bag off of me, twisting to put it behind us. I noticed the book of CDs on the floor and hoped Raizel wouldn't mind as I picked it up.

No, I've never driven stick. I flipped through the CD book. Bob Dylan, Janis Joplin, and Johnny Cash, all wonderful. The car vibrated as we sat and waited for the engine to warm.

No? Never? It's awesome; you should give it a go.

Actually, I've never driven. Period.

Raizel laughed and I tried to sink lower into the seat, to shrivel away.

Yeah right! Guess I'll have to teach you.

The slight trembles in my stomach subsided as the car began to move away from the sidewalk. I continued through the CDs, finding artists I had only faintly heard of--Bikini Kill, Le Tigre, the Distillers, Peaches, Metric, so much to choose from. I removed a CD and held it up.

Can we listen to this?

Raizel glanced at my hand.

Of course! Her wavy locks swayed. Ani's my favorite. I would kill to see her live.

We sat silently for the rest of the ride, listening to the tunes. I admonished myself for having never given Ani Difranco a chance before. I was too shy to ask if she was the guitarist, but whoever it was had some real talent. Her collectively soft and hard voice made me feel like I wasn't in a cold little Canadian city.

Do you like this song? Raizel took her eyes off the road for a moment to smile at me. Her teeth were so white.

Love it.

After ten minutes she turned down a road I'd never been on. Golden Street, read the little green and white sign on the corner. All of the houses were different sizes and colors, unlike the row of duplexes in Oakwood. Raizel parked and cut the engine. I mimicked her, only reaching for my door handle when she reached for hers. I grabbed my backpack and stood on the sidewalk while she locked the doors. The air wasn't as cold there in the suburbs, as the abundance of buildings shielded us from the wind.

The houses and apartment buildings were all blatantly old, but undeniably beautiful and unique. They were destined to be described by Dr. Seuss; some were big, some were small, some were short, some were tall. Raizel lead me up the driveway of a narrow, three-story house, blue with white trim and a one-car garage. Everything was shaded by three trees, their red leaves having fallen in dramatic poses along the lawn.

We traipsed through the front door into a sunroom full of junk--snow shovels, boxes of newspaper, sports equipment--and left our snowy shoes on a mat reading, *Come On In,* just like Raizel had said before I'd entered her car. She led me through another door, thin and wooden, into a kitchen. The flowered wallpaper and old appliances reminded of every elderly person's house I'd been to. A big set of glass doors leading to the backyard allowed light to stream in. The countertops were clean and I pictured people drinking hot cocoa at ten p.m. while playing cards at the table. I thoroughly enjoyed the four mismatched chairs.

Do you like orange juice?

Yeah.

Raizel pulled open the fridge door, of which every inch was covered with photos and magnets. We didn't speak as she poured two glasses almost to the brim. I eyed a bowl of fruit on the counter, wishing I could ask for one of the plump, yellow bananas. My stomach threatened to groan.

She opened the basement door and flicked on a light. The wooden walls lining the staircase reminded me of my childhood. Specifically, I thought of my Aunt Blanche's farmhouse. Down the stairs we went, to a dark room. The carpet was dark orange and the furniture ranged between shades of dark red and dark brown, regular things--a TV and a couch, a coffee table, and two fat armchairs. Behind the couch there was a vanity table with a huge mirror and a rotating stool. I was delighted to find that the air smelled nearly as old as my own family's basement.

Just put your things wherever.

I put my coat and backpack on one of the armchairs. She went into her bedroom for a minute and came back wearing a shirtdress over her tights, a big, white slate of fabric with a pair of black scissors on the front, her pearl necklace dangling down her chest. The shirt hung off her body, making her tight-clad thighs seem tiny.

This is my hair-doing shirt.

It's alright. You look kind of edgy. I beamed with pride. She caught my pun with a laugh.

Okay, sit here. She patted the stool and I sat looking in the mirror. One second after I had silently admitted I looked okay in the toque, she tore it off my head. I didn't have time to feel embarrassed, as her fingers immediately wove their way into my locks and held them up, examination time.

You're going to look fucking awesome.

I smiled shyly and broke our mirror eye contact, looking instead at the stuff surrounding the mirror's perimeter. Pictures from magazines were taped up--shots of skateboarding stunts and interviews with people I assumed she admired. I saw pictures and stickers of some of the bands I had seen in her CD collection, a photo of a big St. Bernard dog lying on a couch, and pictures of Raizel with people who were probably important to her. She was extremely photogenic and I longed to use her as a model. Her friends were nearly as impeccable; someone had managed to capture them in careless moments of laughter. Liam was a star in several of the photos, his ice-blue eyes having become translucent upon the flash of the camera. One photo in particular caught my eye, Raizel and a dark-skinned girl with a wild black afro, arms looped over one another's shoulders, huge grins as though they'd just shared a joke.

Your friends are pretty.

I only talk to pretty people. Raizel smirked at my reflection. Okay, come with me.

We went into the small basement bathroom and I knelt with my head hanging over the bathtub. I quickly became mesmerized by her fingers massaging my fucked up hair, warm water trickling down my face to the tip of my nose. Then she rubbed my head with a towel, stains assumedly having come from previous dyes. When we were back at the table she placed the towel over the mirror so I couldn't see. My hair was so soft from the conditioner that the comb slid through it and touched my shoulders again and again.

Hey, is that your boyfriend? Searching for conversation, I noticed a picture on the mirror's frame, poking out from the side of the towel.

Who?

There, in the right hand corner. I used my nose to nod at the picture, as my arms were trapped under the towel Raizel had draped over me.

The picture was of Raizel with her white-blond hair arranged high on her head in a pile of curls, some pieces down near the front. She wore a black spaghetti-strap gown and her arm was around an attractive boy, taller than her with charming facial features. He was broad-shouldered and dressed well, in a gray vest, black collared shirt, and purple necktie.

Oh. No. She pressed a bobby pin into my scalp. That's my brother Sullivan.

Was that at grad?

No, just the winter formal.

Wow, you guys must be close, hanging out together.

If you say so.

I bit my lip and vowed to stop making assumptions.

I only said that because my brother would *never* hang out with me. He didn't come to my grad. He didn't even ask to.

Mm hmm. Raizel mumbled, bobby pins between her closed lips. How old's your brother?

Twenty, now.

My brother liked doing his own thing. I wouldn't be too offended.

We made small talk as Raizel combed and tugged my hair and clipped pieces up. She took scissors from the top of the desk and pinched seemingly random pieces between her fingers and chopped them off. My armpits got sweaty hoping she wouldn't fuck it up more than I had. I felt lighter, like I only had feathers glued to my head. Then she was tweaking it and putting gunk in it and blowing it dry with hot air. She removed the towel from the mirror like an artist at a painting exhibition.

I opened my mouth and a small yelp came out. She had definitely followed the shortness I'd started. The hair closest to my scalp was a mere centimeter long. All of the hair in the middle at the top of my head had been molded up in a feathery faux-hawk. My hair looked like something that would piss off a set of good parents and impress the group of offbeat kids who'd hung out in the smoking lounge at my high school. I had some bangs toward the left, which I'd never suited, but she had resisted my cowlick with the heat of a flat iron. I touched my hair, which was as wonderfully soft as I'd hoped. I wasn't exactly *beautiful*, but I felt monstrously good. Maybe fucking awesome.

What do you think?

Raizel looked at me in the mirror again. I couldn't look back, not from awkwardness, but from not being able to tear my eyes off my own reflection.

I love it. I continued to finger the healthy edges of my hair that she had snipped. I felt like one of those ignorant ladies on What Not to Wear. I can't believe it. How can I repay you?

Actually, you're going to do me now.

Huh?

I need a trim.

Oh, I can't. I don't know what to do.

You can do it. One inch, that's all. It's curly, so it doesn't matter if it's perfect. She motioned for me to get off the chair and took my spot.

But...it *is* perfect.

In the mirror, I saw my cheeks redden. My stomach got all tight. I couldn't believe she would trust me with her white-blond unicorn hair. I thought it would sparkle in my hands.

7

Did you forget about me today? Tiff asked softly. I felt the beginning of her guilt trip over the phone.

I tried calling you. I was happy that I wasn't lying.

Yeah, well, it doesn't say so on my phone.

I was at a payphone.

Oh. Where were you?

The mall. It's a long story.

So you ditched me to go shopping?

Come on, Tiff, you know I don't have money.

Sophie's team won. I guess she doesn't need your support.

Click.

Fuck. I put the phone down.

My mother glared at me over her Danielle Steele book, smoke twirling up from the ash tray beside her.

Language.

I went to my room and looked in the mirror, holding a smaller mirror up behind my head to appreciate my hair from all angles. I took off my regular black shirt and put on something I hadn't worn in years, a black button-down shirt that matured me a little. Fall had fallen and no would see the shirt under my sweater, unless I met someone that night and did something involving the removal of clothing.

Fat chance. I crossed my arms over my belly and turned to the side to examine my reflection.

Ring ring ring.

Venice! Get the phone!

I stomped to the living room.

Like you can't just reach three feet and answer it, I snapped.

Ring ring.

Like it's for me. My mother sat, smug on the sofa in her smelly afghan cocoon, a new cigarette lit in her hand. She raised her eyebrow when she noticed my hair.

Ring ring.

This is why I need a cell phone. My middleman is a retard.

Ring ri--I swiped the cordless off the coffee table. Hello?

My mother glared at me again, sucking on her cancer stick. My brother Doug has autism, you know.

Took you long enough, Tiff said in my ear.

Hi. I knew she would call back. I retreated to my room while my mother yelled menial things from the couch.

Are we still going to the bush? Tiff acted all coy, like I'd forget she had just hung up on me--which I would.

I am. Wouldn't mind if you came with me. I acted all smug like I hadn't disappointed her--which I had.

Deal. Meet at the corner in ten?

Where are you going? My mother looked up at me from her permanent indentation in the living room couch, biting her nails and smoking a long cigarette.

Ew, since when do you smoke Menthols? That smells like shit.

Venice! Her mouth dropped open. I'm trying to quit. And answer my question--where are you going?

Just over to Tiff's. We might watch a movie, or have a fire. I'll probably come home, but if I'm sleeping there I'll let you know.

Fine. But don't call too late. I work at seven-thirty tomorrow. She tapped her cigarette above the ashtray on the coffee table, flaky gray chunks dumping off the end onto Marilyn Monroe's beauty mark.

Shit. What happened to your hair?

Raizel happened. I reached up to touch a piece of my soft hair.

Huh? Tiff's own red hair hung wildly around the shoulders of her black coat. We stood on the quiet corner down the street from my home.

I tried to cut it myself last night. It looked bad. I got it fixed by this chick named Raizel. Funny story, really--

Ohh. Tiff shoved her hands severely into her pockets. She walked around me slowly, checking out my new 'do. In that case, I'm not mad at you for ditching me. No offense, but you look like a tomboy now. You should wear some makeup or somethin', doll up your eyes a little. Why the hell would you cut your own hair?

I shrugged, cold air pushing at my back and going down past the hood of my sweater. I definitely didn't take offense from anything Tiff said. I made a mental note to badger my mother for a new coat.

How was Sophie's game?

They won.

Oh, good. Speaking of Sophie, here're her shoes. I handed her the squeaky clean pair of Nikes I'd been wearing to job interviews. So what'd you bring to drink?

My mom bought me some Smirnoff coolers, but she only let me take two. She's afraid I'll turn into an alcoholic. What about you?

I should have known she would only bring coolers, the sort of drink people often deemed girly. In our society, girly meant weak and weak meant not drunk. I felt around in my backpack and held a water bottle up under the streetlamp.

What is it?

Tiff gazed at the bottle like it was a creature in the local aquarium.

Bacardi one-fifty. Four shots worth but my mom'll never know because it's seventy-five-percent alcohol. I replaced it with water.

Oh! What a good idea. Can I try it?

We each took fast swigs of the shit, our faces pinching together around our mouths like bundles of material ready for tie-dye. We swallowed and then spat on the sidewalk pa-tew pa-tew and laughed, wiping our mouths. Liquor buzzing in our chests, we walked down Oakwood Terrace, my family's street, toward the field. We ducked behind cars and garbage cans in case my mother saw us out the living room window. She knew Tiff lived in the other direction.

From the road we could barely make out the fire glowing between the trees. As we trekked across the cold grass I started seeing shiny metal, the hoods of cars that belonged to wealthy kids. I heard a car stereo bass and people laughing. The bush was a sure deal--whenever my mother asked, I told her Tiff and I had sat around her backyard fire pit all night, and always proved it by shoving my smoky sweater under her nose.

Tiff, promise me something. I put my arm out like I was driving a car and had slammed on the breaks, protectively stopping her from moving forward.

What? She looked eagerly toward the bush party.

Promise me you'll talk to someone tonight. Someone who isn't me. Especially if *he's* here.

Who? She absently palmed her mass of curls as though *he* hadn't been there for the past ten parties.

K, whatever then. Play dumb. I began walking again.

Venice! Fine, I promise! Now give me some more of that shit!

We both laughed and swigged from the rum before swaggering through the bushes to the clearing. I felt like a queen bee. Less than ten people had gathered, which meant we could claim spots on fireside logs. I wondered if the potion in my bag would explode from heat, smiling at the thought. The liquid was already burning in my belly.

High school kids with familiar faces welcomed us and made small talk. Tiff was quiet, but she put forth her friendliest face, the pretty one that showed all her teeth. Every time the others complimented my hair I thanked them profusely and grinned privately about the strangeness of the past few days.

Looking through Tiff's digi-cam one morning after a bush party, we'd named each group and pointed out what we hated about them.

The log across the circle from us held The Gigglers, the group of ninth-graders who showed up at seven-thirty every night and chugged seven-dollar two-litre coolers, always announcing when they were drunk. Lingering at the trees near the edge of the circle were The Dudes, the guys with gangster hats who lit their joints in the fire, cringing and jumping back every time. The Bitches, mostly from Oakwood Heights, drove Sunbirds and Beetles with specialized license plates.

DADSGRL

MISSY

2HOT4U

I recognized a few of them from my days at St. Timothy's Catholic High School, but we barely paid each other heed.

We drank all the alcohol quickly, getting our tilt on and dancing by the cars when older kids showed up. The Young Adults, we'd named them. When *he* arrived Tiff kept dancing, pretending not to notice.

Hey, Oliver! I hollered above the flames in the pit and summoned him over.

Hey Venice. Nice hair. Oliver grinned down at me, hands in the pockets of his coat, old and woolen.

You like it? I patted the back of my new 'do, careful not to flatten my spiked mini 'hawk.

Yeah, you look like Angelina Jolie. But hotter.

Shit, I thought, the best way to get my friend mad at me for a second time that day. Oliver was joking, something hard for Tiff to pick up on.

Gonna go get a drink. I ducked out of the conversation and the Young Adults mingling by the cars. I didn't look back to see if Tiff was talking to the object of her affections. I stalked up to a skinny guy and offered him a toony for a beer.

You want something better? He led me around to the dark side of the trees. I wondered if he wanted to get it on, but I wasn't afraid because I was big and could throw a mean punch. I'd seen him around there plenty of times and he'd never done anything except stand around and smoke joints. He was probably about to offer me some weed.

I like your hair. The guy's chin jutted toward me.

I could've said the same for him if not for the the hood drawn up around his head, darkening his face. He dug into the deep pocket of his baggy jeans, his hand emerging with one of those zip lock bags good parents put sandwiches for their kids' lunches in. The baggie was full of pills. His speech was slurred and his eyelids kept closing in elongated blinks.

Oh, shit, I dunno. I don't really do that.

Come on, boo, it'll get things going for you. I just stocked up. You interested?

I considered reaching in and selecting a pill the way little kids contemplate which crayon to pull from the box. I could've had nearly any color I wanted, but one look at his slick eyes deterred me from saying yes.

No, sorry. Not tonight.

I've seen you around here. Keep in touch if you wanna do business. He gave me a paper with his number on it.

I wasn't stunned. A lot of weird shit happened at parties. In fact, I was undeniably flattered; my haircut must have made me look like someone with bravery to dabble.

I ended up scoring beer from a Young Adult who was old enough to buy booze and didn't ration it as much as us. When I returned to Tiff, she and Oliver were chatting by the car.

So…I applied to the College of Arts. Tiff gazed up at Oliver's kind smile, encased by the beginnings of a scruffy beard. There was something so mature about him.

Already? I thought, but I swelled with pride for her and couldn't stop myself.

She's a genius.

Oliver raised his eyebrows and nodded. Tiff didn't seem mad at me for barging in.

Artistically speaking. Tiff smiled coyly up at him.

Well, I guess we can go for lunch sometimes. Oliver smiled coyly down at her.

How's school going, anyway? I barged in again.

It's tough. Oliver nodded emphatically. But fun. You should definitely consider uni if you get a chance.

Um. Thanks, but no thanks. I smiled. I *will* consider 'borrowing' your November bus pass, though.

Oh, damn. Oliver raised his eyebrows. October's already coming to an end, isn't it?

Yep. Tiff rubbed her chilled hands together, blatantly hoping Oliver would hold them.

We passed the cans around between the three of us and joked about The Gigglers who were out past their bedtimes. When Oliver's cell rang and he excused himself, Tiff and I took off running to the toilet--a separate bunch of trees where girls could pee. I never went there alone, as Oakwood Terrace was dodgy and anything could happen to a chick whether or not she could throw a mean punch.

We squatted a few feet away from each other, dark grass tickling our bare behinds.

How much do you like Oliver, on a scale of one to ten? I asked my friend, mid-relief.

Thirteen. I like him sooo much, Venice. I love his beard thing. And he's so tall. I just want him to pick me up and throw me around. She cracked up laughing. What about you? We never talk about who *you* like. Do you like anyone at the party?

As much as I enjoyed sixth-grade-like conversations regarding crushes, I laughed drunkenly, my stream of urine heading on the slight downhill toward Tiff's feet. She screamed, pulling up her pants, and leapt out of the way.

We spent the rest of the night as we usually did--getting trashed enough to talk to strangers and make inside jokes we'd forget the next day unless someone had caught shit on camera, though I didn't have one of my own. All the rich kids, and kids with jobs, had mobile camera phones. Shortly after starting at Team Bean, Tiff had bought a cell phone. She also had her own digital camera, a present her dad sent her from New York for her birthday. We sang dirty renditions of campfire songs and hugged people we agreed sucked when we were sober.

Oliver and Tiff laughed together. A lot. She pawed his forearm when he cracked jokes. Watching them laugh together, I didn't have to wonder why she liked him--apparently picking up on *his* jokes wasn't too big a feat for my stone-cold friend.

Later that night as we were walking home Tiff pulled the same maneuver I had earlier, putting her arm out as though she was driving and had slammed on the breaks.

Promise me.

What? I giggled.

Oliver saw you with that Seed guy.

Seed?

Yeah, that drug dealer. The words came awkwardly out of her small mouth, so naïve and unaware of what she was saying.

So? I was asking him for beer.

Just promise me you'll stay away from him. I got a bad feeling about him. He's always, like, lurking in the bushes.

I looked at her in the light of the streetlamp, shivering under her big hoody. I had to make her feel safe. I leaned forward wrapped my arms around her. I squeezed.

Love you, Venice. Tiff hugged me back.

She tended to say those words when we'd drunk too much. Maybe it was the alcohol, but they were the most believable I love yous I had at that point in my life. The words were strong enough to constrict my throat and moisten my eyes and warm me while I slept, if I was really allowed to call it sleeping.

8

Mornings after drinking I tended to prolong lifting my head from the pillow for as long as possible. Things were decent until that moment, and after doing so my whole day was determined by how much the room spun and how many hammers banged inside my temples and how many sailboats were at stormy sea inside of me.

My brother Dana rapped on my bedroom door, saying some old broad wanted me on the phone. I pushed past him and his messy hair and sweatpants. His t-shirt was greasy from the previous night's free large-sized popcorn with extra butter from his job at Phantom Cinema. I wondered who dared to wake me so early.

Hello?

Hi, Hon. It's Rhonda calling.

I yawned as she spoke, delaying my next words.

Rhonda who?

From The One Buck Store.

Huh? Oh! Good morning, how are you?

Don't you mean good afternoon?

I looked at the microwave: nearly one p.m.

Yes, sorry. I immediately tried to sound like a respectful young lady as I carried the cordless back to my room.

Hon, I'm calling to let you know the position's been filled.

I wanted to ask her what I'd done wrong and how I could change her mind, but instead said, Thank You, and hung up.

As I lay back in bed and played with the phone antenna, I contemplated calling Raizel. After I'd trimmed her hair she had driven me home at five-thirty, a time when the sun shimmied to the horizon and the sidewalk looked a pale shade of blue. I didn't want her to see that I lived in a brown duplex with a shitty roof like seventy others around it. Her house had character and mine had cracks. But, pulling up, she hadn't looked outside; she had pushed the hair out of my eyes, fixing last details on her piece of work. We'd exchanged numbers as awkwardly as possible. I'd gone inside, engulfed all of Dana's leftover pizza, and crashed for three hours so I'd feel like going out with Tiff.

A number of things stopped me from calling Raizel. She was probably working. Or sleeping, like I should've been. She would probably think I was desperate for friends.

Besides, I couldn't ditch Tiff again. The Autumn-Afternoons-After-Graduation Plan: she and I would sleep-in however late we wanted and then one of us would call the other. We altered the plan for days when she had to work, which was usually just twice a week. We'd walk around the block wishing we had a car so we could go through Tim Horton's drive-thrus and ask for things they didn't sell, like Big Macs and Whoppers. Sometimes she brought her camera and she posed while I shot, dramatic and flamboyant expressions on her little face. She often took candid pictures of me talking or eating--my tongue half out, double-chin doubled.

Getting big cappuccinos from 7-11 had become a ritual, after which we'd take the bus around the city. I never had money, since my mother barely had enough for herself and her stinky smokes, so my best friend paid for everything. First off, she had a job. Secondly, her mom still got a child-support check, all of which went to Tiff's wallet. I always told her I'd pay her back and she always told me to think of it as a present from her dad, even though I'd never met him because he lived in the states and I'd never left Canada.

The day I got rejected by Rhonda the One Buck bitch, my head didn't hurt too badly. Tiff and I took our cappuccinos on the bus and went to the downtown library, a big, magnificent old building I'd held dear in my heart since I was a fetus. Maybe I dragged my feet more than usual that day. After renting a billion DVDs Tiff said she'd treat me to fish 'n' chips at a nearby restaurant.

So, wasn't last night fun? Tiff said, toying with her napkin on the glass tabletop. I watched her tear the little red fish in the center of it.

Yeah, man. The parts I remember, anyway.

Do you remember that creeper when we were dancing?

I looked up, searching my mind. I tugged my bottom lip between my fingers.

Oh my god! Yeah, he was nasty.

Sooo pervy. I can't believe he wanted us to make out.

I can. Guys love that shit.

Do you think Oliver does?

I dunno, maybe you should ask him. We could do it for him sometime. I wiggled my eyebrows.

Um… Tiff looked down at her napkin, ripping the fin of another fish. That's a little weird. You're like my sister.

Oh god, as if you can't tell I'm joking.

Whatever. Oh, and remember that weird Seed guy talking to you?

Yeah. He's actually pretty nice.

Drug dealers aren't nice.

Remember all those rumors last year about that kid who was dealing from his locker? Isn't that crazy?

Exactly, Venice. There's a reason they sent him to prison.

Hey, I wonder if that was Seed.

Not possible. That one kid's totally still in juvy, or maybe adult prison by now. Hey, I have an idea. You should apply *here*.

We looked around at the servers with their black aprons and frilly George Washington shirts, the black and white checkered floor, the crystal-framed mirrors lining the walls.

Nah. The wound's still fresh. I'm gonna wait a few days before trying again. I swirled my Coke around with my straw. Besides, who wants to work at a place where they serve straws with pop? You're never supposed to drink pop through a straw.

Even at Micky D's?

Okay. McDonald's can do whatever they want and it'll still taste good. Mmm. Greasy, delectable--

Venice, I have to tell you something. Tiff looked down at her napkin massacre. I'm afraid of art school.

I knew it! I laughed, clapping my hands successfully. You're afraid of talking to your classmates, aren't you?

She gave me The Look, the one usually directed at her mother.

Whoa. Don't give me The Look.

Don't act like I'm not stepping out of my shell.

Sorry. You were great at the party last night, talking to Oliver for more than a minute. I laughed and sipped my drink.

Your new hairdo has made you a bitch. By the way, he came over when I went home. Who needs to talk when there's other stuff to do?

I snorted, nearly shooting soda up into my nostrils.

Why didn't you tell me?

She shrugged, shredding her napkin with her fork.

How far did you go?

Not as far as you and Kale.

Excuse me? I put my drink down and stared at her. She could be bitchy, but I could always intimidate her to death. She kept her eyes down and I tried not to feel guilty for anything.

I'm sick of fighting with you. She sighed.

Who says we're fighting? I nudged her foot under the table and smiled, wondering if she actually thought I should apologize. By the way, he e-mailed me the other day.

Who?

Kale.

Well, what'd it say?

I'll show you later. It's funny.

After the meal Tiff wanted to treat me to more stuff. She said it was because I was her best friend, but I knew it was because we'd had tension. Buying stuff was like wearing blemish cream. We could pretend the pimple was gone, but it would still be red and throbbing when we washed our faces at the end of the night. We got ten-dollar esthetic school manicures, drinks from Booster Juice, and then she wanted to buy me my first lottery ticket.

My mom gets them all the time. She won a hundred bucks once. And since I turned eighteen I haven't bought one.

She was right; she'd turned eighteen in August while I'd remain a tender seventeen until December. We passed the One-Buck Store so I could spit on the window and its advertisement for one-dollar toenail clippers. We were a block from our destination when I realized where she was leading me.

I looked forward to seeing Raizel, but I wasn't prepared. I liked her. She was pretty and different and nicer to me than a stranger had ever been, despite the fact that she'd suggested I take drugs. In the back of my thoughts all day I had been wondering when I should phone her. I imagined how obsessed she'd think I was if I coincidentally wandered into her work. Again.

The drug store loomed at us a block away, its red and blue sign shining in the sky.

MAIN STREET PHARMACY
for your personal and pharmaceutical needs

I slowed my walk, claiming to have cramps from the food. I worried about what Tiff and Raizel would think of each other. Tiff would probably pinpoint Raizel as one of those prissy rich chicks she could never get along with. She would hate her for being so warm and blond and for trying to look like Marilyn Monroe, and for trying to steal me, and Raizel would probably think Tiff was cute and try to straighten her luscious red curls. I would have chuckled if nerves allowed it.

Upon arriving, I made Tiff enter before me, just like I'd made Dana go up the attic stairs first when I was tripping and scared. I couldn't see anyone, but heard voices at the back of the store.

Let's get this over with. I rang the bell on the counter. While Tiff peered through the glass case at the lottery tickets, I looked around and tapped my foot.

Hey, girlfriend. Oh my god. Your hair looks *so* good. He appeared, lanky Liam with his black hair, pale skin, and tight, purple jeans. He gestured to my hair, eighty percent of his fingers that day adorned with rings.

Tiff raised her strawberry-blond eyebrows behind her glasses. Oh shit. I'd been so consumed by how my friend would perceive Raizel that I didn't consider how she'd perceive Liam.

Thanks. I smile all big and proud. I didn't feel like introducing two clashing rebels to each other, as they obviously both thought they were genuine representations of an era they were too young to have experienced. I had to admit, Liam had an interesting spin on 'punk'.

Liam looked through Tiff and her talking eyebrows at me.

So, what can I get for you? Smokes?

We don't smoke. Tiff turned to look at a wall of gum.

I rolled my eyes, smiling at Liam. I didn't know anything about the lottery, so I just pointed at the Halloween specials.

Two of those. I glanced over my shoulder a few times, but couldn't see Raizel or that older dude.

Tiff gave me money. As I was handing it over the counter Liam spoke again.

What're you up to later?

Surprised, I looked at Tiff again and back at Liam.

Not a whole lot. Maybe going to the bush at Oakwood.

Oakwood? Like, *old* Oakwood? That's so dodgy. And it's cold outside. You should come party at my friend's place.

Yeah? Maybe.

Tiff stared with her mouth open. I couldn't help but relish her eyes darting back and forth between us. Liam wrote his number on the change, a five-dollar bill, and grinned as he told me to call him at nine.

When Tiff and I got outside I gave her one of the lottery tickets. We leaned on the cold wood of a bench and scratched the gray ticket parts with a couple of pennies.

Who's he?

Shit sorry, I forgot to introduce you. That's Liam. I met him yesterday.

So, what, is he gonna be your new boyfriend or something?

Seriously? Don't you think he seems gay? I smiled.

Yes, he does. I was gonna warn you, just in case you were interested. Which I'm glad you're not. What a jerk, calling Oakwood dodgy.

Oakwood *is* dodgy!

He reminds me of Ellie from Degrassi. Tiff's lip curled up.

You're the redhead.

Bitch. You win anything?

No. You?

Nah.

We stuffed the tickets into a trashcan and walked toward the bus terminal. My fingertips were cold and I noted the first sight of my breath. When I could see my breath there was barely time to put on a sweater before winter would screech around the corner.

Are you gonna go to that party? Tiff stamped her feet for warmth.

I dunno. I wished more than anything that she would encourage me to go. I don't exactly know him.

Don't go. Let's have a movie night. We did rent all that shit from the library.

Okay. I agreed without agreeing.

Can I have my five bucks then?

I tried not to feel anything as I gave her the fiver and Liam's number.

9

Tiff requested an action movie, one with guns and cars and grunting men trying to save a girl taken for ransom. Beside me on the couch, Tiff sipped happily on the chocolate milk she'd brought over. She squealed when every car chase began. The more she wiggled and grabbed my elbow, the more I fought the urge to fling her away from me.

I moved to the computer and curled my legs up under me and checked my e-mail. I wanted to phone Raizel. I thought it had been long enough, and the point of exchanging numbers was to call each other, but I worried about what Tiff would say.

Why do you want to be friends with her? That's a weird way to make friends with someone. You don't even know her.

Hey, can I read that e-mail from Kale now?

I looked over my shoulder at her.

Sure.

I opened the e-mail, getting up so Tiff could sit in the computer chair.

This isn't exactly to *you,* Venice. It's just one of those forwarded questionnaire things.

Yeah, but look at the list of recipients. Only my e-mail address shows up.

True, true. She scrolled down with the mouse. Over her shoulder, I re-read his words.

What's your full name?: Kale James Shepherd.
How old are you?: It's a secret ;)
What's your boyfriend/girlfriend's name?: Don't have one

That was good. The next questions made something move around in my belly.

Where are you?: In my bedroom.
What are you wearing?: Blue plaid boxers and a wife beater…not that I have a wife ;)

Also good.

I couldn't stop it from entering my head.

We're in his little room listening to the Ramones, each on our third Heineken. He makes fun of my Punk Attitude purse and I slap his forearm. He grabs my wrist, quick despite the booze. My hair is long and black, dangling in his lap.

I deny wanting anything from him until my lips fall upon his. The music blazes the air while I climbed onto him. The computer chair creaks, his tongue in my mouth. My legs around his waist, he picks me up, the first person to lift me since I was three feet tall. I push his hands off my fat waist. He throws me on the bed and I imagine he's a puppeteer and I'm a small, pretty rag doll.

We'd fuck for ten minutes.

Afterwards, he smokes a cigarette out his bedroom window, in consideration of what my mother might say if I go home smelling like a sports bar. He doesn't know she's a chain smoker. I watch him standing naked and wonder if he'll crawl back under the sheets. The beer closes my eyes and he tells me not to fall asleep.

Why not?

I'm not through with you.

Sure thought you were. I motion at his thing, hanging limply like the cigarette in his fingers.

He pauses, looking at me.

You say the weirdest things.

Really? Is that a good thing?

You're just not...like...other girls.

Good. I smile.

He stubs his smoke out and throws it out the window. I feel guilty, wondering if it will fall in an old lady's hair eight stories below. Kale comes back to the bed and spoons me and claims he's too drunk to drive me home in his Jeep, not that he wants me to go, anyway. He kisses the back of my neck and breathes on me with beer breath that I purposely mistake as the scent of an older man.

He has me again, standing up against his bedroom door, where people in the apartment across the alley can see everything. Nearly everything. Even with their best bird-watching binoculars they would never see that we were something other than a girl and her boyfriend in passionate mid-afternoon throes.

I'm gonna get some pickles and crackers, you want anything? I asked Tiff, tearing away from memories. I stretched my arms up high, trying to dispel my dirty thoughts. I stifled the urge to whistle the way people do in cartoons when they're being casual.

Really? I'll come up with you and check out the pantry. Tiff pulled her legs out from under her butt and stood up.

No, it's okay. I chewed the flesh inside my cheek. You relax. I'll find something good and bring it down.

Okay. I'm gonna check my Facebook.

Good. That would tide her over for a bit.

You want me to make you a profile?

What, on Facebook?

Yeah. Come on. It's really fun.

No, I really don't. But thanks. I ran out of the basement, skipping every other stair, and shut the door behind me. I was quick about it, taking the cordless into my room. I scrambled to find the right pocket of the jeans I'd worn that magnificent day, and after three heavy breaths I punched seven digits into the phone.

Bang bang bang. My heart. I found myself doing something I'd only ever seen happen in movies. My mind made my fingers press End right when I was going to press Talk. I chuckled, disbelieving what I'd just done.

I managed to redial the number, press Talk, and wait while it rang. Before I could wonder how long was too long to wait, a voice was in my ear.

Hello?

It was her.

Hello?

H--I coughed. Hey, what's up?

Who's this?

It's Venice. What's up?

Who?

Venice…you did my hair yesterday. I tugged the round collar of my t-shirt away from my neck, glancing at my bedroom doorway.

Ohh. You must want Raizel. I'll go get her.

Oops. Yeah. Please.

I looked at my watch and waited, trying not to hum in the silence. I had already been upstairs for three minutes and Tiff would start to wonder.

Hello?

Hi, Raizel?

Yeah, Venice? Her voice leaked across the phone and tickled my ear.

Who was that? She sounded just like you.

My sister Abby. Everyone says that. Sorry if she pretended to be me and said stupid things.

No, don't worry. I chuckled and cleared my throat. I was just calling to see what you're doing this weekend.

Working 'til five on Friday, and I have Saturday off.

Oh, do you wanna get together Friday night?

Okay. I got invited to a party if you wanna come. Hey, you can meet Abby.

That sounds cool.

Should I pick you up?

Yeah, what time's good for you? I grinned into the phone.

About six-thirty. I like to start early.

Deal. Do you remember where I live?

Clear as day.

When we hung up I giddily gathered things from the fridge and leapt down the stairs. Tiff didn't notice how long I'd taken, eagerly reaching for the jar of pickles. She was concentrating on her Facebook profile pictures, ninety-eight percent of which she'd taken with her family's webcam. I didn't ask what I'd missed in the movie.

We continued with the Autumn-Afternoons-After-Graduation Plan for the rest of the week, since Tiff didn't have any more shifts until the weekend. For her it meant getting out of the house while her mom blasted love ballads and cut middle-aged women's hair in their basement. For me it meant filling the absence of responsibility with drinking coffee and renting things from the library.

Whenever people annoyed me, Dana or my mother, I remembered my plans with Raizel and her sister. I cleaned the house Friday morning only after everyone had left for work, because they would overanalyze the situation so much that things would be dusty again before they realized they should thank me. My mother would feel guilty for having become a slob over the past six months.

I vacuumed the rug and washed the dishes and folded the clean laundry. I organized the front closet and, after deciding she wouldn't miss it, took my mother's old winter coat from the floor and added it to *my* closet. The jacket wasn't too puffy or old-lady-ish, just this sleek black thing with a drawstring around the middle.

A typical supper at the Knight house: one of us would boil a no-name can of chicken noodle soup, or tomato, or cream of mushroom. If Dana was there, we'd need two cans. He was a growing boy. Then we'd share a sleeve of saltine crackers, letting the crumbs get all over the table or counter where the pack was opened. Throughout my life I'd become creative at dipping things in soup--melba toast, sandwich meat, celery sticks, pickles, potato chips, pasta, and one experimental time, a forkful of peanut butter. I was the master at savoring. I knew that if I was lucky enough to get cheese, I should put it at the bottom of my soup bowl and pretend to forget about it until the soup was gone. I knew, when I re-discovered the cheese all melted and stringy, how to wrap it around my spoon and suck it off, savoring.

We'd take our bowls to the living room and sit in a row on the pilled sofa, chatting between bites. Sometimes one of us, or all of us, would be in a bad mood and we'd avoid talking. One time we put ER on, but I shouldn't remember that. I just looked through the colors and the people and their voices, stared at the reflection of my family. There I was with my flat hair, my brother with his bulbous belly, and my mother with her head tilted down, raccoon eyes trained desperately on things flashing on the screen of a little electric box. I stared at her for ten minutes and waited for her to move or notice how zombie-like she was. Nothing happened. I think I looked away out of boredom, but also because I felt a tiny bit sad.

I was a tough girl, but little things sometimes made me sad.

The difference that Friday and every other weekday since I could remember was that when my mother came in with her chapped lips and cheeks all red from the wind, she looked straight in my eyes and smiled before lifting her bowl and shuffling out to the living room sofa. She had noticed the absence of crumbs and dirt crunching under her socks as she trekked across the carpet, had noticed the records and books neatly piled on the shelves instead of toppling over one another and spilling across the coffee table.

I wondered if she had noticed the absence of gooey brown tobacco stains etching their way from the ceiling down the walls, or the faint ache in my shins from tiptoeing on a chair.

10

We were on a gravel road. Abby was driving us to this bonfire party on the outskirts of town, and I was squished between the door and a brown paper bag of booze. I was forced to trust her to drive ten kilometers above the limit and check her text messages at the same time. She had fuzzy blue covers on the seats. My backpack was at a weird angle and I was concerned about its contents descending to the dirty car floor--my battered house keys and the rape whistle I'd picked up for free at the Sexual Abuse Prevention Convention at my school in grade eleven. When Raizel saw it she made fun of me, asking who had time to pull out a whistle and reef on it while being attacked. I'd kept it because it was a gorgeous shade of purple.

That sunny evening we raced along a road I'd never met and all I could smell was green tea air freshener dangling from the rearview.

Ten minutes later we arrived, parking Abby's clunky old car beside several others in the driveway. We were at a small gray farmhouse with all the fixings, wooden birds sticking out of dead geranium pots, a thin metal rail meant for scraping mud and manure off boots, a small windmill creaking in the breeze. None of us quite knew who lived there, a friend of a friend of one of Abby's college classmates, but we didn't care as long as the party was good.

Abby knocked on the front door while Raizel and I shot the shit by the car and put one-liter bottles of Coke and Jack Daniels in our coat pockets. I possessed a definite pride about having been a drinker for so long, as I was the one to suggest pre-mixed liquor. We wouldn't have to take swigs of shit that made us cringe before we chased it with something soft. We wouldn't have to pour the liquid anywhere but down our throats, something that could be difficult when we were too trashed to even button our jeans properly after squatting in bushes. We wore mitts and draped long-ass scarves around our necks. Raizel took a blanket out of the trunk. The chill had me more than happy to be wearing my mother's rejected closet-floor jacket.

No one answered the door for Abby, so she led us behind the house. Three guys sat around a wooden picnic table. They introduced themselves as Ian, Kyle, and Gary. I knew I'd remember Ian because someone had written *Prada* in big, messy black letters across the front of his hoody. They seemed older than us, broad-shouldered and tall when they stood to grab us some lawn chairs. They were all good-looking and gentlemanly, yet abrasive with their jokes about each other. The girls and I sat giggling in our seats with the booze held between our knees.

Dinnertime in autumn--I had never realized that a farm was the perfect place to be. The sun took forever to set on flatlands surrounding us, hot pink in a sky streaked orangey-red and purple and dark blue and eventually black. I was reminded of the gorgeous painting Tiff had made for me when we met, the one with little faraway people indelibly rooted to the ground like trees.

I'd loved that painting and had immediately put it up in my room. The first time Tiff had come over and seen it her cheeks had become warm and she had smiled all shyly behind her glasses. I had asked her why there were four people in the painting and she had said, 'You, your brother Dana, your mother Kathy, and the other person who made you'. That was the clearly defined moment in which I began loving her. I'd gotten to look at the painting until spring when water had come in through the cracks in my window and slid down the wall. The moon had dissolved in the sky and the sky in the people and the people in their roots and the ground and onto the rest of wall and all the way down to my carpet. Then it had looked more like the painting *I* had made for *her* when we'd first met.

The other advantage of being an experienced drinker was that I knew how strongly emotions tended to come on. Thinking about Tiff saddened me and made me wish she was there and that she liked making new friends as much as I did. Art school would be really hard for her. But still, that was a hole she seemed weirdly willing to dig. I stifled my thoughts and zoned in on what was being said around me.

Abby was damn good at getting attention. She drew the boys in with her petite figure and radiant smile. Her hair wasn't as blond as Raizel's, and it was long and straight, and she wore jeans instead of cool tights, but her voice carried further and she said whatever she wanted. First meeting her that evening she had looked me up and down.

You're right, Raisin, she's fucking sexy.

I had on my loose-fitting jeans and my high-tops, not as special as she made me out to be. I wondered if Raizel had actually said such a thing. Something didn't feel right about comparing Abby and Raizel as sisters; I could barely tell Abby was a year older. They were more like mates from boarding school who told each other everything. As far as I knew, siblings weren't supposed to talk about smoking pot and stealing from an overpriced lingerie shop, in case they let something slip at the dinner table.

That was girl talk. With the boys, Abby talked about reality TV and how her purpose of living was to get on Canadian Idol so she could moon the whole country. Within five minutes of conversation I knew that she hated two things--bad fashion and North American reality television.

People started showing up when I was half done my drink, which meant I wasn't shy about introducing myself. For a moment I stood atop an incline in the field. I couldn't spot any Gigglers, Dudes, or Bitches, just some Young Adults amid a smattering of Older Young Adults.

Ian and I were the ones to get the fire going, building a teepee out of small chunks of wood and crumpled paper. Everyone made a circle around us to block the wind and I fell into my whiskey-tainted imagination. The pit blazed and I got to chuck logs in like a rustic woodsman working hard to keep his family warm. Ian threw me over his shoulder like a sack of beans and dropped me outside the circle in a bed of tall grass. He plopped down beside me and shared his flask's contents with me, scotch that scorched my tongue and warmed my chest.

Anyone could have seen it coming. One glance at his smile and his elbow nudging my drunken body into the grass, and you could predict it. I let things go the way they were supposed to, the way romance fanatics watching the movie of Us would have appreciated. I let him kiss me even though I had seen snot in his nostril a second earlier. I let his tongue march across mine and his hand hold my head until the ground's frost soaked through the back of my jeans. I shivered and detached my face from his.

I'm gonna go piss. I went meandering through the crowd to find my people. My friends. Faces smiled at me from under parka hoods with faux-fur trim.

I found Raizel standing facing the fire sucking on her Coke bottle, nearly empty.

There you are, V! She unfolded the blanket so we could hug inside it for warmth.

Someone started singing *My Heart Will Go On* and people caught the tune like dynamite strings catching flame, lighting the night with our drunken voices. The farm was better than the bush at Oakwood; the farm was bigger and there was no one around for a mile to complain of our noise. Raizel put her colds hands inside my jacket, between my sweater and t-shirt. I shrieked and let her keep them there even though they had discovered my big marshmallow of a belly.

Raizel must have been frozen in her miniskirt and cupcake tights. Thankfully, she had on her pea coat and her fire-engine shoeboots. I hugged her back for a minute, resting my chin on top of her head, like I did with Tiff when we were drunk enough.

We finished our drinks quickly and tossed the bottles in the fire. I enjoyed the way they crinkled and disappeared at the coals. Soon, Abby sauntered up to us, empty-handed and complaining that the whiskey and Coke hadn't been enough. I was bigger than her and definitely feeling it, but not to the point where things were unclear. I thought to myself, I should have brought more. I could handle more.

I wish we had something better. Abby tucked her long hair behind her ears and looked around.

I doubt we'll find anything out here. Raizel sighed.

Yeah, it's not exactly my scene. Let's go get the car. Abby turned toward the driveway.

I was going to say that I was enjoying myself and that I couldn't imagine a better way to spend the night, but Raizel looked at me dead-on.

You wanna go, V? Her eyes were all big and inquisitive.

I couldn't pass up the chance to experience the alleged 'something better' with her. That moment when I looked at the party it was different, groups of people cuddled by a dim fire, content with their beers and their hot dogs on sticks and low laughter, inside jokes. I suddenly felt as though we were intruding on a cozy gathering of friends. Some guy was sitting on the ground somewhere, waiting for me with his tongue hanging out of his mouth.

Of course, let's hit the road.

The three of us flattered ourselves by covering our heads with the blanket as if anyone would ask us where the hell we were going. We ran in the cold around the house to the driveway, which had filled up with cars in the past two hours. Our fists bounced off the hoods of all the other vehicles as we ran by, for no reason other than to hear the clang of metal on an October night.

I suspected Abby was tanked, but I wanted to get back to the city so badly that I couldn't bring myself to say anything. We sat on fuzzy blue seat covers with the car heater on for five minutes before we peeled out. My worry subsided as Abby drove steadily in the dark. The city lights appeared soon enough and then Abby was texting on her phone again. The night was absolutely ours.

Okay, I think I can get us something. Abby held up her phone.

Sweet! Raizel cheered.

If not, my brother Dana can pull for us. I smiled, excited to keep the party going.

What? Abby glanced over her shoulder at me.

Watch the road! Raizel sternly ordered her sister. Venice, she's not talking about booze.

Oh?

No, man, I'm talking about Daisy, Abby clarified, facing forward. Besides, *I'm* old enough to pull.

Who's Daisy? I was like the dopiest of the Seven Dwarves.

E. Raizel glanced back at me again and smiled, cocking her head.

The drug had many nicknames--E, X, ecstasy, but I'd never heard daisy before. When I was in grade twelve our whole school had endured a lecture about E; it'd happened right after some kid was caught dealing out of his locker at another school in Sloam. I'd read about it in the paper and heard all sorts of things--he'd been polygraph-forced into admitting the names of all his customers, who'd subsequently been sought out and charged with possession. The boy himself had been arrested, detained, and expelled. He'd been sent to a strict juvenile center where he probably still remained. The newspaper had quoted his ashamed parents:

We didn't raise our son to deal drugs. We sent him to a nice school in a nice neighborhood. We just want to know what we did wrong.

Then in school, we'd been warned about the possible consequences of taking E--mental instability, comatose, strokes, and death. I didn't know about the upsides firsthand, but people used the drug at raves to achieve feelings of a completely euphoric nature. Calling it daisy seemed to simplify it as sweet and happy and safe.

The music in the car was nice, caressing my thoughts about the choice I had to make. To be or not to be; to do chemical drugs or to...what? I clearly imagine what Tiff would say. I pushed her voice out of my head before I could be influenced.

Who is this? I poked my face between the front seats. I looked at the houses flying past, thankful for dull traffic and therefore fewer things for Abby to crash into.

Tegan and Sara. Raizel flashed a smile over her shoulder with her crazy-white teeth. Don't you love them?

Oh. I've never heard of them.

WHAT? I don't believe you.

They sound good. I shrugged.

Good? They're AMAZING.

Better than Ani?

Abby laughed then, interjecting.

You can't argue with her about Ani. But she's right, Tegan and Sara are the shit.

Cool. I smiled, mentally adding the band to my checklist of Things to Borrow from the big, magnificent, old downtown library.

A few minutes later I recognized Golden Street; we drove past Abby and Raizel's Dr. Seuss home, all of its light off and Raizel's Camaro parked docilely out front. We stopped at an apartment building at the end of the street. Abby cut the engine and dialed a number on her cell phone.

Can we come up?

I noticed my reflection in the rearview mirror--wide eyes and pale skin. I had to remember to stop by Raizel's work for some blush, if I could squeeze money out of my mother. We all crawled out and put on our hoods, protecting our ears from chill. Tummy butterflies skipped me across the apartment parking lot.

Despite our lazy whiskey limbs, we made it up to the fifth floor, which smelled exactly the way people think apartment buildings smell--like cats and old newspapers and foreign foods. The walls were off-white and the carpet bore a reddish-purple paisley pattern usually designated for senior citizens' sofas.

Standing outside door 508 and knocking, Abby and Raizel and I smiled at each other.

The first thing I saw when the door opened was an afro--a freaky, pin-curled black afro seemingly untouched by chemicals and heated tools and anything else you can think of that damages hair. I also saw big, black eyes and glowing brown skin and a warm, pink-lipped smile. Despite the recent commencement of fall, she wore a short orange dress showing most of her legs, thin legs that went on forever, a dark river leading to bare feet on the front entrance linoleum. I stopped breathing for a moment. Gold bangles clanged around her tiny wrist as she thrust her hand at me.

Hi. I'm Amara.

Um. I'm Venice. I took her hand and noticed a gap between her teeth. The narrow black slit looked like mine, but somehow she remained flawless and I remained a big, blundering blob.

Don't worry if you stop breathing. Abby slid past me to enter the apartment. Everyone does when they see Amara.

I wondered how weird being a model would be--that is, for everyone to know your job before you tell them. I shook the afro girl's soft hand, entranced by her grin.

Amara's place was so warm, we peeled off our hoods and scarves and mitts and coats onto the front landing floor. We drank orange juice and sank into living room furniture, Raizel and I on the sofa, Abby and Amara in respective armchairs. The apartment living room was particularly average, with DVDs strewn about, a bookcase, and framed Walmart wall art, the kinds of photographs I personally had the capability to create. I vowed to never be sold at Walmart. My stomach was a dolphin begging for fish, flipping over and over again

Flip flip flip.

I desperately wanted to understand the big fuss about pills, little colorfully compacted chemicals. Apparently, they were something better than whiskey and out-of-town bonfires.

II

Amara undid the string on her necklace satchel and withdrew several orange, circular pills. I watched her afro shake when she smiled and turned her hand, dumping the pills onto the coffee table. I wondered if she had intentionally matched her dress with them.

Abby and Raizel both passed Amara money, though I didn't see how much. When I dug my wallet to see how much I could scrounge up, Raizel put her arm out.

I got you.

Thanks. I smiled.

Don't they remind you of your grad? Amara's eyes flashed up at Raizel.

Yeah. Raizel smiled, a memory bubbling in her mind. But those had percentage signs on them, right?

No. Amara shook her head. Dollar signs.

Oh.

We each picked up a pill and held them between our forefingers and thumbs. I examined mine as casually as possible, realizing there was a picture stamped on it. Was it Buddha? I barely had time to think before Abby raised her glass.

Cheers, baby!

We all popped them onto our tongues and took heavy swigs. The orange juice was sweet, refreshing, and cleansing, in that no one outside that room could've told what was in my esophagus, or possibly already my stomach. I couldn't feel it and therefore didn't have to believe it existed. Amara put on a CD, this compilation of artists I'd never heard before. Their voices and lyrics were genius. While Abby and Amara got into a heated conversation about feather jewelry, I moved down the couch toward Raizel.

Hey, I wanna tell you something. Well, two things.

Shoot. She looked at me and smiled, white-blond waves hanging around her glowing cheeks.

Thanks for my haircut. I love it.

No problem, V. Thanks for mine, too. She sipped her orange juice. And what's the second thing?

Can I call you Raisin?

She laughed, displaying a row of milk-white teeth, and pulled the cup away from her lips.

You're about the millionth person who thought of that. I give you props for asking, though. Sure, call me Raisin.

Whoa. Amara pulled her thoughts from Abby to put her orange juice down on the coffee table. You must be special.

She got down on the carpet and sat cross-legged, drawing her dress halfway up her caramel thighs. Amara was even skinnier than Tiff, so skinny she could have comfortably worn her bracelets around her thighs. She sifted through a pile of CDs.

Yeah, Abby added. She doesn't let, like, anyone call her that. Just me and Mom and Dad. And Sullivan used to.

I smiled into my plastic cup, sipping. I felt like the juice was sweetening me, body and soul, reaching under my fingernails and between my hair follicles.

Raizel leaned back into the sofa and looked at me with her eyes half-closed, a smile taking over her face.

Who's Sullivan? I sipped my orange juice again.

Raizel and Abby made eye contact and I used my x-ray photographer's goggles to understand a whole conversation in their split-second glance. *She doesn't know? Doesn't know what? Doesn't know about Sullivan, silly. What about him? Aren't you going to tell her?*

Their brother. Amara stared down at her collection of CDs. Sort-of.

Not really, now, Raizel spoke. A whole other time, an *era,* passed through her radiant eyes.

Oh my god, I thought. *Did he die?* I remembered Raizel's hair-cutting mirror, and cringed at what I'd said.

Wow, you guys must be close, hanging out together.

The conversation passed dully. Everyone moved eagerly onto another topic. Soon I noticed a presence in the room, something climbing under everyone and pushing them up. My new friends tilted their heads while entertaining thoughts, necks slack like newborn babies'. Abby tapped her toes and all ten fingers. Amara kept changing the music. I was in a warm place. Everything was vivid; the colors in the room were alert and exaggerated--the blazing blue sofa, candy red carpet, and shiny orange goldfish in its bowl by the window. Everything was pretty. I wanted to stand up.

Um. I looked around, my head tilting like theirs were. I blinked for a full two seconds, during which the sides of my mouth rose into unstoppable glory. I think Buddha's arrived.

Y'think? Raizel softly replied, picking my arm up from its docile position on the couch. She slung it around her back, my hand resting on her shoulder and her hair three inches closer to my cheek. I couldn't stop smiling about our newfound companionship.

Your dress looks really cool. I looked away from Raizel at Amara. It's like a tangerine.

Hey, wow! Amara looked down. How nice.

She grabbed the edges of the skirt and got up off the carpet to twirl like a child in a Sunday morning church dress. After a minute I realized the lumps protruding through her tight dress material were hip bones. She turned up the music on the big stereo system, an artist I finally recognized, and gave a big, gap-toothed smile.

I love Radiohead! I shouted.

It's Thom Yorke's solo album! She cried back. Come dance with me!

I accepted her hand and she pulled me off the couch. Raizel stretched out on the cushions. Amara and I threw our arms up, bouncing and swaying. Every time my toes reconnected with the soft carpet jolts of enjoyment sprung up my shins. My legs and hips matched the beat dead-on. Seeing Amara's beauty, I was reminded of my own. I was twice her size, but felt like a feather. I danced carelessly with my cool new hair.

Abby got Raizel up off the couch and we all grabbed hands in a messy round of Ring-Around-the-Rosie. I was floating again, up up up, like when I'd taken the Gravol, but to an entirely different place.

HELLO? Abby shouted into her cell phone. Amara had changed the CD to techno and there was no avoiding the noise. Abby covered her ear with her hand. LYLE?

Raizel, Amara, and I shrugged at each other, which was when I noticed their gigantic, black pupils. My own eyes felt sprung open the size of pancakes. When I reached for the stereo's volume knob, I looked at my hand and wondered how it could be so different from other girls'. My fingers were stout and had square tips, while theirs were all long and slender.

Here lemme get that. Raizel was near my ear, leaning on my shoulder to reach past me and turn the music down. Her hair smelled like peaches.

That's better. Abby uncovered her ear and stationed her hand on her hip. Who's this?...Kyle? Uh huh?...I know. I remember you. You told me a funny penguin joke...Uh huh...Who? Ohhhhh.

Abby looked up and nodded directly at me, grinning.

I looked away from my hand and turned to Raizel.

Who do you think it is?

No idea. Her lips played with her labret piercing.

I looked at my left shoulder, down my arm to my elbow, and down my forearm at my fingers, my strange, mannish hand entwined with a pretty one. Her thumb skin rubbed softly against mine.

Oh my god. Even her arm had blond hair.

Oh my god what? Raizel asked.

Okay. Okay. I'll tell her. She'll be tickled pink. Hold on a sec, k? Abby looked at me. The guy you made out with wants to do it with you.

I opened my mouth.

What? Who?

Ian or something?

Ohh. I couldn't believe that had happened in the same evening. What does he want to do with me?

Huh? When did you make out with someone? Raizel dropped my hand, a hot piece of toast.

Is he hot? Amara asked, a giraffe swaying to the music on her hind legs. She seemed to be clenching her jaw, the bones in her face hard with concentration.

Ew, Amara. Raizel tsked.

He wants to know if you'll go out with him tomorrow. Abby leaned on the wall and closed her eyes, cell phone hanging at the end of her flaccid arm.

I felt my cheeks turn a hot, buzzing red.

Raizel moved away from me to turn up the music and grab Amara's hands, putting them up and hopping. Amara was taller and looked down at Raizel in such a loving way I could've cried. Lauren Hill was busting a lung. The girls' skirts moved flirtatiously with the music, Amara's bare feet and Raizel's cupcake tights pawing the rug.

Abby plugged her ear again and spoke.

GIVE US HIS NUMBER AND SHE'LL CALL HIM TOMORROW.

We all danced for a while, shouting the lyrics when we knew them. Amara stopped changing the CD when she became so entranced by a techno song that a house fire couldn't have torn her out of that living room. She stood with her eyes closed, toes moving around on the carpet like an anteater feeling its environment. I was beyond fascinated, running my hand up and down Amara's bare arm, Abby doing the same to her on her other side. I had never known how many different smiles one person could have. I closed my eyes.

When I opened my eyes I moved my head around.

Hey guys, where's Raizel?

Amara's eyes fluttered open briefly, like the wings of a butterfly, before she re-closed them and continued swaying.

Abby twirled, clenching her jaw, and shrugged.

Doin' her thing.

She's been gone a long time. I noted their nonchalance. I floated away from the others, across the carpet to the dim hallway, seeing three doors. I felt like I was on a game show and had to choose the door with the best prize behind it. I led my fingers rub against the wall as I walked, enjoying the tingling sensation on the back of my hand. Door number one, on my right, led to a pantry. Door number two, on my left, led to a bathroom.

I looked straight ahead at the third door, wondering if Raizel had gone to sleep. If so, I'd be sure to call her a party pooper. The night was just getting started, and continuing without her didn't feel right, for she was the glorious one who had brought me there. Looking down, I saw a light in the space between the carpet and the wooden door. The light was instantaneous, a laughing red and then a whispering blue, like police lights.

Raisin? I breathed her name, knocking carefully. When I pressed myself against the door the cool feeling of wood caressed my body through my clothes.

Soon it opened and I tumbled as gracelessly as possible into the police room, landing on the carpet on my hands and knees.

Shut the door.

I quickly obeyed and squinted through the flashing lights to see her sprawled across the huge bed. The room was the largest in the apartment, and I thought at the time that it smelled like potpourri, though later came to know the scent of the fruity hookah contraption on the dresser. An electric disco ball on the bedside table mercilessly slapped colors across the walls and ceiling. My favorite was orange, for it seemed on fire and reminded me over and over again of Raizel's Camaro and Amara's dress and pills with Buddha on them.

I stayed on my knees and crawled to the bedside, my head near Raizel's.

Are you okay? I tried to see her face.

Yup.

I soon realized she was grinning from ear to ear, eyes closed, body smothered in a blanket and the hood of her sweater drawn around her face as though the room was cold.

I'm just watching the lights through my eyelids. You should try it.

Okay. I leaned back against the nightstand and let my eyes close. The lights became alive, clown yellow and flamingo pink and jungle green, gently moving. This is *so* pretty.

Have you ever watched a disco ball on daisy before?

Ummm...No. I opened my eyes and watched her, burrowed peacefully in the blankets. I debated telling her I was an all-around newbie. Have you?

Ohhh yeah. It's my favorite. Just ask Abby.

Do you guys do daisy a lot?

Raizel's eyes opened, two dark almonds.

Not too often. You?

I wondered what was not too often. I wondered what was too often.

This is my first time.

Shut up! Raizel hoisted herself up on her elbow. If I'd known that I would have taken you to the club or somewhere cool.

This is pretty cool. I smiled. Can I come up there?

Of course. She smiled back, moving over and holding the blanket open. I crawled in and lay on my side, facing her with inches between us. Now, I'm gonna give you the best first trip ever. Pull your hood up like mine.

I followed her instructions, appreciating the soft warmth around my head.

Now take this.

We each used one of her iPod earbuds. She flipped through her tunes, the device casting light over her cheeks and nose. My eyes felt distracted by her labret ball, wanting to touch it.

I wanna get a piercing.

Yeah? Where? Raizel glanced up at me before continuing to scroll.

I dunno. But I really like yours.

Thanks, V. Okay, are you ready? It's The Silly Rainbows.

The Silly Rainbows? Is that the band name?

The music came on and I closed my eyes, imagining a band in a blank white room. There was a soft guitar melody, and then a simple drum and the clash of a symbol, and then the same keyboard note repeating again and again and then an instrument I couldn't recognize but which sounded like someone running a wet finger around a wine glass. The singing was interesting; no words, but voices humming happily, and soon my ears were delighted by a quietly grand entrance of trumpet.

The song was over too soon, the instruments leaving one by one just as they'd entered, and then there was nothing but the guitarist alone in the white room. I felt a spark of something, though at the time I couldn't discern whether it was love or inspiration or plain old orange Buddha daisy.

Hey, do you feel like talking? The first time I met daisy I was with Amara. I talked her ears off. I talked about everything that came into my mind. How are you feeling?

I feel really weird, Raizel. *Raisin.* I feel like I'm floating, but not like a cloud. More like a bee, near the ground. And this blanket is *so* soft.

We giggled together, rubbing our cheeks on the quilt.

Just in case you don't know, some types of daisy are different from others. Actually, almost all pills have different effects on different people. I had a downer once that made me feel like I was sinking into the floor. I cried the whole time. Then this other time I was wired for twelve straight hours, dancing my ass off. Then there's the perfect medium--some pills make you feel like you love everything, and you'll be satisfied doing anything, whether that means making out or watching something really bad, like an action movie. And sometimes pills have *no* effect on people. We call them bum pills.

Oh, really? I didn't know that, actually. I thought daisy always made people want to dance and suck on soothers and ignore everyone else. Hey! You don't like action movies either?

Hate em. Raizel laughed. And I've never been a soother gal. Hey, do you wanna know what I like about you?

Hmm? I clenched my jaw, feeling the sudden urge to rock back and forth on my side. I curled and uncurled my toes, made and unmade fists.

You know when there're raffle draws at parties and big events, and everyone sits around with hopeful expressions on their faces? Even though the prizes are always, like, t-shirts and water bottles and shit? Well, you almost *always* have that expression on your face, that hopefulness. That's what I like about you.

12

The next morning Tiff called when I was definitely supposed to be sleeping. Dana tossed the phone on my bed without answering it, letting it bounce off my motionless body. The ringing pierced my heard directly behind my eyes, my least favorite kind of headache if I had a choice.

I yawned and uttered my first word of the day.

HhHAAallo?

I have two big things to tell you.

Sometimes I pretended I didn't know the people I knew; I listened to their voices and speculated their mannerisms to determine how I would judge them if I was a stranger. Three adjectives for Tiff's voice were childish, conceited, and cheerful. A strange combination.

Venice?

Do you know what time it is?

It's eleven. You're still sleeping? What did you do last night?

I grunted, not wanting to explain.

Stayed up late watching a movie.

What movie?

I dunno.

So, do you want to hear the good news, or the good news?

What. I was a blank slate, hardly in the mood to play games. I picked at my eye boogers.

I got accepted! To university!

I raised my voice, knowing what she wanted to hear.

You go girl! YaaAAWwn. When does it start?

January. I'm so fucking excited. I should have applied in the spring and gone this semester.

Sweet. Sorry, I'm pretty tired.

We've established that. But guess what else.

What?

Monica said you can start on Monday.

Start what?

Well, I gave her your resume.

What? Really?

Yeah. We start at nine, so we should meet at the bus stop at eight-thirty. And don't bring lunch. You'll get something at the orientation. Plus we're off at two.

But I didn't even have an interview.

I know. You seemed so bummed the other day, I decided to go ahead and tell Monica you rock.

Oh. She pitied me.

Well, thanks.

Geez. Don't sound so excited.

THANKS TIFF!

That's more like it. She laughed.

When we'd hung up, I got to thinking about the changes in my life since high school had ended. I hadn't worried about my weight much, not being surrounded by older female teachers in their high heels and sleek business attire, and by girls in their skinny jeans and tight capris and short shorts and stretchy tank tops and sports bras and thong panties in the change room during phys. ed. I wasn't huge compared to everyone else, but I had a rectangular block body. I had always felt like they were sizing me up and trying to figure out if I was actually a girl under all the black sweaters and hoodies and big jeans from the men's section at Winner's, the cheap and comfortable ones that didn't squeeze my upper thighs.

I picked up something of Dana's off the floor of my closet, a red plaid flannel shirt he'd given me after deciding he hated how it clung to his swollen stomach. I popped it on over my sleep camisole, buttoning it up and turning to the mirror. I couldn't believe I'd never tried it on before, loving how the material hugged my chest and shoulders and not my belly. I glanced up at my hair, shocked to realize how fabulous it was though I'd just awoken; lying placidly on my head was my fluffy mushroom-brown faux hawk.

I returned to bed with my new, old warm shirt and thought about Dana and our lack of altercations since my graduation. He had even invited me to make an attic hangout with him. I reveled in the fact that my mother had been so busy with work that she hadn't been able to watch over me--as much. I couldn't wait until my first payday so I could buy something new and confuse her as to how I'd paid for it.

I turned to my bedside table, seeing the ripped piece of newspaper on which Abby had written that Ian guy's phone number. I reached over and crumple it up, chuckling.

Raizel and I had stayed in the bed sharing her iPod until Abby and Amara had barged in, announcing they were fucked up and needed to lie down. Four monkeys in a bed, we'd spooned and sang bad nineties' pop songs until someone banged on the wall from the apartment next door. Then we'd lain dozing in and out of conversation, listening. I'd never before heard the sounds of morning in an apartment building, creaky floorboards, a crying baby, a coughing man, a radio announcer on high volume, toilets flushing and pipes running.

By eight a.m., most of the noises had ceased as people tramped down the stairwells to their cold vehicles. Though I'd insisted on taking the bus, Abby and Raizel had driven the twenty minutes to drop me off at my duplex doorstep. I'd thanked them profusely, noticing gray hoops under their eyes.

Upon asking myself if there was a chance that I was finding happiness, or belief in such a thing, I stretched my arm up to knock on my bed's wooden headboard.

We met on the bus stop corner halfway between our houses, like we'd been doing since the ninth grade. Waking up early had been no easy feat.

Are you nervous?

Tiff bobbed up and down on her heels. I had barely noticed the cold air.

No way.

I tried not to throw up my Shreddies on the sidewalk.

Don't worry, Mondays during the day are slack.

Pulling open the glass door at Team Bean, I breathed in a scent that had become familiar to me since Tiff had started there. Rich coffee aromas swirled around my nose and I immediately craved one of the robust, steaming mugs customers all around sat drinking.

This is a slack day? I silently wondered, triggering my nerves.

Tiff smiled at a lady who was already working the front counter, leading me behind the counter and down a narrow hallway to the staff room. Seeing the sofa, round table, and dirty microwave, I beamed at the thought of belonging to something as exclusive as a staff room.

This is where my picture'll be in November. *She* only got it this month 'cause she's here all the time.

I looked above the microwave at a wooden brown plaque on the wall, encasing a photo of an older lady. The engraved text under her curly hair and wrinkled smile read

Patty Gavinsford
Honorable Staff Member
of Team Bean Café
October

And this is my locker. Tiff swung up open the metal door of her foot-wide locker. You can put your stuff in here 'til they give you one.

Sweet.

Is that what you're wearing?

Tiff motioned at my hand-me-down red plaid flannel and my baggy jeans.

Yeah. What's wrong?

It just seems unprofessional. Like pajamas or something.

Aren't I going to wear one of those stupid aprons over it anyway?

I guess so.

She removed her own jacket to reveal a white button-down shirt. I had assumed she would be wearing black, the only thing I'd ever seen her in. The stupidest color one could possibly wear at a coffee shop job was white. I forced myself not to say anything, knowing I should be extremely grateful that she'd hooked me up. I brushed away her words of speculation. I was thankful for my excuse--my hair was too short to pull it into a strict ponytail like Tiff's and our boss Monica's.

My new boss Monica had the kind of post-pregnancy curves women liked to complain about, but I didn't mind them or her big, brown chestnut-colored ponytail. There were some weird things about her, though. She smiled a lot, like she'd put Vaseline on her teeth as a reminder, and her eyes didn't move. She had no sign of crow's feet or other late-thirties/early-forties wrinkles from a lifetime of happiness. She just let her mouth curve up at the sides and that was the extent of each grin. The other thing was her mole, a brown dot above her eyebrow about the size of a pencil eraser. As a photographer, imperfections didn't bug me; it was the hairs spurting from her imperfection and hanging in her eye that held the power to make me ill. Luckily, I'd met her on various occasions and thus didn't have to spend that Thursday morning adjusting to the creepy aspects of her face.

Good morning, Venice, I'm so glad for the opportunity to work with you.

I noticed how short Monica was, only reaching my chin.

You know, we wanted to hire you before, but summer's our slowest season and I guess Tiffany beat you to the punch. I'm sure you understand. Well, it's nice to see you.

We shook hands.

Oh my dear! Your hands are freezing. Go ahead and choose any drink you want, on the house.

I tore my eyes off her mole.

Cool. Thanks, Monica.

Oh, and Venice, I *love* your shirt. Plaid's all the rage this fall. Tiffany, would you mind making Venice's drink and bringing it back to the crew room?

Monica retreated into her office. I laughed, nudging my friend. Tiff scowled.

Okay, what do you want? And by the way, we get a free drink every shift so don't feel too special or anything.

Um, okay. What do you usually drink?

Cappuccino, of course.

I'll take one.

I went back to the crew room where I proceeded to watch a video about food safety and customer service. I couldn't believe I was getting paid ten dollars an hour to watch movies and drink coffee.

At lunchtime Monica ordered Chinese food and we ate together in the staff room. She kept her smile on, showing me the work schedule on the staff room wall, my name written on Wednesday and Thursday afternoons the following week.

Don't worry, we'll give you lots of training.

She showed me pictures of her bald, fat-cheeked baby. I felt surprisingly comfortable and a little guilty for all the times I'd badmouthed her to Tiff. I admonished myself for judgmental comments regarding moles and big butts.

When we finished eating, Monica had Tiff train me on the cash register. There wasn't even another person working. Tiff had been right about the slackness after all; two old women sat silently sipping lemon tea and looking out the window. Tiff showed me which buttons to press for regular coffee, cappuccino, mocha, vanilla latte, tea, chocolate chip cookies, and blueberry muffins. The menu was extensive, but the till was electronic and everything was written in plain English.

At four o' clock a short woman in her mid-fifties came into the restaurant and opened the door to get behind the counter. A sticky web of hairspray clung to her short perm. She looked over her glasses while talking to me, speaking briskly like someone of great distinction and authority. Or someone who had recently been awarded Honorable Staff Member.

I'm Patty. What's your name?

I'm Venice.

What in the who now?

Tiff and I made eye contact.

Her name's Venice, Tiff said. Like the city. In Italy.

Oh, you youngsters. I once knew a woman named Olive. Like the vegetable. Or is an olive a fruit? Anyway, what a peculiar name. She was a peculiar lady, though. Not saying you're weird or anything. But this lady, she'd do the weirdest things with her plants, like leaving them on the apartment balcony 'til noon, then bringing them in until nine at night. Isn't that strange? I only know this, mind you, because she lived in the apartment across from me. She'd also sometimes walk around naked when she thought no one could see her. Imagine my mother setting the table for Thanksgiving dinner, looking up, and seeing a pasty white arse across the alley.

I didn't know whether to laugh or nod in agreement; thankfully Tiff did.

Sorry, Patty, but we have to catch the bus.

Oh, don't let me keep you. Patty waved her hand and stumbled into the bathroom, her perm waving goodbye.

Run!

Tiff and I broke into laughter. We rapidly untied our chocolate and cream-splotched aprons and grabbed our things from Tiff's locker. My plaid shirt had miraculously remained unscathed by the day's hard work. I still hoped my mother would smell something on me and realize I'd been at my *job*.

No such luck, through her curtain of nicotine.

13

Liam called me, saying he'd gotten my number from Raizel, and asked why I'd never called. I apologized, sincerely.

On Tuesday at six, he called me again.

By Wednesday, I was ready for our gabfest, the cordless fully charged. I surprised him by dialing his number. I lay on my bed with my feet propped on the wall, gazing up at my Andy Warhol guns. We took turns talking. We took turns listening.

He told me about his boss's beer belly.

I told him about Monica's mole.

He told me about the cute guy who kept coming to the pharmacy.

I told him I'd only ever come there because I didn't want to wait for the bus in the cold.

We pondered the thought that we'd never have met if I hadn't had that shitty One Buck Store job interview. We'd never have met if I hadn't been fucked up in grade ten, had taken drivers ed, had gotten a loan and bought a shitty secondhand car so I wouldn't have to take the bus. We'd never have met if no one had invented buses.

We laughed.

He complained to me about the sound system in his car.

I tried to talk Tiff up, making up for her impoliteness at the pharmacy.

He told me people always stared when he was out with Amara.

I told him I hated my teeth, but loved his.

He said he loved my teeth. He told me he hated his.

We agreed to swap.

Then we laughed.

Then we agreed to steal Raizel's perfect teeth.

We only ever hung up when my mom or Dana barged in.

On Thursday, my second five-hour shift at Team Bean came and went easily, as I was still being shown the ropes. I received disposal training--choosing which parking lot bin to throw things in, according to their material. Patty led the training session. I wished it could have been Tiff, but Monica said Patty was more experienced. I learned how to mop the floor so bits of dirt would come out from between the tiles. She also told me how to wipe a window with paper towel instead of a cloth, so it wouldn't streak. The whole time, she talked about her grandkid's chicken pox. Tiff stayed behind the counter and laughed at me between customers.

I stifled the urge to kung-fu fight Patty.

When we were off at six, Tiff and I eagerly grabbed our things.

Bye, Monica! I called toward the office.

Bye, girls! See you! Monica called back, leaning in her computer chair to wave us out.

We were getting off the bus in Oakwood when Tiff spoke to me.

Bush party tonight?

She bunched up her shoulders to block the wind.

Sure. Oh, and hey. Thanks for getting me this job. I think I really like it.

No prob. Call you later.

The wind bit my cheeks as I lurched down the sidewalk. I hugged myself tightly, vowing to buy some mittens as soon as I got paid. The thought of having a payday floated like a cloud across my mind. I walked up the path home, to our little brown duplex, and pushed open the front door, my nose immediately greeted by a greasy, cheesy, doughy, tomatoey smell. I untied my sneakers and followed the aroma through the living room to the kitchen.

I'd been planning on setting up in front of the basement computer with mushroom soup, crackers, and a can of no-name diet soda, but entering the kitchen, I stopped in my tracks.

Taking up our whole kitchen table was a creation from Chester's Pizza Parlor, oozing with cheese and sauce. My mother was pouring herself a drink and Dana was taking plates down from the cupboard. My mouth immediately pooled with saliva.

Hi, guys. I stood over the table, breathing in the pizzalicious steam.

Our mother looked over her shoulder at me. I noticed that into her pop she was pouring some of the Bacardi 150 that had fucked me up at the last bush party.

Hi. What did you do today, my peach?

I--

Lemme guess, you were with Tiff. She smiled, sipping her drink.

I crossed my toes that she wouldn't think her concoction was watery.

Well, yeah, but today we--

Do you want some pizza? Dana cut me off, turning to the table with three big plates. He rolled up his sleeves and grabbing the metal pizza slicer.

Are you kidding? I used my hand to waft the smell toward my nose. I *love* pizza.

That Leo guy called for you again. He left his number. My brother handed me a greasy napkin with a number scrawled across it in blue marker.

Hmm...oh! His name's Liam. Thanks. I folded the napkin and put it in my jeans pocket, though I already knew his number by heart.

We've been waiting for you, Day's got some big news to share. My mother leaned back on the counter.

I was genuinely surprised that she didn't ask about Liam.

Well. Dana shrugged. It's not *that* big.

What's up? I accepted a plate from him, heavy with pizza. I licked my finger when a bit of sauce touched it.

Wait a sec. Here, Mom. He handed our mother a plate. After he'd gotten his own plate ready, he held it in the air. Cheers.

Sure, those days I'd cheers with anything--booze, daisy, why not pizza? We stood in the middle of the kitchen and tapped the edges of our plates together. Clink.

So, my boss 'n' his wife are getting a divorce 'n' my boss is looking for a tenant. Dana bit his pizza, looking down at it.

A what? I held my pizza slice up, poised to bite the tip. I let my teeth sink in, salty buttery flavorful goodness filling my mouth. The sauce was the best part, hot red paste infused with basil and parsley.

A tenant. Someone to live in his basement suite.

Our mother nodded, beaming.

The house is real nice.

Where? I swallowed my food, doughy lumps traveling down my throat.

Somewhere by Broadway. Isn't that awesome?

I paused.

Broadway? Isn't that far away?

Sure, but I can walk to work and to get groceries and everything. It's the best area. Dana pushed the Desperately Celebratory pizza into his face, sauce surrounding his lips like a toddler.

And how are you going to afford this Broadway basement suite?

He got promoted to manager. Half of our mother's Obviously Celebratory drink was gone.

Huh? I pulled the pizza away from my face, one bite taken off the end. I felt my cheeks get hot, wondering how she knew things and I didn't. You think being manager of the shittiest movie theater ever is some amazing opportunity? That's retarded.

Venice! I told you not to use that word derogatorily. My mother scowled. She finished her drink and began to pour another.

I slit my eyes at her back and her scraggly brown locks.

Venice. Dana scowled before biting into his second slice of pizza. I thought you'd be happy for me.

Congratulations. The best of luck. Farewell. Bon voyage. I held my plate in one hand and opened the basement door with the other.

Where do you think you're going? Tell us about this Leo guy. My mother leaned on the counter with a cigarette in her mouth. She went cross-eyed as she lit her smoke. Is he cute?

Very. I didn't care to see their faces. I flicked on the light before descending to the first step and letting the door click shut behind me. I went down the stairs, put my pizza on the coffee table, and curled into the sofa's butt indents, wrapping a fleece blanket around my toes and pressing my face into the cushion.

I didn't turn the TV on or anything, just listened to the noises above me. They laughed sporadically, my brother and my mother who had become best friends behind my back. I'd had no chance to tell them about my job. They hadn't even noticed that I was wearing something other than black for the first time in four years. I heard the sink running, must have been dish water, and wondered when either of them had begun cleaning.

Maybe he'd chosen to leave because I'd been a rotten little sister. I hadn't hung out with him often enough. I hadn't complied with his attic hangout idea.

Looking around for something to wipe my nose with, I pulled Liam's number out of my pocket. I reached for the cordless.

14

Bundled in my plaid shirt, black hoody, and my mother's old winter coat, I stood in the dark by the front door and waited for headlights to appear on the road outside. I had the rest of my mother's Bacardi 150, about five shots' worth, in my backpack, and a burnt compilation of Ani Difranco and Tegan and Sara playing in my disc man.

Behind me, light from the kitchen crash-landed on the gray living room carpet. I turned around and took out an ear bud to hear my mother opening and closing cupboards. Shit. She was looking for her booze. I peered back out the screen door's window, my heartbeat rising.

Venice? VENICE?

What? I turned so my backpack was facing the dark.

Have you seen my Gravol?

Phew. My heart slowed down and I touched the heavy bottom of my backpack.

No. Maybe you finished them.

My mother appeared in the kitchen doorway, her slim figure a dark silhouette against the light. She groaned and rubbed her belly as she stepped toward me.

Can you go buy me some more?

Huh? Hearing the rumble of an engine, I looked outside. Streetlights shone on the hood of a black car. No. I'm going out.

Her face morphed, lip lifting in disdain.

Where are you going? Can't you bring me some on your way home?

Out. I'll get them if you give me money.

Okay.

While she limped down the hall to her room, I opened the screen door and waved at the vehicle. *One minute*, I wanted to say, but knew I wouldn't be heard through the bass of the car stereo.

I snatched the ten dollar bill out of my mother's hand, trying to ignore her pained expression, the one where her lip curled up and her eyebrows pushed together feebly. I opened the door to skip gaily down the front steps without looking back, so she didn't have time to drill me about my plans for the night. When I reached the car I opened the passenger door and hopped in, leaning back against my bag.

Hey, V! Liam turned down the music and flipped his black bangs out of his eyes, his signature move, and showed his slightly crooked teeth, his signature smile. He wore skintight jeans and a hoody with rainbow lines zigzagging every which way.

Hey. Nice car. And nice sweater. I put my Discman in my backpack and pulled out the Bacardi 150. You wanna get a lil tipsy?

Heck yeah, girlfriend.

He pressed the gas and we shot forward down the street. Zooming past buildings, I watched our duplex become a dot in the side-view mirror.

So how was work today? I relaxed into my seat.

A little busy. Raizel and I barely got to hang out.

Oh? I looked at him, cocking my head curiously. So...what's she up to tonight?

She went out of town, to Bowville. There's a Millie Fischer concert.

I wondered who Millie Fischer was.

We stopped at the edge of town at the 7-11. The confectionary was in the strip mall connected to Chester's Pizza Parlor, so I spat on the greasy window like I'd done to Rhonda and her One Buck Store. I watched my saliva slide down the window and onto the brick below, wishing I could spit on everyone who'd ever betrayed me. I stalked into the 7-11 to help Liam choose what to mix the rum with.

I like Dr. Pepper. He looked at me out the side of his eyes. I recognized the redness surrounding his pupils. What about you?

Yeah, whatever. Anything that kills the taste.

Okay. He leaned in and spoke quietly. I'll go ask directions if you put it in your bag.

What? You mean steal it?

Shhhhhhhh!

His peppermint breath grazed my cheek. Usually the 7-11 had a security guard, but I supposed his shift hadn't started for the night. I glanced at the front of the store to see the clerk leaning on the counter reading a magazine.

K, whatever. Let's do this.

Liam strolled down the candy aisle up to the register. The young chick working looked up at him and smiled. I watched him say something and she laughed with her mouth wide open, swiveling to point out the window behind her. I turned my back to the security cameras mounted on the wall, shoving a one-liter Dr. Pepper into my backpack.

I guess they don't have it. I came up from behind Liam, speaking louder than necessary in a two-foot radius.

Oh. Too bad. Let's go.

Uh, what are you looking for? The girl behind the counter batted her lashes and gazed up at Liam.

Um. He flicked his hair out of his eyes. Mentos.

They're right behind you, silly. The girl smiled.

I turned around and examined the shelf.

Oh. He means *papaya* Mentos. We're really craving them.

She raised an eyebrow blatantly full of doubt.

I didn't know they made those.

Well. Thanks for your help, girlfriend!

Liam grabbed my hand. We darted for the door, laughing.

Oh God. I shook my head at Liam, grinning. What did you ask her for?

Directions to Venice. If only she'd known she could just point at you!

Oh, wow. Are you sure you can drive?

Yeah, I'm okay. But if you're uncomfortable you can drive.

Oh…I don't have my license. It's okay. Let's go drink this shit.

Liam sped the car around a couple of corners, stopping at a playground, still near my duplex. We got out and ran to the structure.

I used to play here when I was little. I put my foot on a kiddie swing and swayed. With my brother Dana.

The weight of my backpack pulled me off balance. I jumped, pushing my high-tops into the sand, remembering. I remembered the slide and the sandbox and the monkey bars. I'd *owned* that playground before growing tits.

Me too. Liam sat on the tire swing. He was so tall that his feet dragged in the sand as he swung.

Really? When? I looked over at him. I stepped down and dug the ingredients for our drink out of my backpack.

Just kidding. But I bet we would've been friends. I probably would have pretended to crush on you.

Mmm hmm. I swigged the Dr. Pepper and Bacardi 150, letting it slide down my throat and ignite my belly. I walked over and passed it to my new friend. It's not too bad.

He drank a bit, scrunching his face at the bitterness.

It's alright. I prefer something *better*, though.

Oh? I tried to remember where I'd heard those words before. Oh. Do you mean 'daisy'?

Yeah. It's so wonderful. I love it because I can say whatever I want, and not worry about what anyone thinks. I can just hang out with the people I love, and not think about my parents or my future or anything, y'know?

Totally. So, you know where to get something better?

Nah…usually Amara gets it from someone at work. But she's in Bowville with Raizel.

Oh. I perched my butt on the opposite edge of the rubber tire swing. I wondered what Bowville was like. All I knew was that it was two hours away, but crossed a border into another province.

We let the tire drift back and forth, the toes of our shoes dodging the sand. I knew my inhibitions were still intact, because I didn't lean over and whisper that the future didn't matter, like I wanted to. When the breeze picked up I shivered.

Oh my god. I just got an idea.

Yeah?

Liam's eyes lifted from the ground and met with mine, excited. He flicked his bangs to the side and waited for my plan, stopping the tire swing with a lurch like a first-time driver stalling a standard.

Yeah. You'll love it. Let's go.

We got back to the car and I pointed the way as he drove. I wasn't worried, as we had drunk just enough to warm our innards and not to liquefy our limbs. I giggled at every corner, clutching the holy-shit handle.

Gray smoke rose lazily from the trees toward the pitch-black sky. The campfire's scent tickled our nostrils. Liam held the rough branches to the side and let me enter the clearing before him, finding kids sitting on logs, mingling around the fire clutching bottles and red plastic cups.

Hi, Liam and I said in confident unison. A few kids grinned and raised their drinks. Liam smiled at everyone dazedly and flicked his bangs.

We found Tiff at our usual spot by the cars, where the Young Adults hung out with their doors open and stereos blaring Eminem and Jay-Z. She was on the hood of Oliver's car, back to us with her shiny red curls dangling around her shoulders. Approaching, I realized Oliver was leaning against the cars between her legs, and they were doing something with their mouths that I didn't care to see.

Get a room! I stomped closer to sling my arm across Oliver's shoulders. He immediately tore his face away from Tiff's to see who'd interrupted them.

Tiff squinted through the dark at me.

Venice? Oh my god!

She jumped off the hood of the car and embraced me, cold hands pulling at the back of my neck. I wrapped my arms around her and squeezed, disbelieving how small she'd remained since apparent adulthood had begun.

What are you doing here? I thought you were too tired from work today.

Yeah, but I mustered up some energy. You remember Liam, don't you? I patted the colorful arm of Liam's sweater.

Hi. Liam smiled and extended his hand.

Hi, I'm Oliver. Oliver stepped forward and accepted Liam's hand, shaking heartily.

Tiff slit her eyes, shooting her boyfriend the infamous Look.

Yeah. How nice to see you. Tiff smiled with pursed lips. She pushed up her glasses and craned to look up at him.

You too, girlfriend.

I stifled a laugh, watching Tiff's face change as she tried to figure out an appropriate response.

Listen guys, I'm gonna go find some beer, so just chill out for a bit. I took a few steps toward the bush.

Oh wait. Liam dug into the back pocket of his jeans before handing me twenty dollars.

Wow, that's nice of you, Liam. Oliver smiled. So, do you play hockey?

I walked across the long, trampled grass, shaking my head and grinning. I pictured Liam turning an icy hockey rink into a catwalk. Upon returning to the clearing I stood warming my palms over the fire and scanned the faces of fellow partiers. Some of The Bitches sat on a log and took pictures of themselves, a shame to all photographers. Beside them was a couple making out, and next to them The Gigglers dipped marshmallows in Kahlua and charred them in the flames, shrieking when they caught fire.

As time passed, I glanced back at the cars. Shit. They were probably already wondering what was taking so long. I crossed my fingers in hopes that Oliver was still making an effort with Liam. I pictured Tiff sitting with her arms crossed over her chest, complaining about the cold.

I was about to accept defeat when I noticed a couple of The Dudes coming out of the bushes, these guys dressed in skate shoes and baggy jeans and toques pulled low over their heads. I approached them, glancing around and tugging at the straps of my backpack. That was when my stomach did its flipping trick.

Flip flip flip.

I kept my voice low.

Is Seed back there?

Yeah, dude. One of the guys looked me up and down. What's up, shorty? You havin' a good night?

Sure, but it could be better. I smiled and winked. If you know what I mean.

Finding Seed wasn't hard, him in a gray zip-up with the hood over his head. His jeans were baggy, nearly dragging on the grass like the ones I'd worn all throughout high school. He was halfway through a joint, watching the party from outside of the bushes, evidently waiting for business to happen.

Remember me?

Caught off guard, he looked up at me. His eyes were different than before, not flitting around nervously. Light from the fire seeped through all the branches and twigs of the bushes, letting us check each other's faces out.

Sure, boo. I gave you my number. But you didn't call me.

Uh yeah, I lost it. The lie hung in the air between us like the useless limb of a war veteran, lame.

So what do you want?

I couldn't get over the difference between his calmness then and the last time I'd seen him.

I want three pills. I breathed out heavily.

Pills? He raised both eyebrows, waiting.

Um. E. Some people call it daisy?

Weird. Daisy. He fished around in one of his jeans' lower pockets, a huge one that hung casually around his knee. Do you know why they call it that?

Come to think of it, no. I glanced around.

Listen to the last part of the word. Ecstasy.

Uh, Seed? I coughed. How much for one?

He looked at me and squinted slightly, thinking for a moment.

Ten bucks. Usually fifteen, but you're special.

My cheeks became warm as I slipped him Liam's twenty and the ten bucks my mother had given me earlier that night. I'll take three.

He handed me the smallest plastic bag I'd ever encountered, about the size of a postage stamp and covered in smiley faces.

You wanna come party with us? I felt guilty about seeking him out specifically to acquire something. At the time I didn't know that drug dealers expected to be used, to be phoned and asked for things and to be given money instead of friendly chatter. He declined, saying he was going to find some customers.

The tiny bag lay perfectly encased in my fist, burning a happy hole, my stigmata.

15

When I found the car, Oliver and Tiff both had their butts on the hood, holding hands and talking quietly. Liam was bent beside the car, fixing his hair in the tiny side mirror.

Hey, Venice. Oliver smiled at me.

You're back. Super. Tiff's voice was flat. She pushed her glasses up. Where's the beer?

The back of my neck became hot. I squeezed the smiley face bag in my hand.

I couldn't find any. That's what took so long. Besides, I don't feel so well anymore.

Oh? Liam straightened, settling his hair with the ol' flick of the bangs. Want me to take you home?

Or we can. Oliver slid off the hood of his vehicle, the metal popping out.

Tiff rolled her eyes, crossing her arms exactly how I'd pictured her earlier.

What's wrong with you now?

My stomach really hurts. I just don't think I should drink beer. I think I drank too much coffee today. Coffee's a diuretic, you know. I clutched myself around the waist and leaned on the car with my hand. I scrunched my nose and groaned, for full effect. I leaned over and whispered through Tiff's red mane. I have the shits.

Oh! Tiff widened her eyes behind her glasses. That sucks. You should eat bananas. I hear that hardens your--

Okay! Thanks, Tiff. Call me tomorrow.

Okay, feel better.

Liam and I walked back toward the street where he'd parked his car, though not too quickly, in case Tiff was watching. As the sounds of laughter and thumping beats faded in our ears, I breathed in deeply.

We returned to our tire swing at the park, sitting on the edges with our legs in the middle. Liam wrapped this blanket around us, a big, black thing covered in lint; he'd dug it up from the backseat. Deserted grass fields surrounded us. There was no sound but the wind playing with fallen leaves.

Ready?

I sucked the insides of my cheeks to gather spit. Liam did the same.

Oo ook ike a fiss. I tilt my head back so as not to spill the pool of saliva under my tongue.

Oo do too. A playful glint passed through Liam's eyes.

I opened the smiley face bag and held a pill up under the playground lights. Stamped with lemons, they were the same shade of blue as a baby boy's blanket--or a girl's, if her parents were twisted enough. They were almost as blue as Liam's eyes. I remembered Raizel's words of wisdom, and wondered what blue pills would be like--high energy, low energy, or the happy medium. My fingers shook as I handed one to Liam and gripped one for myself.

Flip flip flip. My stomach.

Cheers. I passed on the tradition.

We tapped pills before tossing them into our mouths and swallowing. Down it went, a tiny blue lemon tumbling into a cave, an abyss. I could hardly wait for it to explode--sour peel particles would be everywhere, tickling me from the inside out. I laughed.

This should be fun.

Come here, V. Liam hoisted his legs up on either side of the rubber tire swing and held his arms out to me. I crossed my legs over his, enjoying the warmth of his thighs under mine. We embraced each other and swayed like a pendulum.

So, how was your conversation with Tiff? My head came to rest on Liam's shoulder.

Oh, god. More like un-conversation. The only thing she said to me was that my pants were awfully purple. And girly.

Sorry.

Yeah. So. Whatever. But her boyfriend seems cool.

Yeah. Oliver's a really great person.

I lifted my head off Liam's shoulder to test the effect of the daisy. I wondered if it would come on as quickly as the last time, or if that had actually been slow and my mind had been too impaired by whiskey for proper judgment.

Hey…V? Liam's head tilted to the side in copycat experimentation of the daisy.

Yeah?

What do you think of gay people?

I raised my eyebrows at him, our faces a foot apart.

They're like everyone else. They're just people. Why do you ask?

Well, what does Tiff think? I just can't believe *she's* your best friend.

I know. Don't get me started. You wanna hear a story?

Tell me. Liam leaned his head on one of the metal chains from which the tire swing hung.

Once upon a time, two girls graduated from high school. One had long red hair and really skinny legs. The other was slightly chubby and a little mannish.

What? You're not chubby. You're just big boned.

Whatever. So we graduated from high school and decided to have a little party in Tiff's backyard. Tiff's mom got us booze and let us have people over.

Liam grinned his crooked-tooth grin, eyelids dropping slightly as he listened.

So I invited this guy, Oliver. Tiff pretended to be pissed off, even though *everyone* knew she liked Oliver. Me and Sophie and Tiff started playing drinking games--

Who's Sophie?

Oh, sorry. Tiff's older sister. So we sat around drinking until Oliver came over. He brought this guy called Danny with him, at least we thought Danny was a guy until he sat by the fire and then we were all like, holy shit, Danny's a girl. Seriously, she looked just like a dude.

So, we played drinking games until we were wasted. I just watched everyone else, like a fly on the wall. Tiff talked to Oliver and Sophie flirted with Danny, giving her neck rubs and shit. It was really obvious that Tiff was trying to ignore them. But THEN!

My words bounced off the metal slide ten feet away, echoing. I looked around, surprised. Liam widened his eyes.

What happened next?

Danny grabbed Sophie and started making out with her, or maybe Sophie grabbed Danny. I can't remember. But Tiff was like, Sick, what are you doing, and Oliver was like, Go, Danny! Because he was best friends with this chick.

Then Tiff freaked out, calling Sophie a dyke and threatening to tell their mom, swearing and spitting everywhere. It was really awkward. THEEEEENNNN--

What happened then??? Liam leaned forward, his ears magnetized to my words.

Then Sophie kissed Oliver.

What?? Why?

I guess she wanted to prove to Tiff that she wasn't gay, or a lesbian or whatever.

What'd Tiff do then?

From what I can remember, I mean, I *was* super drunk, Tiff went in the house and wouldn't talk to any of us for the rest of the night. She wouldn't even talk to me and I'm her best friend in the whole world. Pretty much ruined our grad night.

Did she ever forgive her sister?

I dunno, but she still goes to her ringette games and cheers for her. But I think now that she's seeing Oliver, he's not hanging out with Danny.

So is that the end of the story?

Yeah, did you like it?

That's so stupid. Stupid shit. Liam looked out at the field, which stretched a long way in each direction.

Hey Liam?

How's your daisy?

I think I'm rolling. What about you?

I dunno. I'm not really feeling it. Do you wanna split another pill?

Sure.

I removed the third baby-blanket-blue lemon pill from the little bag, put it between my front teeth and chomped down. Chemical dust exploded in my mouth, bitter debris. I cringed and swallowed the little chunks as quickly as possible.

Shit. I looked at what was left of the pill and held my palm open for Liam to take it. I'm really sorry. It's the small half.

That's okay. Thanks. He popped it into his mouth and swallowed. You wanna lie in the sand?

We pulled our legs out of the tire swing and fell to the ground, not caring about our clothing. The lower we got to the ground, the warmer we felt, dodging the wind. Liam tucked the blanket around my toes and calves before crawling under and wrapping his arm around my waist. We lay face-up, hands playing with millions of minute pebbles, eyes playing with billions of vividly twinkling lights on the black canvas above us. That was the only thing the night sky had ever shown me--a disturbingly symmetrical pattern of stars. I wanted constellations. I wanted to see a meteor fall. I wanted the blackness that comes with a cloud-covered moon. I wanted the myth of Aurora Borealis to light up before my eyes.

Liam? I cleared my throat and spoke toward the sky, closing my eyes when the stars spun too rapidly. Why did you ask how I feel about gay people?

I guess it's because... Liam took his arm off of me to wrap it around himself. I get attached to people way too easily. When they find out I'm gay they usually, like, *recoil.*

Really? In this day and age?

Really. Especially family. He looked away from me across the sand, gazing at the bottoms of the jungle gym's support poles. So many people say they love gay boys, but when it comes down to it, they don't really wanna know. They just want fashion expertise. Especially straight chicks.

Liam, I would never bail on you. You're awesome. When he wouldn't look at me, I poked his side, feeling his ribcage through his shirt.

He rolled his head back my way.

I *really* like you, Venice. Not in the way the world wants me to, but I do. The first time I saw you I thought, I wanna be friends with her. I just had to make sure you knew what you were getting into.

I reached one arm under his body and one over his front, pulling him toward me for a tight embrace. We stayed that way for some time, the passing of minutes and hours indeterminable. The warmth of our bodies smoothed each others' senses like a knife spreading icing on warm cake. Soon my legs were jumping around. I clenched and unclenched my jaw, rolled my shoulders around on the ground.

Ohhh, fuck. My voice vibrated. I pushed my back up off the ground. I'm so fucked.

What? Liam sat up, putting his arm around my shoulder. Are you okay?

I stood up and kicked the sand before coming to a standstill over Liam. I leaned on his shoulders with both hands.

My shoes are too tight. Can you undo my laces?

Yeah, yeah. Liam responded quickly, kneeling before me and tugging at my laces. My knees shook. My head was about to float away.

Up up up.

Fuuuck.

V? Are you okay?

Yeah, I'm just, wow. I slipped my feet out of my shoes and tore off my socks, tossing them over my shoulder. I just needed an anchor. For my head, you know. You probably think that sounds weird. Ahhhh, that's better.

I pressed my bare feet into the sand, feeling its rough softness massage my toes. I reached out to touch Liam, who was still kneeling before me. He closed his eyes as I smoothed his bangs down on his forehead.

Not as soft as Raizel's, but pretty good. Oh, sorry. No offense or anything. Her hair's just amazing. Did you know she let me cut it?

Yeah. She told me. Every time we get high together she lets me stroke her hair. She's like a little kitten.

Wow, cool. I wish I could stroke her hair right now.

Oh yeah, if you really wanna trip out, stick your hand in Amara's 'fro.

That sounds cool. Hey, Liam, do they know you're gay?

They?

Raizel and Amara.

Liam laughed, looking at the ground and shaking his head. He laughed for a long time, so long that I began to wonder about the effects of blue daisy.

We met at Mars.

You went to Mars? What were you on? I stuck my tongue out at him.

The gay bar.

Where?

Seriously? You don't know about it?

No… I frowned, jogging through my foggy memory.

It's downtown. Liam tossed his bangs out of his eyes.

In *Sloam?*

Um, yeah.

Hey! You said you were eighteen. How did you get into a bar?

Amara works there. She lets me and Raizel in through a back door.

What? That's crazy. And really cool. Is she gay? I mean, a lesbian?

Raizel? Yeah.

WHAT? RAIZEL'S GAY? I meant Amara. How can Raizel be gay? I pictured her cute tights and pretty, curly hair. Amara, too. She was even more girly with her bangles and her dress and her necklace satchel thing.

Liam shrugged.

They both are. Show Raizel a picture of Ellen Degeneres and watch her face. She blushes and gets all giggly. Those two went out for a while. They didn't tell you?

Raizel went out with ELLEN??

No, dufus, Liam slapped my calf, sending a jolt crawling up my skin under my clothes. He flicked his bangs out of his face again, ruining my smoothing job. I reached out to stroke his hair again.

She went out with Amara.

WHAT?? I tore my hand away and put my fists on my hips. Are they still together?

No. They broke up in August.

Why?

Actually, I don't know. They didn't tell me. Wow, you know what?

What?

I'm reeaally fucked, too. Liam lay back down, shaggy hair splaying around his face.

Make a sand angel. I smiled.

My eyes dove around without the rest of me as Liam stretched his skinny limbs as long as they'd go, waving them back and forth in the sand. He wiggled like a jelly fish. When we got up we both gazed through the dim light at his creation.

It's *so* beautiful.

For the next few hours we walked around the playground, arms outstretched, letting our hands bump against the metal poles and wooden platforms. Across the field I watched pieces of loose-leaf, homework, love notes, hates notes, riding the wind. I liked when they hit the chain-link fence and flattened out, trying to get through.

I stood in the middle of the sandbox and closed my eyes, feeling night-time. Before I re-opened my eyes I knew that everything would be the same. The flagpole, bike rack, ball diamond, and elementary school would stand where they always had. My heart fluttered.

Raizel and Amara's alleged gayness flew around in my head. Liam was right, I could be a dufus sometimes. I wondered if Raizel would have more fun if I was there instead, in Bowville. Who wanted to hang out with their ex, even if their ex was a tall, older girl with an afro and a smooth complexion and a perfect gap between her teeth? They probably held hands during the Millie Fischer concert and wished they'd just met each other in the ticket line.

I went down the spiral slide sixty times, obsessed with the feeling of flat coldness under me as the tunnel manipulated my body. Every time I landed I lay for a minute however I'd fallen out the end of the slide, wishing I had a camera so I could make Liam photograph me. I could get a Facebook account and post the pictures so everyone who knew me, and didn't, could see how happy I looked. Every time my body tried to detach itself from my mind I touched something new, reminding myself of where I was.

We came down together, parked outside the playground with our legs tangled in the backseat. Liam smoked a spliff while I bopped the last daisy petals out of my system, listening to bass beats on low volume. Every time I lay my head back on the seat, I had to bring it up again and rock back and forth, clenching my jaw. Five o' clock rolled around, and then six, approaching seven.

The sun opened itself like a lily blooming over rooftops, the windshields of cars on the street, and peoples' front yards. I looked across the browning grass field at the playground and wondered how we'd been so enchanted by hunks of metal and splitting old wood.

16

Hey Monica. I walked into my boss's office at a quarter to nine on Sunday morning. What's up?

Morning, Venice. Monica swirled around in her computer chair, brown ponytail turning with her. She gave me her same old smile. I'd seen so much of her mole that weekend that I barely glanced at it before making eye contact with her. It was *so* crazy this morning.

Oh, like yesterday?

Exactly. So, what's up with you?

I was wondering something. I downloaded some music last night and made a CD. I dug it out of my backpack. Do you think we could listen to it today?

Monica kept smiling. She took the CD from me and looking at the song names I'd written neatly on top.

As long as there's no swears, or screaming, I don't see why not.

Of course not. Even that really old guy will love it.

You mean Old Man Winter? My boss laughed and popped the CD case open.

Fifteen minutes later I was at the front end of the store, scrubbing the counter around the coffee makers, Millie Fischer's soft voice and folk acoustic guitar soothing my ears and those of the few customers we had. I nodded my head to the melody, thinking she was like a quieter, more innocent Ani Difranco. I didn't blame Raizel and Amara for going to Bowville, even though they were ex-girlfriends and it might've been awkward. Or maybe they'd been so close with each other that nothing could ever be awkward between them again. Maybe they'd gotten back together, as I imagined often happened at Millie Fischer shows.

When Tiff arrived she stopped in her path, seeing me behind the counter.

No wonder you weren't home when I called this morning.

Yeah. I figured I'd make some extra money.

Wow, you seem to know what you're doing. She nodded at the counter, where I'd rearranged the sugar and creamers and coffee filters and tea bags.

Doesn't it look better this way? More inviting?

I guess so.

Tiff took off her purse and her coat, relieving the same white blouse she'd worn on Thursday. I, however, had opted for a black t-shirt, not wanting to ruin my new favorite red plaid flannel top, and my old baggy jeans for the same reason. She pulled her hair strictly away from her face.

Do you wanna put your stuff in my locker?

No, I got my own yesterday. The one next to yours.

Yesterday?

Yeah, I had a six-hour shift. My training's finished now.

Oh my god, I can't believe you're working so much.

Yup.

Then the best thing happened. A squat figure that was Old Man Winter came strolling up to the counter; rather, he shuffled up in his old man slippers, a blue cardigan stretched over the hunch on his back. His eyes were wrinkled at the corners and the skin underneath sagged with age. Atop his head was the most convincing white-haired comb-over I'd ever seen. He didn't smell bad, for an old person, just a bit dusty. I looked down at him, about to complete what I didn't know at the time was a daily ritual at Team Bean.

Hi, there. I greeted the old guy, conscious of not softening my voice. Monica had given us a talk about treating the elderly just like everyone else.

Hello, dear. He wheezed a bit.

What can I get for you? I ran my finger around the perimeter of the till, noticing the brownness coming off on my skin. I made a mental note to clean the till later.

One coffee.

I pressed the button reading COFFEE. Quickly, I erased it and pressed SENIOR COFFEE instead.

Now--wheeze--would you mind--wheeze--making it half hot water and half coffee?

No problem. I wondered how to ring it in, but there was no one around to ask. I pressed EMPLOYEE DISCOUNT, knocking the price in half. Anything else for you today?

Yes. He took out his cloth handkerchief.

A woman and her baby entered the coffee shop and stood in line behind him. While he hacked into the cloth I prepared his coffee, setting the hot mug on a tray. The woman and her baby and I waited as he stuffed the hanky back into his blue cardigan pocket beside his smokes and crossword puzzle pens.

So what else can I get for you? I awaited his answer.

Oh, dear. Old Man Winter's eyes rose from his pocket, moist and pink when they met with mine. From his mouth came a chuckle, a noise rusted with phlegm. A warm blueberry muffin, hold the butter.

I started all over, deleting 50% SENIOR COFFEE and hitting SENIOR COFFEE/MUFFIN DEAL, after which I hit the EMPLOYEE DISCOUNT button, since he wasn't drinking a whole coffee or having butter.

Okay, and that's it?

That's it. Old Man Winter hacked briefly into the sleeve of his sweater before pushing up his glasses with a shaky, wrinkled finger, its tobacco-yellowed nail due for a clip. The woman behind him adjusted her baby from one hip to the other, trying to peek at her wristwatch.

That'll be fifty cents. I stepped toward the coffee makers to grab a rag. I wiped the perimeter of the till while he took out his change pouch and handed it to me.

These old eyes. He tapped his glasses, leaving a smudge on the right lens. Take what you need.

I plucked out two quarters and handed the pouch back to him.

Thank you. I'll bring it out to you when it's ready.

He smiled briefly before shuffling back to a table to set up his crossword book.

Sorry, I'll be right with you. I smiled as brightly as possible at the woman with the baby, so she couldn't possibly get pissed off at me. She bounced her baby a little, staring at me while I took out a plate and put a blueberry muffin in the microwave.

Hi. Tiff came down the hall from the staff room and stopped at the till to greet the woman. Welcome to Team Bean.

I smiled to myself. I spotted Old Man Winter in the lobby and carefully walked out to place the plastic tray on his table.

Stop! I cried out sharply when he reached for his mug.

He looked up at me from his seat.

Sorry. It's really hot.

Oh, my. Say, you must be new around here.

I found his voice to be far more proper than that of anyone I'd been associating with--he had a keen way of starting sentences with 'why' and 'now' and 'say'. I believed I could successfully give him the time of day without becoming annoyed.

Yes, it's true. I wiped my right hand on my apron pocket and held it out to him. I'm Venice.

Why, what a lovely name. Venice, like in Italy? He reached up gingerly.

Yes. What's your name?

I'm Walter.

We shook hands; his skin was so soft, my working girl's fingertips must have indented his elderly palm.

Nice to meet you, Walter.

The pleasure is all mine. Don't-- He interrupted himself, voice on the verge of another coughing fit. Forget your tip.

Ding ding ding. A light went on in my head at the thought of a couple extra bucks. I looked back to see him opening his worn leather wallet. He pulled various things out, setting them on the table.

Well, it's your lucky day. Walter slowly pushed up his glasses, subsequently smudging the other lens. He rested his tender, aged hand on a bill and slid it toward me. This is the smallest I have.

I opened my mouth as I picked up the beige hundred-dollar bill. I took a quick glance around. Tiff was still serving the baby lady, and other customers were quietly minding their own business. I couldn't remember the last time I'd seen such a large bill, but recalled Tiff telling me elderly customers often paid with them.

Would you like me to change it for smaller--

No, dear. You could use it to buy some new trousers, or a nice blouse. He gestured toward the frayed, dirty hem of my jeans.

I looked down. My jeans *were* pretty bad, but I had a nice pair at home.

Thank you *very* much, Walter. Can I get anything else for you now? Would you like us to turn the thermostat up? Are you comfortable?

I got back around behind the counter just as Tiff's customer was walking away. Unable to stop smiling, I couldn't wait to tell her about the money. Then she spoke.

Bitch. I followed her gaze toward the café door, which fell closed behind the woman.

What's wrong? I pretended to scratch my nose, hiding my smile behind my hand.

She was trying to get the coffee-muffin deal for only fifty cents.

Oops.

At least there are no other customers. Can I make you a drink? Cheer you up a little?

Sure.

I swayed to the music as I poured Tiff a cappuccino, wishing I knew Millie Fischer's lyrics so I could sing along. I handed her the drink and we leaned against the counter, waiting.

Thanks. Hey, isn't this music weird? I swear Monica's trying to be young and hip or something. Maybe her baby's bringing out her youthful side.

I raised my eyebrows and touched the outside of my jeans pocket, stroking a bump of folded money.

I like this music.

Really? It's so different. She removed the lid of her drink and blew, cooling it. Steam darted up into her face and she laughed, squinting at me through foggy lenses.

Different from what?

Alexisonfire. *Tell* me you still worship Dallas.

Diversity, my friend. Besides, he has a softer side, too. City and Colour?

Oh. I guess so. Hey, you wanna watch movies tonight, or go to the bush? Tiff's glasses cleared up to reveal her bright green eyes.

Neither, I thought.

Let's go to the bush. I'm avoiding my mom.

Why?

Nothing. She's just being a bitch.

I'd opened Liam's car door at eight on Friday morning, stepping like a newborn fawn onto the sidewalk with my untied high-tops.

Take care, girlfriend. He'd gotten out behind me, shivering despite the linty black blanket wrapped around his body.

You too, Liam. Hey, I almost forgot something. I'd opened my backpack and pulled something out. Here.

He'd widened his icy eyes and taken the old, floppy beige toque from me.

Are you serious?

Of course. It'll warm you up. Besides, it looks much better on you.

Oh my god. Thanks.

Liam had pulled the hat down over his hair, bangs flattening on his forehead. Pulling me forward for a hug, I'd felt his chest against my ear, knowing it wasn't just daisy that had made him profess his love for me hours earlier. We were meant to be friends. I'd squeezed him back.

See you later.

I'd trudged away with my Discman restfully giving me Tegan and Sara.

Along the walk I hadn't been able to think of anything but a slice of toast, a big mug of orange pekoe tea, and our comfy basement sofa. Turning onto our road and scanning the line of duplexes, my stomach had risen into my chest, beating like a heart. My mother's ratty old car was in our driveway instead of in the parking lot at bank. She drove the kind of vehicle obviously meant for teenagers--cheap, old, and broken.

My mother had heard me kicking my shoes off and had come down the hall to me. I'd stopped in my tracks upon seeing her still in her sleepwear, a salmon pink slippers and a ripped gray robe.

Hi. I'd leaned against the closet door, putting my head against the wood with a sudden wave of exhaustion.

Nice to see you, did you have a good night? Her brown bangs had been matted back on her head, revealing pink skin around her eyes.

I'd felt my face frown, the rest of my head falling asleep.

Are you sick?

I've been awake all night with a stomachache. She actually had looked in pain, clutching her belly like it would fall apart if she didn't. The biggest truth was the lack of a cigarette in her mouth.

My mouth had dropped open.

Oh! Shit. I'm sorry, Mom. I forgot.

Language. What were you so busy with?

I was at Tiff's. We had a fire pit, then started watching Titanic, you know how long it is. I just got completely carried away. Here, smell my sweater, I swear I was at Tiff's.

I'd pulled the shoulder of my shirt up and waved it near my mother's face.

No. She'd scrunched up her face and stepped back. Then she'd watched me close the front door and slip into the kitchen and pour a gigantic glass of water. She'd even followed me to my bedroom, peering in.

Look, I'm sorry. I'd turned back at the doorframe so she couldn't enter. Do you want me to go get some Gravol now?

I'd crossed my toes inside my socks, hoping Tiff was awake so I could go over and borrow ten bucks.

Dana already got me some. You should've called.

She'd crossed the hall to her room and shut herself in.

I'd removed the tight jeans I'd been wearing for almost three consecutive days. They'd become not-so-tight, only slightly creasing my skin with the denim's lines and folds. I'd fallen asleep mere minutes after burrowing bare-legged under my blankets.

Five minutes before the end of my shift that Sunday, Monica came out to the front counter to hand me a piece of paper with my name typed on it in bold letters.

This is a progress report. I'd like to go through it with you.

Tiff, who was on her break at the time and sitting in the lobby, looked up from her book.

Progress Report: Venice Knight
Punctuality and Attendance: 5/5
Sanitation: 5/5
Speed and Accuracy: 5/5
Attitude: 5/5

When I got to the bottom of the paper I froze.

Appearance: 10/5

Ten out of five? I looked up at Monica, taken aback.

She stuck her tongue out through her permanent smile.

There's not really a report for appearance. But if there was, you'd pass! By the way...today a customer gave very good feedback about you. He said your customer service skills are extraordinary.

I chuckled.

Thanks, Monica.

17

Tiff came home with me. The place was quiet. Dana was in his room and my mother had left a note on the kitchen table.

Out. Back around six.
Mom

She was probably on a cigarette run. I crumpled the note and threw it out, along with weekend newspapers and fliers. Then I cleaned the dishes piled in the sink, a pot from the previous night's soup dinner, plates crusted with pizza sauce, cereal bowls--in which the milk had solidified and created its own fragrance, and the cups wet with Kool-aid remnants. I set them upside-down in the cupboard so they wouldn't get dusty.

Tiff and I gave Dana some money, arranging for him to pick up some booze at the neighborhood store. Then I put my burnt Tegan and Sara CD in the living room DVD player and got started in the kitchen.

I was chopping the vegetables and Tiff was stir-frying the button mushrooms when the phone rang. I ran to the living room, tomato juices dripping from my pinky to my elbow when I picked up the cordless.

Hello?

Hey, girlfriend.

Liam! What's up? I tried to lick my elbow.

Nothing much. What are you doing tonight?

Right now I'm cooking supper for my family, and my friend Tiff--

I remember her. Aw, how sweet of you, cooking.

Yeah, I guess. I don't really know what I'm doing. What are you up to?

Just bored. I'm at the pharmacy, here 'til one in the morning. We're doing inventory.

Bummer. I walked back into the kitchen and wiped my arm on a dishrag. Is Raizel there too?

Who is it? Tiff had stopped stirring and was looking at me. Nosey, nosey Tiff.

Huh? I heard Liam say. No, man. She's still in Bowville. Amara just texted me, she said they'll be back tomorrow afternoon.

Ohh. My bad. I picked up a knife and continued chopping vegetables on the cutting board, which looked as though it'd never been used.

I think we should all get together tomorrow.

I pictured Liam when we'd first met, splayed out on a milk crate, flicking his bangs. I realized I'd become the person he was talking to on his cell phone. Something sizzled inside of me.

That sounds fun. Call me tomorrow, k?

By the time we hung up, Tiff had figured it out.

Your boy toy? She held up her wrist up and letting her hand fall limp.

Yup. Jealous?

Please. Oliver calls me every day. And sends several text messages. Tiff leaned forward to adjust the stove heat, her curly ponytail nearing touching the mushrooms. Sometimes I'll be standing there, doing nothing, and he'll send me a text saying, 'I wanna be with you', or, 'I can't wait to see you'. It's *really* sweet.

You win. I put chopped onions, cucumbers, tomatoes, black olives, and feta cheese into the biggest plastic bowl we had, the one Dana used for the free popcorn he always brought home from work.

So... Tiff tossed her ponytail to the other side to glance at me. You're hanging out with him tomorrow?

Yup. I waited for her to invite herself. She said nothing, keeping her eyes on the stove.

I was opening the oven when Dana walked into the kitchen toting two brown paper bags.

Hey bro', I sang, moving my shoulders up and down with my new favorite music.

Why are you so happy?

I'd known the questions would come sooner or later.

I have good news.

Did you finally find a boyfriend?

No. Did you?

Ha ha. What is it then? Dana looked between Tiff and I.

Wait and see, my good brother, wait and see. Oven warmth surrounded me as I poked at the lemon-and-pepper-seasoned trout.

Dana hung around, putting the liquor the fridge, a six-pack of beer, a box of white wine, and a brand new bottle of Bacardi 150 for my mother. He even pulled the table away from the wall so four chairs could fit, and set it with plates, napkins, forks, knives, and wine glasses.

My mother came in around six o' clock, just as she'd written in her note. She walked into the kitchen with a furrowed brow.

What smells so good? She rubbed her red hands together and held them near the oven. Oh my god, and you've cleaned. It looks wonderful.

I, we, cooked dinner. There's fish, and Greek salad, and stir-fried mushrooms. I wiped my hands on a dishtowel.

My mother looked at the clean black button-down shirt I'd changed into, then at the table.

Where did you get the money for all of this?

Let's sit down. Tiff pulled out her chair.

We sat around the table, steam and the scent of butter from the open dishes teasing our nostrils. Throughout the cooking process I'd been silently planning my speech, but somehow forgot it all. I looked at my mother and her scrunched, suspicious face.

I got a job. I cracked my knuckles under the table. Pop pop pop.

Where? My mother and brother exclaimed in unison.

With me, at Team Bean. Tiff beamed. I helped her get hired.

No kidding. Dana sized me up from across the table. I looked away in remembrance of how I'd acted about his promotion.

That's fantastic, Venice! My mother clasped her hands on the tabletop. When do you start?

Tiff looked confused.

I...started last week. Under the table I tried to crack my knuckles again, to no avail.

Seriously? Dana asked. Why didn't you tell us?

Oh, you know...I didn't want to steal your thunder. I allowed my eyes to glance up and meet with my brother's.

Well, congratulations, my peach. My mother rubbed my shoulder. That's great.

Thanks. Now I'll finally be able to afford a camera.

Totally. Dana nodded and gave me a smile. Congrats.

You too, Dana.

Should we eat? Tiff's eyes flitted between the three of us. I'm excited to try the food.

Oh yeah! I jumped up from my chair and pulled open the fridge door, displaying its innards like I was Vanna White. I thought we could have some celebratory drinks.

Wow. My mother's jaw dropped at the copious amounts of liquor. Well...why not?

I laughed successfully, a high-pitched bird-like melody. I got Dana a beer, rum and Coke for my mother, and wine for Tiff and I, after my mother had confirmed that Tiff was allowed to drink. My mother trusted my best friend so much that she didn't even phone Pam.

Tiff wasn't used to drinking anything but cocktails and coolers; the wine was so strong that she had to sip it delicately between bites of trout, though she soon warmed up, quite literally, patting her reddened cheeks with the back of her hand. Everyone raved about the food even though the salad had grown warm and the button mushrooms had grown cold and the fish was chewy. Dana had room in his belly for a second helping, and then a third.

We were clearing the table and my mother was on her third or fourth drink when she pointed at me.

Did you just get a job just for an excuse to drink with me?

I smiled.

My brother, having downed four cans of beer, and starting his fifth, offered to do the dishes. I thanked him even though he was getting water all over the floor I'd just swept. My mother slipped away for a cigarette. Tiff and I removed the box of white wine from the fridge and ran downstairs three steps at a time, laughing when a bit of the sweet liquor splashed on the rug. I rubbed it in with my sock.

It's all good. It's clear.

I put some music on the computer, my play-list of Tegan and Sara and Ani Difranco and Millie Fischer. We sat on the carpet, agreeing that the cool cement beneath it felt especially comfortable that day, and passed the wine box back and forth with its heavy innards sloshing around inside.

Hey, wasn't Monica playing this at work today? Tiff cocked her head to listen.

Actually, I was. I tipped the box back with the opening over my mouth.

Oh. Sorry. This reminds me of the stuff Olly listens to.

Olly?

Oliver. That's my nickname for him. You know something? He loves wine. I bet he'll be surprised when he finds out I'm drunk. I mean, not when he finds out that I'm drunk, but that I'm drunk off wine. I'm really excited to tell him. Oh my god. I can't get enough of this stuff. She wiped the back of her mouth with the sleeve of her precious white blouse, the one she'd worn at Team Bean, and while we'd cooked, and all the way through supper.

I flicked some congealed salad dressing off her shoulder.

What? Tiff flinched away from me and looked down. Ew. Are we still going to the bush?

Yeah…?

I don't want Oliver to see me in this! Or smell me in this!

I laughed.

This isn't funny, Venice. I think he might be the one.

The one?

THE ONE I MARRY.

I slowly pulled the box away from my lips.

You're, like, eighteen.

SO? She breathed heavily, face having reddened drastically. Like a tomato in a microwave, she was about to pop.

Okay! Relax. I'll lend you something.

Fifteen minutes later we were crossing the field to the bushes, the box of wine bumping around in my backpack. Though we'd made a dent, at least half of the booze remained. My smallest black t-shirt hung off Tiff like a sleeping bat, its hem sneaking out from under her puffy winter coat.

When we arrived we sat on a log, waiting while some of The Dudes lit the fire. Their method that evening was to cover a ratty blanket with a can of someone's sister's aerosol hairspray before tossing it over the flickering logs. Wild orange flames embraced the blanket, smoke immediately erupting from the pit.

I coughed and leaned back, shielding my face with my arms. My heart jumped when I nearly fell to the leafy carpet.

Ugh. Tiff?

Yeah?

Don't you ever get sick of this? I gestured around us, at The Gigglers and The Dudes, and The Bitches with their North Face jackets and pretend-ripped jeans.

Yeah... Tiff's wine-glazed eyes scanned the party. I see what you mean. Sometimes I wish there were other things to do, besides this and watching movies and wandering around downtown.

Hmm. I glanced back at The Dudes, stroking my chin. I wondered if Seed was in his usual spot outside the bush, waiting for business. The Dudes had always actively displayed their pothead-ism.

Tiff swigged some wine, eyeing me in her peripheral vision. I heard the box thud as she set it on the ground between our calves.

Okaaay. Clearly, you have an idea. Out with it. She chose that moment to jab me in the side with her skinny Tiffany Abraham pointer finger. I shrieked and grabbed her hand, forcing it away.

We could try-- I laughed as her finger persisted, nudging its way between my ribs. No one paid us heed, busy in their own drunken games. We could try something else.

What? Tiff cocked her head, like she had in my basement when I'd played Millie Fischer. The fire shone off her curls. What do you mean, something else?

Something better. I shrugged, toeing the dirt with my dirty sneaker.

Like...?

Like E, or something? My eyes were reluctant to meet with hers.

Venice!

Tiff jumped up. I caught the log's balance by slamming my hand into the soil, its moisture encasing my fingers and palm.

I can't believe you.

I rubbed my hand on my ratty work jeans and opened my mouth.

Or not. I was just thinking out loud.

What's going on with you? Tiff hissed, a dot of saliva hitting my nose. Wearing red, listening to shitty music. It's that Liam guy, isn't it? And what's up with your mom? First you say you're avoiding her, then you make her a huge meal and buy a bunch of alcohol. I don't even like wine. Where did you--

You're being a lot like her right now. I stood up. Way too nosey. And my music is *not* shitty.

You know how I feel about drugs. They ruin peoples' lives. Haven't you ever seen Intervention? She crossed her arms over her chest the same way my mother did when she wasn't impressed. I *know* you have. We watched it together.

I glanced around at the other partiers, longing for the first time ever that I'd arrived with anyone but Tiff. The Gigglers were singing the alphabet backwards and trying to walk in a straight line. The Bitches were comparing gel nails.

Okay. I'm done with this. I'm going home.

I was reaching down for the wine box when Tiff snatched it up and held it over her head, arms bent by the weight of the box's contents.

I'm done with this, too! She turned to the fire.

Stop! I yelled.

There's a fight! Someone announced.

Punch her!

Fight! Fight! Fight! They chanted.

It's gonna blow!!! Someone screeched, probably one of The Bitches.

Does wine explode? There's alcohol in it, right?

Someone laughed.

Their words twirled in the air around our bodies, frozen like a scene on a scratched DVD. Everyone had stopped what they were doing to watch us. Being the center of attention had never felt worse, including the time I'd puked on stage during my third grade Christmas concert.

One of The Dudes came up from behind Tiff, easily grabbed the wine box, and dropped it on the ground near the logs. My friend shrugged, blinking heavily.

I left her there and moved through the partiers, who were obviously disappointed that there hadn't been a catfight. I could have flattened her face with one hit. I pushed tree branches aside to escape, the dark engulfing me, and stalked across the field, kicking the long grass and dragging my jean bottoms in the dirt.

I picked at bits of dried mud from between my fingers.

18

I once experienced the flying of time. The determiner of happiness. I was really young. Clock hands spread like bird wings and soared around corners.

Seasons.

Puberty.

I'm a kid and my bike is a dictionary illustration next to the word 'dilapidation'. The wheels on everyone else's bikes slice through puddles and flick droplets my way. I secretly pretend to be the guard following troops and keeping everyone safe. My bicycle is a red piece of metal my mother may or may not have found at a garage sale.

Mom took wire-cutters to a schoolyard on the other side of town and cut the lock off that bike and stole it from some kid. You're riding stolen happiness. My brother told me this once, poetic and stupid.

Shut up Fatso. Mom's an angel.

I didn't let him know I believed him.

People make fun of Dana because he has a girl's name. They make fun of me because I'm Dana the Fatso With a Girl's Name's Sister. I never tell Dana that I love him, even though I do. He sometimes calls me Bitch, but besides that he's okay, and that's why I put up my shield and don't let words get to me. Other kids have never come home to the macaroni and cheese Dana cooks and shares with me; they've never wrapped up in our smelly basement quilts and played Sonic the Hedgehog with him on a cold winter day.

We don't spend as much time together in the spring. Spring is when I break free from our tiny duplex and go for bike rides. At first I go out alone, ten minutes away to Oakwood Heights. I pass clusters of kids playing Hop Scotch or Red Butt against the wall of eight-car garages and tell myself not to think about joining in because I'm from elsewhere.

Dana told me a story once. Once upon a time, construction companies puked on a map of Sloam, our city, and decided to build mansions where spots of regurgitated meatloaf landed. They called it Oakwood Heights as though it was remotely similar to Oakwood Terrace's short, sloppy buildings, homes to single parents, plumbers, and illiterate seniors.

These three girls from school start riding around my neighborhood. They slow down when they pass me on their bikes, not minding when I eventually trail along. I give them cool points for daring to enter 'sketchy' territory, not that they need cool points. They are among the most popular girls at school, East Indian Marity with humongous eyes and a sleek black braid, Janet with her small nose and strawberry-blond lion's mane, Cecile with her gymnast thighs and year-round healthy summer glow.

Cecile Grey, who I used to hang out with, but who ditched me a long time ago, when the boys realized she was cute and the girls realized she was skinnier than them. I still have baby fat and my hair dangles around my shoulders, uneven from my mother's sewing scissors. She's never sewed anything so they're more like Wreck My Kids' Hair scissors. I keep everything pulled back in a scraggly, knotted ponytail.

As we ride, the girls discuss who likes who in our eighth grade class, who would make a good couple, and who doesn't like each other. Sometimes they include me.

Venice, what do you think? Do you like Thomas?

I bet she does. *Every* girl does.

I blush and they glance at me for the rest of the ride, laughter in their eyes.

Whenever we pass the park with the hill we ditch our bikes at the bottom and run up to the apple tree plethora. I wonder why they call it Dole Mountain when the sign near the street reads something different.

Humphrey Park

We shake the trees until apples fall like bombs, and when I chomp on them everyone screams that I have to wash them first.

Sometimes the apples don't fall and the others pout because we're all too short to reach. I roll up my sleeves and hoist myself onto the lowest branch, where I can balance on tiptoe and reach any apple they want. They laugh every time.

Thank you times a thousand.

They put the apples in their backpacks to share with their families later--after they've been washed, of course.

Then some ass hole takes my bike. One minute I'm up in a tree, everyone spotting me while I teeter on a branch, and the next minute we're stumbling down the hill to three bikes instead of four, heads swiveling frantically. Janet and Cecile and Marity stand around, chests huffing, glancing at each other. They silently wonder why someone had taken my bike when it was lying with three beautiful, sparkling mountain bikes with pink streamers. Maybe someone running by grabbed the first thing they saw, but I secretly suspect karma. *Blame* karma. My mother really *has* stolen it, and someone is returning the favor. Because of karma, I'm not supposed to get pissed off, but I'm holding an apple and can't help slamming it into the ground and making bits of white fruit fleck my shoes.

After that, I start riding Marity's bike while she perches on the handlebars like a bluebird. Sometimes I balance on the pedals and let her have the seat behind me, hands squeezing my sides when I catch speed. Janet and Cecile called us lezzies. Then they apologize because it's not my fault my bike has been stolen.

Those friends of mine take up all the room in my diary. I write about how we're all going to go to the little high school in Oakwood Heights together the next year, St. Timothy's, even though my family isn't Catholic. I write about how cool my friends are, how funny, smart, and sophisticated. I write a profuse amount about their beauty, Marity's, in particular, and how I'm a blob in comparison. I can still picture Marity on Dole Mountain, her skin shining in the sun, bronze. I describe her to my diary as poised, dark, and stunning.

Three years later I realize Dole is a brand of apple juice. We never have anything but Kool-aid in our weathered duplex fridge.

Time has *flown.*

19

On Monday afternoon I found Seed's number where I'd left it as a bookmark in my high school yearbook.

When he picked up, I explained who I was.

You said you lost my number. He coughed.

I found it.

Well, I guess we're both in luck. What's up, boo?

'Boo'--the nickname made me feel like we were in a music video and I was a half-dressed lap-dancer. Considering my giggles, I must have liked it. I assumed I wasn't too special; he probably called all his chick friends 'boo' and other names Tiff and I made fun of--'shorty', 'babe', 'lil mama'. I pushed Tiff out of my mind, not caring to think about what'd happened the night before.

Bang bang bang. My heart. I thought about the boy who'd been arrested for selling E in high school. I didn't know much about it, but knew cops had ways of finding out anything. I decided to be extra careful, not saying E, or daisy, or pill, or anything of the sort. I knew enough to never discuss quantity or price via phone.

Can I...come by?

Seed lived in a sixteenth floor apartment with a view of Wainmont, an area out past Broadway. When he opened the door the first thing I saw was a rectangle fish tank so big I could've fit inside and invited my friends to join me. Maybe Liam was too tall, but Tiff could fit. My mind stung. The tank was stocked with black, blue, orange, and yellow fish, some striped and some dotted, swimming through the clear, blue water around a bundle of plastic coral and neon stones.

Don't bother with your shoes. My cleaning lady's coming tomorrow. Seed led me around the tank.

The second thing I noticed was Seed's head, no longer covered by a lurking-in-the-bushes hood. Blond dreadlocks would've hung to his shoulders if not pulled back by an elastic band.

The third thing I noticed was how abrasively the sun lit the place, so high up. The apartment was surprisingly nice, though a little messy, things tossed about at random. A cloud of pot hung in the air, presumably fresh bong exhalations. All I could smell was weed. Weed, weed, and weed, though there was none to be seen. I wondered if he ever sat on the balcony smoking a spliff and watching people get mugged. Wainmont wasn't safe, but it was the place to live if you wanted to spend on things other than your home. I wondered how old Seed was, but didn't think it was appropriate to ask drug dealers personal questions.

Have a seat, boo. Seed pointed at the long, sectional sofa.

He probably made more money than my whole family's monthly income combined. I thought of that night at the bush when his eyes were practically rolling back in his head. Watching him dig into a tube of Pringles, he just seemed like a regular kid, stoned and chilled out, a Wii game paused on the sixty-inch television. He was living the dream.

So, what would you like? He made me feel like we were at fast food restaurant and he was behind the counter--though a McDonald's visor wouldn't have fit around his dreads.

I was hoping to get some more daisy. No beating around the bush.

Okay. Seed balled up his fists and rubbed his eyes. When he pulled his hands away, his peppermint-green eyes shone at me. How much do you want? Wait a sec, are you a cop?

Do I look like one? I looked down at my outfit--high-tops, jeans, baggy shirt, faux-hawk blow-dried and sprayed into three-inch erection.

Joking.

Seed didn't see me blush as he took things off the wooden coffee table--envelopes, blank CDs, a Bob Marley ashtray, six Bic lighters, Febreze air freshener. When the tabletop was empty he lifted it to reveal a secret trunk meant for things like blankets and knitting needles. Instead, stacked neatly inside were little boxes I could only assume contained drugs and drug-related paraphernalia. I wondered if the cleaning lady ever looked inside.

Do you have a pill box?

No, I was just gonna put them in my wallet. I shrugged.

They might break, boo. I got these real trippy ones on sale if you want.

Seed dug his arm into the corner of the trunk and withdrew a stack of little colorful plastic boxes. As I browsed through them, he lit a joint and took a big hoot, eyes on me. Before I could feel perturbed by his stoned gaze, he handed the joint over.

For a few seconds I just stared at the object in my hands, at that point having never smoked anything in my life. I decided to regard it as a cozy, tightly rolled burrito, except I wouldn't bite the end and dip it in salsa. I thought of my mother and her disturbing tobacco addiction, but marijuana was different. It couldn't give me lung cancer--could it?

I took a quick puff and gave the joint back, feeling indifferent about the skunky aroma. I didn't cough. I wondered who had smoked weed in the first place and how they'd imagined it would get them high. When thought of that way, people who invented things like light bulbs and toilets and telephones didn't seem so mighty. They were only experimenting too, and happened to create things deemed crucial by the world as opposed to plants beholding the potential to diminish pain and irritation.

The pill boxes were eye-catching, but obviously cheap, covered in patterns and sparkly pictures--butterflies, happy faces, and stars. They reminded me of arcade vending machine stickers. I didn't *really* want one, but felt like it was expected of me. I picked up an Asian-inspired one with cherry blossoms and a koi fish.

How much? .

Fifteen bucks.

Are you kidding? I flipped it around in my hands, liking how the fish's tail caught the sunlight streaming in.

If you buy it today I'll give you an extra pill. He indicated toward the trunk and handed the joint back to me.

I took another puff before speaking.

I dunno. I'm kind of--

No problem, boo. Two free pills, cause you're cute. He ashed the joint in a Coke bottle.

Cool. Thanks. I tried to stifle a wide smile.

Seed reached into the trunk and pulled out a baggie of yellow pills.

Oh! They're yellow. Do you have any of those blue ones?

The ones with the lemons? No such luck.

Oh. I really liked those.

Everyone likes those. He smirked. They fucked you up good, hey?

Yeah. It was amazing.

I'm trying to get them again, but--cough--they're in high demand. These are the next best thing. And look, they got little lips on them. Like kisses.

He put one in my palm and I examined it. I giggled.

That's cute. But why don't they put lips on the red ones?

Seed looked at me, smoking the last of the joint. Oh, fuck. I must have sounded so stupid. Maybe they *did* put lips on the red ones. Suddenly he laughed, coughing at the same time.

I have no idea. They put little trees on the red ones. Why don't they put trees on the green ones?

Because they put french fries on the green ones?

We looked at each other, both having sunken into the sofa, and laughed. Everything was comfortable about it--my arms, legs, eyes, and mind. I wanted french fries.

That night I showered and re-dried my 'hawk to stand up, and put on clean clothes, a black muscle shirt and black cardigan meant for occasions like weddings and funerals and Easter. I'd washed my nice jeans so they were tight again and clung to me in the right places. If I was someone who liked girls I'd probably approach myself and say something along the lines of, Come here often?, even if we were at a bus stop or something. After payday I was going to convince my mother to sign a parental consent form for a facial piercing.

At nine o' clock someone knocked on our front door.

I'll get it! I yelled, running into the hallway from my room. My mother lay in her usual place on the sofa with her crocheted afghan, a novel, and a cloud of smoke around her brown hair.

Not so loud. She eyed my hairdo.

Hungover? I laughed, recalling the boozefest.

It's not funny. She sunk into the couch cushions. And we're really busy at work.

I turned away from her, still smiling, and jumped over a pile of shoes to open the front door.

Raisin! I exclaimed, seeing Raizel through the screen door, hands shoved in the pockets of her gray pea coat. I yanked the door open.

V! Raizel threw her arms around my waist and squeezed.

Shh! My mother hissed at little Raizel with her curly white bob and red shoeboots.

I rolled my eyes and stepped outside, hoping my mother hadn't caught a whiff of pot. The cement stoop chilled my bare feet. Her Camaro sat near the sidewalk, engine quietly rumbling. Putt putt putt.

Raizel took her arms off me and played with a lock of her hair.

Is that your mom? She's *so* pretty.

Please. Are you high?

Maybe. She giggled, shoving her hands back into her pocket. I just smoked one in the car with Liam.

I pulled my eyes from Raizel to glance at the car. Liam waved from the passenger seat, his cell-phone glued to his ear.

So, how was Bowville?

Meh. Raizel's smile fading slightly. Parts were good.

How was Millie Fischer?

She fucking rocked!

Language! My mother called from inside.

Sorry, Mrs. Venice! Raizel called back.

Oh my god. I laughed and went back inside to grab my bag. I filled my backpack with socks, clean underwear, and my toothbrush. Considering the contents of my koi fish and cherry blossom box, odds were high that I wouldn't return home that night.

Are you going somewhere in that nice sweater?

I whipped around to see my mother leaning on my bedroom doorframe, still wrapped in her afghan. My heart jumped and I squeezed my fingers around the little box, inching from my dresser toward my backpack.

Yeah. I'm going out.

Who's that girl? My mother yawned.

She's my friend from high school. I slipped the pill box into my backpack and closed it.

I don't remember her. My mother frowned. What's her name? And where are you going?

Raizel. She thinks you're really pretty.

Sure she does. My mother laughed, limp brown locks shaking with her head.

I zipped up my coat and pulled my backpack straps over my shoulders.

So, Raizel invited me to sleep over. First we're going clubbing, though--

If only you were old enough, my peach. My mother laughed again. Phone me before bed, okay?

A minute later I scampered out the door and across the lawn to the Camaro. Raizel got out. I ducked under her seatbelt to throw my stuff on the backseat, sliding onto the cold leather after it.

Geez, it's smoky in here. I caught a lungful of weed.

Playing at low volume was yet another artist I'd never heard, drums and electric guitars and some chick with an excited voice. I was sick of asking and being the naïve girl. I wrote some of the lyrics in my mind, knowing I could look them up later.

Liam twisted in the passenger seat to give me an indolent grin.

Hey, girlfriend. How nice to see you.

The sides of my mouth turned up when I realized he was wearing the beige toque. I caught Raizel smiling at me in the rearview mirror as she reversed out of my driveway.

Liam met someone. Raizel giggled.

The row of duplexes disappeared behind us as Raizel edged the car off Oakwood Terrace.

What's he like?

His name is Ben. Liam flicked his bangs out of his eyes. He's--

Sexy. Raizel laughed, interrupting. But so girly that *I'm* almost hot for him.

I blushed and rested against the backseat, clasping my hands around my knees. The air in the car chilled me limb by limb, bone by bone.

Where'd you meet him?

At Mars. Liam pulled a mirror out of his pocket, checking the placement of the toque on his head. He'll be there tonight.

Nice. And Amara's working there tonight, right?

Yup.

We figure we'll stop at Morgan's for a bit, then head to Mars. Raizel glanced back at me briefly. Is that cool with you?

Sure. I nodded. I grinned into the dark.

20

Raizel weaved the car in and out of streets I'd only ever seen from bus windows--the city's older streets, near Broadway. The moon was small that night, a sliver of light hinting at leaf-covered lawns, naked trees, and chipped brick buildings. My brother's basement suite was somewhere nearby, waiting for him to move in and grease the place up.

Raizel pulled the car over on a side street, cutting the engine. She left the keys in so the heater and the music stayed on. Then she leaned across Liam to pop the glove compartment, taking something out. That band was still on, the one with the high-pitched singer. I was trying to decide if I liked music like that when Liam stretched his arm into the backseat, bearing gifts.

What? I took the item from his hand, something cool and hard, possibly glass. I held it like a baby chick. The stereo cast a bit of light across my hand, and I saw a small, purple pipe, its bowl full of marijuana. Ohh.

Here. Raizel handed me an orange Bic lighter. She and Liam both twisted in their seats to gaze at me through the dark.

I weighed my options. I had already smoked up once that day, and it hadn't been so bad; in fact, I had sort of made a new friend. Looking at the pipe, I suddenly lusted for the laughter I knew it would bring.

I. . .don't know how to do it. Fear crawled like a pink spider up my neck.

What?! Liam exclaimed. Are you kidding me?

Liam! Raizel punched his skinny shoulder. That's okay, V. You don't have to.

I handed the pipe back to Raizel and sank against my seat, watching as she rolled her thumb on the lighter and let it hover over the weed. I wished I wasn't such an awkward loser. We made eye contact, light from the tiny fire flickering on her angelic face. After a moment she moved her forefinger away from the hole on the side of the pipe, inhaling. Then she coughed, and like a bomb had hit her mouth, gray smoke flew out and covered everything, a skunky blanket.

Woo hoo! Liam cheered.

You okay? My voice meandered through the post-cough haze.

I was too afraid to ask if I could try smoking the pipe, just once.

When they'd finished the bowl, we opened the doors and let the smoke flow out into the dark. I crawled out Raizel's door under her seatbelt. She removed her gray pea coat and tossed it into the car, revealing tiny, black shorts over vertically pin-striped tights, a heather-blue v-neck shirt and her pearl necklace dangling between the two little bumps on her chest.

Wow. I looked her up and down. I can't believe you're wearing that.

Raizel lifted her arm to run her fingers through her white-blond hair, shifting her stance so her right hip jutted out from under the shirt. I caught a glimpse of a beauty mark on the skin above her shorts. I wondered how she would pose, as a model. She gazed at me, eyelids partially closed over her dark eyes.

What's that supposed to mean?

Oh, no, nothing bad. Really. I mean, I wish I could pull off an outfit like that. If I wore those shorts I'd look like a big fat clown.

I felt like sewing my mouth closed.

Well… She moved her hand from her hair to my head, stroking the short hair above my ear. At least your hair looks awesome. Not many people could pull that off.

My scalp smiled at her fingertips.

Okay, lovers. Liam stood ten feet down the sidewalk in his purple jeans and the toque. Let's go.

You just wanna go see Ben! I called back.

Raizel laughed and slammed the car door before turning to strut after Liam. I let them lead me to a three-story house. We tramped across the lawn. Though it was only nine-thirty, house music boomed from inside, spilling across the yard. Anticipation bubbled in my stomach when I thought about my backpack and yellow kiss-imprinted objects.

We walked straight in without ringing the doorbell or knocking. The people inside wouldn't have heard us anyway, not a chance with that music. Teens lingered in the front entranceway, trying to find their shoes in a huge pile. We kept ours on.

You don't wanna lose those. I put my mouth near Raizel's ear and pointed at her Docs.

So, you like 'em? She twisted her head to speak into my ear.

I smiled at her stoned grin and shrugged. We walked through a short hall to find a few partiers in the a well-lit kitchen, lingering around a table covered in party items--pop, a bowl of chips, stacks of plastic cups. No booze was in sight; if someone left their booze on the table at that kind of party, they'd hardly taste it before it was gone.

Stairs out of the kitchen led us to a second-story hallway and another staircase.

Two bucks each! A kid stood at the bottom of the staircase pointed up the stairs. He came straight, or not so straight, out of an American Apparel ad with his mustard jeans and frizzy, blond hair pulled high with a scrunchie. His turquoise tank top had armpit holes that dangled halfway down his sides; first signs of armpit hair meant he couldn't have been older than fourteen. I glanced up the stairs and wondered what was so good that we had to pay to get in.

Hey! Liam rested his arm on the wall beside the boy's head. You're new here. What's your name?

Oh my god. Raizel laughed and squeezed her eyes shut. She leaned toward me. Watch him do his magic!

I thought we could've afforded the six dollars, in fact, even *I* could have paid for everyone and had money left over, but watching Liam flirt was more than entertaining. He flicked his bangs out of his eyes and said something near the kid's ear.

Okay, come on. Liam grinned, taking Raizel and I by the hands and leading us up the stairs. The boy's number was on Liam's forearm in neat, bubbly writing, along with a name. Jack.

A familiar sight greeted my vision--flashing electric disco ball lights, but instead of in a bedroom, they fell on peoples' heads in a sea of darkness.

Some people sat on sofas around the room's perimeter, while what seemed like a hundred others in the middle of the room danced. My mouth fell open when I realized they were dancing. While I could think I was King Shit for knowing the ropes at a house party, I had never been to one where people *danced.* I caught a glimpse of the room's unfinished walls and concluded that someone had gone through the trouble of making two bedrooms into one gigantic party room.

Oh my god! I can't believe this.

I said the words, but knew I wouldn't be heard. Music quaked the floor and reverberated in my knees. Glow sticks hung from peoples' heads and necks and ankles and wrists, coloring the air when they pumped their arms to the heavy beat. Ceiling fans also donned glow sticks, swinging them along with the tunes.

Liam still grasping our hands, we moved along the edge of the crowd. We jumped over the legs of couch people, who lay with far-out, shut-eyed expressions on their faces. I guessed they were all teenagers or in their twenties, bodies entwined like they'd been friends forever. On our other side, people spun, swayed, and jumped, some of them sucking on pacifiers.

I laughed as though someone had told a joke.

As we neared the back of the room, peoples' attitude seemed different. I got the feeling that they were concentrating on something, collectively. Everyone faced a wall of windows, hands raised as though cheering someone on. We snuck through the thickening crowd, people smiling at us when we touched them, instead of punching our guts like I imagined happened at most music concerts. Their warm bodies encased us. I took off my coat.

You'll wanna take this off, too. Raizel pointed at my funerals-and-weddings-and-Easter cardigan. I complied.

Two girls in sparkly backless t-shirts and blue short shorts from a seventies' phys. ed. class danced in jazzy unison on a platform at the back of the room, long ponytails whipping their cheekbones as they twirled. If not for other things going on around us, I may never have torn my eyes off their sweaty backs and the tanned bare skin between their shorts and white knee-highs. I hugged my stomach over my muscle shirt.

To left of the girls was a long, black booth, a tangle of neon green, pink, and orange cords duct-taped to a power bar on the floor underneath. Atop the table were a soundboard, microphone, laptop, and a million other pieces of equipment I didn't know the names of. On each side of the table was a speaker as tall as my shoulders, subwoofers shaking with the beat. Behind all of the equipment and the electricity was a skinny young guy in a muscle shirt like mine, short, dark hair framing his face, fiddling with dials as his shoulders jabbed the air, his own body mesmerized by the beat. He waved a tattooed arm and muttered into the microphone.

Make some noise.

The crowd whistled in response, shoving a smile onto the DJ's face. He hugged his tiger-striped headphones, owning the room; the way anyone moved from that point on depended not on noise but on the music spewing from his fingertips.

Raizel leaned over to yell at me.

That's Morgan. Doesn't she remind you of Samantha Ronson?

I laughed at my mistake. The DJ didn't look remotely like a girl. I nodded and added the name to the list of things I'd google later. We stood in a circle to the side of the crowd, my lower back gathering sweat under my bag, which was heavy with my peeled layers.

I can't dance yet. Liam crossed his arms over his chest.

Sure you can! Raizel closed her eyes and raised her arms, drawing her v-neck up. I caught a glimpse of the skin above her shorts where the top of her tights hugged her flat belly.

I can't either. You guys are stoned and I'm not on anything. I looked down at my own body and pulled my backpack off. But--

Wait ten minutes. I usually get something from Morgan. Liam glanced at the DJ.

Yeah, Liam has friends in high places. Or we could just drink. Raizel pointed in the dark at a door-side bar, people in the line dancing and looking over their shoulders toward the DJ. I wondered how Morgan felt, a hundred people at her beck and call.

But guys. I knelt to unzip my backpack. I looked up at their inquisitive faces and raised my voice. I *have* something.

My new friends got down on their knees, right there where people had probably spilled drinks and puked, Liam in his skintight jeans and Raizel in her shoeboots and tights. We hunkered over my backpack and I pulled out the cherry blossom koi fish box.

Hey. Raizel reached out. Her black fingernail slid along the side of the box, dark eyes aimed at my face. Where'd you get this?

Why? I shrugged. I bought it.

Nothing...it reminds me of someone. It's pretty.

I smiled and opened the latch on the side of the box, popping it open to display the four yellow pills I'd gotten from Seed earlier that day. They were the shade of yellow parents chose for nursery walls when they didn't know the sex of their unborn child. I figured I could share with them after they'd been so generous to me. Liam hugged me before going to grab some water from the bar.

Raizel scooted toward me on the floor, putting her face near my ear.

V, you don't have to do daisy if you don't want to. It doesn't matter.

My cheeks and forehead got all hot, like someone had lit candles underneath. I looked down and closed my fist around the pillbox, regretting telling her that night at Amara's had been my first time ever meeting daisy. A girl stumbling by narrowly missed stepping on my backpack. I pulled it into my lap and covered my stomach. I stared at my fist.

Hey. Raizel nudged me with her elbow. Or you can do it. It's your choice. I just wanted you to know I think you're cool whether you do it or not.

The candles under my skin went out in a whoosh of exhalation. I smiled and looked back up at Raizel, noticing how her hair glowed in the black-light.

21

Liam returned and we each plucked a pill from the container, the rave roaring around us.

Cute lips. Liam held the pill between his thumb and forefinger. I've never seen these before.

To tonight. I smiled and tongued the gap between my two front teeth.

We took turns gulping the water and throwing our head backs to swallow the pills, no one around us paying heed. The little object slid down my throat before a familiar waiting period, limbo, purgatory between earth and absolute heaven.

As time passed I felt as though I was climbing a ladder rung by rung, up up up. Nothing could touch me. Raizel and Liam and I danced in a circle near Morgan's booth, feet supposedly on the ground. The music pounded at the same time as my heart. I felt disco ball lights pass over my closed eyelids, red, orange, yellow, green, blue, purple, an infinite rainbow. When I re-opened my eyes the crowd had doubled; glow sticks and soothers were everywhere.

I borrowed Liam's phone and slipped down the stairs, letting the boy with the mustard jeans stamp my hand. When I'd escaped to the cool air, I sat on the sidewalk and dragged my hand around on the lawn behind me, frosty grass licking my skin.

Hello? My mother answered our family phone.

Hi mom. I prayed she couldn't hear the house music. Her end of the line was quiet. I pictured her under the dim light of our living room lamp.

Hi. Where are you?

We're at Raizel's house. You'd love it, Mom. It reminds me of Dr. Seuss.

Oh? How?

I paused.

It's really. . .big.

Oh fuck. I was so obvious.

Anyway, we're having a *great* time.

Are you drunk?

No. Maybe tipsy. Her parents let us try their wine. It's home-brewed. In fact, they offered to give me a bottle for you. I think you'll like it.

The more details I gave, the more credible my lies were.

Hmm. That sounds nice. When are you going to bed?

Right away. We're just watching a movie now.

What movie?

The. . .it's called The Morgan's House. I slapped my leg. Stupid. It's not very good.

Okay. My mother laughed. Are you working tomorrow?

No. Day off. I'll come home in the morning. Bye!

Back in the house, I flashed my stamp at the boy before running up the stairs, giddy with freedom. Raizel tossed her curly hairy around, jumping whenever the song changed, arms up like she could grab the sky if there was no ceiling. She was a fairy-tale creature. I watched her closed eyes and wondered what she was thinking. Maybe she was feeling instead of thinking. Tiff popped into my head. I imagined her dancing at that party, a Barbie with unbendable limbs. She would've made a scene.

Some guys made their way to our circle and surrounded Liam, putting their arms up and chests as close as possible without touching. Something about Liam attracted people like magnets. He had the best crooked-toothed, bang-flicking face out of everyone I knew. He grinned and danced as the filling in a sandwich between two well-built shirtless guys.

I suddenly felt a surge of love for Liam. Explaining what a surge of love feels like is hard; the feeling just happens and if the hamster's running on the wheel in your head, you recognize it as it is and don't make it out to be something suggested by society, such as a crush or infatuation. I loved him as a friend, a handsome friend who made me laugh when I was high and rubbed my back while I came down. I stroked his fore-arm and knew he felt my love travel along his pores and to his soul where he could care for my feelings if he so chose.

Raizel and I danced together, bobbing our shoulders to the music. We jumped together as though we'd eaten a whole bowl of sugar, the thought of which making me laugh as I pictured the acne I'd have if I did such a thing. Adrenaline. The beat came up from the floor through our feet and to our hips. I felt as beautiful as my companions looked, not caring about anything, the buttons on my shirt begging to pop open as I threw my arms up and swayed to the rhythm.

Soon a remix of a Tracy Chapman song came on, made faster for raves and clubs. I forgot about everything, the way I'd hoped I would. I forgot about the clocks ticking in the world and about Tiff and her coldness. All I could think about was bettering my life. I vowed to start doing things that would help me in my future as a famous photographer. I would start saving money for a really, really great camera and some extra lenses I could use for pixel-perfect close-ups. I imagined photographing all the people around me and their permanent smiles seething happiness. I promised myself I'd make a better effort with my mother and Dana.

When taking daisy, there came a time when the taker of said daisy asked herself if she was high or if she'd run into a bum pill. There were two ways to know. The first way was to look at the seventies' phys. ed. class dancers with their long hair and fit legs and admire them instead of feeling jealous. The other way to know was to let my daisy companion stand behind me and trail her fingers from my sides forward and press her body against my back. When I turned around Raizel grabbed my hands and we danced like an old couple doing a slow polka at a wedding reception. Her smile smelled like a rose and I became a cat gazing down at her face.

I'm so fucked up. I purred.

Raizel laughed, playing with her labret ring with her teeth. She pulled me toward her for a tight hug, a prism of warmth between our bodies. I'm soo glad we can share this together, she said. I felt her mouth graze my earlobe, felt her breath skip and hop its way into my head. I understood the core, the heart, of 'something better'. No amount of whiskey, wine, beer, or Gravol could have elated my entirety in such a manner. Yellow lips were not bum pills.

We danced on and on, amazingly seeming to never break a sweat. My feet didn't even hurt inside my high-tops. Raizel suggested a water break, so she and Liam and I grabbed hands and squeezed through the crowd to the bar. I held my bottle against my neck, cool condensation drip drip dripping off the plastic down the back of my shirt as we headed downstairs. The boy with the scrunchie and mustard jeans stood on the bottom step with his hip jutted to the side and his back arched.

Hey, baby. He looked up at Liam. You can't go back in if you leave now.

Yeah? Says who?

I don't make the rules. The boy crossed his arms. I just work here.

You work at a house party? A smile crept up my cheeks.

Yeah. The boy popped his gum, looking me up and down. And it's two-thirty, so we're not letting anyone back in.

Shit! Raizel exclaimed. It's two-thirty? Are you sure?

Liam whipped his cell phone out of his back pocket and pressed a button to check the time. The screen lit up his face.

Oh, fuck. We gotta go, guys.

See ya. The boy waved us out. Call me!

Traffic was sparse. Raizel had no problem driving, saying she'd pretty much come down anyway. I wanted to believe her, but still felt my fingertips and toes buzzing. She turned up the music and we bopped in our seats.

Raizel cursed when we stopped at a red light. She picked her cell phone out of the dashboard drink holder.

Amara finished at one. She tried calling me six times.

She called me, too. Liam looked at his cell phone. And Ben tried twice.

Maybe they're still there. I watched the old, brick buildings speed by. I wondered if Mars was such a beautiful building.

No, V. Liam turned to look at me. Amara tends to freak out over shit like this.

I clenched my jaw.

Liam dialed Ben, but couldn't get an answer. Afterwards, he phoned Amara.

Hello? Yeah, it's Liam. I'm so sorry, Amara. Yeah, she's with me. Sure. He handed his cell phone to Raizel.

Are you at home? Yeah? We're on our way. After hanging up, Raizel cursed again. Fuck. She's pissed.

I leaned forward to rest my head on the back of Raizel's driver seat. Liam looked at me.

You'll have to lie to her, V.

What? I took my head off the seat. Why me?

Because she can tell if we're lying. If you do, she'll believe you.

Okay, but what should I say?

Minutes later we pulled into the apartment parking lot. Raizel cut the engine in the spot designated for flat 508. We left our coats and bags on our seats, barely feeling the cold as we darted up the stairs to the fifth floor. The reddish-purple paisley pattern of the hallway carpet screamed at my eyes, brighter than ever.

When Amara opened her apartment door she stepped aside, letting us enter. She had on sparkly eye makeup and her hair was pulled back with a white braided headband, the poof of her 'fro poking out the back. Her skin contrasted neatly with the tiny white dress she had on. I glanced around to assure myself I hadn't wandered onto a Victoria's Secret runway.

Hi. She gazed at the three of us. I averted my eyes, my telltale pupils.

Hey.

We discarded our shoes and followed her to the dimly lit living room.

How was work? Raizel settled in the sofa and tucked her ankles under her butt.

Good. Amara sat beside her, stick-thin legs poking out of her dress. Beside Raizel with her black booty shorts and pinstriped tights, they were a sight for sore eyes, an image meant to be captured on film.

I plopped into the armchair across from the one Liam was in. He looked at me pointedly.

Listen, Amara, we *really* wanted to come to Mars tonight. I put on my most mature voice. Sometimes when talking on daisy, I felt like I was sitting outside of myself, listening to someone else. I've never been there. I thought it would be fun.

But?

We...wanted to surprise you. We called my dealer and stood outside his apartment for, like, *three* hours. He kept telling us to wait.

Amara's eyebrows went up, distorting her thin, dark face.

Why didn't you just get something from Morgan?

Because we weren't getting daisy. We were gonna get coke.

Raizel and Liam's mouths suddenly dropped open. Shit--my story was too far-fetched.

But Amara nodded in apparent belief, glancing swiftly at Liam and Raizel. She tugged at the satchel around her neck, which must have been empty.

So, does that mean you didn't bring anything?

No. A quick champion smile ran up my cheeks. I reached into my backpack and pulled out my cherry blossom box.

Is that a pill box? Amara craned her neck toward me. Where did you get that?

I bought it. I frowned, wondering why everyone kept asking about the box. Raizel eyed my hand. I pulled the last yellow lips pill out and handed it to Amara.

Have you guys already taken it? Amara frowned at me.

We *just* took them. Liam nodded. Like, ten minutes ago.

We stayed with Amara, dancing on her living room carpet and pretending we weren't coming down while she was reaching her clouds. I wished I didn't have to give her the last pill, but understood the sacrifice for friendship. Around five o' clock, Liam stretched out on the sofa and fell asleep more swiftly than a sunbathing cat. I thought it a damn good idea when Raizel wanted to retreat to Amara's bedroom and lie with the disco ball lights serenading our closed eyes.

I think these pills are shit. Raizel winked at me before yawning at Amara. I don't feel anything.

That's so weird. Amara clenched her jaw, swaying to the tunes blasting from her stereo. I *really* feel it. I'll come with you guys, though.

She flicked the music off.

We flowed down the hall and closed the bedroom door. Amara turned on the disco ball light and we dove into her big bed like it was a swimming pool in July. Under the duvet my new friends hugged me from either side, my back to Raizel and my face in Amara's neck. I thoroughly enjoyed the weight of their hands resting on my side. Amara's coconut body lotion was soft on my nostrils.

Oh my god. I whispered against Amara's skin. I'm soo comfortable.

Raizel hummed quietly, holding me from behind, her nose in the back of my neck at my hairline.

Amara giggled, her hand rubbing my side, and moved down so we were looking into each others' eyes.

Groovy. I watched her makeup sparkle in the colorful lights.

You're groovy. Amara blinked for three seconds, smiling when she re-opened her eyes. Her teeth were glowing pearls in the dark. Yup, you're still here.

I saw her moving forward at full speed--a cougar running through a field toward a herd of elk. Did cougars prey on elk? No time to think. She put her dry lips against mine. I closed my eyes. If I didn't reject a boy who drank scotch and sat me on the ground without caring that it was cold, I had no justification to reject a girl who held me like she would an egg and who gave me orange juice and let me cuddle in her bed in her warm apartment. Our mouths moved together for a quiet minute, her hand pawing my waist. I eased the braided band off her head and wove my fingers in her 'fro, getting lost, remembering Liam's recommendation.

If only *she* wasn't here. Amara whispered.

Behind me, Raizel's throat emitted the tired humming of slumber.

22

I awoke to the sound of nothing, lying on my back with my head half under the pillow, weekday morning noises having come and gone. I groaned and stretched my arms, my fingers brushing the cool brass of headboard railings. I pulled the pillow off my face and curled my body around it, the fly of my jeans digging into my belly.

I was on the right side of the bed, the cool window beside me. Amara was face-down on a pillow, but Raizel was nowhere to be seen. I watched Amara's dark back move up and down each time she inhaled, her top vertebrae jutting from under her skin. On the nightstand beside her, the disco ball purred and clicked with electric exhaustion, its colors lost in the light of day. I reached over her and turned it off. Amara barely stirred.

I padded past the unlit bathroom and the pantry door out to the kitchen to pour a tall glass of tap water. My shins ached as though I'd been running to raise charity money. The microwave told me it was half past nine. I found Liam lying on the living room sofa, smoking a joint with the beige toque pulled down over his face.

Psst. Good morning.

Liam pulled the toque up to reveal his icy blue igloo eyes.

Morning, V.

Did you see Raizel? I plopped down in an armchair and rubbed the backs of my calves with my knuckles. I wished I had ten arms, each of which could rub a different hurting part of my body--especially my head.

Yeah. She started work at nine. She gets off at five. That's when I start today.

You're kidding. She must be tired.

Yeah, but our boss lets us do whatever. Want some?

That's awesome. I nodded. I took the joint from Liam and sucked on it, glad he wasn't using a pipe. Smoke flowed into my mouth and looped around my lungs before spiraling back out. I groaned, wondering if Raizel had noticed Amara and I kissing.

Hmm? Liam looked at me.

Last night, Amara and I--

Made out?

Yeah, how did you know?

Raizel told me.

Ugh. I shook my head and took another puff. Was she pissed?

I dunno. Why would she be pissed?

Because that's her ex. I don't wanna mess with their shit. I handed the joint back to him. I'm not even gay.

Liam laughed heartily, a whoosh of gray flying out and surrounding his face.

What's so funny? I watched the pot smoke twirl toward the windowsill fishbowl, sunshine trespassing between the curtains shining off the sides of the goldfish below. Hey, can I ask you something?

Do it. Liam chuckled.

Do you know why everyone keeps asking about my pillbox?

Your pillbox?

Here. I looked around for my backpack and immediately remembered our hurry to get up to the apartment. Oh, fuck. My backpack's in Raizel's car. And my jacket.

That sucks. Did you mean the box with the fish on it?

Yeah… I felt my stomach flop.

Raizel used to be with this Asian girl. They were like, *really* in love. Your pillbox probably reminds her of Hannah. It's got an Asian design, right? It's got those Asian trees on it, anyway. How many times did I just say Asian? He laughed, his red eyes squinting.

Oh. Hey, are you hungry? I frowned and leaned my pounding head on the chair's armrest.

We left a note on Amara's coffee table, leaving her to sleep. Coat-less, I hugged myself on the walk down the street to Liam's car, which was parked in front of Raizel's family's tall house. I wondered if Abby was home. We ducked into the car and blasted the heat, techno music slipping tiredly from the speakers.

We went through a McDonald's drive-thru for breakfast, spending the rest of my hundred-dollar tip. I nibbled my McMuffin and sucked my Coke and stared out the windshield at traffic, busy people with errands and priorities. After working all weekend, having Monday and Tuesday off felt wrong. I was a glutton and had spent all of my money, with nothing to show for it. I could barely finish my sandwich. I worried that I'd completely fucked up my friendship with Raizel.

Liam took me home and we stayed in my basement with the curtains on the tiny window drawn, tucked under blankets to keep out the cold. Liam didn't care that they smelled like dust. We took turns resting our dancing shins on a heating pad. We drank tea and watched two movies I hadn't been able to convince Tiff to watch, artsy French films with actors we'd never heard of. The movies had brilliant violin and piano soundtracks. Tiff had complained sourly about the subtitles and we'd gotten into an argument because she was an artist who couldn't find it in her heart to respect others' work.

Tiff called at three o' clock. I'd never been more thankful for call display, muting the ringer when 'ABRAHAM P' flashed on the little screen. I'd call her later and say I'd gone to the doctor. Or the dentist, or something. My head wasn't in the right place to revive our friendship.

Half an hour later, Liam's phone vibrated on the coffee table, moving toward the edge as it buzzed. He read the text message.

Raizel wants to hang with you tonight.

What? Really? I wrapped my hands around my lukewarm tea mug.

Yeah. She tried calling, but no one answered.

Oops. The ringer's still off. I picked up the cordless and scrolled through the call history--ABRAHAM P, ABRAHAM P, MN STRT PHRMCY, MN STRT PHRMCY, ABRAHAM P. I smiled.

We rolled up to the pharmacy in Liam's car. I'd showered and teased my 'hawk to a standing position even though the bare tops of my ears froze in the wind.

Ugh. Liam groaned as we walked up to the door. I'm so tired.

It'll be alright. I imagined him smoking a doobie on the stack of milk crates, texting some lucky boy--or several.

We pulled the glass pharmacy door open and I heard the jangle of the bell.

Hi. To my left, Raizel leaned on the cash register counter with her elbows. She twirled her fingers in a lock of her stunning hair and waited blankly for us to respond, faint purple blotches under her eyes.

Hey. I spoke softly.

Liam took off toward the back of the store, down the very aisle where Raizel and I had first met. I walked to her and placed my hands on the counter above the lottery ticket case.

Sorry I didn't answer when you called.

It's alright. She looked down and played with her chipped black nail polish. So, I thought we could go get Halloween costumes tonight.

Oh. Sure. I bit my lip. My wallet was empty, but for two dollars. What're you gonna be?

I dunno yet. But I'll be off in... She leaned over to check the time on the till. Two minutes. We'll go pick up Abby and Amara, then head to Value Village.

Oh.

What? Raizel looked away from her nails and back up at me with her vibrant eyes. You don't like Value Village? They have the best old stuff. It's so random. There's nothing wrong with second-hand--

Raisin. It's fine. I felt my face turn red, as it'd recently begun doing. I remembered the feeling of Amara's bed before certain things had happened, the wonderfulness of new friends. I wasn't sure if I was meant to apologize for things that seemed out of my control.

You look pretty tired. Raizel walked out from behind the counter. Let's take caffeine pills.

Do you like this?

I turned away from the wall of Halloween supplies. A limp black pirate hat rested atop Amara's 'fro. She held a red corset up to her torso.

They don't really go together… I picked up an old man mask with puffy white hair spurting out the top, wondering how anyone could think old men were scary. On the inside they could be just like Walter.

Ew. Amara stepped toward me, her high heel crushing a pack of fake nails. I'd never seen her outside of her apartment. With heels on she was nearly six feet. You're not thinking of covering your face, are you?

Amara reached down to stroke my jaw-line, my nose catching the perfume on her wrist. I glanced around to see who was watching. The huge second-hand store boomed with old people, some of whom would surely be offended by a couple of lesbians--not that I was one--not that I had a problem with those who were. I wondered if Raizel was hiding behind something, plotting revenge against me with a plastic sword.

No. My fingers toyed with a pack of fake blood. I'm just looking.

Well. Amara took the pirate hat off. She picked up a pair of cat ears. Halloween is the best excuse of the year to dress like a skank.

I laughed and pretended to agree, remembering Halloween in high school when girls would show up in tights and ice cream cone bras and claim to be Madonna.

Amara wandered away down the aisle, her long arm tousling a stack of colored feather boas. I turned and scampered into the men's section to hide behind a rack of ties, inhaling the second-hand scents of other peoples' fathers.

Why are you hiding?

I jumped. The caffeine pills Raizel and I'd taken had really worked, pulling me out of my post-daisy funk into an abyss of sweaty palms and hyperactivity. Abby was beside me.

Oh, hey. I'm not hiding.

Okay. So, what's up? What do you think?

She smoothed her blond hair away from her face and leaned down to pull a wig over her head. When she came back up, sleek black polyester strands hung around her shoulders. I noticed how close in shape her and Raizel's eyes were, though Abby's were more the color of kiwi skin than sparkling seaweed.

Are you gonna be a cat? I looked down at the rest of her outfit. She had on leopard-print leggings and frayed brown suspenders over a white shirt.

Ugh. I really wanna be Karen O, but I don't think anyone will get it.

Karen O?

Lead singer of The Yeah Yeah Yeahs?

Ohh. I nodded emphatically. Right. Maybe you could be Josie from Josie and the Pussycats.

Abby's kiwi-colored eyes squinted. Suddenly she laughed, looking down at her outfit.

I could, couldn't I?

I grinned and stood on my tiptoes to scan the store, wondering where Raizel was or if she'd found anything. Amara was still in the Halloween section, holding a short-skirted plastic nurse costume up to her long body. Everyone who walked by stopped and stared for a moment, wishing she'd put the costume on and strut around with her tiny ass hanging out.

Hey! I have the best idea! Abby suddenly exclaimed. She began sorting through a rack of men's' jeans. What's your size?

After finding costumes for ourselves, Abby and I met Amara and Raizel by the changing rooms. I wondered if they'd been talking about me or had simply stood in silence the whole time. They let us cut in line and we stood with baskets full of stuff while the old ladies behind us glared over their bifocals.

Abby got a room first, leaving the three of us standing in an awkward circle at the front of the line. Then Raizel got a room, skipping away with her stuff. She'd Abby what she was thinking of dressing as, but had sworn her to secrecy. In the space under her fitting room door I saw her set everything on the floor, catching a glimpse of white material. I watched Raizel's dangling hand unlace her red shoeboots.

Come on. Amara nudged me.

Huh? Oh no, you can go first.

No, we can go *together.* She grabbed the handle of my basket.

One at a time. The teenaged girl in charge of the change rooms stood in front of us with her hands on the hips of her red Value Village smock.

We're sisters. We need each other's advice. Amara flashed her a sweet, gap-toothed smile. She yanked my arm and we darted past the girl into Fitting Room Number Six. Amara was strong for someone with spaghetti-like forearms. She closed the door after us and put our things on the floor. The room was so small it barely allowed us to stand facing each other with a foot between us and a tiny chair in the corner meant for children to wait while their mothers tried on pair after pair of four-dollar jeans.

You wanna do something fun? She wiggled her eyebrows.

Um. I clenched my fists into sweaty, conglomerate balls. Oh, god. I was going to get with a girl. At Value Village. In a room the size of a pantry. I pressed my back against the wall, hands in the pockets of my hoody.

Amara looked in her over-the-shoulder blatantly fake Chanel purse. Her skinny fingers emerged with a tiny, plastic bag of white powder, the top sealed with a rubber band. She dangled it in the air between us.

23

Is that cocaine? I looked around, as if anyone could see us. I caught my reflection in the full-length mirror, stone-cold expression buried in my eyes. I was having a good hair day. I touched a stray strand.

Shh. Amara held a finger to her lips. And you'd better start trying things on. They can see our feet under the door.

Right. No peeking. I pulled a pair of men's jeans out of my basket. I turned away from her to unzip my own jeans. In the mirror I saw that she wasn't paying attention at all, but that she had sat in the kids' chair and was using a bank card to divide the coke into lines on the back of an Elton John CD case. I slipped my jeans off and wondered what she'd think of the cellulite patches on the backs of my thighs.

After last night… Amara evened the powder with a bank card. I got to thinking.

I gulped and leaned down to slip my feet through the pair of men's' jeans. I pulled them up quickly.

I mean, after you mentioned you guys were trying to get coke, but couldn't, I decided I really wanted to try it. Have you ever tried it?

Whew. She wasn't talking about *other* things that had happened the previous night.

No. I shook my head. I fastened the fly on the jeans, disbelieving how they barely squeezed my belly. I looked in the mirror to enjoy how the pants straightened my legs and drew attention away from my thighs.

So I called up this guy I met at Broken String, that little bar next to Mars. And he hooked me up, just like that. FNMPHHHH. Amara sniffed.

I turned around to see the CD case resting on her bare knees, her face and bushy hair hovering over it, rolled up five-dollar bill in her hand. She looked me up and down.

HEY! Those look pretty good. Now get down here.

We traded spots, me teetering on the kids' chair wearing amazing jeans and Amara standing in front of the mirror. She pulled her dress up over her 'fro. I looked down and stuck the fiver in my nose, plugging my other nostril with my left forefinger as I'd seen Amara do. I laughed when I realized she'd created a white heart around Elton John's face for me.

Flip flip flip. My stomach.

FNMPHHHH. I sniffed, feeling the coke sting my nostril walls like a thousand bees. One half down, one to go. FNMPHHHHFNMPHHHH, I snorted again, double power. I put my hand over my nose and sniffed, not wanting the blow to fall out and go to waste, no matter how badly it scorched and sizzled in my face.

I gazed up at Amara. She'd not been wearing a bra under her dress, and stood before the mirror in a pair of neon pink underwear. Her breasts hung like grapes on a vine, a long dark vine that was her bony chest. I wanted to give her a cheeseburger. I looked up past her delicate neck, past the gap in her two front teeth, at her big, brown eyes. She blinked at me.

Sorry. I looked away, sticking the CD case back in the fake Chanel purse. Collarbone up, my skin was burning.

Don't be sorry. Amara offered me her hand.

I took it and stood up, stumbling. My head buzzed.

Whoa, easy. She put her hands on my shoulders to steady me. I felt like a horse in a stable stall, no choice but to look directly at her.

Sorry. It's just that my friends and I don't really change in front of each other. And by friends I mean friend. My friend Tiff would *never* change in front of me. So--

But we're different. Amara put her hands on my waist and stared down at me. She pulled up the waistline of my hoody.

H-how? I saw her enormous pupils, blackness spilling like coffee into her irises. Along with my hoody, my t-shirt came up over my head and fell into our pile on the floor, my fleshy blob of a body exposed. Under my sports bra my belly made a slight roll over the top of the jeans. I didn't care. I was on fire, in my nose and my heart and under my skin.

We have a connection. Amara kept her voice down to a whisper.

The bees that had flown into my nose zipped around my forehead and ears. My body smiled while my mind told it not to.

You're very interesting. I didn't know how else to respond. The coke seemed to have counteracted the caffeine pills, diminishing the sweatiness of my palms. I placed them on Amara's waist where her ribs poked out. Her skin was cool and smooth, a piece of paper.

She put her mouth on mine and pushed me against the mirror, jarring coldness on my bare back. I closed my eyes and let it happen. I sank into the mirror and pulled her with me, our tongues entwined like snakes, swirling round and round. She rubbed her flat chest against my sport bra and I inhaled before our stomachs could make contact. My hands traveled up and down her spine. She shivered.

We made out for a mere minute before standing with our heads alert and our eyes glowing like embers. We had a hushed conversation about how fun Halloween would be at Mars. She was excited to show me where she worked. She giggled and bent over, her stomach barely wrinkling, to shove her plastic nurse costume into my backpack.

What are you doing? I stared at her pupils. We already look suspicious, the two of us in here together.

We all shoplift. There aren't any cameras.

But it's bad karma.

Aw. You believe in karma, too? Amara stroked my cheek with her pointer finger, seemingly her favorite seductress move.

Of course.

Well, I always think of it this way. If you donate stuff from your house, more than what you take, you should gain store credit.

I thought for moment.

Okay, I see what you're saying. It's not like I have money, anyway. I gestured to the men's jeans. And I really want these.

Throw 'em in! Amara exclaimed, unzipping my pants. Take whatever you want. What are you going to be, anyway? We should totally dress as a couple. You should be my bloody patient. I'll tend to all your wounds. And what do you *mean* you don't have money?

I'm broke.

Don't you have a job? At a coffee shop or something?

Well, yeah. But my first payday is on Friday.

Oh. Good. Then you can give me thirty bucks for the coke, right?

Are you serious?

Normally I wouldn't ask for money, but it was really expensive. A girl's gotta eat.

Sure. I glanced at her stick-thin legs.

On the way home, Raizel stopped the car near a playground so we could smoke two big ones and discuss Halloween. Amara offered to pick up pills for us, as long as we paid her back. I noticed how Abby and Raizel's voices droned, while Amara's and mine still carried on excitedly. I whispered to Amara that she should share some coke with them, but she dug her bony elbow into my ribs so hard I might've keeled over if not already sitting.

There's none left. She snaked her arms around me in the backseat. I wondered how that could be true, considering the last time I'd seen the baggie it was still half-full of blow. We'd left the changing room at the same time, my backpack laden with theft.

I was starting to crave another hit.

Abby and Raizel were none the wiser in the car's front seats, nodding their heads to something instrumental. The music reminded me of the stuff Raizel and I had listened to on her iPod the first night I'd met daisy.

Is this The Silly Rainbows? I put my head between the driver's and front passenger's seats and scooted my body forward, slipping out of Amara's gangly arms and awkward lies.

Wow! Raizel leaned her back against her door. She smiled at me and puffed her joint. Someone's got a good memory. A plus.

I beamed.

They dropped me off at eight-thirty, as Raizel had begun to yawn behind the wheel and was no longer responding to our discussion. She still hadn't told

Amara and I what her costume would be; neither had I spilled about mine, though Abby and I exchanged a secretive glance when the others prodded me. I definitely wasn't going to be someone's sidekick surgeon. I gave Amara her crinkly nurse costume before crossing the lawn to my humble abode. I entered the duplex to find my mother snoozing on the sofa, her back to the world and afghan strewn across the floor. I crept past her so she wouldn't wake up and ask me about non-existent bottles of home-brewed wine.

I sat in front of the basement computer and tapped the desk with my fingers while I searched for all the things I'd been telling myself to. I found out that the band we'd listened to in the car, the night of Morgan's party, was Le Tigre, who specialized in feminist and gay-related lyrical content. When I searched Samantha Ronson, the only thing that came up was her face beside Lindsay Lohan's, because they'd apparently had a relationship. I supposed she did resemble Morgan, being a gay DJ, but wondered how many people had actually considered Samantha Ronson's musical career.

I hoped direly that one day, when I was a famous photographer, people wouldn't hear my name and comment, Sure, she's talented, but have you heard about her indecisiveness? Maybe by then I'd have married and divorced, and while flipping through my latest coffee table book, called *The Expressions of the Polar Bear and Other Icy Creatures,* people would speculate that I'd struck again with my inability to carry on a proper relationship. They'd conjure up their own reasons as to why I'd never made it to college and my fans would defend me with reasons they hoped were true--'I heard she won the lottery at age seventeen', and, 'I bet Venice Knight didn't have to go to college because she was born knowing everything'.

When I searched Karen O, lead singer of The Yeah Yeah Yeahs, I was relieved to find that her sexuality wasn't broadcasted, and therefore couldn't sway people toward automatic admiration. Abby was a genius for wanting to be Karen O for Halloween, as she was known for having the most dramatic and imaginative wardrobe in the current world of rock. I also reflected that, despite raised eyebrows around my baby-tomato-sized Asian-inspired pill box, Raizel's own sister was going to dress as a woman with an oriental background.

Next I searched the idea Abby had given me for my Halloween costume. I was pleased to discover how easily I might pull it off, especially with the items in my backpack. I watched a couple of videos to get my moves down pat.

I just had to make one big change.

24

At noon on Wednesday, I went to Tiff's house, knocking on the rickety wooden back door with my fist. I looked around the yard while I waited. The fire pit was covered with its metal winter lid, lawn chairs having been folded and set in the space under the porch. The trees were naked, branches darting erratically into the sky while the lawn below adorned brown leaves.

Hey, Tiff appeared behind the screen door, hair creating a red veil around her shoulders. What do you want?

Can I come in?

Yeah. My hands are painty though.

I wiped my shoes on the wooden porch steps before pulling the door open and stepping onto the kitchen landing. Tiff stood before me in a professor's coat, the white material splattered with a gang of paint colors. The sleeves were rolled up to her elbows and she held her hands out limply, fingers donning a red sheen.

I saw you tried calling me yesterday. I rubbed my chilled hands together.

Yeah. Come on.

I peeled out of my shoes and we went down the hall to Tiff's bedroom. I stretched out on her bed and she sat at her painting desk.

I haven't heard from you in two days. Tiff picked up a fat brush to swirl its hairs in a pitcher of murky water.

I got really sick.

Oh? She took the brush out of the water and looked over her shoulder at me, pushing her glasses up in the middle. A red dot remained on her little nose. Are you okay?

Now I am. At first I thought it was that food that I cooked, but my mom and Dana didn't get sick. Did you?

Not at all. She shook her head. I didn't get sick from the wine, either.

Yeah, see, I thought maybe it was a hangover, but I was puking for two days straight.

I see. She eyed me before turning back to her. You do look a bit thinner.

I put my hands behind my head and relaxed into her pillow, my eyes sashaying around the walls. Paintings were everywhere--abstracts, landscapes, a few orchestrated by geometric shapes, and some I referred to as 'those dotty ones'. Tiff specialized in pointillism, either looking at a subject or conjuring something up in her brain, then creating an image by dabbing with a variety of brushes an array of colors hundreds of times across a page. On the wall beside me, just two feet up from the mattress, was my personal favorite of all her paintings.

Looking closely, the middle of the picture contained a series of brown, beige, peach, and gold dots. The perimeter of the eight-by-eleven computer printer paper from her mother's office was made up of lollipop colors--cherry, citrus, blue raspberry, and bubblegum.

Not looking closely, a man stood with his hands in his trench coat pockets, face hidden by shadows. He appeared to be standing with a hunched back in a colorful abyss that Tiff had told me was the hue of the world. For some people, the most difficult thing to comprehend was mustering up brightness while the rest of the world had long since achieved such a thing.

What are you working on? I propped my elbows on Tiff's pillow to look at her table.

Something for Olly. She moved her chair so I couldn't see the painting.

Oh. Tiff, I'm sorry about the other night. I didn't fully believe I should be the one to apologize. I wondered if she'd ever make *me* a painting again.

Really? She looked back at me.

Yeah. Doing drugs was a stupid idea. I know you wouldn't ever do that.

I'm sorry too. I think I overreacted. It was just an idea, it's not like you actually tried to give me E. I know you wouldn't do it, either.

Yeah. I glanced at the trench coat man in a prison of brightness. But I *have* smoked weed.

I bit my lip and waited for her to throw her paintbrush at my face. Maybe she'd be using green and it would land on my cheek in the shape of a marijuana leaf.

Really? She set her brush in the pitcher of swamp water and swirled in her chair. With who?

Ummmm, I did it with Liam.

What was it like?

At first I felt all spaced out, like I'd just woken up or something, then I got all giggly, then I pigged out on Pringles.

So nothing bad happened?

Like what? You seem really interested, Tiff.

It's just that...Olly smokes weed sometimes, and he said people can freak out if they're not in the right state of mind.

Weird. Nothing bad happened to me. Do you wanna try it sometime?

Maybe. Tiff looked down and picked at the paint on her fingers. If Olly can be there. I don't wanna 'green out' or something.

I laughed. Suddenly Amara popped into my mind, the strangest thing on my list of recent events. I wanted so badly to tell Tiff what'd happened and ask for her advice. We'd always talked about boys together and I didn't see why girl-on-girl relationship advice should be any different. Not that I wanted to have a girl-on-girl relationship with Amara. Or anyone else. I opened my mouth, but other words came out.

Oh hey, I almost forgot. Does Pam have an opening today?

Why? You want *another* haircut? Tiff motioned at my 'do, assumedly already too short by her standards.

No, no. I wanna dye it. I bit my lip to save from telling her it was for more Halloween costume, knowing she wouldn't approve. I was doing all too much that she wouldn't' approve of. Can we go ask her?

Sure. What color?

It's a secret.

In my mind, I left my Amara problems sitting on a bed in a little room, waiting for me to return. I didn't know how long it would be before I'd return. I closed the door to the mind room quickly. We trekked down to Tiff's mother's basement hair salon, past the sign hanging from the ceiling:

______ & Pam's

'Nathaniel' had been scratched off the plastic board during The Divorce--before I'd met Tiff. Chemical fumes wafted over, begging to run up the stairs and out of the salon.

Hey girls. Pam glanced up from a People magazine, leaning her heavy frame on a vanity table. She stood near an elderly client whose short locks were clipped to a floor-mounted hair dryer.

Hi, Mom. Do you have an opening for Venice this afternoon?

I sat in a hairdressing chair for the second times in two weeks, flipping absently though Pam's copy of People. Because of all the movies Tiff and I had ripped and watched, I knew who the celebrities were, but I couldn't say I knew why people cared about their personal lives. Still, a tiny part of me hoped there'd be an article about Lindsay Lohan, just so I could find out if she'd had trouble getting over the great Samantha Ronson.

I missed Raizel's mirror-side collage of pictures and stickers. Tiff went upstairs to work on her painting and I felt my mind float away from the magazine. In my mind I walked through the room with the patiently waiting Amara problem. Behind me, Pam worked her gloved fingers through my faux-hawk, hair product aromas seasoning the air around my face. I smiled at her in the mirror before staring at the corner of a page, pretending to read.

Wow, who cut your hair last? Pam raised her eyebrows.

Um. I touched the edges of my surely jagged fingernails, wanting to look down at them, unable to move my head. My friend Raizel. She wants to be a hairdresser.

Wants to be? It's well done.

Oh, really? Thanks.

You really do look good, Venice. A smile crossed Pam's vibrant face. I'm starting a new diet, too. With Weight Watchers.

I would have shrunk into my chair and crawled away if not for the goop in my hair. My face in the mirror didn't look so different, the same round shape, pink lips, eyes the color of my mother's cigarette ashes.

Thanks. I smiled back up at Pam. How's that going for you?

It's a lot of math. You know, counting calories. She leaned her elbow on my shoulder to fetch a butterfly clip from the side of the mirror. But I think it's going well.

Oh, yeah. You look great, too.

I only started it yesterday, but thanks, dear. And when did you start your diet?

I blushed.

I haven't really started a diet.

I know what you mean. She nodded while she scrunched her nose. I've already snuck in three chocolate chip granola bars. That's about…let's see…six Weight Watcher's Points. Or is it eight?

For the next hour and a half, I let her explain how Weight Watcher's worked, not because she was my best friend's mother, not because my hair depended on her. Her face glowed secretively when she spoke of temptation and calories and exercise schedules. I thought Tiff to be lucky as an artist; if I was a painter who wanted to capture the essence of livelihood, I would envision Pamela Abraham's face for inspiration. As a photographer, I'd have to take actual pictures of her, and explain why I wanted to, after which I'd probably receive quizzical looks and awkward quietness. A painter could just take a mind picture and be on her merry way.

When my hair was done I hardly believed my reflection. I'd achieved what, once upon a time, I'd desired so badly. I gazed at myself for a while, trying to decided if I like being blond.

Holy shit! Tiff cried when I pushed open the door of her bedroom. She dropped her paintbrush and got up to walk around me. Her painting smock was even more paint-splattered than it'd been before.

Well? I tapped my toe.

It's…different. Damn.

What does that mean? I bent my knees and looked into her bedroom mirror, tousling my locks a little. I pulled my bangs away from the side Pam had slicked them to.

Damn, my mom's good!

So you like it?

Yeah. It's such a pretty color. It looks so natural. She nodded and I could hardly believe her enthusiasm. She stuck out her tongue. But you still look like a boy. How much did she charge you?

Nothing. I crossed my toes, hoping Pam wouldn't tell her how I'd pulled out my empty wallet and pretended I'd left my money at home, and how Pam had said it didn't matter and that it was an early birthday gift.

Are you serious? She really likes you, you know.

I know. I stuck my tongue out. Anyway, we should get going, right?

25

I'm gonna make a cappuccino. Tiff pulled open the door at Team Bean. You want one?

I sighed, thinking about Pam's Weight Watchers wisdom.

I'll have the biggest, blackest coffee possible. And four sweeteners.

Jesus! That stuff contains aspartame, you know.

So?

It gives you cancer.

At least I won't be fat anymore. I tsked, waving my hand idly in her direction.

What? Tiff turned her head to me, her red ponytail brushing her cheek. Her mouth hung open. Since when do you care--

Hey, girls! The chatty woman with the perm stood behind the till, counting tip jar change. I'd forgotten her name, but felt the sudden urge to turn around and crawl into my bed at home. I yawned.

Hey, Patty! Tiff walked over to make our drinks while I took our stuff to the crew room.

I read the sign on Monica's office door.

Gone for supplies.
- Mon

Having no manager around to account for my punctuality, I took my time putting on my apron. I desperately didn't want to hear any more about Patty's neighbor's plants or 'pasty white arse'. I caught my reflection in the mirror above the microwave and nearly spun around, having forgotten my new hair color. I realized how dark my eyelashes looked, bringing out bits of silver in the cigarette ashes that made up my orbs.

I pondered the possibly that I had eyes to catch others' eyes.

When Monica returned she propped open the shop door and called me over. I left Tiff at the front counter with Patty talking her ear off about a customer she'd had earlier.

Whoa. Monica and I stood outside, wind whistling through the trees at the edge of the parking. Your hair.

My hair...? I teased, pretending I hadn't changed the color drastically.

It's nice. Monica turned to motion at her van, the side door of which lay ajar, displaying a pile of cardboard boxes. Can you help me bring these in?

Of course. I stalked over and chose a box; peeking in, I saw that it contained a big, sloshing bag of cream. I picked the box up and shuffled toward the coffee shop entrance, knees daring to buckle. When I got inside I bent my legs the way I'd seen done in my orientation video, setting the box on the floor near the walk-in-cooler.

Oh my god, you lifted the cream? Tiff appeared before me, wiping her hands on her apron.

Yeah…? I breathed in heavily.

No one can lift the cream. Wasn't that, like, really heavy? You could've taken the bags out and carried them separately.

What? I lifted the bag of cream and realized there was another one underneath. Ohh. Oh well.

I went back outside, wondering why I was the only one made to unload the van. I didn't dare complain, for fear of lowering my review scores. Monica talked on the phone in her office, Patty read the newspaper, and Tiff made commentary on my lifting techniques. I picked up a box of bottled water, huffing and puffing while I brought it inside and set it on the front counter.

Come help me. I glowered at Tiff with my surely reddened cheeks.

Me? Tiff wrapped her hands around her cappuccino.

Yeah, you.

We went outside and I chose for Tiff a medium-sized box of sugar packets from the van. She made a noise as I handed the box over. Oof. Then she walked with her back bent toward the entrance of the store. I picked up a box of teabags and sailed by her.

You shouldn't bend your back. I stuck my tongue out. You'll hurt yourself.

Monica came out of her office when we were nearly finished. She poked her head into the van.

Wow, you guys are amazing. And Venice, how did you ever recruit Tiffany to lifting duty?

I looked at Tiff with her red cheeks, rubbing her arms where most people had biceps. I wondered what it was like to be a girl who didn't have to do things just because she was too skinny. I wondered if Amara ever had to lift boxes of beer at Mars, though I didn't see that as a possibility. I couldn't even picture her standing behind a bar taking orders, either.

Amara. I wished I could tell Tiff.

Let's talk about Halloween. Tiff made the suggestion near the end of our shift when we had no customers. Patty had long since gone home, and we were waiting for the clock to turn eleven.

Okay. What are you going to be?

Probably a pregnant lady. Monica said I could borrow some maternity clothes and a book of baby names. You? Tiff sprayed a tabletop and wiped it lazily with a rag.

I laughed. She *would* choose such a lame costume. I gathered a pile of newspaper from the sofas in the corner.

It's a secret.

Well, what do you wanna do? Do you think we're too old to go trick-or-treating?

Hold on a sec. I took the bundle of newspapers in my arms and went outside, October wind assisting me across the parking lot to the huge paper recycling bin. Empty coffee cups skittered like mice on the pavement around me. I tossed the papers in the metal bin and stood for a moment, watching cars roll by with glaring headlights and warm interiors, the hair on my own bare arms standing at attention.

When I made it back inside the clock on the till read eleven-oh-one. Tiff was in the office with Monica, probably doing research for her 'costume'. I took off my apron and pulled my winter coat on, covering my chilled arms.

Let's go, Tiff. I don't wanna miss the bus. I shivered for effect. It's cold out.

I'll drive you guys home. Monica smiled past Tiff at me.

The next day dragged on, waking to watch a movie until three-thirty in the afternoon, when I got dressed and go to Team Bean. Because of the cold winds and my newfound passion for serving coffee, Tiff and I gave up on the Autumn-Afternoons-After-Graduation Plan. Team Bean was dead; no one wanted to leave their homes for a hot cup of java when the trees dared to fall on them. I couldn't complain, as Monica let me sit in the lobby with a book and a black coffee when I was done cleaning.

Friday was special for two reasons, one being Halloween and the other being my first payday ever. Monica was finishing payroll in her office, talking on the phone and hurriedly typing things into the computer. I started work at nine, realizing as I read the schedule in the crew room that Patty would be my co-worker all the way through to three p.m.. I poured myself a black coffee to prepare for an earful of unimportance.

Nice costume. I gestured to Patty's blue wig. I assumed the furry red ball on her face was meant to be a clown nose. The polka-dotted apron was also probably a pre-meditated aspect of her ensemble.

Thanks, Venice. Oh my word, I can't get over your hair. Anyway, I found this in my grandkids' dress-up trunk. Oh, they're the dearest things, my grandkids. They gave me a Halloween fashion show yesterday and you'll never guess what they've decided to be.

The clown nose apparently restricted her voice to a nasal whine.

What? I had no choice but to ask. I blew on my brimming coffee and wished I'd remembered to leave room in the cup for cool water.

Well, Katie, she's fourteen, she's going to be a witch, and Samuel, he's nine, he's going to be a lion.

Very original. I smiled. When I was nine I was probably something of the animal variety, too. I faintly remembered a polar bear costume, the ears of which I'd crafted myself out of construction paper because my mother had forgotten to help. When I was fourteen I didn't bother with a costume, as that was the year I'd begun drinking. I'd crawled out the attic window onto our duplex roof and dared nighttime to scare me, as books and movies said darkness should. There was nothing frightening about a sliver of moon or a glimpse of smoke from a nearby field's bush party.

--and in Elm View, and then we'll drive them to Oakwood Heights-- Patty continued speaking.

Are they going to trick-or-treat around Oakwood Terrace?

Heavens, no! Patty's eyes popped wide open. She removed her furry nose to itch the skin underneath with her dry, old nails. That's no place for children.

What do you mean? I took a hefty gulp of my coffee, enjoying its black liquid warmth careening down my throat.

It's just not a good area. There's always something on the news about Oakwood Terrace, break-ins and muggings. I feel sorry for kids who grow up there. They grow up way too fast. Did you know that if something bad happens to a person before they become an adult, a part of their brain stays that age forever? It's clinically proven. My friend Midge--

Ouch. I nodded and sipped my coffee, smiling as if Halloween and my first payday ever hadn't been slightly ruined.

Team Bean got busier after lunch, about two p.m.. We were next to the financial district of town and often drew clusters of important people on their afternoon coffee breaks. Besides the suits and pencil skirts and cardigans the colors of fall leaves strewn delicately about their shoulders, I didn't mind businesspeople. Helping someone achieve the best part of their day was wonderful; they smiled while we asked them their favorite questions.

What size would you like?

Cream or sugar?

Anything else for you today?

They dropped loonies and toonies in the paper coffee cup near the till.

Tippaccino. Thanks a latte.

All of our regulars passed through, Walter and the other oldies, placing their orders and sitting down. When I first started at Team Bean, I had trouble remembering who was who, who ordered coffee and how they liked it, and which muffin they wanted, if they wanted one at all. But that Friday, Halloween and payday, I discovered something.

The secret to being a successful coffee bitch was to make correlations between people and their orders. The cranberry muffin went to the man in the red turtleneck sweater. The small coffee went to the smallest, most shriveled old lady in the whole store. The dark roast went to the lady with the baby, as she undoubtedly needed extra caffeine, having a child who constantly pulled at her earrings and the collar of her blouse.

I watched the time.

At three o' clock a new employee came in, this big chick Monica was going to train that evening. She wore glasses and all around her dirty blond hairline were dots of sweat. I thought it a shame that Monica had worked all day and would have to continue that evening--she should've been taking her baby door-to-door, his little arms stuffed into a bumblebee costume.

Hi. My name's Meaghan.

Hey. Sup? I'm Venice. I smiled and shook the new girl's warm hand, remembering to make eye contact. I debated telling Meaghan the secret of being a successful coffee bitch, but couldn't wait. I became a cocker spaniel untying my apron and skipping down that narrow hallway to the shop's tiny office.

Monica got out of her wheely computer chair and handed me an envelope with my name written in delicate cursive on top:

Venice Knight

I giggled and jumped a little, my heart beaming with pride. I tore through the glue that'd sealed the envelope shut. My fingers reached in.

Congratulations on your first payday ever. Monica grinned.

I unfolded my pay-stub, eyes scanning the numbers and columns.

I don't get it. How much am I getting paid?

Here. Monica leaned over me and I caught a whiff of baby powder. Where it says 'income'.

Two-hundred-and-fifty-six bucks??????????????????????????? That's awesome!

Oh, wait a sec. No no no. That's before taxes. Here's the real amount. Monica's finger slid on column to the right, stopping on a red highlighted number.

Oh. Two-hundred-and-thirteen?????? That's still great!! I'll take it! I bounced on my heels again, pounding my fist in the air.

Whoa. Patty came bumbling down the hallway, Meaghan in tow, her big hips swaying. What's going on down here?

Payday, babay!!! I retrieved my backpack and jacket from my locker. I wanted to yell, *I'm outta here, suckers!* but stopped out of consideration for Monica. See you guys later. Nice to meet you, Meaghan.

You too. She smiled, covering her teeth with her hand when they dared to pop out from between her lips.

I squeezed past all of them and danced out of the store, pulling up the hood on my coat. Wind pushed at my back immediately, urging me forth.

26

I jogged down the sidewalk to the bus stop, ducking into the glasses shelter next to a woman with a baby carriage.

Happy Halloween. I smiled. Though her mouth was concealed by a red scarf, her eyes crinkled at the corners.

When bus 58 arrived, I helped the woman lift her carriage up the squat steps. I squeezed my bus fare in my fist, standing with my body half out the door.

Are you going near Anchor Road?

Anchor Road? The driver scratched his gray beard, pondering. What area?

It's in East Bay. I gotta make it there by four fifteen. I looked at the clock near his steering wheel.

3:14

Okay, let me ask someone. Sit up front here and I'll tell you where to transfer. He ripped a transfer ticket off the stack by the fare bucket.

Oh, I didn't pay yet. I stepped up and opened my fist over the fare bucket, my coins falling in through the slots clang clang clang.

An honest girl, she is. The driver used both arms to twist the steering wheel, pulling the bus away from the sidewalk. He picked up his handheld radio and signaled another bus driver, long black cord dangling to the rubber floor mats.

I sat down, realizing the woman and her baby and I were the only passengers. She pulled out a book and I pulled out my Discman, putting Ani Difranco on low in case the driver needed to tell me something. Through Ani's soothing voice I heard the wind rapping at the windows lining the vehicle's sides. My stomach twitched inside of me as my plans for the evening flashes into my mind.

At four o' clock the bus pulled up somewhere Very Far from my home, at a bus terminal with bus schedules posted neatly on the backs of clean glass rectangle shelters. A hundred feet away was a three-story building with a sign out front.

East Bay Shopping Center

The parking lot nearly full of vehicles. A long banner hung from the building's roof, advertising:

Get your Candy and Costumes at The Holiday Store.

Here we are, young lady.

I pulled my earbuds out and got off my seat, standing beside the driver.

Which bus do I need?

The thirty-one should be here in a minute or so.

Thanks.

I got off the bus, wind whipping my cheeks immediately. I sauntered over to the bus shelter to sit on the metal bench with an old lady. She looked down at my jeans. I crossed my arms and leaned back, looking straight ahead at the wall of the shelter, catching my reflection in the glass. Ah yes, I had forgotten about my blondness. I moved my head from side to side, checking out my 'do. My faux-hawk had flattened slightly, but there wasn't much I could do about that. Later I'd shower and raise it to perfection once more.

The 31 pulled up and I dug my transfer ticket out of my pocket, hopping up the few steps onto the bus.

Can you tell me when we're on Anchor Road?

The woman driving squinted at my transfer ticket, making sure I wasn't one of those cheap-asses who kept transfers and tried to trick drivers later on.

Sure. We'll be there in five minutes.

I glanced at her dashboard clock

4:12

Shit. I wished for a millionth time that I had a cell phone. I'd yell into it, Don't worry! I'm still coming! I'll be there soon!

The bus pulled out of the shiny terminal and away from East Bay Shopping Center, going down a road lined with neat gray sidewalks and dainty trash bins. I knew the general area--I'd been to the bay a few times, but had never been down that road before. I liked the road's hill-like declination and the skinny trees with their bare twig branches, leaves having been raked from around their bases, probably stuffed in trash bags and carried back through the city to the landfill near Oakwood.

When we neared the bottom of the steep road, near the tiny harbor and the wooden walkway lining the bay, the bus suddenly careened to the left. I craned my neck to catch a glimpse of shiny gray water before it was out of sight. Soon I saw a big green sign with crisp writing hanging off a set of traffic lights.

Anchor Road

The houses a few roads away from the bay were nice; not as overwhelming as Oakwood Heights and not as underwhelming as Oakwood Terrace. Like good daisy, they were a happy medium, no Lamborghinis or Ferraris in sight; neither were there station wagons from nineteen eighty-two.

Anchor Road! I heard the driver call out. The bus slowly halted alongside a bus shelter.

Some passengers boarded the bus, talking to the driver. I went out the back door and stood on the sidewalk, hugging myself. When the bus pulled away I crossed the road toward a mini-mall of businesses, wind persisting against my cheeks.

I saw my destination.

SCPB
Sloam Citizens' Personal Bank
of East Bay Area, Sloam

I gazed at the tall building, fresh bricks made to look old, like those jeans people buy already covered in specks of paint. Tiff hated those entirely, said they were a disgrace to all painters. When the wind bit the tops of my ears I stopped gazing and pushed my way through the revolving door. I immediately caught the tangy scent of new carpet.

To the left were a few ATM machines, straight ahead a customer service desk, and to the right a line of bank tellers behind a red velvet rope, so people knew where to line up. I scanned the tellers' faces before marching up to the customer service desk.

Welcome to SCPB, may I help you with something? A middle-aged woman smiled brightly, encouraging me to respond.

Hi, yes, I'm looking for Kathy Knight.

Ah, I see. Do you have an appointment?

Sort of. I mean, she's my mother.

Oh! The woman pulled her glasses down her nose, looking at me over a rim of silver. Alright then.

She didn't have to say it. I knew we didn't look alike, especially since I'd become a bleached blond faux-hawk kind of girl. Plus my mother was trim and petite, probably from all her cigarettes. I remained a blundering broad-shouldered square-hipped big-boned blob, but I'd never take up smoking, not in a million years, not even if it made me slim and desirable.

The woman led me away from her desk down a hallway of little rooms with automatic sliding glass doors. A clock at the end of the hall told me it was four-twenty. I wondered if Seed was smoking a doobie in his sunny apartment.

Here she is.

The woman nodded her head and strutted off in her bulky cream-colored heels. I looked through the glass at my mother. She looked so serene, reading glasses pushed as close to her eyes as possible, chewing on the end of a pen while she skimmed something on the computer.

Mom. As I reached up to tap the glass, the door detected me and slid open.

Oh, good, my peach, you're here. She double-took me. Oh my god, your hair!

Oh yeah. I forgot we hadn't even crossed paths at home since I'd had it done.

Tiff's mom did it. Is this your *office*? I gestured at the loveseat, the small water cooler and the fan perched on her desk shelf. I pointed at her computer. You have a *Mac*?

Yes, for the time being. It doesn't have a view of the bay or anything. No window, actually. She spoke so matter-of-factly. Have a seat. You look cold.

She filled a ceramic mug with hot water from her cooler, and then reached in her desk drawer for a paper packet of hot chocolate.

For the time being. I should've known the bank would give her something and take it away, even after all her hard work. I stirred the hot chocolate. My mother kept her eyes on my hair.

I guess I like it. It'll take some getting used to.

So…I wrapped my hands around the mug, watching steam rise. How do we do this?

Well, I've filled out most of your paperwork, written down what you need. You just need to sign here. She pointed at the bottom of a page. And here.

I signed my name. Venice Knight.

Now what?

We went through everything else, all of the papers and information, and she showed me how to use my online banking account, let me choose a password while she looked away. We went out to the teller and used a little machine that let me type in my very own made up four-digit PIN, then deposited my paycheck.

Back in my mother's tentative office, she handed me my very first debit card ever, a screaming red piece of plastic containing one-hundred-and-ninety-three dollars, because I'd withdrawn twenty bucks cash. She hadn't snuck a look at my PIN. She was my nosey, overprotective mother, but this was something I'd earned; it was my own money and I could spend it how I liked.

Your hot chocolate's getting cold. Drink up, peach, then we can hit the road.

Sorry, Mom, I'm not really thirsty.

Come on. It's cold out. The car heater's not working right today, either.

Because she'd helped me with everything and hadn't embarrassed me in front of her coworkers, I stifled remembrance of Pamela Abraham's calorie counting. I chugged the hot chocolate, lukewarm liquid sashaying lazily down my esophagus. I couldn't forget the taste quickly enough.

We zipped our coats up as high as they'd go and marched out of the bank. The customer service woman was off duty at the same time, and stood by her SUV in the parking lot to aim a hearty wave at my mother.

Bye Kathy! Have a great weekend!

See you, Sandra.

I couldn't remember the last time I had ridden in my mother's dirty white car. We dove in from either side, slamming the doors tight for wind protection. All day the vehicle had sat in the parking lot, cold seeping through the windows into the seat fabric.

I couldn't wait to put on my costume. I couldn't wait to call my friends. I couldn't wait for that night.

I'm glad you finally came down, my peach. So, what do you think? My mother steered the car away from the fancy building, heading down Anchor Road the way I'd come from.

It's very nice.

Very nice? That's it?

I licked my lips and tasted remnants of powdery chocolate.

Okay. It's way nicer than your old branch. But it's too far away.

But the *area,* my peach. Have you seen the bay? Here, let's take the scenic route. She turned left off Anchor, going down the steep road with the skinny trees.

Mom, I've seen the bay before. I really wanna get home.

What's the rush? We're just in time to catch the sunset.

At the bottom of the hill we turned left. Suddenly we were the last car in a line of traffic passing the bay.

'The bay', as we called it, was a man-made lake the mayor of Sloam had deemed important to budget for a decade earlier. I remembered the day the project was finished and the public was allowed to walk along the sidewalk with the crisp white railings overlooking an expanse of turquoise, oceanic water. A person standing on one side could see trees and traffic on the other side, but the main idea was the clear, cleanness of the water. Motorboats weren't allowed in the bay, but there was a small loading dock for paddle-boats.

While the trees and lawns and boulders around the bay had remained scenic, the lake itself had lost its surreal brightness throughout the years, gathering litter from passersby and illegal swimmers. I looked out the window at the now-dark water, which sparkled under the orange sky. One glimpse was enough for me. I willed my mother to drive fast and take me home. Me and my red debit card.

I couldn't wait for daisy.

27

Bump bump bump. Before Liam parked the car downtown, we heard the bass of Mars' music.

I never go without pre-drinking. Liam handed me a can of beer.

Why? I took a deep swig, careful not to flatten my 'hawk on my seat's headrest.

Drinks in the bar are way more expensive than the liquor store. You'll see.

I didn't tell him I'd never been in a liquor store.

Liam pulled down the sun flap over his driver's seat, checking his eye makeup. I followed his example, examining my face in the mirror above me. I'd borrowed my mother's mascara and drawn it across my lashes, making my gray eyes pop.

Do you think I'm wearing too much blush?

Oh my god. Liam turned to me, his beautiful blue eyes framed with black liner and fake lashes. You're, like, barely wearing any makeup. But you look hot.

Thanks.

We downed our beers, stepping on the cans when we got out of the car. Crinkle crinkle crinkle, they went. Bump bump bump, went Mars. I pondered the fact that my belly burning with quickly consumed liquor was one of the best feelings in the world. I'd left my backpack at home, the only things in my pockets being my house keys, shiny new bank card, and twenty-dollar bill.

My mother hadn't even asked where I was going. She probably assumed I'd be playing Ouija Board and watching horror films with Tiff.

I'd straight up told Tiff I was going out with Liam that night, because he'd asked me first. She'd pretended to be mad, but was obviously thankful for alone time with Oliver.

Liam led me through the dark alley, his head held high. He was a tall, black widow spider, eight fabricated legs attached to his back, white cotton hanging off some for the illusion of a woven web.

Two bars were squashed up beside each other, one with a dark entranceway and a black sign reading

Broken String Bar

The other had a sign over its doorway in rainbow lettering

mars
previously known as freedom bar

I breathed in the remnants of cigarette fog and fruity cigars from people loitering outside. Their faces loomed, but intoxicated voices rose excitedly over the darkness. I enjoyed their shadows cast on the brick, graffiti-splayed walls. A couple of drag queens towered over everyone else in their platform heels and back-combed wigs. One of them nodded at Liam.

We kept walking, right around the corner.

Hey. Liam held his phone to his ear. Amara. AMARA. Can you hear me? WE'RE HERE. YES. WE'RE OUTSIDE.

He flipped his phone shut and jutted his hip out, frustrated.

Oh my god. I think she's pissed already. It's...what? Ten thirty?

What does it take though, really? One beer? I pictured Amara's narrow, nude body in a Value Village changing room.

Liam laughed and patted my shoulder. We stood outside a red metal door, no handle on the outside so no one could try getting in. I soon heard noises on the other sides of the door, thumping and jangling keys.

Watch out. Liam pulled me to the side, his manicured nails denting my arm.

The door flew open and Amara tumbled out in her short short short crinkly plastic nurse costume, tiny white hat with a red cross resting precariously on her 'fro.

Fuck! Liam grabbed the door at the last second. You almost locked us out!

Oops. Amara giggled and stumbled forth in her white six-inch heels, pretending to fall into my arms. Catch me!

I grabbed her hips to steady her and pulled the edges of her skirt down to hide her bright green panties. She towered over me, monstrous.

So what do you think, V? Amara pushed me back and struck a pose, her skinny arm over her head so her hand hung limply. Doing so, her skirt rose again, revealing her gitch and the tops of her dark, dainty thighs.

Yeah, you look good.

Amara didn't say anything about my costume; I wondered if she even noticed my hair.

Guys. Liam was already inside, leaning out the door a few inches. Let's go in before we get caught.

Right.

I followed them down a dark hallway, stepping over a few boxes. It was inconceivable as to how Amara made it through that hall without falling. We walked past a kitchen with fluorescent lights. The cooks paid us no heed, busily creating platters of nachos and deep-fried delights. Light from another room spilled into the corridor, and beyond that I saw a pair of swinging doors, flashing lights from the bar crossing the tiny circular windows.

I couldn't wait.

Amara put her fingers to her lips, hushing Liam and I as though we'd be heard through the thumping tunes invading the air. She motioned with her hand one finger, two fingers, three, and we scampered past the doorway. Curiosity made me steal a glance of someone I could only assume was Amara's boss, a robust man in a Santa costume talking on the phone in his tiny office.

I could barely take the situation seriously, imagining Santa catching us sneaking in and spanking us over his knee.

You've been naughty. Coal for your stocking this year.

We pushed through the swinging doors.

Welcome to Mars, baby. Liam squeezed my forearm.

I immediately caught the warmth of other people, seeping through their costumes and laughter. Music welcomed us, remixed songs turned techno coming from speakers at the end of the room, though I couldn't see a DJ. No one was dancing.

One section of the room was filled with tall, wooden tables and high chairs. Several middle-aged guys lingered there, clutching mugs of beer and pretending to chat while their eyes wandered. They looked like teachers. They looked like doctors. They looked like peoples' fathers. My eyes settled on a brown-haired guy, daring myself for a moment to believe he drove the number eighty-four bus. When his eyes stopped on me I quickly looked away.

Those are the makeout couches. Amara touched my shoulder and pointed at a corner lined with sofas. Maybe see you there later.

She was clearly starting to get the wrong impression of me. I turned away to scan the room, my belly dancing before the rest of me.

Nearly everyone wore a costume. Mickey Mouse and Spiderman squeezed past us to go up a spiral staircase. Sitting at a table together were Cher, a tube of toothpaste, and a witch.

What's up there? I asked Liam, my attention wandering up the stairs.

We'll go up there later. Liam leaned over, holding his brightly lit phone. Raizel's outside.

Liam took the keys from Amara and scampered back through the swinging doors down the dark hallway. I crossed my fingers that he wouldn't get caught. Or maybe he'd want to be caught, and Santa would be just as glad to be the catcher.

Here you go. Amara's arms came around me from behind. She rested her chin on my shoulder and popped her hand open in front of my face.

Thanks. I grabbed one of the eight pills, yellow with lips like the bunch we'd done the other night. They must have been circulating the town, between *all* the dealers. I wondered if Seed and Amara's dealer knew each other. Maybe they were friends, and tested the pills together, getting fucked up and watching the stars on Seed's balcony. I wondered if they stopped each other from doing stupid things.

Hold on a minute. Amara walked to the bar, her tiny hips swaying, and ducked under a countertop. The male bartenders, each dressed as one half of a broken heart, grinned at her.

Engulfing the bar was a crowd of Playboy bunnies, disco queens, fairies, devils--people like Amara who'd used the holiday as an excuse to dress like a skank. I was beginning regret my costume choice. It wasn't like high school when I'd been too embarrassed to wear something funny--I was in a wild place where people could be whatever they wanted. I could've been a monkey. I could've been a monster. I could've been Tom Hanks in Cast Away with a beard and a volleyball.

Amara returned with a bottle of water.

I can't open this. She reached out to stroke my jaw, her condensation-moistened fingers fumbling toward my ear.

I took the bottle and backed away, pretending to be on the lookout for Liam. I glanced at the double swinging doors with the little, circle windows. I was starting to doubt that Mars was the best place to do daisy. There wasn't even a dance floor.

Don't worry, they'll come in soon. Amara grinned down at me. She breathed near my face with her musty mouth. She still smelled like a cave and a sponge from under the kitchen sink. I couldn't believe I hadn't noticed the odor before, not even when we were kissing.

I squeezed my pill in my sweating palm and twisted the cap of the plastic bottle.

Hey, girlfriends! Lanky black spidery Liam skipped toward us through the throng of partiers, dark cotton appendages bouncing behind him. I assumed the girls were making their way through the crowd after him. I couldn't wait for an excuse to get away from Amara.

Janis Joplin, wearing circular sunglasses, came out from behind Liam--a girl whose blond hair had been backcombed to look like she'd stuck her wet finger in a socket and then slept on it for three hours. A long peace-sign necklace dangled between her breasts in her floral poncho. She pulled the sunglasses down and revealed her stoned eyes.

Abby! I laughed, pointing at her huge bellbottoms, my pill still trapped in my hand. Nice jeans.

Hey! Abby wrapped her arms around me and squeezed, familiar skunky pot fragrance surrounding us. I looked over her shoulder at the crowd of people and animals and animated inanimate objects.

My eyes stopped on a girl in the crowd. She stood still in an expensive-looking low-cut white dress with a puffy skirt, her slender arms hanging long at her sides, head turned away. All of her light hair was pulled back from her face, like I'd never seen before, into a low bun at the nape of her neck. I would never have thought Raizel would choose to be something as ordinary as a bride. Or maybe she'd meant to dress up as Beautiful--and had certainly pulled it off.

Flip flip flip. My stomach. I hoped she wouldn't be offended that I had changed my hair.

Abby and I let go of each other. I felt Amara's hands grasp for my lower back like a football player and a ball on a rainy day. I was drawn forward.

Raizel's bare, vulnerable face turned. Her eyes landed on me.

V! Oh my god! Raizel lifted her arms exactly as her little sister had, to wrap them around my neck. Her mouth was an inch from my ear. You look so different!

Raisin! You look so beautiful. Do you know who I'm supposed to be?

No, but Abby said it was her idea.

I grabbed Raizel's wrists from the back of my neck and held her a foot away from me. Together, we looked down at my white t-shirt, manly sweater vest, men's jeans. I danced for a moment, letting her guess.

She shook her head and lifted her face, flashing an earth-stopping smile.

Ellen Degeneres. She grinned.

I laughed, remembering Liam's words.

Show Raizel a picture of Ellen Degeneres and watch her face. She blushes and gets all giggly.

Go get a pill from Amara. I pointed over my shoulder with my thumb.

I dunno if I'm gonna do daisy tonight. Raizel shrugged, still smiling. Maybe just drink.

Seriously? I felt my eyebrows rise. I moved my mouth closer to her ear. Maybe I will too then. I don't wanna be rolling on my own.

You have Amara. She's *always* down for that shit.

While Amara went behind the bar to score half-priced bottles of beer, the rest of us stood around checking each other out.

You look hot.

You do. I want to stroke your spider legs.

I want to stroke your poncho.

Do it.

V, you really do look hot, in more ways than one.

Thanks. I'm not too bad, though. This vest is breathable.

You're breathable.

Thanks...I think?

Raizel, you almost have cleavage. That's hot.

So do you, Liam. So do you.

Liam, where did you learn to do makeup so well?

Magazines.

Amara returned with the beer and we claimed some of the high chairs by the dance floor, squishing in around a small circle of a table top. After a ten-minute struggle in my mind, I threw my head back and swallowed the yellow lips. Liam and Amara did the same, though Abby and Raizel refrained. People kept filing into the bar through the front door, packing us in like sweaty sardines. Amara perched on her chair with her neck stretched tall and crossed her arms over her chest, green triangle of panties ever-apparent under the shiny white hem of her costume.

Let's go upstairs, guys. Abby slumped off her chair.

We moved slowly across the room.

Raizel struggled to lift the hefty sides of her wedding gown. After a moment of laughter, I took her arm and pulled it over my shoulders. In a swift motion I wrapped my arm around her waist and lifted her legs with the other. Raizel giggled while her hands clung to my neck, the train of her dress dragging on the stairs as we ascended. I couldn't believe how light she was. The others followed us.

Oh, Ellen. Raizel laughed in my ear. You're so strong.

Damn. You're lighter than two bags of cream.

What? I don't get it.

Oh my god. I laughed back, suddenly noticing her feet. You're still wearing your shoeboots?

Shoeboots? I don't get that either. You have some funny lingo, Ms. Degeneres.

When we got upstairs I set Raizel down on the floor in the bit of light splaying out from the unisex bathroom, helping her smooth her skirt. People standing in the line glanced at us. A heavy, shorthaired girl in a construction worker costume looked me up and down. I only knew she was a girl because of two lumps under her white muscle shirt. My eyes scanned the tattoos trailing down her arm. I imagined her thoughts.

What's that straight girl doing here? Fag hag. Wannabe dyke.

After a moment her eyes flitted away from Raizel and I, probably to Amara's crotch.

Like a school of fish, my friends and I turned to move down a wide hallway that seemed to lead to a pit of darkness. From top to bottom, the walls appeared to have been molested by drunkards with glowing paint. Through the handprints I read messages, many of which I didn't understand.

I banged john jacob jingle heimer schmidt
katie + nina = luv
mitchell d. & chris r. = forever
lets get I thing straight…I'm not
jen & sam married july 9, 2007
shane & carmen were the best
no, alice & dana were
long live the drag king
pride fest. 1993 don & mickey were here (and queer)
lez b friends
richard's a bitch
try sexual
I made it onto the chart
Freedom Bar Forever, r.i.p. Kelly Hansel
come out come out wherever you are

One message in particular caught my eye, written neatly as if to deliberately stand apart from the others.

If you're not proud enough to wave your flag
you'd better find a different one.

I got the immediate sense that I was on the outside of a secret club. No--I was inside a club I didn't belong to. Every person who passed us in the hall probably wondered how I got in, not because I was a minor, but because I didn't have other credentials. I averted my eyes and followed Liam's skinny black legs.

I didn't have *any* flag to wave.

We moved steadily down the hall, assumedly because my friends had read all of the messages time and time again. They had probably written some themselves, laughing while their humongous daisy-induced pupils danced with the vivid greens and fuchsias.

Music lit my ears like firecrackers as we entered a dark room, finally happening upon the DJ, whose booth was raised to one side. Faint lights spun over the people on the massive dance floor, their icy drinks in glasses raised above their heads to avoid spilling the expensive liquid.

The high-rise ceiling was splattered with hundreds of plastic glowing stars. They reminded me of the seventh grade when I'd pocketed some from the dollar store and had used them to create messages that would come alive on the ceiling when I flicked the lights off and lay on my bed. They'd been unreadable to anyone but me--my diary of glowing stars.

CGIAD (Cecile Grey is a ditcher)
TLIAP (Thomas Lars is a pervert)
ISDNCD (I stole Dana's Nirvana CD)
IGTL50P (I'm going to lose fifty pounds)
SDE (Santa doesn't exist)
NDG (Neither does God)

I tugged Liam's arm, pulling the side of his face toward my mouth.

This place is *so* cool.

D'you like it? It used to be a movie theater.

I grinned, feeling my shoulders move alongside the music like a duck with a river's current. I longed to swim into the middle of the dance floor and crawl up on the platform, to feel someone against my back and someone else against my chest. I longed to let the music beat in place of my heart.

This is where *I* work. Amara leaned toward me with her sink-sponge breath.

I *know.*

No, I mean, this room.

Cool. I nodded and swigged my beer.

Cheers! Abby shouted above the music.

We all touched our beer bottles together, the glass clinking. I sucked the opening of my drink again, cool bitterness cleansing my dry throat.

Let's go dance! Liam waved his arm in the air and pointed at the dance floor. His makeup sparkled.

28

Why are you so angry? My eyes flicked around and my toes tapped, daisy amping me up.

Up up up. We were stationed in the hall next to the glowing messages. I read the one behind Amara's head.

can I bum a fag

Nothing. You still owe me for that pill, by the way. It's just-- Amara closed her eyes for a long moment, swaying. I put my arms out, preparing to catch her. You guys dressed up as a couple. That was supposed to be you and me.

Who's dressed as a couple?

You and *Raizel.* Or should I say Portia?

Portia? I repeated the name, letting it roll across my mind. Oh. Oh my god. Portia. That's Ellen Degeneres's girlfriend, right?

More like super life-partner. And what's worse is you guys look like Ellen and Portia on their *wedding* day. Or commitment ceremony day. Or whatever.

My cheeks burned worse than if I'd sat in the sun for six hours. My eyes darted into the dark movie theater room to Raizel, who danced clutching the sides of her dress, shiny red shoeboots showing underneath. Maybe Amara was wrong and Raizel had simply dressed as a bride.

And don't tell me you didn't plan it. Amara's eyes were still closed. I wasn't born yesterday.

But-- I moved my eyes from Raizel to Abby, innocent Abby with her funny shades and flowing poncho, dancing and holding her little sister's hands.

We didn't.

Later, I excused myself to the bathroom. I gritted my teeth and swayed against the stall door as I pulled up my jeans. I pushed the flimsy metal latch with my sweating fingers and floated to the sink. I looked up from the tap and saw myself in the mirror, surprised to be greeted by my own eyes, made-up. I'd never been the kind of girl who wore makeup, no matter how hard Tiff tried convincing me. That Halloween, my first payday ever, my first day as a blond, my first time in a bar, I was the kind of girl who *wanted* things. I wanted to show the world something more than eyes the color of cigarette ashes flicked carelessly. I wanted to be noticed, like

seaside boulders

feathers of a loon

pregnant clouds on a July afternoon

Hoping she'd see such things, I purposely let my eyes flail across the mirror and meet with those of the tattooed construction worker girl I'd thought was judging me earlier.

Happy Halloween. I grinned, try not to look goofy with my gapped teeth.

She smiled and nodded politely.

I drifted away.

Up up up.

A blooming daisy.

29

The next morning I awoke to a humming noise reverberating in the walls of our duplex. I rubbed my eyes, feeling bits of crusty mascara on my closed fists. My bedroom clock told me it wasn't even nine yet.

Hey.

I shot up, alert.

Oh my god. You scared the shit out of me.

Amara lay beside me on her stomach, cheek on the pillow, bare bony back and lime green panties a shocking sight amid my off-white bed sheets. She still had on her heels. Nausea hit me when I imagined my mother or Dana peeking into my room that morning. Immense confusion would have been an understatement.

I spotted her shiny nurse costume on the carpet by my desk, her black winter overcoat beside my crumpled vest and man jeans. I ran my hands under the sheet to skim my own bare thighs and the elastic hem of my underwear. A baggy t-shirt concealed my top half.

Amara closed her eyes dreamily into the pillow.

I tried to remember. We'd had some beer, popped pills, danced our asses off, had some beer, popped more pills, and moved to the beat until the DJ announced Last Call. Then I'd left the bar and ridden around with the others in Liam's car. Oh my god, he'd driven drunk and high. I remembered being dropped off and shouting goodbye and Happy Halloween in the middle of the road, probably waking my own mother and someone else's down the road. I couldn't remember inviting Amara into the duplex. Surely, my sober self would never have done such a thing.

Questions flipped around in my head as though on a ping pong table, my own rationale acting as paddles. What had we done? Had we drunk more or taken something upon arrival at my place? I looked around for cups, or a bottle, or a debit card with white powder along the edge.

I *hoped* I still had my debit card. I slipped out of the bed and knelt on the carpet, reaching for the jeans I'd worn. I felt the pockets, breathing heavily when I happened upon my card. I remembered using it at the Mars ATM after paying Amara for the daisy. I remembered Amara asking me to give her the thirty bucks I owed her for the line of coke at Value Village, and taking another forty out. I remembered getting pissed off that I couldn't take out ten-dollar bills or fivers.

Did I spend lots of money last night? I plopped onto my butt and hugged my shins, looking at Amara for all of the answers.

Mm mm nnn. She turned toward the wall, back facing me, and drew the thin sheet up around her body. It's fucking cold in here.

Her spine popped against her skin like stepping stones in a dark passage of water.

Bang. I heard the front door slam. The humming outside persisted.

Well, I'm getting up.

I pulled the jeans up my legs and went into the hall, shutting my bedroom door behind me, closing something I didn't want to deal with. Cardboard boxes lined the hallway, their duct-taped flaps labeled with a black Sharpie in a vowelless code:

lvng rm
ktchn
bthrm
bdrm

I heard people talking in the living room and wandered toward them, my bare feet crunching crumbs and bits of dirt that had gathered since the last time I'd vacuumed. I happened upon my mother and a middle-aged man standing in the living room, looking out the window.

What's going on?

Hi, my peach. This is my daughter, Venice. This is Gabe, Dana's boss. He brought his truck over to help with the move.

Phew. My mother showed no signs of knowing what time I'd come home; her brow wasn't furrowed, hands not clasped anxiously, fingers not twirling a lock of her knotted hair. Or maybe it was a facade; maybe she was interested in Gabe and didn't want to come off as a wench. First impressions could last forever.

Hi. I crossed my arms over my chest, braless under my t-shirt. The first impressions I sometimes made had me yearning to crawl backwards into a dark hole.

Hi, there. The man spoke through a thick brown mustache, which matched the mop of hair on his head. He gave me a swift nod before turning to open the screen door.

Morning, Venice. Dana entered, cheeks reddened by the wind. He rubbed his sneakers on a bit of newspaper on the landing like a bull meditating an attack.

I caught the source of the humming, a black pickup truck running its engine, the back loaded with my brother's discolored furniture. I wondered if Gabe had noticed where I'd once used a knife to carve SCREW YOU atop Dana's desk. I wondered if, because of that, he was reconsidering letting Dana be his basement suite tenant.

Dana moved past me, down the hall to retrieve a box. I followed him a few steps, leaving my mother to talk to the mustached wonder.

I didn't know you were moving today. I kept my arms crossed, though suddenly for a different reason.

Yeah, well. It's the first. I gain possession of the place today.

Oh, yeah. It's November. Trippy. I looked down at my toes.

Hey, I think I left something in your room. My brother reached for the brass handle on my bedroom door. Do you mind if I--

No! I mean yes, I do mind. It's a mess in there.

What? Why does that matter? Dana used his sleeve to dab at the sweat on his forehead. I'm just going to get--

His chubby hand turned the knob. I inhaled sharply. The jig was up. I was about to come out of the closet, which made less sense than anything, as I'd only accidentally wandered into it in the first place.

Argh! Dana jumped back. Shit. Why didn't you tell me you had someone over?

I stood on tiptoes to peek over Dana's shoulder, realizing Amara was fully clothed--well, as full clothed as it seemed she ever got. She stood in the middle of the room wearing my red plaid flannel shirt as a mini-dress. I assumed my black belt was too big for her, as she'd tied it severely around her waist instead of using the notches.

Hi. Amara flashed my brother and I a bright white grin and reached up to tousle her 'fro. A big, springy black curl landed on her forehead over her dark eye.

Dana, this is my friend Amara. Amara, this is my brother Dana.

I remembered the reaction I'd had upon seeing her for the first time. I didn't blame my brother for retreating slowly into the hall without responding. He picked up one of his boxes and shuffled away, his jeans drooping at the back like a plumber's.

I entered my room and closed the door, staring at Amara.

That's my favorite shirt.

It's hot. You don't mind, right? I only have that nurse getup with me.

I guess it's alright.

Plus I like how it smells. She tugged the collar toward her nose and sniffed, waiting for my reaction.

Amara, I think we should talk. I shuffled to the bed and perched on the edge. Afraid she would take a nonexistent hint, I jumped up and moved to my desk chair.

Yeah, actually, so do I. Amara sat on the bed where I'd been seconds earlier. She leaned down to rub her bony ankle, probably sore from her vicious heels. Why did you just introduce me as your *friend?*

I'm not exactly out to my family. I mean, not that I should be. There's nothing to be out about. I picked up a pen and dragged it across a paper on my desk.

What do you mean? You should totally tell them. I can help if you want. When I told my--

No, I mean--

Knock knock knock.

I jumped up and swung my door open.

Peach. My mother leaned her head in, brown hair dangling down the door frame. She sucked a Menthol cigarette. Hi. I'm Kathy.

I'm Amara. Nice to meet you. Amara crossed her legs, nearly flashing my mother.

My face burned.

Mom, this is a smoke-free zone. I coughed dramatically and waved my hand through her smoke.

Sorry. She kept looking at Amara. I'm trying to quit. You know, it's hard.

No, you're not, I thought.

I bet it is. Amara nodded sympathetically.

Anyway, my peach. My mother finally turned to me. She brought the cigarette to her mouth and exhaled into the hallway. Dana left a pile of things he's getting rid of.

Oh. Like what? A bag of old popcorn?

My mother laughed.

Go look in his room.

Dana's bedroom carpet was plagued with rectangular dents from his dresser and bed, the walls' paint chipped where tape had been torn off. He'd gone without even saying goodbye. Nothing was left but closet hangers and a large assortment of junk in the middle of the carpet. Amara plunked herself down, cross-legged. I avoided looking between her legs at her neon gitch, gazing instead on the pile.

Raizel was right. Your mom's bangin'.

Oh my god. I frowned. You're sick.

So, what's this? Amara picked up a long paper, rolled up and held together with a rubber band.

Give me that.

Her eyes widened when I snatched the paper away. I almost definitely knew what it was. I tugged the elastic band off and threw it over my shoulder.

I unrolled the paper slowly and lay it on the carpet, using books and a deck of cards to weigh down the corners.

What the fuck? Amara laughed.

I touched the large poster, black but for two sketched bananas--one lemon yellow and the other bell-pepper red.

It's an Andy Warhol print. I didn't think I should have to explain, but I remembered the framed flower photographs from Walmart in her living room. It matches the gun design in my room.

Oh. Okay.

I suddenly got the feeling that Amara was the wrong person to go through the pile with. And I knew who it was supposed to be.

I'm really hungry. Let's go eat.

Sure.

After a breakfast comprised of tea, stale toast, and eggs, I scraped our plates off into the kitchen trash can. Neither of us had eaten properly, Amara probably because she never did, and myself probably because I was busy trying to figure out how to get rid of her. Finally I told her that my mother and I were going over to see Dana's new place, and that I'd walk her to the bus stop.

We stood on the sidewalk in the cold, hands shoved in our respective coat pockets. Halloween's wind had calmed itself, not threatening to lift Amara's skirt--my favorite shirt. The air bore a frostiness that hung listlessly, unmoving.

The eighty-four came hissing and rolling around the corner after a few minutes.

See ya later. I turned to walk back home.

Wait, wait, wait. Amara grabbed my hand, pulling me toward her.

I caught sight of the vehicle's few passengers peering out at us, waiting for us to get on board. I turned my head at the last second and let Amara's lips land on my cheek near my nostril. Her breath smelled old, musty, cave-like.

Sorry. My face got hot.

It's okay. I know you're not ready. Amara clunked up the bus steps in her enormous heels, drawing everyone's attention from the sight outside to the spectacle inside. She made her way to a seat, plunked down, and turned to wave out the window.

Call ya later. She mouthed the words and shaped her hand like a telephone, wiggling it by her ear. A curl still dangled above her eye.

30

Riiiing. Riiiing.

Hello?

Hi. Pam? Is Tiff there?

No, sorry, dear. She left for Team Bean already.

Oh, I didn't know she was working today. I glanced at the clock.

10:50

Yup. If you call her cell you might catch her. She doesn't start 'til eleven.

I hung up and quickly dialed Tiff's number, letting it ring until the receiver hurt my ear. She'd probably already silenced the thing and thrown it in the metal box of her locker. I was about to press End on the cordless when I heard her voice.

Hey. Make it quick, I'm about to start my shift.

Oh hey, Tiff. When are you done?

Seven.

Wow, an eight-hour shift?

Well, yeah. I *am* saving for school, you know.

Right. Well, do you wanna get together later? We can hang out or watch a movie or talk about last night. How was your Halloween, anyway?

I really can't talk right now. But later I have a date with Olly. Sorry. The new schedule's up, though, and we're both working tomorrow at eleven.

Oh. Who you working with today?

That new Meaghan chick. I think I gotta help train her. Oh shit. It's eleven now. Gotta go.

Click.

For a second, I actually missed her.

I retrieved my mug from my shitty breakfast with Amara, picking out the crusty teabag and pulling a new one from the orange pekoe box in the cupboard. I filled my mug with scalding hot water and moved down the hall to Dana's room, which wasn't really Dana's room. I wondered what to call it--The Empty Room or The Room That Echoes. Maybe my mother would make it into an office, one she could call her own.

I set my mug on the carpet and picked up a Lego man, putting it off to the side in my Don't Want pile. To the same pile I added a dictionary, a comb, an empty picture frame, a padlock with an unknown combination, a bottle of whiteout, a remote control for an unknown electronic device, a Bart Simpson mouse pad, and a turquoise mitten.

The first item to hit my Want pile was a coffee table book featuring photos of farmers in other countries. I remembered the mail carrier ringing our doorbell one day after school and Dana signing for the package that was the book, even though he clearly wasn't Gretchen Sesley and we clearly lived at eleven Oakwood *Terrace*, not Heights. Neither of us had felt guilty.

I added more things to the Don't Want pile--a Slurpee cup, a bag of Q-tips, and a wallet made of duct tape. I remembered making fun of him for looking up instructions on a do-it-yourself website and then actually using the wallet.

A couple of clothing items lay atop the pile. I picked up Dana's old phys. ed. shirt, our high school's logo splayed across the front, and proceeded to throw it on the Don't Want Pile. I was beginning to think I was wasting my Saturday when I picked up a pair of camouflage-print shorts. Although they were far too big for me, I could probably wear them with a belt, if I ever got mine back from Amara.

I'd been so busy considering the shorts that I hadn't noticed what lay beneath them. My mouth hung open, a hole of gawk. My brother must have arranged the items in the pile specifically to surprise me.

I picked up Dana's old gray, metallic digi-cam. I remembered him buying it shortly after he'd started at Phantom. He'd shown it off all around our house, taking close-ups of random things--salt grains on the kitchen counter, smoke rising from our mother's ashtray. I'd only been allowed to touch the device when Dana wanted shots of himself poppin' lame wheelies on his BMX, and then I'd purposely zoomed in on his bulbous, grease-induced pimples.

I pressed the power button and heard a little chime. A tiny, circular red light appeared. The screen lit up, royal blue.

Memory Card Empty

I aimed the camera and pressed the button, a light running dully through the room. Three seconds later the picture appeared on the screen, a tiny square of a closet haunted with empty hangers. I pressed a lightning bolt button on top and re-took the picture, a blaring light greeting my eyes and the rest of the room. I brought the farmer picture book and camouflage shorts and banana Andy Warhol print back to my own bedroom.

So, the flash was a bit dodgy and the memory card lagged. When important things happened I would probably feel like a limping old man in a race across the country. But I couldn't care--I had a camera--my *own* camera.

I felt asleep until six p.m., when my mother opened the door and stuck her arm in, hand encasing the cordless.

That Amara girl's on the phone. Oh, sorry. Why are you sleeping?

I don't feel good. Tell her I'll call her later.

My mother retreated into the hall. I glared at the closed door.

On Sunday I woke up chipper, immediately putting on Tegan & Sara and hopping around my room between bites of cereal. I used safety-pins to alter the camouflage shorts so they hung low on my hips, but not too low, and paired them with my black button-down shirt.

When I looked in the mirror, seeing my outfit and my short, blond hair, an unfamiliar sensation came over me. I turned from side to side, even putting my back to the mirror to look at my butt. I lifted my arms straight in the air, letting my shirt ride up and reveal my belly. I put them back down and smiled, checking my teeth for Cheerio remnants. The gap between my teeth stared back at me, a tiny black slit.

Tears came from nowhere, fat salty drops that stung my just-barely wind-burnt cheeks. I blamed them on my approaching time-of-the-month.

For the first time in my life, I felt *beautiful.*

31

Tiff and I caught the bus to Team Bean together. Sloam had become a big refrigerator, cold docile air settling around everything. I keeled over on the shiny brown bus seat, rubbing my chilled bare calves.

Tiff smiled the whole way. She kept checking her phone for bittersweet text-messages.

Friday night was soo good. My mom let me stay out 'til however late I wanted. I think she *loves* Olly. He's such a gentleman, you know? And not even just in front of her. He always opens the car door for me and pulls out my chair. We watched that Saw movie at his house, but I don't really remember it, if you know what I mean.

Wow. Romantic. Does he live with his parents still?

Yeah, but they stayed upstairs and handed out candy.

So, like, did you guys do it?

Shh. Tiff spat and her cheeks reddened. An old woman sitting in front of us glanced back with raised caterpillar-thick eyebrows.

Sorry. I lowered my voice to a whisper. Did you guys do it?

No. Tiff smiled. But maybe soon. I know he's The One, but I want to be ready, you know?

Oh yeah. I remembered losing my v-card, once upon three years ago. I know.

Plus-- Tiff paused to laugh. I was wearing my pregnant lady costume. I think it scared him a little. Hey, by the way, you wanna come to Sophie's next game? It's on Thursday.

Not really, I thought. I'd made plans to hang with Liam and the others on Wednesday night, which meant I definitely wouldn't feel like doing anything the next day.

I dunno. I might be working.

Oh. Okay. So…how was your Halloween?

It was okay. I looked out the window as we entered Elmview. Pedestrians in Sunday mode walked leisurely to their street-side mail boxes or to the corner store for potato chips. They were all so *normal* in their hikers and finger gloves. I decided, then and there, to tell my best friend about Amara. I opened my mouth.

How's *Liam?* Tiff lifted her arm as she'd begun doing, mocking the dainty limp wrist associated with gay men.

I closed my mouth again and shrugged.

When we got to Team Bean, Monica was standing at the front till with Meaghan, the new girl, pointing out different buttons.

Hi girls. Monica glanced up.

Though she wore her usual smile, I swore I noticed something in our boss's eyes--an apology, unhappiness. Five minutes' leeway 'til our shift started, we moved down the hall to the crew room. I was opening my locker when Tiff gasped.

Oh my GOD.

What? I turned around, unzipping my coat.

Oh my god. She pointed at the wall above the microwave. I can't believe this.

Patty Gavinsford
Honorable Staff Member
of Team Bean Café
November

What? Monica just hasn't changed the plaque yet.

No way. Tiff jabbed the inscription with her pointer finger. It's fucking November.

Oh. Right. I paused and looked at her.

Tiff averted her eyes to some bits of lettuce on the floor around the sofa eating area. Her red ponytail dangled, hiding the sides of her face like a horse's blinders.

Oh my god, don't cry.

I'm just so *sad.* Tiff looked back up at the plaque, saliva catching her words as her mouth twisted painfully into a sob. I tried so hard.

You know what? We'll just ignore Monica today, okay? And Patty. Rubbing Tiff's bony shoulder, I realized I hadn't touched her in a long time. I pointed at the work schedule, on which my name had only been written four times that week. I regretted the next words long before my mouth emitted them.

Look. I have Thursday off. I can go to Sophie's game with you.

32

Sloam's autumn wind seemed to fall asleep, like a kitten full of milk. Everything was so calm that I couldn't listen to Alexisonfire without cringing at its displacement in the air. Millie Fischer was the one for me.

Click. One second. FLASH. Three more seconds.

The model appeared on my camera screen, gray faux-fur hood of some old winter coat framing her fair skin and peach lips under the streetlamp. She stood with her sneakers sunk in the crispy dark grass at the start of a field, flashlight in my left hand cutting her chin with shadows. I moved my hand up, lending embers to her cheekbones. Darkness lurked in the folds of her clothing.

Perfect. Don't move. Don't even smile.

Click. I waited. A strand of white hair whipped across her nose. Dim flash. Three more seconds.

I'm ready. The other model came from behind me, high heels quickly stabbing the pavement. She hopped up the curb and onto the grass, bending her knees. Though she swayed to one side, she was easily a foot taller than the other girl.

Wow, that's an interesting combo. On my camera screen I checked out a short pink pea-coat, seemingly meant for a child, and ripped fishnets hugging her toothpick legs.

I picked this up at Value Village. She grinned, a black gap separating her two front teeth.

The first model ducked quietly off the camera screen, back to her suitcase of clothing at the side of the road. I'd told them each to bring random clothes to model for me. I'd suggested borrowing things from their families and the taller model had made a face, as hers lived 'out of province'--what that meant, I didn't know.

Click. I waited a second. Dim flash. Three more seconds.

Um. I peered at the two-inch screen on my camera, holding it closer to my face. Let's try that again.

She lifted her arms over head, hands draping along the sides of her 'fro.

Click-wait-dim flash-wait.

Okay. I guess that one's better.

The girl teetered off the grass toward her own collection of clothing, a bursting black garbage bag set at the bottom of the field's Do Not Trespass sign.

The other model stood ten feet away with nothing on top but a black bra, wavy white-blond locks covering her face as she bent to pull some jeans up around her slender thighs. Sitting precariously above the white hem of her panties was a large, dark birthmark. So the perfect *could* be imperfect. Before thinking, I raised my camera.

Click-wait-dim flash-wait.

Venice, you perv. Are you taking pictures of us changing?

I glared at the pink pea-coated girl.

No. I was aiming at the car. I pointed a few feet away at the orange Camaro.

What's so good about a car?

Hey! the other model objected, jeans buttoned and zipped. She began slipping into a long, puffy parka. That's my hunk of burnin' love.

Anything can be beautiful. I snapped a picture of the long car, my camera lens embracing its orange-peel hue.

I sat in my family's basement, toes tucked under my butt, waiting while the pictures uploaded onto the computer. Forty-eight percent complete. Seventy-three percent. Ninety-one. The first photo appeared, the one I'd taken of Dana's closet immediately after happening upon the camera.

I clicked through the next pictures, my bedroom and my new Andy Warhol print. My toes. In the dead of the afternoon on Saturday, the street outside my bedroom window. My eyes remained dark in the bland light streaming in from outside.

Finally I happened upon the first pictures from the photo-shoot, Amara with her arms crossed leaning against the streetlamp, legs running eternally toward the ground. She'd accidentally blinked.

The next pictures were of Raizel and Amara posing together in bright eighties' wind-coats. I'd instructed them to jump and their hair had gotten in the way every time the camera had decided to shoot. I'd hollered at them to pretend they were at Mars or Morgan's instead of some shitty field with dying grass at the edge of a town called Sloam. My voice had ricocheted off the metal posts.

Next were some photos of Amara in her silly pink pea-coat. Damn. She'd closed her eyes again in all but one--one where she'd turned her body and completely erased her arm. She may as well as have hidden behind the lamppost.

Next I found the ones of Raizel, practically swimming in her long parka and jeans falling sloppily over the tops of her red shoeboots. I wondered if the jeans belonged to her dad. I wondered if he'd laughed when she'd asked to borrow them, or if she hadn't had to ask.

Raizel stood gazing dead-on at the camera, eyes slit cleverly, arms in the air as if she was bigger than the darkness around her. Blond curls spilled out the sides of the hood, a small pink smile resting above the ball of her labret piercing.

Something inside of me leapt. I'd taken an *amazing* photo.

I clicked the arrow at the bottom of the computer screen and suddenly happened upon the photo of Raizel with no shirt, bent forward. The camera's flash had completely illuminated the inch showing of her pitch-white panties and her nearly-as-white hair cascading over her face. My eyes fell to the birthmark that had caught my interest.

I pressed ZOOM three times, making everything bigger on the screen, Raizel's slim waist and the oversized freckle at the bottom of her flat belly.

Was it a birthmark?

I pressed ZOOM again. It was a tattoo. I could have sworn I'd seen something the night we'd gotten out of the car at Morgan's. Seeming to flow together like a river, the dark script probably came from a language considered far prettier than English--Thai, Arabic, Somethingese.

ZOOM. ZOOM. ZOOM. I suddenly found that I could understand the inked lines and letters while not understanding at all.

Like waves relying on beach I'll be waiting for you

Are you okay down there? My mother's voice flowed down the stairs from the kitchen. I heard her feet on the first wooden steps. What are you doing, my peach?

Nothing! I called back, quickly closing the photo. I didn't want to imagine what my mother would think if she found out I was looking at half-nude girls on the computer.

I already had enough people who thought I was gay.

33

We went up the steps at the rink's entrance slowly, me towing a blanket, Raizel with a bucket of cookies she'd baked, and Amara with her high heels, a mile away from the hem of her dress, click-clacking on the cement. I'd spotted Pam Abraham's family van in the parking lot, so I knew they'd arrived. My stomach flipped as I yanked the door open.

Flip flip flip. At the reception, I paid the two-dollar entrance fee for each of us, glad it was so cheap. I'd spent nearly half of my money on Halloween, and other such nights, and payday was still a week away.

We poked through the second set of swinging doors and breathed in the fragrance of concession-stand hot dogs and damp socks. Through a cold, white puff of exhalation I scanned the black wooden bleachers surrounding the rink. Little kids, assumedly having just finished a beginner's lesson, sat all around, their parents kneeling before them to untie their skates. They probably didn't know how lucky they were.

The night before, we'd gotten up to no good, just as I'd suspected would happen, hitting up a couple of bottles in Amara's living room. We'd gone over after supper, Liam and Raizel and I, to start as soon as possible with shots of spiced rum, chased by Malibu, chased by orange juice. I'd pitched in twenty bucks for liquor and had gotten substantially fucked up. Some people Amara knew from Mars had come over, a girl named Queenie and a couple named Robby and James.

After warming our cheeks and toes with booze, we'd all rolled our jeans into capri-pants, as Amara had turned the thermostat to twenty-eight degrees. She'd claimed twenty-eight was the perfect temperature, while the rest of us toasted like Pop Tarts. Raizel had complained that she couldn't roll her tights up at the bottom and we'd all demanded she just take them off. She'd refused, blushing.

Later in the night Queenie had looked at me across the living room and asked where I was from.

Here, I'd answered her, surprised. I mean, Sloam.

I mean, where do I know you from?

You know me?

You're so familiar. Her eyes glittered, booze-moistened.

I'd raised my cup of Malibu, alcoholic liquid zipping along my tongue and down my throat. For a long moment my eyes had born through her fedora, nose ring, and plump, rosy cheeks.

I know. I'd snapped my fingers excitedly. Do you have any tattoos?

Yup. Queenie had rolled up the sleeves of her cardigan, revealing a pin-up girl riding a motorcycle up one of her forearms, a couple of cherries on the other.

I talked to you in the bathroom at Mars. I'd smiled. On Halloween.

Ah, yes. Queenie had nodded, rolling her sleeve back down.

Sorry. I was really fucked up that night.

So was I. She'd ginned hugely. You didn't seem it though, don't worry.

Girlfriend, show me that tatty again. Liam had gotten up from his spot on the floor and reached for Queenie's arm.

Thus, the start of the tattoo exhibition.

It's so hot in here, anyway. James had undone his jeans and pulled them down, right there in the living room. He'd shown us his huge under-the-sea thigh tattoo, octopus tentacles reaching for the hem of his briefs. Then he'd sat back down, jeans strewn near the coffee table.

Liam had held his hair away from the back of his neck to display a tribal knot I hadn't known about. He'd claimed it meant freedom. I hadn't had to ask why freedom was important to him.

Robby had whipped off his t-shirt, revealing a blazing pink graffiti-style back-piece.

Liam had nearly drooled on the carpet, looking at Robby's chest.

I'd expected Raizel to show off her own tattoo. She'd kept it hidden, quietly admiring the others' ink.

Venice! Over here!

Over there. Raizel pointed toward the top of the bleachers. Is that her?

I spotted Tiff, orangey-red hair draped around her shoulders looking longer than it ever had. I led my new friends up the aisles between the bleachers, kids around us munching after-practise snacks. I caught one of the fathers eyeing Amara's legs.

Hey. Tiff smiled at me. She nodded quickly at Raizel and Amara before looking down at her hands.

Guys, this is Tiff. Tiff, this is Raizel, and this is Amara.

Amara let her arm dangle, hand brushing mine. I crossed my arms before Tiff saw anything. I pretended not to hear Amara's huffing noise.

Um, you can sit here. Tiff took her big thermos off the seat beside her.

I couldn't believe she was doing it, being all normal.

I sat beside Tiff, Amara sat beside me, and Raizel on Amara's other side. A zamboni circled the ice's rectangular perimeter.

Oh, before I forget. Tiff reached into the pocket of her puffy jacket. Your bus pass.

Thank you so much. I took the flimsy blue card from her, sparkly snowflake decals on the front welcoming winter. Outside, real snow had yet to arrive. Tell Oliver I owe him one.

Okay. Tiff zipped her pocket closed.

Is this hot chocolate? I pointed at the thermos between her leg and mine.

Yup. Tiff pushed up the bridge of her glasses with the back of her hand. Just like last year.

I grinned and rubbed my hands together, knowing I was feigning more excitement than I actually felt. I pulled my hands into my sleeves and pinched the ends closed to keep out the cool air.

So, your sister's playing, right? Raizel leaned forward to look across Amara and I at Tiff.

Tiff's eyes flitted around behind her glasses for a moment, probably trying to take in Raizel's eyes and blinding shade of hair. In my sleeves, I found myself actually crossing my fingers that she wouldn't give her The Look.

Yeah. Tiff grinned, flashing all her teeth before she put her hand over her mouth.

Well, you'll have to point her out to us. Raizel smiled back, drawing attention to her labret ball.

Just look for number 5.

Deal. Raizel settled back, leaning her elbows on the bench behind us.

Beside me, Amara stirred.

Where's the bathroom?

Apparently wanting to make a big effort, Tiff spoke up.

It's on the other side of the rink. See that door that says LADIES over it?

Amara raised her eyebrows. Shit. Tiff had been doing so well.

Come with me. Amara squeezed my thigh before I could swat her hand away. She stood up and pushed passed Tiff's knees and suspicious face.

The zamboni was leaving the ice as we entered the cold bathroom, a long line of olive-green metal stalls stretching along one wall. The players' warm-up music, The Pussycat Dolls, trickled in from the rink outside and slammed against the bathroom tiles.

What's up with your friend? Amara leaned against the outside of a stall door. She reached into her stupid Chanel purse for a pack of cigarettes.

You smoke?

Yeah. So? She lit the cigarette, bracelets clinking around her wrist.

There's a 'no smoking' sign.

Why do you *always* follow the rules? She pulled a long, white cigarette from the pack and held it out to me.

No, thanks. I shook my head. And I *don't* always follow the rules.

Wanna do something fun, then?

Like what?

Amara puffed her cigarette for a moment, elongating her neck as she leaned back and blew upward. I wondered if she'd set off a fire alarm.

Look in the back zipper pocket. In a swift motion the purse came down from her shoulder and hung before my eyes.

I pulled her necklace satchel out of the pocket, undid the drawstring, and removed a familiar rubber-banded baggie of white powder. Ah, yes. Drugs were never actually called by their names--something better, something fun.

Shit. I heard voices near the bathroom door, and quickly stuffed the baggie up my jacket. What if it was Tiff? Judging by her anger at my mere suggestion of E, she'd never forgive me if she actually *caught* me with coke. Was coke worse than ecstasy? Ecstasy lasted longer, but coke hurt more.

We shuffled into the big, wheelchair-accessible stall without looking back to see who'd entered the bathroom.

I don't know. I pulled the baggie out from under my coat, and lowered my voice drastically. It's really bad for you.

Okay, mom. Amara spoke, not caring to whisper nearly as quietly as me. She sucked on her cigarette, probably contributing to her caveman, under-the-kitchen-sink sponge breath. Raizel doesn't seem to think so.

What do you mean?

Footsteps passed our stall. A sink turned on.

We did it earlier, in her car. Didn't you see the powder on her dashboard?

Shh! I have a photographic memory. Truthfully, I hadn't known to be looking at the dashboard when we were in the car. I peered through the crack between the stalls, seeing the back of an older woman as she left the room. I don't remember any powder.

Whatever. Anyway. Didn't you like it when we did it before?

I thought of the buzzing, the immediate happiness, the inability to worry.

Of course I did.

My voice cracked, jumping between the tiles and into the drain.

The game was starting when we got out of the bathroom, the warmup music having ceased. I wondered if Tiff and Raizel were pissed at me for leaving them in awkward silence. *Did you fall in?* I imagined Tiff sneering.

I scanned the ice as we circled back around the rink to our bench. Girl after girl, all in heavy padding and red jerseys, zipped past the plexi-glass windows. Finally I spotted tufts of red hair spilling out under a helmet, a solid white five stamped on her jersey.

Hey! Sophie! I slapped my hand against the plexi-glass, the banging echoing throughout the whole rink.

Sophie barely noticed, skating toward her team's side of the ice. The opposing team, in menacing black jerseys, spilled out of the change-room at the end of the rink. They trampled the floor clumsily with their skate blades.

Amara laughed and grabbed my hand, pulling me forward, eyes averted. We scampered up to our seats. Amara's heels banged against every metal step. I sniffed and dragged the back of my hand across my nose, making sure. I drew my hand back into my sleeve.

Hey guys. Sorry we left you guys alone. I realized Tiff had slid down the bench to sit with Raizel.

No problem. Tiff smiled.

We were just talking about her mom's hair salon. Raizel twirled a bit of her hair in her fingers. I caught her eyes darting between Amara and I.

Cool. Yeah. I nodded emphatically. It's awesome.

After waiting a moment for Tiff to move back to her spot on the bench, I realized she wasn't planning on doing so. Amara plopped down. She squeezed my hand, reminding to sit down, and we pulled my blanket across our laps. I giggled and let her keep holding my hand, not caring if Tiff saw and thought *things*. I didn't understand what was so wrong about a girl with a soft hand trying to hold the soft hand of another girl. I felt my thumb stroke Amara's skin.

The cold seat buzzed under the back of my thighs. I tried to steady my shaking knees, thankful I could blame my twitching on the room's low temperature.

Did Raizel tell you she's the one who cut my hair? I turned to Tiff, whose eyes were busily following the players as they flitted around the ice.

Yup. Tiff nodded.

That's not all she's good at. Amara leaned over me, peering at Tiff. You should try her baking.

Oh, Amara. Raizel tsked. Don't overrate me.

Oh yeah, I forgot you brought cookies. I nodded. Let's try them.

Okay, okay. A light peach hue filled the tops of Raizel's cheeks. She bent to retrieve the Tupperware from under her seat.

Woo hoo! Amara hollered toward the ice, though she probably had no clue what was going on. I realized Sophie had caught the ring around her stick.

Go, Sophie! I yelled. Tiff, look!

Beside me, Tiff tensed up as she watched her sister speed across the ice, ring in tow.

Woo hooOoOo! I cupped my hands around my mouth to gain volume.

Several benches in front of us, a group of parents glanced over their shoulders. I stuck my tongue out at them.

Sophie swung wide, letting the ring slip through the gaping legs of an opposing player, straight into the net.

YES!!! Tiff jumped up from her chair. The rest of us stood up and cheered, fists pounding the air.

We sat back down.

Shit. Beside me, Tiff snapped her fingers. I forgot my camera.

Hold on. I hopped over the empty bench in front of us and turned around. I dug into my flimsy backpack and pulled out my digi-cam.

Where did *that* come from? Tiff raised her eyebrows. Is it your mom's or something?

Oh. I held the camera a foot away, its silver front gleaming before me. Dana gave it to me when he moved out.

Oh my god. Amara grinned, reaching out to touch the camera. Was it in that pile of junk he left in his room?

What pile of junk? Sitting on the cold bench, half a cookie in her lap, Tiff deeply resembled a lost lamb.

You know what I *really* want pictures of? Aurora Borealis. The Northern Lights. Wouldn't that be *so* trippy? But they don't happen 'til spring. I looked it up on the internet. Spring is *prettiest* season. Besides fall. Winter's cool, too. Literally. I laughed. And summer's alright.

When my laughter ended, I caught Tiff's eyes resting on mine for a moment too long.

I held the camera up to my face before she could notice my pupils.

34

Monica considered nine to five the *perfect* working hours, which was what she scheduled for me that Friday. She said, as I was no longer the new girl, Meaghan would be taking the random shifts. Seven to eleven. Eleven to three. Three to six. Six to eleven.

Since doing coke for the second time with Amara, I'd been feeling low on energy. One minute we'd been flying high and the next I'd been ready to fall asleep on those cold, black bleachers, mentally willing myself to make it through the game. I'd whispered to Amara that I wanted more, and she'd whispered back that she did to, but none was left. Then I'd developed a headache, blood pulsating in my temples and forehead, barely able to cheer when Sophie's team won four to two.

I wiped the counter around the coffee machines, straightened the tea bags, bent and took out a bag of plastic stir-sticks, poured them in the container labeled Stir Stix, stocked the cooler with bottle drinks, and brewed fresh coffee, constantly turning to check if a customer was lingering, waiting for me to demonstrate the finest slavery. I trudged through the motions of being a Coffee Bitch.

Even a dark roast black coffee wouldn't do the trick.

Straight after work that evening I lay in bed under the covers, listening to Tegan and Sara and dozing in and out of sleep. I heard the phone ringing outside my bedroom door, but could barely wake myself. I reached over and pressed pause on my CD player, perking my ears. I heard the SHHHHHH of running water and concluded that my mother was taking a shower.

Dana! Can you get that?

The loud words left my mouth before I could think. They seeped under my bedroom door into the hallway outside, into the room my brother had left empty and dark. I hadn't even gone to his new basement suite yet.

I darted into the hall, thinking Liam or Raizel was calling. ABRAHAM P, the caller ID told me. I sighed and considered leaving it to ring. Tiff was probably going to ask me to go to the bush or have a movie marathon in my basement.

Hello? I yawned exaggeratedly, padding back down the hall to my room.

Hey, it's me. Tiff replied in a singsong voice.

Hey. Sup.

Did you have fun yesterday?

At the game? It was okay. I got a really bad headache, though.

For reasons I can't tell you about.

Yeah, that sucks. Your new friends are interesting.

Oh, yeah? How so? What did you think of them?

Raizel was really nice. Tiff paused. And *really* pretty. And her cookies were good.

And?

Okay. What's up with that Amara girl? She's really pretty, but super anorexic. And she would barely even look at me. How old is she, anyway?

I think she's twenty-four. Sorry. She can come off as a bit snobby.

Like you.

So what are you doing now?

Lying in bed. I'm really tired.

Oh. So I take it you don't want to watch movies?

Sorry. I want to, but I'm really sleepy. I worked all day. What about tomorrow?

Tomorrow *I* work all day.

Yes!

But we should hang out at six, when I get home.

No!

Okay. Sounds good.

Outside my room, I heard the pipes close and hissing water stop. My mother was probably reaching out her shower door for a towel, fog blinding her vision.

I fell back asleep.

RIIIIIING!

I snorted, waking suddenly, and reached for the cordless on my bedside table. I didn't even bother looking at the screen.

Hello?

Hey, girlfriend.

Liam... I realized I hadn't talked to him in a few days. What's up?

Aw. You sound so tired.

I *am.*

Do you want me to hang up?

No. You have a soothing voice. Don't mind if I fall asleep.

But I have something important to tell you.

Let me guess. You got new jeans?

Nope. He giggled.

A new scarf?

No...one more guess.

Oh my god! Did you meet someone?

Yes! Giddiness tinged his voice, words unable to leave his throat quickly enough. You remember that guy I told you about?

Um... I thought. You mean Ben?

No. I think Ben's over me. At least, I'm over him. But you know that guy I said always comes into the pharmacy?

Yeah?

Hottay. He sang. He gave me his number today.

I imagined that when Liam was in love he danced around doing good deeds and wearing tap-shoes. I decided I had to ask all the right questions before he exploded into a million bite-sized pieces.

What's his name?

Christopher. He wears a tie. Can you believe my luck?

That's amazing, Liam. How'd you get his number?

When Liam and I had finished talking, I relaxed against my pillows. My mother was creating an orchestra of pots and pans in the kitchen. I'd probably never fall asleep.

RIIIIIIING!

Ugh.

Hello? I frowned, pushing my eyes against my pillow.

V?

I listened for a moment, hearing laughter, wherever the caller was.

Raisin? I propped myself up on my elbow, so my voice wasn't muffled.

It's me. What are you doing?

Listening to music.

That's all? Just listening to music?

Okay. I smiled. I was also trying to sleep.

Sorry! I'll call you later, or tomorrow, or something.

No! It's okay. Where are you?

I'm at home. Just about to eat dinner. Why?

Oh. Did you know Liam met someone?

He meets someone new every week. Her laughter fell like a sprinkle of cinnamon on my end of the phone.

I giggled.

A pause. I heard a man talking in the background. Probably her father.

What are you doing tomorrow? She asked.

During the day? Nothing. I bit my fingernail. You?

Working during the day. But do you wanna hang out after?

Ugh.

I'll take that as a no.

No, no. Sorry. I *really* want to hang with you. But I just told Tiff I'd watch movies with her.

Oh.

I know. Why don't I ask her if you can come?

Oh, I couldn't impose. You guys have fun.

It's really no big deal. She likes you, anyway.

Really? She said that?

Yup.

Riiiing. Riiiing.

For a change, I was the caller.
Hello?
Hey, Tiff?
No, it's Sophie.
Oh, hey. Congratulations with your game yesterday.
Thanks for coming to it! Hold on a sec.

Hello?
Tiff?
Hey, Venice.
Hey, about tomorrow--can someone else come?
Who? Your lover, Liam?
He's not my lover. I sighed. Do you mind if Raizel comes?
Um. She paused. I don't mind. But, like, can I be honest with you?
Yeah?
Can you not invite that Amara girl?
Okay. You really don't like her, hey?
Yeah. Something about her just bugs me.
That's okay.
Hey, I have an idea. Her voice suddenly perked up.
What's that?
Why don't we watch the movies at my place? We can probably use Sophie's TV.
Why? You don't like mine anymore? I teased.
No, it's just that Raizel seemed really interested in the hair salon. Maybe my mom will show it to her.
Aw. I smiled. That's so thoughtful of you.

I heard the static buzz of the living room TV turning, on, a distant hum. Noises penetrated the duplex's stale air, voices of characters and the show's background suspense-building music.

Riiiing. Riiiiiiing.
As much as I didn't want to, I *had* to dial Amara's number. I lay flat on my back and watched my bedroom light until my eyes gathered water.
Riiiiiing. Riiiiiing.
Yes! I was off the hook.
Hello?
Fuck.
Hey, Amara. I blinked the eye water away.
Who is this? A car honked behind her voice. Raizel?
No, it's Venice.
Oh my god! More honking. Sorry. What's up?

What're you doing?

I'm on the bus. On my way to Mars.

Oh. Working or partying?

Working. She sighed. I work, like, every weekend.

You mean you're working tomorrow night?

Yeah. Why? Her voice suddenly grew friendlier, like she was trying to stroke my jaw through the phone. You wanna come see me at work?

I thought about it. Mars was a fucking fantastic time, but I was being allotted the perfect way out.

I have a movie date with Tiff. As I said it, something made me neglect telling her Raizel was coming. I was going to invite you.

Aww. Come on. What's a better time--getting fucked up and dancing or sitting around watching movies?

Sorry. I made the commitment. She's my best friend.

Whatever. Hey, maybe I can get out of work tomorrow.

Shit.

Isn't Saturday, like, your best night for tips? A stab in the dark--I had no idea if she even made tips.

Yeah... She sighed again. Alright. Well, can you visit me at work tonight?

Ummm, sorry, I kind of have a headache. I'm really tired from working all day.

Sure you are. Amara hummed. What about Sunday?

Mind tired, guard down, I was unable to think of anything.

Sure, I guess so.

Finally, I could rest. My burnt Tegan and Sara CD had ended, so I replaced it with Ani. Invisible cigarette smoke traveled under my door and infected my things--my clothing, my curtains, my face. I closed my burning eyes.

RIIIIIIING!

For fuck's sake. I pressed TALK.

What? I snarled.

Hello? A man responded.

Hi?

It's Dana.

Oh. Hey.

Is something wrong?

I just--A pause here in an effort to soften my voice--I'm trying to sleep. And, like, fifty people called.

Sorry. I know how you get when you're tired.

Yeah. So how's life.

I'm all unpacked now. You guys should come check it out soon.

Sure, sure. I muttered, disbelieving the words even before they were out.

So, can I talk to Mom?

Hold on.

I pulled the comforter off my body and stumbled into the hallway.

Mom? I followed the smell of smoke.

I stood in the living room and held the cordless out for my mother, who sat with her back against the couch, eyes wide open, ashes on her cigarette having grown long.

I thought you were quitting.

She kept her eyes glued on the television.

MOM! I shouted

For fuck's sake! She shouted back, turning to slit her eyes at me.

In our home, my mother only swore when she was truly angry about something. As much as I wanted to reprimand her for having a potty mouth, I knew I was on testy waters.

What's wrong? I let my arm fall to my side, cordless a dead weight. Ninety-eight percent of me didn't *really* want to know what was wrong. Two percent was curious.

I come home and find you sleeping, and then you hog the phone all night. Who the fuck do you think pays the phone bill? And were you too busy to make me supper?

Uh… I swallowed. I hated rhetorical questions. I was working all day, too.

You think I can quit smoking when I'm so stressed out?

Nice to see you, too. Dana's on the phone. I tossed the cordless on the couch and it bounced on the taut cushion beside my mother.

Hello? She put on a polite façade, as though Dana hadn't heard our conversation.

I went back to my room to slam the door and lock it. I climbed into bed and let Ani hum beside me.

35

On Saturdays, my mother usually stayed home all day, festering in her nightgown and the television, meaning I *had* to go out. I couldn't stand the cracking sound her ankles made each time she went to the kitchen for a tea refill. I couldn't stand how her lips pinched together around her cigarette like she was eating a lemon.

After a brunch of Shreddies and the spoonful of milk left in the carton, I pulled on my winter coat and a neon scarf from nineteen eighty-three, just high enough to shield my ears from the wind.

Going to work, my peach? My mother glanced at me from the couch, her legs folded up in a nightgown afghan cocoon.

No. Just going out.

Okay. She gazed at me for a moment, the black rings under her eyes not doing her justice. Oh! Before I forget, Dana wants to know if we can eat supper with him Thursday night.

Where? At his new place? The words slid from my mouth as though tasting bad.

No, he's gonna come here with his girlfriend.

Girlfriend? I let my hand fall off the doorknob, turning to face my mother.

I know, right? Her eyes seemed to sparkle in the strip of sunlight through the living room curtains. Wouldn't that be a nice, to meet her and have a nice meal?

What's her name?

Molly.

Ew. I turned to the door again.

Try to come, okay? She looked back at the television. Book it off work.

My own Autumn-Afternoons-After-Graduation Plan:

I took the short bus ride to Team Bean, loving being greeted by bitter, rich aromas when I wasn't on shift. Three customers lingered in the lobby, two of whom looked about ready to go back to work, their jackets on and brief cases closed. The third customer was a white-haired lady in the sofa corner, resting her eyes while her tea cooled off.

Tiff and Meaghan leaned with their elbows on the front counter, ponytails dangling around their heads as they read opposing pages in a magazine. I looked down the long hallway behind them, noticing that Monica's office was dark.

Wow. I pulled my hands from my pocket to rest them on the counter. Busy day? It doesn't feel like Saturday.

Both girls looked up, wide-eyed. Tiff grinned. Meaghan quickly pulled the magazine off the counter, placing it near the coffee machines behind her.

Welcome to Team Bean, what can I get for you?

I felt my eyebrow rise involuntarily.

You don't remember me?

Meaghan cocked her head.

Psst. Tiff's elbow pressed into Meaghan's round side. She works here.

Oh my god. I'm sorry. Her cheeks turned a shade of red I'd not known was possible. Her chubby palm smoothed the dirty blond baby hairs missed by her ponytail. It's Vanessa, right?

Close. Tiff smiled.

Not even close! I slapped Tiff's bare forearm. It's Venice.

Oh, right. Meaghan nodded and smiled, once again letting her hand cover her teeth before they were revealed. Can I get you a coffee or something?

Yeah, I'll get an extra large dark roast.

Cream or sugar?

Four sweeteners. I eyed Tiff pointedly. She rubbed her arm where I'd hit her.

Coming right up. Meaghan turned to the coffee makers, taking one of the biggest paper cups of its stack.

Meaghan's mom subscribes to Cosmopolitan. Tiff grabbed the magazine from behind her, setting it on the counter between us. Did you know there are five hundred different ways to do it?

Do what? I smiled, glancing at the page. A woman and man lay in a pitch-white room, their feet tangled in bed sheets, private parts nearly exposed. They seemed to share a secret.

It. Meaghan looked pointedly over her shoulder, not realizing I was teasing.

Really? How many have you tried?

Meaghan couldn't have been older than twenty, but seemed even younger than Tiff and I, eyes widened in a display of innocence. She ignored my question and began typing something into the till.

You're gonna charge me? I wrapped my hands around the huge coffee, warming my wind-chapped skin.

It's half-price, right? Meaghan glanced at Tiff, who was enthralled a section of the article titled *The Red Rover.*

Tiff shrugged.

Come on, guys. Monica's not even here.

Okay, fine. But you have to leave a tip.

Here's a tip. I pulled my scarf back up around my ears. Try sucking his toes. Boys like that.

Really? Meaghan cocked her head again.

I laughed.

Venice? A man's voice was in my ear. Why, hello, dear.

I turned around, coffee in hand, to face an old man in a long parka, gray hair combed back. I got lost in the crows' feet behind his thick glasses and the brown sun marks on his skin.

Walter. I smiled. How are you?

After he'd ordered, I escorted Walter to his favorite table, the one near the window where he watched traffic and pedestrians.

Shaking hands slowly snapping buttons open, Walter successfully removed his coat. I mustered the courage to ask him something.

Walter, can I take a picture of you?

What's that, dear?

Well... I felt my cheeks become warm, pulling my backpack off my back. I have this new camera, and I was wondering...

Oh, my. Is that one of those computer cameras?

Yes, yes. Have you ever used one? I pressed POWER and handed the device across the table.

Why, you look so lovely. Let me see... Walter lifted his arms, steadying his trembling elbow on the window to focus.

With half a cup of coffee left, I caught the bus to the downtown library, the change in my wallet further diminishing. I'd have to hit an ATM, but at least renting from the library was free.

I walked in past the censor bars and dropped the DVDs Tiff and I had previously rented into the slot at the front counter, glancing at the elderly librarian. She eyed my coffee and I quickly turned away from her, breathing in the scents of paper and dust and perfume of housewives in the cookbook section. I made my way to the DVD aisle, turning my head sideways to read the labels.

After choosing a stack of DVDs, I remembered Raizel telling me she didn't like action movies, either. Jostling my coffee and the pile of thin, plastic boxes, I returned half of what I'd chosen. I ended up with two romantic comedies, one horror film, an inspirational sports movie, and one psychological thriller.

Let me help you with those. The librarian who had been eyeing me appeared, offering a plastic carrying basket like the kind used at grocery stores.

Oh. I smiled, dumping my selections in. I took the basket into my arms. Thank you. I like your glasses.

Oh? Thank you. The woman reached up to touch the fuchsia frames around her eyes. Then she turned to go, her flowery skirt waving as she moved. She reminded me of someone--perhaps a kindergarten teacher I'd had, or a friend's aunt.

Excuse me?

Yes? The woman looked over her shoulder.

Could you please tell me where the music is?

Go to the basement. She flashed me a rosey, lipstick-dressed smile.

Toting my basket with me, I went down the stairs at the back of library, into a brightly lit room. I couldn't believe how quiet that basement room was, besides the tapping of the desk woman's fingers on her computer keyboard and the soft flipping of the pages in books of sheet music.

The CDs greeted me immediately, a long row of drawers labeled as easily as possible, solely in alphabetical order. Someone, somewhere, agreed that not everything needed to be labeled by genre. I moseyed to first drawer and pulled up a squat, plastic stool.

BAM. Right in front of me was Alexisonfire, the album that had come out that fall, but which I hadn't even heard. I slowly placed it in my basket, along with Adele and Ani Difranco and the CD of a band I'd never heard of called Ask Amber.

By the time I'd finished looking through the C drawer, my basket was teeming with items, most of which I couldn't bare to leave behind. I lugged it, and my empty coffee cup, to the desk.

Excuse me. I whispered, trying not to blow coffee breath across the counter. Can you throw this out for me?

The young woman at the counter pointed at a trash bin near the room's entrance.

Oh. Okay. I continued whispering. And, how many CDs am I allowed to take out?

Wordlessly, she peered over the brim of my basket and began taking things out, dragging them across the censor on her desk. The only sound in the room was the beep of each bar code. Three CDs were left when the woman eyed the computer screen.

You've reached your limit. She spoke without whispering and began wrapping the CDs and DVDs in bundles with elastic bands. Return everything in a week, okay?

Sure. I replied easily, knowing I could just rip them all to my computer and enjoy them at a later date.

When I arrived at the downtown bus terminal, a great portion of the afternoon had passed. My stomach growled with every step and I considered stopping somewhere before my destination. One glimpse of Liam's and Raizel's car lined neatly on the sidewalk, and I couldn't wait to see my friends.

I pulled open the door of the pharmacy.

Hey, girlfriend! Liam waved over from the counter, whooping.

You're crazy! I wandered over, resting my plastic bag of library items on the counter. What's up?

Not much, Liam sang in his giddy voice.

Did you see Christopher today?

Maybe. It was the kind of maybe that definitely meant yes. Liam turned to the back of the store. RAIZEL! LOOK WHO'S HERE!

V!!!! I heard her squeak, from a hidden location. I craned my neck to get a better view of the store. A man perusing the chip selection looked up, ears perking at the commotion.

I found it hard to believe that only weeks earlier I'd been afraid of The Main Street Pharmacy, had found it to be an intimidating place.

Chris is on his way. Liam flicked his bangs away, revealing slightly made-up eyes. Oh my god. You can meet him!

I dunno if I'm gonna stick around. I clutched my stomach for emphasis. I'm really hungry.

RAIZEL, BRING US THE PHONE BOOK! Liam hollered.

The store's sole customer brought his Lays to the counter, digging in his pocket for money.

Here it is. Raizel appeared from the depths of an aisle, lugging Sloam's thick phonebook. She'd parted her hair on the far right, leaving the rest down and wavy. 'Sup, Venice?

Not much. You look cute.

Really? She fingered her locks. New hairstyle.

Mmhmm. I smiled, before pointing at her tights. Those are cute, too.

These old things? Raizel pulled the zebra-print stocking away from her skin before letting it snap back.

The door closed behind the man with the Lays, and then we were alone. I fought the urge to yell, the way Tiff and I had always joked in high school when my mother left the duplex--*Party!*

Ladies! Focus. Liam leaned over the counter and snapped his fingers, the metal of his rings flashing. Should we get Chinese or Vietnamese?

Whichever has debit on delivery. I patted my backpack.

Waiting for the food, the three of us sat on the milk crates at the back and smoked a fat one--a joint nearly as thick as my pinky finger. Liam had turned off the front lights, tricking customers into thinking the store was closed.

We put on one of the CDs I'd borrowed from the library, something called Crocodile Attack. We fell laughing off milk crates when it turned out to be the soundtrack of a kids' movie, and switched it with Atmosphere. Liam wanted to throw Crocodile Attack out the door, but stopped when I told him I'd have to steal his identity for a new library card.

We ate spring rolls and noodles and fried rice and deep fried shrimp dipped in plum sauce. The crazy thing was that, after I'd eaten double what I normally would, my fingers kept picking at everything and bringing bits to my mouth. The three of us soon found ourselves in sloth-mode, hands folded over our robust bellies.

I'm pregnant. Liam's belch cut the air. I'm gonna have a food baby. Due date is in one hour.

I wonder what it's like to pregnant. As Raizel spoke, smoke wafted out of her nostrils. She gazed at the ceiling, hand idly passing a newly lit joint to Liam.

Yeah. Liam nodded, taking the stick. He sucked the end, embers momentarily glowing orange. I wonder if it makes you feel, like, *whole*.

You'd always get a seat on the bus, I piped up.

Liam and Raizel looked at each other and laughed.

Do you guys want kids? I asked softly, unsure if it was a taboo subject in the gay community. I accepted the joint from Liam.

Of course. Raizel smiled, labret ring bobbing. I want lots of kids. But I don't want to be one of those super overprotective mothers who makes her kids call her all the time.

I looked at the floor and wondered if they ever swept it, noticing crumbs and bits of dirt. As far as I knew, their boss never made them do anything.

I wonder if Christopher wants kids. Liam spoke dreamily, imagination seeming to lilt in the air with the curlicues of marijuana. He suddenly snapped to reality. Speaking of which--where is he?

When Raizel's shift ended, we hugged Liam, whose lover had never shown up. We said goodbye and dodged through the chilled air to the Camaro.

What should we bring over? Raizel twisted to pick her CD book up off the floor in the back seat.

Oh, nothing. They usually have a pantry full of goodies. I reached into my library bag. Here--why don't we put this in?

What's that? She took the CD case from me. The Butchies??

Yeah. I laughed, having rented the CD solely for her sake. I thought you'd like them.

Actually, I kind of do. She nodded, pushing the disc in the player.

Oh, you've heard them before?

Well, a really good song of theirs is on The L Word.

Is that a movie?

Oh, my dear. She laughed.

Recalling the first time I'd ridden in Raizel's car, I realized I no longer felt the need to curl shamefully into my seat when she laughed.

36

We pulled up outside of Tiff's with a bag of stuff from the Oakwood 7-11, Raizel having convinced me it was the polite thing to do. I suspected she was secretly in the mood for munchies, coming off her weed high. She'd tried to pay for everything, but I'd insisted on paying half. I longed to zip into the future to the day when I'd receive my six-figure salary and pay for everything for everyone I knew.

Okay, do we smell like smoke? I took my seatbelt off and turned to face Raizel. Outside, the ground was dark, the sun having fallen for the night.

No--why would we? Raizel undid her own seatbelt.

I mean, from the pot?

Oh, no. That smells usually goes away after an hour.

Suddenly, she put her hand around the back of my neck, frosty fingers jolting my skin. She pulled me toward her and sniffed the collar of my jacket.

You're good. A smile hid under the twitching sides of her lips. Why are you so worried, anyway?

I don't want Tiff's mom to know.

She won't.

We got out of the car and lugged everything around to the back door.

Holy shit! Tiff exclaimed as she opened the door, eyeing our snack-filled arms. We had potato wedges, tortilla chips and salsa, Sunchips, Pringles, Fuzzy Peaches, and a tray of Slurpees.

I slipped out of my shoes. Raizel copied, following me up the short landing into the Abraham family's immaculate kitchen. Wordless, we padded down the hall to Tiff's sister Sophie's room. When the light flipped on, my eyes were immediately drawn to the photo-covered walls, courtesy of her Wal-mart employee discount. I wished I could afford to do such a thing with my *own* bedroom.

This isn't my room, Tiff said quickly, kicking a pair of her sister's jeans toward the closet door. It's so messy.

Are you kidding? Raizel laughed, looking around. She perched gingerly on the edge of the made bed.

Yeah. I giggled. You should see Raizel's room.

Raizel stuck her tongue out at me.

Oh, yeah? Tiff smiled. I bet it's cool, though. My sister is *so* weird.

This one, right? Raizel pointed at a photograph taped to the wall, one of Sophie and her ringette team.

Yeah.

Tiff? Pamela Abraham's headed poked in through Sophie's bedroom door. Her eyes lit up when she saw Raizel. She stepped into the room. Oh! Hi! I'm Pam.

I'm Raizel. Raizel reached forward and shook hands with Tiff's mother.

Well, it's *so* nice to meet you. Pam grinned, eyes trained on Raizel.

I stared at the floor, praying Pam wouldn't notice the stoned redness of Raizel's eyes.

You too, Pamela. Raizel smiled, not knowing exactly how nice it was for Pam to see Tiff making new friends.

Well, which movies did you get? Tiff glanced at me before shuffling awkwardly to the TV stand in the corner. She gave her mother The Look, but Pam continued gazing at Raizel.

Has anyone ever told you you have the *prettiest* hair color?

Not quite. Raizel smiled lazily.

And, *you,* my dear. Pam turned my way. Your roots are coming in nicely.

Thanks. I held my breath, hoping all remnants of our skunky perfume had truly vanished.

What's that smell? Tiff piped up, nose wrinkling under her glasses.

What smell? I stepped away from her, sniffing deeply for emphasis.

Raizel's face remained calm while I unzipped my coat and slid it on the floor near the closet.

It smells good. Like... Tiff wiggled her nose like a rabbit. Like Chinese food.

Raizel grinned.

I breathed out.

Oh my GOD! Pam glanced at the bags on the bed, next to Raizel. Are you girls really going to eat all that junk?

The three of us perched on the edge of the bed, Raizel to my right and Tiff to my left, watching Pretty Woman with the chips in bowls before us. We laughed in unison at all the right parts. I wondered if Raizel felt uncomfortable watching a heterosexual romance film.

Such thoughts diminished as we all came to stretch out on our stomachs, hugging Sophie's pillows, eyes widening at the movie's climax. It wasn't at all like watching television with my family, plugging my nose when my mother lit up, ignoring Dana while he picked his toenails. Scraping the bottom of my soup bowl in desperation for flavor.

After the movie, I was certain Raizel had had enough--one could only spend so much time with Tiffany Abraham. But I was the first one to throw my jacket on and ended up waiting while Raizel's eyes wandered up Sophie's wall of photos.

We carted the food wrappers and empty chip bowls--we'd devoured everything--down the hall to the kitchen. Ten o' clock had rolled around, the window over the sink presenting us with a sea of blackness. Tiff's mom came bumbling up the stairs.

Oh, hi, girls. Hey, Raizel, Tiff told me you want to be a hairdresser. Do you want a tour of my salon?

Yes. Very much so. Raizel glanced at me. I'll be right back, okay?

They disappeared into the portal of perm fumes and heartfelt pop tunes.

I sighed and pulled a chair away from the kitchen table. I rested my forehead in my hands.

Why are you in such a hurry to leave?

Huh? I looked up at Tiff, who leaned against the kitchen counter with her arms crossed. I'm just tired.

So, you got a Facebook account?

Yeah. Just to post some pictures I took.

I know. I saw them. Tiff began chewing her pinky fingernail. By the way, accept my friend request.

I will. But how did you see the pictures if we're not friends on there yet?

You didn't make them private.

Oh. Well?

Okay, fine. Tiff pulled her hand away from her face, holding it up in defeat. The pictures were fucking fabulous.

Aha! Which ones did you like?

Lots of them were good. I have to say that one of your models seemed more…together. She pointed at the kitchen floor, meaning the girl below us, wandering around her basement.

Suddenly the outside door pushed open, following by a whoosh of frigid air and a woman with a long, red ponytail much like Tiff's. Sophie Abraham slammed the door and stamped her feet on the welcome mat, seemingly trying to will blood back into them.

Oh. It's *you.* Tiff pulled her arms up, shielding her own body from the outside air.

Hey, Sophie. I offered a smile.

Hey, guys. Sophie began unzipping her coat, tomato-red fingers slowing the process. It's *so* cold out.

Wuss. Tiff punched her sister's jacket-padded shoulder. Do you complain to your teammates when you're on the ice?

Ha. Ha. At a loss for a good comeback, Sophie scrambled out of her coat and hung it over the back of the chair beside me.

Raizel pushed open the basement door and stepped up into the kitchen, followed by a proudly glowing Pam Abraham.

Oh. Hi. Sophie turned toward her mother and the strange girl with the white-blond hair. She slit her eyes. You look familiar. What's your name?

I'm Raizel. Raizel wore her eye-catching smile, one that could undoubtedly coerce police officers into vetoing speeding tickets.

We stood around talking for a moment before I made the first move, inching toward the door. I slipped into my high tops before we'd even announced we were leaving.

Bye! Nice meeting you!

You too!

Thanks for coming!

Thanks for having me!

Call you tomorrow!

We skipped down the steps of the small house and ran around front. Raizel kicked through the leaves on the lawn, unaware of how many times Pamela Abraham had begged her daughters and their friends to use the walkway.

V?

Yeah?

You wanna try driving?

Um. We stopped walking, feet away from the Camaro. I can't.

You don't wanna learn? Raizel grinned, pea-coat rising as she bunched her shoulders around her neck. Is there a parking lot or something around here?

Sure. I gave in, smiling back.

Flip flip flip. My stomach.

I directed Raizel toward St. Timothy's Catholic High School. As it was a Saturday night, the parking lot was entirely empty, a flat black expanse of concrete.

We got out of the car, crossing each others' paths at the hood. In the light of the parking lot lamps, I flashed Raizel a mischievous grin solely so she'd wonder if she was making a mistake.

Okay. First, do up your seatbelt.

Okay. I giggled. You'd better put on yours, too. Now what?

Adjust the seat. Can you reach the pedals?

Yeah. And then some. How do I--Oh, this bar thing on the side, right? As I pulled the cold metal stick to the left of me, my seat inched back. Okay. Perfect.

Adjust the mirror so you can see behind you.

Check.

Here's the key. Put it in the ignition and turn it.

I took the metallic key from her. I did as she'd instructed. The car came alive under us, the engine coughing slightly before coming to a smooth rumble. The headlights came on automatically, spreading a carpet of light across the parking lot before us.

After ten minutes of jerking forward, stalling, turning the engine back on, and laughing nervously, I was ready to quit.

Come on, V, keep trying. Push the gas harder right from the beginning.

I followed her instructions. We lurched into motion before the car went silent.

I'm just not cut out for this. I gazed at my hands on the steering wheel, hoping she couldn't see my red cheeks in the dark.

Just try *once* more. This time, let the clutch go as slowly as possible. And go heavy on the gas.

I sighed, igniting the engine again. I pressed the gas pedal and a sound like thunder surrounded us. The noisy squeal of car tires filled the air as I eased off the clutch. We crawled forward. Going fifteen, I kept a steady pace, steering around the lot.

Good job! Okay! Now press the clutch and put your hand on the gear shift.

Her hand fell like a claw over mine, gripping hard. Together, we yanked the gear shift into its second position.

Gas! Gas!

We shot forward again, but didn't come to a halt as had been happening the whole time. Something came over me and I pulled on the steering wheel, a sharp turn. Beside me, Raizel laughed and bumped against the passenger seat door.

I was flying.

We came to a stop directly in front of the high school's front entrance, the car's lights illuminating the building. Over the glass doors stood a robust white statue of a cross and the school's name--St. Timothy's Catholic High School.

Dude. Raizel peered out the windshield. Was this *your* school?

Kind of. For a year.

And then what?

I switched to Milton Wrights.

Oh. Raizel relaxed into her seat.

Where did you go?

Duhill.

Cool. I nodded, eyeing her labret ring. Hey, I wanna get something pierced. Maybe my eyebrow. Do you know a good place?

Well, I got my labret done at this place called Tatty Land.

Tatty, as in tattoo?

Yup.

So, can I ask you something else?

Shoot.

What does *your* tattoo mean?

Raizel cocked her head, white-blond locks nearly glowing through the night air between us.

Or, you don't have to tell me. I shrugged.

It's kind of a heavy story. She held up her arm and pulled back the leather bracelets on the inside of her wrist.

I couldn't believe I'd never noticed it before--a bold, black symbol written in an Oriental language.

Is it about Ha Na? Uttering the words, I felt like punching myself in the teeth.

Huh? Raizel's eyes widened and she let her wrist fall to her side. How do you know about Ha Na?

I dunno. Inside my shoes, my toes pinched each other. I've just heard things.

It's not about Ha Na. Why would you think that?

Well, it's, like, an Asian character.

Fair enough. Raizel's eyes softened. She brought her wrist up to gaze at it again, forefinger stroking the skin. But Ha Na's Japanese. This is Korean. It's for Amara.

Really? Does she have one, too?

No.

Does it mean 'love'?

Raizel chuckled, her mouth stretching wide across her face.

I wasn't in love with her.

I see. My toes loosened, inside my high tops. What does it mean, then?

It means 'strength'. I got it when Amara had problems, you know, to help her out.

What kind of problems? I asked, though I was sure she meant an eating disorder.

Sorry. I feel weird talking about this with you.

Don't be. I won't say anything.

Promise?

Promise. I held up my pinky.

Raizel accepted, winding her own small pinky around mine and shaking.

Amara used to be addicted to coke.

The air in the car suddenly felt dead. If it was summer, I would have been comforted by crickets outside humming their song. There was nothing but the noise of her breathing and mine. The night of Morgan's, Raizel and Liam had asked me to lie to Amara, and I'd been the one to mention coke. I was so fucking dense.

When did she…stop? Amara flashed into my mind, an image of her bent over in the bathroom at the rink, a key full of coke near her nose.

After I broke up with her. But even though we're not together, I have to be there for her. Liam and I are pretty much the only solid rocks in her life. And I guess you, now.

I guess. I got an image in my mind of my own hand dipping the key in the bag before drawing the coke toward my face. I'm not that close with her.

Aren't you together? Like, girlfriend and girlfriend?

What? Me and Amara? I shook my head forcefully. No no, nothing like that.

Are you kidding me? She's telling *everyone* you're her girlfriend.

37

I awoke to an empty house, silent but for the ticking clock on the kitchen wall. My mother had probably gone to run errands. I moved into the living room and peeked through the picture window curtains, discovering an empty driveway.

Throughout the night, something white and pure had appeared, on the roof of the house across the street, on the tops branches of the dead trees lining the field, covering the sidewalk and our tiny front lawn.

I grabbed my camera from my room and, in my sleeping shirt, slipped into my sneakers. I went onto the front steps, the snow's brightness blasting my pupils. I didn't feel the goose-bumps my uncovered skin was surely gathering. I didn't acknowledge the elderly couple across the street pointing at me out their front room window. I turned off the flash on my camera and snapped pictures. The first snowfall of winter was always the best, inexplicably soft and clean.

That night I walked to the 7-11 for a bottle of Diet Coke, slipping into the kitchen when I got home. I looked under the sink and, as I'd suspected, found more than half a bottle of rum left from the time I'd cooked dinner for everyone. I had bought it for my mother with my first tip ever, which meant she couldn't protest if I borrowed some back. I poured out a quarter of my soda and replaced it with the potent liquid.

I lay atop the scrambled blankets on my bed and sucked the concoction, wincing every time my tongue met the bottle opening. I took my camera out of my backpack and flipped through the pictures.

I paused when I got to the photo Walter had taken of me, a close-up of my face. I'd tried to put on the blankest facial expression, a stone called Venice.

My eyes seemed alive, silvery irises catching the light from the window beside us. My hair looked bright and my skin glowed. Seemingly, the only fault with the photo was the pursing of my peach-hued lips. I pouted at the photo, making fun of myself. I couldn't believe I didn't look fat.

I swigged the tainted Diet Coke, my mouth having accepted the bitter bite of rum.

Around nine o' clock I heard my mother move from the living room to her bedroom bathroom. Feeling in a surprisingly bright mood, I left a note on the living room coffee table.

Gone out. Call you later. Your peach, Venice.

I wrapped my scarf around my face and got on the bus, sitting at the back. I took small sips in an effort to draw out the lifespan of my drink. Broken Social Scene, which I'd never heard of but had borrowed from the library, blasted in my ear. The first few songs were instrumental, reminding me of The Silly

Rainbows. I wondered if I'd ever get to see any of my new favorite artists in concert. I'd never been to a concert, besides some random guys called The Things coming to our school in the sixth grade. I'd never been to a *real* concert, not even to see Dallas Green.

The bus looped through Broadway, a few blocks away from Phantom Cinema where Dana worked. The night was young and I could have gone to see him, to say hi and score free popcorn. But the last time I'd gone to visit him, nearly six months earlier, he'd been too busy ripping ticket stubs at the admission stand to say anything more than:

Hey, Venice. Enjoy the show.

I let the bus take me across the bridge over the river, heading downtown. We came to a stop in the bus terminal and I peeked shyly toward the corner pharmacy, the lights of which were off. Probably everyone had gone home for the night. I sniffed and turned the other way, stalking down Main Street with the ends of my scarf flapping against my back. When I finally saw the discreet sign for Mars I wondered if, long ago, when the idea of a gay bar had come up, someone had suggested hiding it and its patrons in that alley where it would hardly be noticed.

I approached the bar in my tipsy swagger, bass bumping against the walls of the building, trying to get out. Because I didn't have a cell phone, I stopped at the payphones outside the front entrance, throwing in a dirty quarter. Beside me, a line was forming in the bar's doorway.

Riiiiing. Riiiing.

Hello? Amara called into her cell phone.

Amara! It's me.

Venice? Is that you?

Yeah. I glanced at the line to get in, noticing a big bouncer perched on a stool, back to me. I tried to keep my voice down. Should I come around back?

Huh? Just go to the back door, okay? I'll be right there.

Moments later, Amara and I were hopping over the boxes in the dark back hallway. The office door was closed, giving no apparent chance for the manager of the place to catch us. We skipped past the kitchen. Amara held my hand tightly and I let her lead me, pull me, invite me in through the swinging doors with the little, circle windows.

The dim lights of the room allowed me to see Amara, her puff of tightly curled hair surrounding her smiling face. She had on the tiny white dress she'd been wearing the night Raizel and Liam and I had come over after Morgan's, and the white braided headband. Instead of her usual sky-high heels, she had on white ballet slippers, ribbons winding halfway up her dark shins.

You look innocent, I said, trying to talk over the music.

Huh? Amara leaned toward me, her hair brushing the side of my ear.

I said you look nice.

I'm so glad you came. Her smiled widened and she squeezed my hand. Take this.

I felt the pill drop from between her forefinger and thumb into my palm. I closed my hand.

The club wasn't as crowded as it'd been on Halloween, yet we found ourselves squeezing through warm bodies to get our drinks. Amara scored us each a free rum 'n' Coke from the bar, short glasses that'd probably be gone in an instant, especially through straws. We didn't bother mingling with the crowd on the first floor, the middle-aged men with their hints of mustaches and tight shirts encasing their chests.

As we walked through the wide glow-paint hallway, I felt as if the colors had faded. I rubbed my eyes with closed fists. The stars in the remodeled theater didn't play with my pupils in such a stunning matter as they had; in fact, they seemed misplaced on the ceiling above the crowd of bobbing heads.

But the music was alive; I moved through the room with the beat coming up through my legs, into my torso and down to my fingertips. I rolled Amara's pill around in my closed hand.

Hey!

I felt someone touch my elbow, through my coat. Ahead of me, Amara didn't look back, letting go of my hand. She weaved through the dancing crowd. Sure I'd been caught, I yanked my elbow away and turned around.

Your name's Venice, right? A boy with a dark tan leaned into to yell in my ear.

Yeah. I turned my head away from his beer breath. You're Robby, right?

He was the boy I'd met at Amara's, the one with the graffiti tattoo spanning his back.

That's right. You wanna dance?

Sorry, I came here to see Amara. I motioned toward the crowd. And I think I just lost her.

Is she working?

Yeah.

It occurred to me that there wasn't a bar or beer tub in the room; nor were there any tables to clear.

You don't really get to hang out with her, then. Robby informed me. You just get to watch her.

Huh?

Robby linked arms with me, escorting me through the crowd of what I'd always assumed would solely be manly women and womanly men. They were people--in one second I saw two blond girls kissing, in another I saw a short man dancing alone. I wondered if he was waiting for someone. I wondered if anyone in the crowd had met daisy that night, as they all seemed to be thoroughly enjoying themselves.

Gay--adj. Full of joy.

When we made it close to the DJ's end of the room, Amara was nowhere to be seen. The music pounded in our eardrums, daring us to dance. I looked around, wondering how she could ditch me after practically begging me to come. I decided to go home and listen to some more of my new CDs.

Robby nudged my side with his muscular arm. I followed his gaze up to the stage by the DJ's booth, beside which stood a birdcage just big enough for a person or two.

Amara had climbed into the cage through a door in the back, coming to stand in the middle with her hands poised over her head, nearly revealing her underwear. I wondered if she had on her flashy green panties. She looked like a real ballerina, ankles crossed and toes pointed effortlessly. I popped the pill she'd given me into my mouth, taking a long suck of rum.

Huh. She's here. The DJ leaned over to whisper into his microphone, the amps letting his voice cascade over the crowd.

A-A-A! The DJ called, one A per beat. A red spotlight moved across the room, landing on Amara. She'd put something in her afro to make it sparkle as it caught the light. Slowly, one of her legs came out from her body, grasshopper-like, her foot coming to rest on the inner thigh of her other leg. Around me, people cheered, watching her while they moved their own bodies and sucked their drinks.

M-M-M! Amara's foot came off of her thigh, the ribbons of her slipper shining under the spotlight. She lifted the leg higher, bent up near her stomach.

A-A-A! Her arms moved from their position above her head, grasping metal bars on opposite sides of the cage. The leg began to straighten, upwards.

By that time, everyone in the room could've confirmed that Amara had on white underwear. I couldn't help but look at the smooth skin around the tops of her thighs. The leg left holding the rest of her up was a sturdy stick, unwavering as she moved. My legs had probably never looked that great, even as a child.

RA! RA! RA! Her right leg shot up, knee nearing her nose, pointed toes flying. She used her to arms to give a mighty push, twirling around. So *that* was how she had muscles. The room exploded in cheers. The people dancing nearest the cage reached their hands through the poles, dropping coins in a metal box fastened to the cage's side. Tips.

Peoples' clapping hands fell slowly as they returned to their dancing and their groups of friends.

I began feeling funny, the condensation around the outside of my glass slipping down the backs of my fingers. I looked to my side, straight into a puff that was some girl's teased hairdo. Robby was gone. I inched toward the speaker and bent, leaving my glass on the floor. I hadn't even finished it. I swore I was sweating like a pig, but when I touched my forehead, my hand came down dry. I still had on my coat.

When I looked back at the cage, the spotlight had diminished and both of Amara's legs were down. She swayed freely. She looked as if she may be feeling the way I did. I wondered if the tip of her tongue was numb. I wondered if a helium balloon had gotten stuck under her heart.

I noticed Amara's pinky finger catching on the bottom edge of her dress every time she moved her arm, lifting the hem slightly.

I moved my own fingers, ensuring myself they were still there. I undid my jacket and left it in a black pile beside my drink and the speaker. I wanted to cheer the DJ on like others, to bop my open hands to the music, but I felt as though everyone was looking at me.

I had to talk to Amara. I lifted my arm and waved it at her. When she didn't notice me, I moved closer to the cage and stuck my arm between two poles, touching her ankle. She winced away as if a mouse had touched her. Then her eyes trained on me and she motioned for me to come closer.

I hoisted myself onto the platform and scampered to the back of the birdcage. Amara held the door open and tugged me in by the collar of my shirt.

Is this your *job?* I shouted near her ear, disbelieving such a thing had never come up in conversation. My words went buzzing around the cage's metal rungs. If the floor was soft I would have lain down. A sofa would have been nice.

Yeah, baby. Amara put her arms on either side of my head, grabbing the poles behind me.

I felt the cold of the metal through the back of my shirt, letting my body rest as it'd been placed. I giggled. My voice lay under the noise of the room, roots under a tree.

I watched Amara as she closed her eyes and let her body flow down, a waterfall, lower legs bound tightly in their ribbon. Her body rubbed against mine as she came back up, dress material having shifted so I could nearly see her chest. As her hip pressed into mine, I looked down over her body.

She pressed her mouth into my ear, warm breath.

Dance.

The DJ had put on a song with a slower beat, something to slow my racing heart. Over the drumming, someone whistled. I imagined the track had been recorded from an old man plowing a field.

I swayed, my foot hitting her tip box, which seemed fastened securely to the metal rungs.

Amara grabbed my arms and put them in the sky. Her fingers trailed my skin. She turned her back to me and looked over her shoulder at my face. I kept my arms up and moved my lower body against her. She had cat eyes. Until then, I hadn't noticed how long her lashes were.

I put my face in her hair and smelled her world.

She tore away from my daydream, grabbing the poles on the opposite side of the cage. Amara faced me and danced, coming up on her toes with her eyes shut. Then she put her head down, lower and lower. Her 'fro flipped as she shot back up, pushing her chest toward me. Her body was liquid, moving freely, effortlessly.

I felt the overwhelming urge to slip her braided headband off her head, like I'd done once before. I couldn't keep my eyes off of her.

38

When Amara had been dancing for fifteen minutes, she was allowed a half-hour break. Fifteen on, thirty off, fifteen on, thirty off, so on and so forth. That seemed like a great deal. I hopped off the stage and offered my hand up to her, helping her down. We pranced through the crowd and downstairs.

On the first floor, I kept dancing while Amara went behind the bar for new drinks. While we'd been upstairs, the place had gathered an array of older people, lingering around the tall tables. Some of them danced, but mostly they just sipped drinks and had drunken conversations punctuated by winks. I got the sensation that they were watching me, but I couldn't care. When I danced, my body was centered.

Excuse me.

Oh, sorry. I moved to the side, letting someone squeeze by me.

Actually, I wanna talk to you.

I moved my eyes up, coming in contact with those of a petite woman with short, black hair. Wrinkles around her eyes hinted at her age; she must have been older than my mother.

Hi. I smiled, stopping dancing.

You're a great dancer. The woman smiled back, soft kindness in her eyes.

Thank you. I glanced at the bar, which had gathered swarms of people. Shit. Amara would probably be a while.

What's your name, sweetie?

I'm Venice. I realized I didn't have to back away from her beer breath, for she didn't smell of alcohol.

Wow. That's pretty. I'm Ilene.

I lifted my sweating hand from my side to meet hers and shake heartily. I continued dancing, moving my hips slightly.

Ilene watched me, dark eyes traveling my body. I couldn't tell if she was a creep or I was experiencing drug-induced paranoia. I closed my eyes.

Hey, babe. Amara walked up behind me. She handed me a drink identical to the one I'd had before.

Amara, baby! Ilene cried. You look beautiful!

Ilene! Amara grinned. I wondered when I'd see you.

I sipped my drink, letting my eyes flit between the two of them.

You're not drinking, are you? Ilene nodded at Amara's hands.

No, no. Amara smiled, holding her drink up. These are both for her.

Oh, god. On top of her coke problem, Amara couldn't drink, either.

Venice, this is my *boss*, Ilene.

Ohh. I grinned, sipping more of my icy drink, cooling my throat.

We just met. Ilene smiled. Would you mind coming to my office?

Oh, fuck. I looked around for a way out. She knew I was a minor. She knew I was high.

I left my jacket upstairs. I'll be right back, okay?

It'll be okay. Amara touched my forearm, deep eyes piercing me. Come on.

We followed Ilene through the swinging doors, music muted ever so slightly behind us. I feigned curiosity, glancing into the kitchen as though I'd never seen it before.

Have a seat. Ilene closed her office door and walked around to her side of the desk.

I wanted to laugh when I remembered her Santa costume. She had truly looked like a fat old man.

Amara and I plopped into the two orange, cushioned chairs opposite of Ilene. I squinted, letting my eyes adjust to the bright overhead light. I hoped Ilene wouldn't look straight into my pupils.

So, Venice. Ilene crossed her hands on the desk top. What do you like doing?

Um, I like photography. You?

She laughed, showing her whole jaw of neat, white teeth.

What else?

I like getting so fucked up I can't see. I like when my fingers buzz and my body moves without my mind.

I guess I like...watching movies. Oh, and of course I *love* music.

That's good. So, straight to the point--are you interested in working for me?

HMM??? I sucked back the rest of my drink, the straw creating a whirring suction noise. I set the glass on the desk. Are you serious? What kind of work?

Beside me, Amara grinned. I tapped my shoe against the metal leg of my chair.

Whatever you want. You seem to like dancing.

That would be *awesome*. Amara piped up.

I stopped tapping the chair with my foot. I hid my moving fingers under my thighs.

I'll pay you twelve an hour, cash.

I stopped my mouth from dropping open. That was a hell of a lot more than I made at Team Bean, and seemingly way less work.

Wait--why cash?

It's easier. I'm the owner, and it's a private club, so I do what I want. Oh, plus you'd make tips.

Sorry. I shook my head. I already have a job.

I understand. Ilene nodded.

I don't. Amara frowned.

I shook hands with Ilene again and we left her office, going back down the hall. Amara took my hand and dragged me to the sofas near the bottom of the spiral stairs. *The makeout couches*, I remembered her telling me on Halloween. I let my eyes scan her body, wondering what she wanted to do. I barely even know what two girls *could* do together. We sat with our knees touching, facing each other.

Are you crazy?! Amara exclaimed, eyebrows riding up her forehead. One of her dress straps had slipped down her shoulder. Why would you pass up on this opportunity?

Because, Amara. I wrung my fingers together like a wet dishcloth. I'm only seventeen.

So? It's called a fake ID. Amara pulled up her dress strap. Some of her hair sparkles fell, glittering in the air around us.

Where am I supposed to get that?

I don't know…I'm sure we could find one.

This daisy's really weird. I changed the subject. I held my hand up, watching the tiniest tremble run through it. Bang bang bang. My heart sped up, wanting to catch a ride with the beat of the music. Everything felt out of sync.

It's not daisy. Amara sighed. Haven't you ever done Ritalin?

I'd heard of kids taking Ritalin in high school, but had never believed it would do more than make me hyper. My heart pounded furiously. I floated up to the starry room and retrieved my jacket, the whole right sleeve having gathered dusty footprints. Amara eyed from her gigantic birdcage. The music raped my eardrums.

I pretended I didn't hear Robby calling my name as I left the room. I left the club out the front door, hiding my face from the bouncer.

Outside Mars I leaned up against the dark alley wall beside a crowd of smoking boys. I put my palm on my forehead, enjoying the coolness, trying to soothe my racing heart.

Are you okay, honey? One of the boys asked.

I kept my rum-tipsy head down, lower and lower until I got sick on the pavement, a liquid pile that steamed in the year's first inch of snow.

Oh my god, I heard the boy say to his friends. Ew.

My eyes stayed on the ground, watching fiery orange cigarette butts land beside my supper.

Then I was alone.

39

On Monday morning, I recovered. I took a Tylenol and lay on the basement sofa, a steaming mug of tea on the table before me.

I worked from noon to five at Patty's side. She talked to me about her dog for an hour before I walked away. She followed me to the hand-washing station and asked if I was feeling okay. I told her I was just tired.

Tired of listening to you, I fought the urge to say.

I went straight to bed after work, ignoring my mother when she hollered for me to help with the groceries. I heard her once an hour later, telling me Amara was on the phone. I kept my eyes closed when she peeked into my room.

I swore I heard music in my dream. Raizel and I were in her Camaro, but I wasn't driving. We just went around town and talked. She told me she used to be a dragonfly. I told her I liked dragonflies. I couldn't make out who was singing on the car stereo, so I played with the volume. It got louder and louder until I realized I was the one singing.

The dream was so vivid that I awoke confused about my own bedroom and the Tuesday morning sun greeting my curtains.

It's June of grade ten and Tiff has noticed Oliver, who's a year older. She likes him so much that she's been dreaming about him. Now she's obsessed with dreams. She starts researching dreams on the computer and scouring our school library for information. When she's not satisfied, we plan a trip to the bag, magnificent old downtown library. That day, she reads things aloud to me on the bus ride home--the different meanings of different events in dreams.

Everything white means you're going to die. Losing your teeth means someone you know is going to die. A happy peacock symbolizes lost love. Wow. She closes the book and deadpans me with her green eyes. It's weird that peoples' subconscious minds know these things before we've even realized them. I mean, *love?* It's just crazy.

I don't buy it, any of it. We're all going to die, Tiff.

Obviously, Venice. But the dreams can tell us that, too.

And everyone loses someone they know. It's a part of life.

Duh. Tiff refuses to step down from her silly new belief system. What about love? What do you have to say about that, Smarty-pants?

With that, she puts me in my place, as she knows I've only ever been an official couple with Gus Jenkins and that I certainly never loved him.

Going even further back--April of tenth grade, and I'm at a pep rally. Tiff's reading a book to my right, and the chair on my left is empty. We're waiting for the volleyball coach to finish announcing the thirty players' names.

All of a sudden this tall guy with hints of dark facial hair plops into the empty seat. He just plunks down and gets comfortable, his warm arm rubbing against mine. His calves, covered in hair, poke out from the bottoms of his long shorts. He turns to me and complains about the bleacher chairs. No 'hi', 'nice to meet you', or 'my name's Gus'.

These chairs are too fucking small. He rubs his hint-of-a-beard. For me, anyway, not for tiny chicks like you.

I'm extremely flattered. We joke around for the whole pep rally. The next day at lunch-time when Tiff and I walk by Gus and his friends, he hollers at me.

Hey, you! What's your number?

I dictate my home phone number while he writes it on the rubber side of his size-fourteen basketball runners.

Gus and I start hanging out at lunch-time, when he's not at basketball practice. But I'm not the kind of girl who'll ditch her best friend for her boyfriend. Most nights, Tiff and I still hang out in my family's basement. She *always* asks me details.

Have you kissed him yet?

What does it feel like?

Does he every try--you know--

She asks such questions with a far-out look in her eyes, probably using the details of my life, but replacing Gus and I with her and Oliver. Living vicariously through me. I stop telling her things, even when Gus undoes my jeans on the soccer field one lunch period and starts touching me, right there where kids a hundred feet away might be watching. I don't touch him back. I don't know what to do with his hairy body. With one look at his shorts, I can see how he feels.

One day Gus asks me to go out with him, on a real date. He says he wants to treat his girlfriend right, take her to a movie or something. And so, that's that--we are boyfriend and girlfriend, something I've been wondering about. Gus also wants to bring his best buddy Darrell to the movie, and asks if I can please get Tiffany Abraham to come. I tell him she's socially inept, and I feel bad saying such a thing about her, but it's true. I guess I don't want Darrell to get his hopes up. Gus says Darrell's super into Tiff and probably nothing about her could disappoint him. I think that's sweet, and Darrell's kind of cute, so I agree.

We end up going to Phantom Cinema, where my brother Dana has just started working, because he has promised us all a family-members-of-staff discount. Tiff and I meet Gus and Darrell by the popcorn stand, but none of us has jobs so we don't get anything. The boys buy four tickets for some medieval movie and we thank them profusely, giggling together as we lead them into the dark theater. We sit in this order--Tiff, Darrell, Gus, me--the perfect double-date.

During the previews Gus grabs my hand and pecks my cheek, saying he's glad I'm his girl. I smile and lean my head on his shoulder even though I have to strain my neck. I'm too shy to say I'm uncomfortable so I lift my head and look down the row. Darrell and Tiff have their heads close together, deep in conversation. I hear Tiff laugh and something flutters in my heart; perhaps she's interested in Darrell. How perfect would it be--two best friends and two other best friends hitting it off? Maybe we're all meant for each other, maybe we'll all get married and get pregnant and give birth on the *exact* same day, and maybe our kids will like each other, too.

We're halfway through the movie when Gus starts laying the moves on, putting his arm around me and kissing my neck. He knows what excites me. The theater is about half-full, but we're in the dark back row, so I don't give a shit. I close my eyes and let Gus touch me the way he's been doing at school noon hour. I like how the elastic of my sweats and panties scolds his wrist. He rubs my parts like I'm a magic lamp and he desperately wants to make three wishes. I finally understand that *Genie in a Bottle* song.

My eyes open and close and I catch flashes of the huge theater screen. The medieval princess in the movie is bouncing around on a horse going up a mountain. Her big breasts are restricted by a dress with an empire waist. I wonder what the rating of the movie is and if we'll get to see what's under the dress. I close my eyes and imagine her nipples, big and dark. I feel like screaming out loud, but so many people are around. I reopen my eyes and watch those breasts being jostled by that horse, and I start breathing all heavy. I feel like I'm the one climbing the mountain and I want so bad to reach the peak; I believe if I can, I will see everything and understand more clearly the ways of the world. A kid is crying and the smell of popcorn is everywhere and I've slumped deep into my seat, but--

Stop it!

Come on, baby.

No! Pssssst. Venice!

One sec. I whisper back, harshly.

Venice! Now Tiff is talking right out loud. I need to talk to you!

I sit upright in my frigid theater chair and Gus pulls his hand away, quickly, guiltily. I lean across the boys and glare at Tiff, whose hair is disheveled. Her lip is trembling.

We slip out of our chairs and tell the boys we're going to the bathroom. Tiff wants to talk right away, but I tell her to wait outside in the royal blue hallway, because I actually do have to pee.

I'm so pissed at her that I can feel the redness in my face. I also feel blood pulsating through me, warming my groin. Inside the bathroom stall I lean against the wall and try touching myself, emulating what Gus was doing moments ago. The metal of the wall is cold against my neck, cooling me down head to crotch to toe. Like a snap of the fingers, I've lost a very important moment in my life.

When I get out of the bathroom Tiff tells me she was just sitting there enjoying the movie when that Darrell kid saw what Gus and I were doing, and got the wrong idea.

I don't mind kissing, but I'm not *like* that, Venice. I don't make-out on the first date.

Oh, and you're saying I do? I cross my arms over my chest, moving heavily.

I'm not saying anything, I just--he was trying to go down my pants, Venice. A boy should--and--anyway-- She gets all flustered and just stands there with her face contorted like a little kid who has just lost her ice-cream cone.

I feel a million miles ahead of her.

The next day at school Tiff and I don't talk much, just sit together in math class and listen to the teacher for once. When I go to Gus's locker at lunch-time, he's nowhere to be seen. He's not on the soccer field either, so I assume he has basketball practice. Tiff and I eat together instead, atop a metal power box outside.

At three-fifteen when school lets out I hang around Gus's locker for a few minutes, until I get the hint. I'm fifteen years old, but I'm not like other girls. I'm not a dog waiting for table scraps.

Tiff and I are two among many waiting for the bus out front. We're just standing there when Gus and Darrell pull up on the road, hanging out the windows of Darrell's brother's car.

Hey, Cock-tease! Darrell yells, addressing Tiff.

Tiff stands there and stares back at him with her infamous Look. I frown at Gus, but he chimes in.

You, too, Venice Knight! Cocktease and Blue-baller! Gus holds a window ice-scraper up near his face and wraps his fist around it, pumping up and down. This is how it's done!

About thirty other kids are watching, some laughing and some wearing sympathetic expressions. Before I can defend us, Darrell's brother rips out of there, tires squealing.

I'd rather be a cock-tease than a slut! Tiff screams at the dust left in the road.

I'm so surprised at Tiff's courage to speak up, even if it's too late, that I put my hand on her shoulder and make an announcement to the crowd around us.

That's Gus Jenkins, everyone! He needs to learn a thing or two! I grin and hold my hand up, wiggling my tongue between my middle and index fingers, miniature legs. I scratch my head and let my tongue drop dead, as if I've forgotten what to do. No one needs to know how good Gus really is; rather, how good his hand is. Plus, he's ruined his basketball sneakers by writing my number on them. Sucker. Mother fucker.

A couple of kids laugh loudly and we both join in, triumphant. Later that night when we're hanging out in my basement Tiff asks if I'm sad about Gus. I laugh right out loud and tell her I couldn't be happier.

I'm only asking, 'cause I think if Oliver and me broke up, I mean, if we got together and *then* broke up, I would be so upset I probably wouldn't eat for days, like my mom when she and my dad split up.

Not me. I shake my head. I'm a free woman. Plus I'm interested in someone else.

Who?

It's a secret, for now.
Okay...did I tell you I dreamt about Oliver last night?

40

I couldn't remember if there'd been anything of significance in my dream about Raizel. I hadn't lost my teeth or seen anything white. There had been no happy peacock. I wondered if Tiff remembered anything about dreams and what she'd have to say about mine.

I worked at nine that day, Meaghan at my side, Monica buried in paperwork in her office. I wasn't sure what I'd prefer, if forced to decide--runny-mouthed Patty or covered-mouthed Meaghan--until the latter brought out her Cosmo magazines. We poured ourselves free coffee and leaned on the front counter, waiting for the seniors to arrive. I stared at an article titled *Ten Ways to Please Your Man.*

When I got home from work the lights were off and the driveway was empty. I stood on the front steps and breathed cold air in through my nostrils.

I heard the phone ringing from outside the duplex, and scrambled in my backpack for my house keys, purple rape whistle and all.

Hello? I breathed heavily, standing on the living room carpet in my snowy shoes.

Hey, girlfriend.

Hey, Liam. What are you doing? I slung my coat over the back of the sofa.

I'm at work. What about you?

I just got home. What's up?

Oh, nothing. I just wanna talk to you about stuff.

Sure. Hold on a sec, okay?

I slipped out of my shoes and kicked them toward the front door. I trudged to my room and closed the door before flailing to my bed, my savior. I dug my toes deep into the abyss of blankets.

So, what do you wanna talk about? How's Christopher?

Well, I dunno. He hasn't called me back at all. But let's talk about you. What's new?

What's new? Um...there's a new annoying girl at Team Bean.

Anything else? Any new boyfriends? Girlfriends?

Is this about Amara? Liam, you know I'd tell you if something was going on.

Is it?

Well... I pictured the two of us in the birdcage together, how hot my face had felt for an instant as I'd watched her dance. I remembered how quickly such feelings had vanished. No.

I think you need to tell *her* that.

I tried.

Try harder.

Okay. I looked at my bedroom carpet, library items strewn around my CD player.

Venice? You there?

Yeah.

I'm not angry at you. Amara's just a delicate person.

How should I tell her?

Tell her you have a boyfriend or something. I'm pretty sure she'll get the hint.

Okay. I will. Hey, Liam, something weird happened on Sunday night.

Oh, yeah? Amara said you left Mars without even saying bye to her.

There's a reason. She kind of tricked me into taking Ritalin.

She tricked you? How so? Didn't you see what it was?

Well...I didn't exactly look at it. The words left my mouth as lamely as a fly with no wings.

You didn't? How is that *her* fault?

I dunno. It's kind of like eating Smarties in a movie theater. You don't have to look at them and choose which color you want. You just know they'll taste good.

Um. Liam suddenly chuckled, the first bit of friendliness I'd gotten from him that night. That doesn't really make sense, but whatever. I don't know what to say. You should be more careful, girlfriend.

So... I heard a card door slam outside my window. Can I tell you about this weird dream I had?

Amara called me the next evening.

Hello? I was sitting in front of the computer, posting more pictures on Facebook.

Hi, is this Venice? Her voice came over the line, a small squeak.

Yeah. What's up?

Nothing. How are you?

I'm okay.

Why did you leave the club on Sunday?

I was really fucked up. I got sick outside.

Aw, baby. Sorry to hear that.

You should be, I thought.

So, I've been wanting to talk to you about something. I pulled my feet up on the computer chair, putting my chilled toes under my butt. I suddenly realized I had a perfect opportunity, the perfect reason to dump her, though we'd never actually been an item.

What is it? Amara inhaled into the phone, holding her breath.

I don't know what you think's going on, but--

Going on with what?

Us, Amara. Someone told me you've been telling people we're together.

The line became silent.

Who said that?

It doesn't matter. I sighed, not wanting to rat out Raizel. But I've been seeing someone else, okay?

The words were a card house, ready to fall over under the slightest exhalation.

Who?

Um--you don't know him.

Him?

Yeah.

You're full of shit.

I looked into the mirror in my bedroom and smoothed my dress. I'd gone straight to Value Village, knowing I could definitely afford something there. One day, I'd be able to shop at places like Broadway and the East Bay Shopping Center.

The dress was a dark blue number with tiny white dots all over, a pattern that instantly reminded me of Raizel's tights. The bodice of the dress hugged my torso and upper arms while the skirt went out from my body, stopping above my knees. Outside the duplex, cold wind probably howled, but my CD player blasted a band called Camera Obscura at me. I tapped my toes and swung my hips, enjoying how flirtatiously my skirt shimmied.

I combed my blond hair so it lay obediently instead of standing upright. I broke through the plastic wrapper on my new palette of eye-shadow, the first makeup I'd ever owned. I'd brought home one of Meaghan's Cosmo magazines, as she'd left them to gather lunch crumbs and coffee stains in Team Bean's tiny staff room. On the page of make-up tips, I duly noted the reasons behind everything. I followed the guidelines of a look called *The Natural Woman--Ladies Night Out,* though in the end my eyes were more made-up than they'd ever been. As promised by the article, the faint purple shadow invited my irises out to play.

When my mother arrived home from work I stalled coming out of my room, cutting my toenails and applying to my neck and wrists a fragrant body lotion I'd found in the basement bathroom. I checked my hair once more before heading to the kitchen.

Hi, Mom. I spoke to my mother's back as she put something in the fridge.

Hi, my peach. My mother kept her back to me, reaching into a brown paper bag from the liquor store. Are you ready for supper? They'll be here any minute.

Yup. I stood on bare tiptoes, peering over her shoulder into the fridge. What did you get?

Well, I got wine and some sushi and other goodies from a restaurant in East Bay.

Sushi?

Yeah-- My mother turned around, interrupting herself when she spotted me. Wow. You look so pretty! You look like a girl!

Thank you kindly. I took the sides of my skirt into my hands and curtsied.

Is this for that boy you invited?

Maybe. My cheeks didn't get warm. He told me he'd be here at six.

Well, don't worry. We still have a few minutes. Oops! I'd better go get dolled up, like you!

When she scampered out of the kitchen I opened the cupboard under the sink, my fingers searching blindly for the bottle of rum. Like a crouching tiger I remained on the floor, throwing my head back for three fast swigs.

I was brushing my teeth in the bathroom when I heard knocking on the front door.

I skipped to the door and pulled it open.

41

Hey, Seed.

He stood on my steps in his Timbaland boots and baggy jeans, a hoody drawn up around his face like the first time we'd met outside the bushes. Over the hoody he had on a red plaid winter parka, reminding me of my flannel shirt, which Amara still had. I waved Seed in, him and his brown paper bag identical to my mother's--the first hint that someone, if not all of us, would get shit-faced that evening.

Nice earrings. I pointed at the diamonds in Seed's earlobes, sparkling despite the dimness of our front landing light.

If not for his job, I'd have doubted the genuineness of the earrings.

Thanks, 'boo. He looked me up and down. Dammmmn.

Hey. I slapped his forearm. Remember why you're here.

Yeah, well. I gotta make it believable. He leaned forward and kissed my cheek.

I took a swift whiff of Seed's neck, making sure his cologne masked the scent of pot, which I assumed he'd been smoking all day.

Hello.

I twirled around to see my mother with her hair swept back, wearing dark tights and a slinky black dress. She hadn't worn the ensemble since my grandmother's funeral. I was going to tell her how nice she looked when Seed stepped forward.

Wow. Seed put his hands together and looked up as if to thank a higher presence. There are *two* of them.

My mother laughed.

It's nice to meet you. I'm Kathy.

'Sup, Kathy. Seed slid the hood off his head, revealing his dreaded hair. I'm Edward.

Did you have trouble finding the place? My mother smiled coyly, not knowing Seed ran most of his own business out of a certain gathering of bushes in a certain nearby field.

No trouble. Seed shrugged. Hey, I brought some drinks for everyone. Where should I put them?

Here. Stifling a smile, I took Seed's hand and led him to the kitchen. We dumped the drinks in the fridge before opening the door to the basement.

Come up in ten minutes or I'm coming down there! My mother chirped from the living room, where she'd probably sit wringing her hands until my tardy brother arrived.

Edward? I whispered at Seed when the door closed behind us. Why didn't you give your real name?

I did. Seed stuck his tongue out, following me down the wooden steps.

Seriously? Now I see why you call yourself Seed.

Yeah. Plus it's good to keep a cover when I'm meeting new customers. He shed his coat on the sofa, revealing a brightly colored hoody.

Oh yeah?

Yeah. Can't be too safe.

I flicked on the television and we sat on the sofa, a cushion between us like a couple of nervous pre-teens.

You want a weed cookie? Seed broke the air between us, patting his hoody pocket.

Yeah, right. I threw him a sideways glance. As if you have some.

He tugged a plastic bag of cookies from his pocket.

I moved over on the sofa until my thigh was touching his, glancing up at the closed basement door. The cookies were circular, and a regular shade of brown with crisp chunks of chocolate.

They look so regular. How do you know there's weed in them?

Because I made them. And there's not weed *in* them. Seed dug one of the cookies from the bag, a ring on his pinky flashing at my eyes. I extracted THC into the butter and baked them with that.

I accepted the soft cookie. I popped the whole thing into my mouth before it crumbled in my hand. Seed laughed and did the same, shoveling chocolaty goodness into his face. We barely had time to swallow before my mother shouted down the stairs.

Venice! Edward! Supper time!

I giggled at his name. I thought, for a moment, that I could have gotten used to his long fingers wrapping around mine as he led me up the stairs in my own home.

We gathered around the living room coffee table, on which the boxes of sushi had been placed. Seed and I sat on chairs borrowed from the kitchen, my mother and Dana and his girlfriend on the sofa before us.

Molly was blond. She wore khakis and a white shirt, blank like the pages in a pad of drawing paper. When she spoke, I found myself turning my head so my ear would be closer to her.

--, ---- do you --, Venice?

Pardon me?

What do you do? For work?

I work in a coffee shop.

I see. She nodded, unsmiling.

Come on, I shouted in my head. *Your boyfriend works at a movie theater.*

Oh, shoot! My mother exclaimed. I forgot the drinks. Venice, could you help me?

We were about to juggle four glasses of white wine and a can of beer when my mother brought her mouth closer to my ear.

Edward's so *cute*. Her nose scrunched up in girly excitement. No wonder you've been going out so much.

The meal went as awkwardly as one would expect, being that my family rarely talked at suppertime, anyway. I'd never tried sushi before, and was finding it difficult to decide whether I should eat each piece in one bite or two.

When I decided on two bites for a particularly big California roll, pieces of rice tumbled into the lap of my dress. My mother giggled, mid-bite her own piece of sushi. The same thing happened to her and we both ended up picking sticky rice off our skirts.

My brother noticed this. He chuckled heartily.

This is how it's done. Dana shoved a whole piece of shrimp sushi into his mouth. He chewed, trying to keep his mouth closed despite the abundance of food within.

Either the wine was loosening me up or the cookie I'd devoured was doing its thing. I realized I had no idea what that meant, but felt relaxed enough to just let it happen. I assumed I would just feel as though I'd smoked a big-ass joint. I giggled at my brother. My chair wasn't very comfortable; the back was too straight and the seat was too hard. I had to remind myself I was wearing a dress with no tights and couldn't sit how I usually did, with my legs spread.

Everyone's cheeks were red when my brother's girlfriend's tiny voice blossomed into something high-pitched and bird-like, however audible. Molly announced she couldn't drink anymore because she was driving. My mother beamed at Dana for finding a girl with such high morals. My brother beamed back and raised his beer. Everyone tapped their glasses together.

After supper my mother and Molly and Dana sat talking in the living room, taking up the whole sofa. I opened a bottle of white wine and invited Seed to my bedroom. I showed him my borrowed CDs. Under normal circumstances I'd have perched gingerly on my bed, a pillow covering the bits of revealed skin around my thighs. I found myself relaxing onto my unmade bed, nodding my head to the music and talking to Seed like I'd known him forever. I even opened the window and let him smoke a cigarette and tell me how to add wax to dreads.

Knock knock.

Shit. I grabbed Seed's cancer stick and dropped it into the wine bottle, watching it sizzle and go black in the inch of off-white liquid.

What the hell? Seed laughed, flipping a lighter around in his hand.

He didn't live with a parent, didn't answer to anyone. I set the bottle on the floor under the bed-skirt.

My mother poked her head in the door.

Hey, Curious George. I giggled at my mother's detective face.

Hi, guys. My mother glanced around, sniffing at the remnants of Seed's cigarette. Venice, you have a friend at the door.

Oh, thanks. I squiggled off the bed, straightening my dress. I nodded at Seed to follow me. On the way out I glanced in the mirror, spotting a girly girl, someone I barely knew. I averted my red eyes as I passed my mother.

We moved past Dana and Molly in the living room, heading straight for the door. Amara stood on the landing in a tight winter coat and leather boots.

Hey. I giggled again, a noise surely induced by recently consumed THC, whatever that was.

Hi…? Amara slit her eyes at Seed. What are *you* doing here?

Amara, this is my boyfriend, *Edward.* I glanced over my shoulder, confirming suspicions that my mother was lurking nearby. She stood near the kitchen door, and pretended to fish through a cigarette pack while she eavesdropped.

Hey, Amara. Seed gave a swift nod, offering his hand to shake Amara's. It's been a while.

You guys know each other?

Not really. Amara turned to go outside, her heels stamping against the linoleum in the landing.

How's Raizel?

Amara turned around, her dark face the palest I'd ever seen it.

We broke up. She's okay, though.

And Abby?

Okay, too.

And Liam?

He's alright. Amara shrugged.

Behind me, my mother told us to 'piss or get off the pot', because we were letting the cold in.

I ran to my room and threw on a pair of leggings under my dress. After thanking Molly and Dana for coming, Amara and Seed and I scampered to the field. I didn't even care that my mother might be peering out the window--she couldn't stop me. Amara told Seed she'd posed in a photo-shoot for me in this very field, and bla bla bla. I cackled into the night air.

I'm so high.

Amara took my great mood as an opportunity, clinging onto my jacket sleeve.

Oh yeah. You want one? Seed, staggering beside us three feet away, drew his cookie bag from his deep pocket.

They're *special.* I giggled, poking Amara in the ribs.

As we moved, Amara held a cookie in her hand. We stopped outside the bushes with the wind tickling our necks. I wondered why she was being so hesitant, when I'd previously gotten the opinion that she would never pass up a chance to get high. I suddenly realized something.

Come on, Amara. Your body's beautiful. You can eat *one* cookie.

Yeah. Seed slung his wine-tainted arm around Amara's tiny waist. You're fucking hot.

I caught the stiffness in Amara's body, trying not to pull away from him. I caught her catching me not saying anything about my 'boyfriend' blatantly hitting on another girl.

Alright. Amara brought the cookie to her mouth.

When we traipsed through to the clearing in the bushes, I had no idea what time it was, but the party was bumping with music and excited shouts. We drew the eyes of the crowd as we staggered in whooping, my attractive fake boyfriend and accidental ex-girlfriend and I. I caught some of St. Timothy's Bitches watching Amara hang off my arm and Seed warm my hand in his pocket. We became a threesome of nonstop giggles, linking arms as bopped our heads along with the music from the cars outside the bush. I inhaled the reminiscence of campfire stench, taking it as my own.

A few people asked Seed if he was doing business, but he said he had nothing on him and he was just there to party. Someone had lugged a couch into the party, a white thing with pale pink flowers all over it. In my head I fast-forwarded the lifespan of that sofa--envisioned perfectly the black cigarette holes and the streaks of mud from girls' shoes as they pounced on their crushes at the height of the party.

The first moment the couch became vacant, Seed and Amara and I swooped onto the cushions like vultures on mice. We'd scored some of the two-litre coolers usually designated for the ninth-grade Gigglers, the thought process being that the drinks were big and we wouldn't have to get up again for a long time. Sunk so low to the twig-filled ground, I took pictures of the crowd that showed up on my camera as a mess of legs and bonfire coals.

Look! I exclaimed, showing Seed and Amara. I'll frame it and call it 'The Bottom Half of a Bush Party'.

Sweet. Amara squinted at the photo. Let's take one together.

I surrendered my camera, letting her long arm stretch out and snap a bright photo of us. Then she leaned away and took one of Seed and I.

So, how long have you two been together? Amara smiled and asked, leaning forward to see both of ours faces. With her eyes stoned red, she looked darker than ever. I wondered if my own eyes were so pink--I didn't yet feel as though the effects of my cookie were wearing off.

Um. I gazed out at the party, which seemed to have grown larger than any other night. Probably, like, a month.

Beside me, Seed nodded absent-mindedly, adjusting the crotch of his jeans.

Really? Amara's hand moved through her hair. So, Seed, do you mind Venice kissing other people?

Huh? Seed glanced between Amara and I.

I widened my eyes, hoping he'd understand.

No. No kissing other people.

It's forgivable, but I'd rather she didn't. Seed looked me up and down, snaking his arm around my waist. He tugged me closer to him on the sofa. I was happy to oblige, considering that under-the-sink perfume of Amara's mouth.

My head floating in the air somewhere above us, I let my face tilt toward Seed, let my eyes drop closed. He put his lips on mine, not forcibly, just warming my mouth. There was nothing distinctly Boy or Girl or Man or Woman about the kiss, just a niceness I told myself I could endure for as long as I had to.

Alright, I get it. I heard Amara talking, but couldn't pull myself away. What do you want me to say? You guys are obviously a cute couple.

Venice?! Another voice cried out.

I moved my head back, my eyes popping open. The light of the fire shone before. Tiff stood before the couch in a superhero-like stance, her puffy winter coat giving the illusion of muscles. She sighed shook her head, wild red curls an ambassador of the flames behind her. I felt my body detach from me, raising my middle finger in her honor. Beside me, Amara broke out in laughter that threw her whole body forth.

Tiff disappeared in the smattering of trees and fire-sparks and hammered teenagers.

42

I returned everything to the library and made way through the CD drawers labeled D, E, and F.

I bought a cell phone when I got paid--a simple, black thing with a SIM card, the cheapest deal I could get. Having forgiven me for outrageous behavior, Tiff sent me text messages all day while she was working. Liam called my cell number so I wouldn't have to leave my room to fetch the dirty old cordless. I figured out how to get different ring tones for different people--The Silly Rainbows for when Liam called. Millie Fischer for Amara. Ani Difranco was for Raizel.

Raizel--a mystery to be solved.

Throughout the rest of November, I developed a reoccurring dream. The dream was about my daily life--going to the library, working, taking the bus--events so ordinary that at all times I expected monsters to pop up around corners. They never came. Murderers never lurked in the bushes. I never drowned and I never caught on fire. The only difference between the dreams and reality was wherever I went, Raizel appeared.

On the first of December, I had the strangest dream of all. Parts of it were blurry.

Raizel and I went to a Greek restaurant. The dream was so realistic I tasted lamb and lemon potatoes. In my dream, Raizel was legally permitted to drink in my dream. I felt like I was actually drinking the three glasses of red wine she ordered and pushed across the table. Garlic tainted our breath. After the restaurant we got into Raizel's car and dug through the glove compartment looking for gum. We happened upon a pack of Listerine mint strips that were supposed to get stuck to the roofs of our mouths and make the air feel cold when we inhaled. They dissolved in our saliva before having a chance to slip down our throats.

We roared down Main in the Camaro, which was when it got weird. Pandas danced on the sidewalks and tried to catch us with ten-foot arms. The air wasn't black, like a normal night. Everything was green, but the snow. The snow was a white, wavering ocean. There were dragonflies in the snow.

Soon I lay on a bed in a tattoo parlor and a man leaned over me, holding a needle. I despised dreams in which I tried to make noise and nothing emerged and then everything sped up and parts went missing. The man hovered over Raizel afterwards and I wanted to scream, *LEAVE HER ALONE,* but felt my jaw lock, unable to open. I somehow knew that if we didn't accept, something horrible would happen.

I went from looking in a mirror and seeing two girls with pink skin and orange eyebrows to sitting beside Raizel in the car in a McDonald's drive-thru. I sucked on a Diet Coke so big I could hardly get my hands around it. I immediately regretted swallowing the soda as it opened my soul, a canyon. We parked in an elementary school parking lot and tried desperately not to look outside. Raizel spoke a language I didn't know. I begged her to speak English, but she couldn't understand me.

What? I asked her, over and over. What? WHAT?

If she didn't understand me, things lurking in the cool greenness outside the car would try to get in. I clawed the door, searching for a lock. I yelled at Raizel to look her own door, so she'd be safe.

Raizel's arms came around me, restraining me and shoving my nose into her neck. I smelled her lilac skin, I really smelled it, and then her cinnamon voice box was four inches from mine, our chests pounding together under our sweaters. I kissed her clavicle and nibbled her skin and used my tongue to trace her faint blue veins. I tried devouring her and then

I woke up coughing. My throat was scratchy. I pulled myself from the depths of my sheets, sweaty from tossing in my slumber. The house was silent as I padded down the hallway to the kitchen. I hated morning breath for making my water taste bad. My head hurt, directly behind my face. Fuck, I was coming down with a cold. I dragged my feet back to my room and lay in bed, disoriented by thoughts.

My mother was at the bank and Dana was at his fancy Broadway basement suite. I moved downstairs with intent to rip CDs onto the computer. I drank mug after mug of orange pekoe tea, convinced I was sick and trying to clear my system. I was rocking my bladder back and forth in the chair before I finally forced myself into our ugly basement bathroom with its cracked tiles and muddy caulking.

I glanced in the mirror on the way to the toilet. I yelped and held in my piss, instantly remembering the time with the Gravol and the allergic reaction I'd imagined and the shock in the mirror. In my eyebrow were two small, sparkly orange balls at the ends of a barbell. I pressed my hands into the edge of the sink and leaned forward for a closer look. When I frowned the piercing stung and begged to return to its place.

I relaxed my face. Dark bags sagged under my eyes.

It couldn't have actually happened. No way. When I closed my eyes, shutting out the sight of my face, the apparent dream twisted in my mind.

Something was harder to believe than the little tangerine above my eye--that I had really come that close to Raizel, kissing her neck and shoulders and ears and everything. Her chest had pressed into mine. My only evidence was a piece of tiny, cheap jewelry.

I peered into the gray flecks that were my eyes and felt synonymous with all the coral destined to live on the ocean floor--unable to surface.

43

On a bus ride to Elmview, I noticed Christmas. I wanted to take pictures of the houses adorned generously with wooden deer, flashing lights, and berry-sprinkled wreaths, but I hadn't been able to find my camera that morning. I thought of my own family's duplex and laughed out loud at how brown and ordinary it would remain throughout the whole year. The woman in the bus seat across from mine heard me laughing and drew her purse closer to her body.

Growing up, I'd never gotten allowance. At Christmas when I'd been nine, my Aunt Blanche had given me a check for a thousand bucks.

Put this toward your education.

She'd given one to Dana, too.

Thanks, Aunt Blanche.

Later we'd complained to our mother, saying we should get to spend the money ourselves and not on something boring, like education. We'd stood behind her as she'd poured coffee one morning, chipping at her trunk like a couple of beavers. That evening she'd given us wads of cash, six crisp hundred dollars each. She'd kept the rest for herself.

For a little while, we'd acted like a lucky family, buying shoes when we'd outgrown them, instead of waiting until our toes had worn holes through the front. Our mother had even given us rides around the city without complaining about the cost of gas. We'd gone to the cinema instead of renting movies with coupons. We'd had orange sherbet and cherries after supper, not canned fruit cocktail or anything preserved. We'd gone to bed those nights with the heat on instead of using six quilts each, and had woken up with hopeful scents of toast and sausages drifting down the hall to our rooms.

Our mother had worn a yellow cardigan. She'd smoked less. She'd whistled.

I'd started making huge plans for the future, including graduating high school on the honor roll and taking a year off to backpack around Europe. I'd decided to learn everything I possibly could about photography. I'd really thought that way as a nine-year-old. My goal had been to sneak up on leopards and take photos that National Geography would write articles about. When they tried to hire me, I'd have already accepted an offer from Vogue. I'd start my own magazine and call it *Tomorrow,* insinuating something ahead of everyone in terms of time, music, and fashion. I'd dreamed of move to a city where bigger things happened than the wind rifling the dandelions lining our yard fence.

We'd been fucking ignorant, Dana and our mother and I. None of us had said it aloud, but we'd looked forward to the next big holiday, Easter, thinking Aunt Blanche would hook us up again. I never knew how she'd found out that we hadn't saved the money; maybe mother's fancy yellow cardigan. Aunt Blanche had barely looked at the three of us that April when we'd driven eight hours to her big estate in rural Alberta. She'd dropped the salad and perogies and mashed potatoes on the table even though they'd been in ceramic dishes and had made clanging sounds. I had copied my austistic uncle Doug, humming with my hands over my ears.

I'd wanted to apologize to Aunt Blanche so she'd forgive us with mugs of hot chocolate at bedtime and kiss our heads when we left in the morning, but I hadn't been able to find the words.

My mother had stopped whistling.

I stopped halfway through the door at Team Bean, finding Tiff behind the counter. Since Meaghan was hired, she and Tiff had been paired constantly. I'd been the one to work beside Patty, listening dutifully to her ramblings. I closed the door behind me, enjoying the warmth of the building.

Hey! Tiff exclaimed across the store.

Hey, Tiff. It's so nice to work with you instead of *other* people. I stuck my tongue out. I'm gonna go put my bag away.

Cool. I'll make your coffee.

Thanks.

I tied my apron as I came back down the hallway. I patted Tiff's back.

I'm sorry.

For what? Tiff slid my coffee toward me.

About Patty. Getting that award *again.*

Pfft. Tiff flapped her hand. Three months in a row. I've kind of come to expect it now.

It sucks. I tried to pick up my coffee, feeling bold hotness immediately on my finger tips.

Tiff squinted at my face.

Oh my god! She pointed at my eyebrow. When did you get *that* done?

Oh, a few nights ago. I looked around the empty store, concluding I wouldn't have to do too much immediate work. I've wanted one for a long time.

Really? I didn't know that. Did it hurt?

Not really. I rubbed my cold skin against my coffee cup. *I don't remember.*

What does your mom think of it?

She hasn't seen it yet.

What? How? She does still live with you, right?

She didn't know I'd been avoiding my mother, her and her nosey nose. Her and her smoking problem. There was no point in calling my mother when I was out each night, as I knew what she'd say. *Come home before it gets too late.*

Too late for what, I wanted to know.

Something's different about you, too. I squinted back at Tiff. Where are your glasses?

Tiff blinked widely, bare green eyes glowing.

Contacts?

Yup. Tiff smiled.

Looks good.

Silently, we brewed coffee in all of the machines so we'd be prepared when--if--anyone came.

So what's new? Tiff glanced at me sideways.

On Tuesday, I hooked up with Raizel. Kind of. Accidentally.

Not much. I took a big swig of my coffee. How's Ollie?

Amazing. I'm trying to figure out what to get him for Christmas.

Hmm. Boys are hard to shop for.

Well... Tiff played with the end of her ponytail. Are you seeing anyone special?

It was crazy that she really might not know such a thing about me.

Kind of.

Maybe we could go Christmas shopping together.

Sure. I *had* to tell her about Raizel. I opened my mouth. But Tiff--

Oh my god! Tiff let go of her hair and snapped her fingers. I forgot to tell you I received my bank loan for school.

Oh. That's good.

It's fantastic. I'm gonna go to campus and get all my books next week. I need, like, fourteen.

Fourteen books about painting?

Oh, no. I'm taking other subjects too. History One-Eleven. Literature One-Twelve.

What? Why?

Just keeping my options open.

Oh. I nodded. I completely understood.

When I awoke on Friday I got the immediate sense that something was missing. I looked in my bedroom mirror, checking my teeth and my skin and my hair. I looked as normal as I'd ever been able to. Everything in my bedroom seemed in place, my backpack hanging on the doorknob and my cell-phone on the nightstand by my bed.

I went out to the kitchen to find my mother seated at the table, forehead in her hands.

Mom? What's wrong?

Stomachache.

Again? Did you have too much milk or something?

Probably. Her head slumped onto the table, chunks of brown hair falling around her arms.

I made myself some toast and tea, bringing it to my bedroom. Safely under the covers, I sat with my breakfast and popped in a Janis Joplin CD. By that time, I was in the middle of drawers J, K, and L at the library.

I stayed in my room all morning, organizing the junk in my desk and the cardboard boxes on the floor of my closet. I happened upon a shoebox of notes Tiff and I had passed back and forth throughout high school, most of which having regarded the most menial things in the world.

what are you doing l8r?
hangin wit you
oh my god! me 2!

amandas skirt is tucked into her gitch
tell her
no! she'll think I'm a creep
you are!

have you ever heard the song where is the luv by the black eyed peas
ya. why?
it's a gooder
no it's not

mr. s keeps looking at me! I think he knows I'm writing a note.
maybe he likes you!
HA HA HA

Some of the notes were heavier.

yesterday my dad called my mom and said he has a new gf and my mom pretended she didn't care but later I heard her crying in her room. but I didn't say anything cause she would know I was listening in on the other phone and would get pissed off. gawd I don't know what 2 do I love my dad but he's being a dick.

you should tell your mom she is 2 good for him cause she is.

I think my brother was smoking weed yesterday. have you ever smoked anything?

oh my god, really? no I've never smoked anything but at my elementary school everyone else always smoked. not weed but still.

I think its so stupid and I would never smoke anything.

me 2 unless I was like really sick and needed something for the pain.

you make a good point.

do you think I'm 2 skinny?
no, and at least you're not big like me. why are you askin anyway?

ur not big ur just normal. that paul guy in my english class said my legs are like toothpicks and asked if he could borrow one to get his lunch out of his teeth.

that's stupid you should ignore him. what a douche.

good idea. but he's sooooo hot I think that's why it matters what he says.

it never matters what boys say.

We'd egged each other on. We'd been each other's advice columnists. We'd just been *there* for each other, an agreement that nothing in the world could have ever broken.

I no longer felt that I could talk to Tiff about everything that was going on with me. Either she'd become too judgmental or I'd become closed, or we'd both changed in unrecognizable ways. The past two months had done a silent number on our friendship.

I couldn't talk to my new friends about my problem. Amara would be pissed off and wonder why I would go out with Raizel and not her, if I was apparently straight. Liam was a good friend, but I wasn't sure if I trusted him to keep a secret. I couldn't talk to Abby, because she was too close to the person who'd helped form the problem in the first place.

I put the notes back in the shoebox and hid in my closet under the shadows cast by my clothing. I opened my bedroom door and walked to the living room, eyes on the back of my mother's head as she watched television.

Mom?

Hmm?

Bang bang bang. My heart was beginning to pound.

My mother hadn't had a boyfriend in years, but she probably knew something about having unwanted attraction toward someone. My brother and I had, after all, been the products of a relationship on the verge of failure, something so inadequate to Todd so-and-so that he hadn't been compelled to stick around for my birth.

I need to talk to you about something. I came around her side of the couch, perching on the arm. Remembering she didn't like that, I sunk into the cushion beside her.

Shh. She stared at the re-run of Friends, laughing when Joey said something. Joey was so silly, but his words flew over my head like a poorly pitched ball.

Okay, what is it? My mother turned to me, an afghan wrapped tightly around her body.

Well, first I want to tell you--

What the fuck?! She exclaimed, frowning hard.

Huh? I looked behind me, expecting to see something horrible. My mother swore when horrible things happened.

What's in your fucking eyebrow?

Oh. I reached up to touch my eyebrow, wincing as it stung. It's an eyebrow ring.

I can see that. Her cheeks reddened rapidly and she turned back to the television. Go take it out.

Shocked, I moved back down the hall to my bedroom. She had no idea what the piercing symbolized for me--the remembrance of what'd happened.

I suddenly realized why I'd woken up missing something. I hadn't dreamt about Raizel throughout the night, or the night before that--not since the weird dream that had turned out to be real.

44

I took the bus to Mars. Halfway out of Elmview I received a text message from Raizel.

I'll b in the parking lot.

I got off the bus and stalked down the alley. When I reached the parking lot I spotted Raizel, perched on the hood of the Camaro with her legs crossed. She had on some of the best tights I'd seen yet, a garden of flowers growing on her legs. Her cheeks were the reddest I'd ever seen them.

Shit. You must be cold.

A little. Raizel nodded, pulling her pea coat as tightly around her body as possible. She held up a tall can of beer. This is keeping me warm.

I'll bet. I tramped my feet on the ground, toes having frozen through the thin material of my sneakers.

You want one?

No, thanks. I wanted a clear head for the discussion we were about to have.

So, you wanna sneak in? There's a drag show tonight.

Can we talk about something first?

Of course. Raizel patted the spot beside her on the car's hood.

Dude, I think I'm too big.

Are you fucking kidding me? Get up here.

I obliged, hopping up alongside her. I couldn't believe the whole hood didn't collapse under me.

So I just want to ask you something.

Raizel just looked at me, waiting. Her dark lashes gathered bits of white frost.

Did you give me something, the other night? I mean, in my drink?

Her mouth fell open.

You really think I would do that? Her voice was small, a baby mouse.

Bang bang bang. My heart.

I guess I just don't know.

Did you even consider that maybe I don't know what happened, either?

So you felt fucked up, too?

I can't believe you just accused me of that. Raizel slid her butt off the car, walking the few steps to the driver's side door. I just can't believe it.

Raizel-- I jumped off the car and stepped toward her.

I'll see you around.

Come on. Don't leave.

She took her wallet out of her pocket thrust a card toward me.

Tatty Land, the card read. *For all your tat and piercing needs.*

If you have questions about *that.* Raizel pointed at my eyebrow. She opened her car door and let it slam behind her.

The whole bus ride home, my stomach tightened more and more. Raizel's offended face bore through my skull, cold eyes suppressing wetness. The walk home from the bus stop, I couldn't find it in me to fear the dark and whatever was lurking in the bushes of my neighborhood. I put up my hood. *Fuck off,* I wanted to scream at the Christmas lights.

Tiff called my cell and invited me out with her and Oliver.

Come on. I have a pack of Oreos with your name on it.

I refused to go.

Riiiiiiiiing. Riiiiiiiiiiiiiing.

Hello? A man answered the phone. Probably her father.

Bang bang bang.

Is Raizel there?

Let me check.

A minute passed.

She's not here, can I take a message?

Can you tell her Venice called?

Sure thing.

Riiiiiiiing. Riiiiiiiiing.

Riiiiiiiiing. Riiiiiiing.

Riiiiiiing. Riiiiiiiiiing.

Raizel didn't answer her cell phone.

Riiiiiiiiiiiing. Riiiiiiiiiiing.

Hey, girlfriend.

Hey, Liam. Are you at work right now?

Yeah. Why?

Is Raizel there?

Yeah. Why?

Can you get her to call me?

I stayed home all weekend, telling my mother I was having my Yearly Cold.

That's weird. You usually get sick in the spring. She moved toward my forehead with the back of her hand, cringing when she saw I hadn't removed my eyebrow ring. After that, she left me alone.

I called in sick to Team Bean both days, telling Monica I'd gotten horrible food poisoning from a certain Greek restaurant. She didn't seem too flustered or angry.

Feel better soon. I'll see you on your Tuesday shift.
Tiff heard I was sick and called to find out what I was really doing.
What's up, Venice?
Nothing, really. *Nothing I could tell you about.* I'm seriously just sick.
Are you sure you're not skipping work to hang out with your secret lover?
Quite the opposite, really.

Liam and I sent texts back and forth.

I told Raizel to call u.
thx
did she call u yet?
no
u'd better tell me soon what's going on w. u 2.

I listened to my music, reading random lyrics over and over again. I flipped through the farmer photo book, becoming slightly inspired to take a new batch of pictures. When I dug through my backpack and clothing drawers, I couldn't find my camera. I slipped back into bed, willing Raizel to return to my dreams and say everything was okay and that I wasn't an asshole.

RIIIING! RIIIING!

I awoke from my nap to pick my cell phone up off the bedside table. A moment later I realized the landline was ringing. I dragged myself out of my room to the cordless in the living room.

ABRAHAM P. I scowled. Tiff knew better than to call me on the house phone. I fell on my back across the living room sofa, where my mother usually lay, thankful she'd gone to run errands.

Hey.

Hello? Venice? She sounded serious.

Hi?

Hey, it's Sophie. Tiff's sister.

Ohh. Hey Sophie. I covered the receiver and yawned. What's up?

Not much. She cleared her throat, casting a bundle of nerves over the line. Um. I was just wondering something.

Yeah? What is it?

You know your friend you brought to my house a while ago? Raizel?

Yeah?

Well, do you know that bar, Mars?

Actually, I do. I smiled, imagining nerdy Sophie Abraham with her red ponytail and Wal-mart Portrait Studio nametag dancing up a storm at Mars. You go there?

Sometimes. Anyway, I've seen that Raizel chick there a few times and I was wondering--

Yes, it's true, I quickly interrupted. She's gay. But don't tell Tiff, okay? I think she just--

No, no, no. I was actually wondering if she has a girlfriend.

I nearly laughed, unable to think of a worse match than Sophie and Raizel. Raizel would never be interested, and Sophie would probably run after her like a panting puppy.

Venice? You there?

Yeah, I'm here. Sorry. I think the phone's cutting out.

Well, I really don't care what Tiff thinks. Could I have Raizel's number?

I'll ask her and get back to you, okay?

Without saying anything else, I hung up and tossed the cordless onto the carpet. I let my eyelids drift closed, not caring that I was in the pit of my mother's smoke lounge. I shivered and pulled the holey couch afghan up my curled body, prepared to sleep the weekend away.

When I slept, I didn't have to think.

45

I watched out my bedroom window until Liam's car pulled up to the curb outside, at which moment I ran down the hall and past my mother in the living room.

Peach? She said softly, looking over her shoulder from the sofa. Where are you going?

Out.

I take it you're feeling better?

Yup.

I bee-lined out the door, high-tops swinging in my hand. My feet, in a mere layer of sock, darted along the snowy pavement.

Hey. I jumped into the passenger seat, immediately turning down the pounding music. Let's go.

Okay. Liam nodded. Without checking whether or not my mother was peering out the picture window, we tore away from the shitty brown duplex.

Liam sped out of Oakwood, through Elmview, toward downtown, and then through Broadway. We kept going, riding night wind all the way to Wainmont, where we'd get what we needed for the evening. I bit my lip when the music stopped between songs, trying not to blab to Liam what was really going on between Raizel and I.

I was still entirely confused, wishing I remembered what had happened. I wanted to remember how her mouth felt on my skin. If I couldn't have that, I hoped to forget.

Liam had brought two bottles of red wine, enough to warm our chests and toes, but we needed something else. I'd warned Seed that we might be stopping by. I texted his phone when we pulled up outside his building.

im here.

come up, boo.

Unsure if I was allowed to invite Liam up, I left him waiting in the parking lot, car engine purring around him. He'd probably have texted fifteen different guys by the time I returned.

I rolled up to the sixteenth floor, checking my reflection in the mirrored back wall of the elevator. My eyebrow ring had become a part of me, no longer stinging as I made different expressions. I sucked in my cheeks, imagining I was someone else--perhaps a woman with her life lain out before her.

When I got to Seed's, he had three friends, or customers, lingering on the couch and the carpet. Before I'd even entered the apartment, I saw them through the massive fish tank. Two boys and a girl, they were definitely high school kids with red eyes and, though it was only afternoon, gigantic bottles of beer.

Hey. Seed reached past me to close the wooden apartment door. What do you need?

Um.

I glanced past Seed at the others, at the girl steadying her Colt 45 with both hands and sipping while she eyed me from under a hooded vest. She probably had a hard-on for Seed, as I assumed most girls did; he was sweet, attractive, smooth, wealthy, and a drug dealer. She wasn't too bad herself, besides the heavy makeup.

I touched Seed's forearm and nodded toward the kitchen. We stepped onto the tiles and stood across from each other in the narrow room.

Do you have anything besides E?

Maybe. He smiled and cocked his head, teasing his teeth with his tongue ring. What are you looking for?

Something not so happy.

Uh oh. Seed's face softened. Is something wrong, boo?

Oh, no. Right now I just don't want to be so...*alert.*

You need me to kick someone's ass? The words morphed his face into a grin.

I followed Seed into his living. He motioned for the girl to take her legs off the knitting trunk before he dug in and removed a bag of white powder. The bag contained at least twice the amount Amara's coke bags ever had, and only cost me twenty bucks.

I don't like coke. I took the bag from his hands, examining its contents.

It's not. It's Special K. It'll get you real low.

During the exchange, the girl on the couch watched us, sucking the opening of her beer bottle. When Seed glanced at her she uncrossed her slender legs to reveal pink gitch under her frayed jean skirt. I considered asking if she knew it was winter. The two guys kept their concentration on some shooter video game.

When I got back outside I scampered out of the building to Liam's car, hugging my backpack to my chest. He'd been peering eagerly out the window, and pressed the automatic lock button as soon as I hopped in. We took off down the road.

What a sketchy neighborhood. Liam motioned toward an apartment building on the right, one with windows made of cardboard and various fabrics instead of glass.

Yeah, well. I kind of grew up around this shit.

Really? Oakwood isn't *this* shitty.

Maybe not. Depends what you're looking at. I pictured the crisp green street signs on the intersection between the Heights and the Terrace, and the Enginergy gas station with its blue raspberry Slurpees and full-service stalls.

Then I pictured the middle of the field with its moldy, decrepit sofa, condoms and bottles astray in the dead grass. I pictured the vehicles parked in the road, pieces of metal left to rust, owners too lazy or drunk to properly dispose of them.

Liam stopped the car near an elementary school park in Broadway, but in fear of the wind whistling around the windows, we didn't get out. We opened both of the wine bottles and sat with the lights off.

On shuffle, the car stereo suddenly changed to one of The Silly Rainbows' songs I'd been listening to on repeat in my bedroom. Soft acoustic led the song into a blast of drums and heartfelt lyrics. I closed my eyes and bobbed my head, clutching one of the wine bottles between my tightly jean-clad thighs.

Meet me again by the tree we loved.
Meet me again in the coffee shop.
When you see me there,
Just stop, please stop.

Oh my god, I almost forgot to tell you something. Liam slapped his forehead.

Yeah? I tilted the heavy glass bottle over my face and sipped the wine. I imagined its grapey redness creating a vine down my throat to my stomach.

The Silly Rainbows are coming to Bowville.

My stomach lurched.

Fuck off. When?

In two weeks. I think on the nineteenth.

Are you going? I tilted my head, imagining the concert. There'd be all sorts of people. There'd be music. There'd be drinks. There'd be dancing. There'd be me, a foot away from The Silly Rainbows.

Of course. I'm surprised Raizel hasn't told you about it yet. You wanna come?

Um. Does that mean Raizel's going with you?

Well, yeah. She'd fucking die if she couldn't.

What about Amara?

She can't. It's on a Saturday.

Oh.

What, you're interested in Amara now?

No. But…I don't think I can come.

Are you kidding? Why?

Me and Raizel kind of aren't talking to each other.

Lover's quarrel? Liam laughed, sipping his own wine. The streetlight outside his window illuminated the green glass of the bottle as it tipped back.

I looked down at my bottle.

Oh my god, girlfriend, you're killing me. What happened?

When I was finished talking, Liam lit a joint and inhaled, silently reflecting on my story of dreams and confusion. He breathed out heavily and pot smoke enveloped me, but I couldn't take the joint from his hands.

What's wrong? You don't like it anymore?

I love weed. I took a sharp breath in. But it makes me eat too much.

So? Liam sucked the end of the joint again. Eating's fun.

Yeah, for you stick-thin people. I'll be good with this. I pulled the bag of Special K out of my backpack, though I had no idea at the time whether it would give me the munchies or not. I copied the trick I'd learned from Amara, dipping my house key into the bag so it gathered white powder. I passed it to Liam.

Thanks. Liam flicked his bangs to the side and plugged one nostril, inhaling quickly with the other. FNMPHHHH.

I did the same, dropping the key into the bag when flames shot up my nose.

Shit. That burns.

Yeah. Liam swigged his wine as if it could deplete the chemical dust riding up inside his face.

I plucked the key out of the bag and brought it to my nose again. FNMPHHHH. I squinted my eyes.

Now both nostrils are burning equally.

I'd better do the same. Liam laughed. FNMPHHHH, his nose went.

Still more than half full, I closed the baggie and dropped it into my backpack. Liam raised his wine bottle and I clinked mine against his, dark liquid sloshing around inside. I drank from the bottle as though I'd run a marathon and had just happened upon a freshwater fountain.

Things began buzzing a little, like coke, but low low low. My head wanted to sink to the floor of the car. Liam turned on a techno song with a strong beat and opened his driver's side door. My legs, unattached to my body, slumped outside and brought me into the car's backseat.

We squished close together under the blanket from the trunk. Every time I lifted my head, my brain felt heavy and soupy. I came to rest my ear against Liam's chest, moving softly alongside his breathing. When he spoke to me I took long moments to respond. I couldn't find the strength to speak loudly enough. Finally we were silent, swigging from our respective wine bottles. The alcohol warmed my chest.

I was lost in a web of thoughts when Liam whispered in my ear.

Sorry about Raizel.

I wiggled my toes, cringing when pain shot up my feet. My ankles were frozen sticks. I opened my eyes and pushed my feet against what I thought was my bedroom wall. When my pupils had adjusted to the tiny bits of lights around me, I shot up, hitting my head on the car ceiling.

Beside me, Liam snored under a big blanket, as cozy as ever.

Bang bang bang. My head and my heart pounded simultaneously.

I rubbed my fingers together, thankful I'd passed out with them in my jacket pockets. I pulled open the car door and dumped myself onto the sidewalk. The sky had morphed from silent black into a royal blue, inviting the sun to come out and play.

Bang bang bang. My heart.

I put my hands on my thighs and leaned over, preparing.

Bang bang bang. My head.

Suddenly everything shot up from my stomach, a dark mess that sprayed the cement and car wheels. Tears sprung from my eyes and I coughed, spitting the rest into the grass at the edge of the park. At least I had short hair that I didn't need anyone to hold back for me.

After relieving my bladder in the grass I crawled into the backseat again. Liam barely stirred as I reclaimed some of the blanket. The section I got was warm from my friend's body, enough to stop the incessant chattering of my teeth. I slipped my shoes off and curled my feet up under me.

Half an hour later, something in my stomach kicked my insides, begging to be let out. I leaned my head out the car door, willing myself to just get it over with. The sky had faded, fair purple. I lurched and coughed and my stomach seized up as I spat potent liquid across the curb.

My cell phone screen lit up, brightness stinging my eyes. It was seven-thirty a.m. and the sun still hadn't peeked out of the horizon. I dialed a number and pressed TALK.

Riiiiing. Riiiiiiiing.

Team Bean, Monica speaking.

Hi, it's Venice calling.

Hi, dear. How are you feeling?

Not so good. That's why I'm calling. I think my so-called food poisoning is actually the stomach flu.

Ohhh. Monica breathed in and out for a moment, thinking. So you should take another day off.

Yeah. I'm really sorry. I put my hand under my t-shirt and rubbed my fiery belly, grateful for the coldness of my palm.

It's okay. Patty and I can handle it.

I lay motionless on my bed, watching time pass as the shadow of a stack of books moved across my desk. As a child, five p.m. had meant coming in from snow-play. As an adult, it meant deciding when to turn on the lights inside. I hated five p.m. for being the time in the afternoon when the sun took the sky up on its offer of darkness.

I picked up my cell phone and dialed.

Riiiiing. Riiiiiing.

Bang bang bang. My heart twitched.

Hello? At the sound of her voice, warmth came over my skin.

Raisin. It's me. Don't hang up.

The phone was nothing but a quiet chunk of metal near my ear.

I'm sorry.

Okay. One word came across the line.

Okay what? I pulled my blanket tighter around my shoulders. Do you forgive me?

How do I know you're being genuine?

I-- I had no idea what to say to that. Because I am.

46

On Wednesday morning I trudged into Team Bean and straight down the narrow hallway. Monica came out of her computer chair and followed me into the staff room.

Good morning. I avoided looking at her face as I opened my locker, shoving my backpack in.

Good morning to you, too. How are you?

I'm a lot better. I rubbed my stomach. Just a little sore.

How bad was this thing? You look ten pounds lighter.

Really? I felt my cheeks get warm as I finally looked at her face. I guess being sick can be a good thing.

Monica stuck out her tongue. Then she put on her usual smile.

I'm glad you're back. You're the only one who will shut Patty up when she gets on a ramble.

I laughed, a robotic sound that wasn't meant to come from my mouth, like a baby falling from a high chair.

Hey, Monica? How do I book days off?

Easy. What days do you want?

The nineteenth and twentieth. It's very important.

Done and done.

I didn't even have to tell her what was so important.

On Thursday when I reappeared at Team Bean, Patty gave me a twitchy smile.

Morning, Venice. What are you drinking today?

Uh. I looked up from the floor. Dark roast.

Cream or sugar?

Huh? She'd never fixed a coffee for me before. No, thanks.

Coming right up! She turned to the coffee machines, her perm bouncing with every step.

Thanks, Patty. I walked down the hallway, the rubber bottoms of my shoes squeaking from bits of melted snow.

Monica wasn't in her office at the end of the hallway, but the door to the staff room was closed.

Hello? I knocked on the door. I had three minutes until the beginning of my shift, and needed to get to my locker. I tried the handle.

SURPRISE!!

I screamed, jumping back.

The lights flipped on and pink balloons flew at my face. Through the streamers dangling from the ceiling I made out the grinning faces of Monica, Meaghan, and Tiff.

Happy birthday! Tiff wrapped her arms around my neck, squeezing.

Oh my god. I scanned the tiny room, admiring the decorating job. A large carrot cake with eighteen candles sat on the table.

Oh, I almost forgot. Monica reached over and pressed play on the CD player. I know you like her.

Millie Fischer's voice filled the room. Although I was in the middle of my first surprise party ever, and it had nothing to do with Raizel, I was instantly reminded me of her. My eyes stung with tears.

Aw. Meaghan looked at the others. She's so happy she's crying!

Here's your coffee! Patty piped up from the hallway.

I accepted the drink from her, not caring if the coffee burnt my fingers through the cup. Knowing I had to say something, I opened my mouth.

I can't believe you guys. I blew the top of my coffee and leaned against the wall.

So you're surprised, then? Tiff smiled.

Duh.

I hope you didn't eat breakfast! Monica bent over the cake with a large knife.

I did, but who cares. Meaghan rubbed her chubby hands together, licking her lips.

Wait! Let's take a picture. I set my coffee down on the table. I rooted through my backpack, checking every pocket before remembering I had no clue where my camera was. I sighed. I guess I left my camera at home.

No worries. Tiff opened her locker to take hers out.

Monica lit the candles and everyone sang Happy Birthday.

They gave me the biggest piece and I licked the icing off, hating myself for every calorie. Then I hated myself for hating myself on my birthday.

Dana came over that night with a case of beer. My mother told me to relax while she and my brother cooked my favorite foods. I watched TV in the basement and chugged two bottles of beer, hating how small the necks were and how slowly it took the liquid to come out. I was rosy in the cheeks when I came back up the stairs.

They'd made tuna casserole, unaware that I'd drunk too much one night in high school and had thrown up everywhere, after which I'd sworn I'd never eat the stuff again. I regretted not swearing, instead, that I'd never drink again.

My mother scooped a big helping onto each of the three plates surrounding the casserole dish. I nearly gagged at the thought of the tuna bits sticking between my teeth. I stabbed a piece of macaroni with my fork.

I got you a gift, Dana blurted out when he'd finished swallowing his first bite.

What is it? I looked into his eyes, gray like mine.

You want it now, or after supper?

Whatever you want. I brought a forkful to my mouth, pushing it to the back with my tongue so I wouldn't have to taste it. I took a quick swig from my beer bottle.

Okay. Dana let his fork clatter to his plate. He dug into the pocket of his jeans, coming up with something blue and plastic.

I took the object from my brother, turning it over in my hands. *4GB SDHC Card*, the front read.

It's for your camera. Dana pointed at the card. Four gigabytes will let you take over a thousand pictures.

Oh. Under the table, I squeezed my fist so hard my fingertips became numb. I nodded and smiled. Thanks, Dana.

Oh! Before I forget. My mother jumped up from her chair, yelling as she moved down the hall. I have something for you, too.

How's Molly? I asked my brother.

She's alright. He shrugged. She's graduating in spring so she's working hard with school.

Cool. I let his words fly through one of my ears and out the other. I didn't bother asking what Molly studied.

And how's Edward?

Who?

Your boyfriend?

Oh. We're not together anymore.

Dana didn't know how to react. He looked at his plate and shoveled some more casserole into his cave of a mouth. I felt myself craving sympathy for the fake break-up between my pretend boyfriend and I.

Here it is. My mother returned, wearing a huge smile as she thrust an envelope toward me.

What is it? I ripped through the envelope and pulled out a birthday card with a frog on the front. Hoppy Birthday, it read. Oh. Thanks, Mom.

Open it up! My mother put a forkful of the tuna creation in her mouth, chomping down.

I pulled back the front flap of the card. A crisp one-hundred-dollar bill landed in the lap of my sweat pants. I picked it up.

A hundred dollars? I stared at the bill, disbelieving it was in my family's house on a regular old birthday.

Read the card. My mother's eyes shone. She swallowed her huge bite of casserole.

Venice,

I can't believe my little girl is growing up so fast. Today is the day you turn eighteen. That means you're becoming an adult. I trust you will make good decisions and flourish with your dreams. Use this money for whatever you want. Wherever life takes you, I will be behind you. Happy birthday, my peach.

Love always,
Mom

P.S. Sorry for my reaction toward your eyebrow ring. It looks cute.

Dana took off shortly after supper, saying he worked in the morning. I shook his hand and thanked him profusely for coming, though I secretly admitted the alcohol was urging me to put on a show. I tried to help my mother clean the kitchen, but she said I couldn't do such a thing on my special day. I left my full plate of casserole on the table and fled to the basement. Three bottles of leftover birthday beer sat on the table before me.

I heard you were coming but I didn't know when
heard you were here but I didn't know where--

I pulled my glowing cell phone from my pocket, The Silly Rainbows' song pouring out the tiny speaker.

Hello?

Hey, girlfriend! Happy birthday!

What? Liam? How did you know?

Facebook reminded me. Why didn't you tell me, anyway? How was your day?

It was interesting.

What are you doing now?

Sittin' in my basement. Kind of hammered.

Sweet. Liam laughed. You're eighteen now, right?

Yeah.

Okay. We're gonna do all the things eighteen-year-olds are allowed to do. Have you ever been to a sex toy shop?

No. I laughed.

Have you ever bought cigarettes?

I hate cigarettes.

Okay, what about going to the casino? Buying lottery tickets?

Sure, we could do that.

And it's totally legal for you to drink in Alberta. *I* know! If you come to Bowville with us, you can drink in the bar at the concert.

Right.

Oh. Sorry...I forgot.

Liam could be so dense sometimes.

Well, I'll get Raizel to forgive you.

No! I'd rather just forget about it. It was a stupid fight, anyway.

When we'd hung up, I got up from the couch and moved to the computer chair, my head spinning. I sat with my toes under my butt. I had no new e-mails, but opened one that had been in my inbox for over a month. My eye darted around the page.

I re-read Kale's answers to the questionnaire, even though they were small talk and I'd come to prefer long talk. His words were brief and they danced on the surface.

I reached for my cell-phone, sitting innocently by the computer speaker, and started a text message, carefully avoiding drunken typos.

r u free tonight? ~ venice

I entered his phone number, still engraved in my mind like bite marks on a pencil.

I clicked SEND.

My stomach churned.

I lay on the couch for the next three hours, willing my cell phone to ring. I kept the phone on the coffee table beside me, checking the battery several times. I'd never forgive myself if dead batteries were the reason I never got to talk to Raizel again. I didn't know why I expected her to call after the conversation we'd had.

Suddenly, in the middle of Amélie, my phone buzzed violently on the glass tabletop.

Bang bang bang. My heart. She was finally ready to forgive me.

I picked it up.

yeah. what u doing at eleven? - kale

Twenty minutes later I stood watching out the front door. My mother was sleeping and the rest of the house was empty, a crevice in an arctic valley. My stomach was knotted. I shivered. As each set of headlights turned onto our road, my nerves rose further, climbing stairs.

Finally a green Jeep appeared, its engine rumbling quietly as it stopped across the street. I let myself out of the house, delicately closing the door. I skipped down the icy gravel driveway and used my high-tops to skate across the road.

I smelled exhaust as I neared the vehicle. The door felt familiarly heavy as I pulled it open and slid in onto the passenger seat. Along with air blasting from the heater, his cologne wafted around and tried to engulf me. I looked at his face after letting the door slam shut after me.

He looked the same, this guy with brown hair, tanned skin, and broad shoulders. Tall, dark, and handsome, Tiff and I had said upon first seeing him in grade eleven. T.D.H. had become a running joke until he'd overheard us and things had gotten awkward, before things had gotten too comfortable.

Hey, babes. He smiled so widely I caught a glimpse of spearmint gum crushed between his molars.

Hi. I was nonchalant, as though we'd traveled back to the old days and had been seeing each other all along. I thought he was going to put his hand on my thigh, but he reached down to the gearshift. I'd never noticed before that he drove a standard.

You changed your hair.

Yeah. Can I drive?

Sure.

He was unaware that I still barely knew how to drive, or that I'd been downing beer all evening. We got out and switched places. I took a deep breath and adjusted the rearview mirror, trying to remember all of the little things Raizel had taught me, which seemed like eons ago. In the mirror, my eyes were red, but calm.

I shifted into drive and took off, something I'd later recognize as an attempt at empowerment. At every red light I slammed on the breaks and felt the triumph in my stomach grow. I wanted him to shrink him into the little passenger seat he should've been in all along. I wanted him to puke on his cocky leather coat.

Be careful, Venice.

I ignored his words, until the wheels slipped on a dark patch of ice and took us three meters past a stop sign. My heart sped up. For the first time, I wondered what kind of trouble I'd get in if the police caught me driving with no license to speak of.

I took us to a dingy Oakwood restaurant where everyone knew the servers didn't ID minors and the shots were cheap. Fake vines ran up and down the walls, surrounding tables with blue and orange suede seat cushions. Statues of mythical creatures separated the booths.

So, how have you been? Kale asked once we'd settled in and ordered two pints.

I'm okay. How's the school? At one point, somehow, I had trusted his dark eyes.

It's okay. I think it misses you though.

You mean you do.

Yeah. He lifted his beer. Well, cheers.

Okay. I clinked my glass against his and took a heavy gulp, realizing something. We've never done this before.

Sure we have. We always used to drink together.

No, I mean...sitting together. In public. Where people can see us. Even if it's nearly midnight, here we are. Like normal people. It's fucked up. I gestured around us, my hand bumping the nose of the unicorn statue beside our table.

Instantly, I felt a cramp in my belly. Raizel's hair came to mind--sparkling unicorn hair. I fingered my cell phone inside my pocket, begging it to pipe up. I wasn't meant to be in that dingy diner.

Listen, Venice, I've been thinking.

Kale's hands, his strong man hands with bits of hair on the backs, lay in the middle of the table where they may or may not have been inviting me to hold them. I could have sworn I saw them tremble. I kept my fingers firmly grasping my beer mug. I took a swig as he continued talking.

Things could be different between us now. Did you turn eighteen yet?

I laughed.

And you're not a student anymore. At least, not my student. You *are* going to university now, right?

Oh yeah. For sure, even though I got an F in the one subject that mattered to me in high school.

I'm sorry. What was I supposed to do?

You're sorry? You were supposed to act like an adult and get over it. Find someone your own age.

You really don't get it.

You're right, I don't. His hands retreated from the middle of the table to around his beer mug, as though it could bring him warmth. He kept his eyes down.

My own drink was almost gone.

Well? What's there to get, Kale? Teacher meets student, they hit it off, teacher fails student to prove he doesn't favor her? I swigged the rest of my beer, three swallows that bulged in my throat.

You sure have a distorted perception of what really happened.

Right. I spat as I spoke, embarrassment the furthest thing from my mind. And you have a distorted way of treating your students.

Listen, I didn't come here to stir up all that shit. He looked back up at me, brow slightly furrowed. There's something I forgot to say, back when you'd listen. Will you listen now?

Sure. I yawned and pulled my phone out of my pocket, trying to focus my eyes.

I'm just so glad we're together right now.

We're not together. We're just in the same place at the same time. I pressed a button and waited for the phone's screen to light up.

Shit. It was dead.

I love you. His words trickled delicately into the air, as miniscule as the drops of liquor stuck in a bottle when everything's been drunk.

I crossed to his side of the cheap orange booth and embraced him, manly shoulders and all, rubbing his leather-coated back. I touched his chin, instantly remembering its scruffiness, and turned his face toward me. Out of everything, his quivering mouth, reddened cheeks, shoulders hunched protectively, his eyes were what caught my attention. I breathed, considering. There was a familiarity about the glistening, black centers of his eyes, something I'd seen in movies with lovers. He was, quite possibly, being truthful. I watched him for a moment, pondering his vulnerability and the silver platter of feelings he'd passed my way. I tried to put myself in his shoes. My heart stung a little, and not from the beer.

Fuck you, man. I floated across the restaurant and out the glass door. He could pay for my beer.

I took the ten-minute walk home light on my feet, unable to fear the dark of night. Christmas lights on every other house lent light to the road, peaceful familiarity of winter. My ears were cold, but my chest was ablaze with life.

Happy birthday to me.

47

I was on the bus to the area of Sloam where Seed lived, out past Broadway. Wainmont was bigger than Oakwood Terrace, and shabbier, if possible--Liam was right. Before meeting Seed and Raizel I'd never had reasons to go there before. The weird thing was how happy I felt knowing I didn't live in the worst part of town.

Every building was tagged at least once, hastily scrawled graffiti spray, broken signs dangling off buildings telling stories of once-owned businesses. The buildings were only slightly familiar, but I stopped at a gas station for directions. My gut tumbled around inside of me and I feared seeing my breakfast again, toast and jam. I walked past a liquor store, a sex toy shop, a bingo hall, and a McDonald's before reaching my destination.

Tatty Land

Each bold letter was painted on the sign like it was dripping green blood. The blinds were drawn, but a neon sign read Open. I pulled open the poster-clad door. Things slowly became familiar, a front counter and a narrow hallway lined with rooms, each sectioned off with a sheet, hospital-like. The walls were covered entirely with pictures of tattoos and piercings and people receiving tattoos and piercings. I inhaled deeply, the abrupt smell of sterilizer flipping my stomach out, the same feeling I got before daisy.

Flip flip flip.

Be ride wit chu. A man's voice came from behind one of the sheets.

I peered into a glass case at the counter, disbelieving someone could put something as thick as a whiteboard marker through their piercing. I fingered my eyebrow, which I noticed didn't sting as much as it once had.

I was perched on a bench flipping through one of the tattoo portfolios when a young, thin girl in sweatpants walked out of the nearest curtained room. She barely glanced at me before positioning herself with her elbows on the front counter. She stuck her ass out like a yawning feline. I wondered what she'd gotten done, as she didn't have any visible tattoos. Maybe a belly ring.

A man in his mid-thirties came barreling out of the same room, removing black plastic gloves and disposing of them in a bin behind the counter. He was heavy and wore a red muscle shirt, revealing a hairy chest and tattoo-clad arms. I noted how closely he resembled Mario with his dark mop of hair and thick mustache. My hands felt clammy as I closed the tattoo album and waited.

One klit peerzing. The man typed up the girl's bill. Sevindy-six buckz.

I stopped my mouth from dropping open and hitting my knee.

I watched the girl dig money out of her pink wallet, wondering if she was going to faint. She smiled, took her receipt, and slowly ambled out of the store.

That girl. I motioned outside with my thumb. How old is she?

Fordeen. The man wiped sweat off his forehead with a cloth before dabbing his mustache. So?

Is that legal?

Id iz wit parendal consent.

Her mother came in here and agreed to *that*?

Yes. Lizzin, toots, I dun have time for diz. How'z dat peer-zing doing?

It's okay. Had he seriously just called me toots? I reached up and played with my eyebrow ring, demonstrating how I could tug it slightly without pain.

Dun do dat.

Oh. Sorry. You know something funny? I don't really remember getting it.

Ya? You were drunk?

No, I don't think so. I was definitely on something. But I don't know-

Daz not funny, tootz. *Dat,* I could git in shit for. You eva hear o that girly wit the fifdy-six axidental starz on er face?

My face quickly got warm. Yes, he had seriously just called me toots.

I want to get something else now. A tattoo. It's something silly, but really important to me. I want it right here, on my wrist.

You on zumdin now? He squinted at me.

No! God no. I'm sober as hell.

You have a pikchur of diz ta-tu?

The word came out of his mouth rough around the edges, frayed like jean shorts. Ta-tu.

Yeah. I pulled a piece of paper out of my backpack and pointed at the inch-by-inch picture I'd chosen. I braced myself for his laughter.

No problim, tootz, I kin do thiz.

Really? How much would it cost?

About a hundred.

A hundred dollars?

Yeah. You wan appoinmin or you ready today?

My stomach churned.

Are you free right now?

In grade eight, a few weeks after we've all start riding bikes together, one of the girls invites me to eat lunch with them at school. I'm surprised that they're willing to be seen with me in public. We sit together and I laugh along with them.

When school lets out for the summer, Janet and Cecile start swimming lessons every day after school. Left alone, Marity and I brainstorm things to do. We sometimes go to the water park or the shitty free youth group at the elementary school gymnasium. Then we make a new hangout for ourselves--The Tunnel, a big metal tube running under a busy street, the safe way for people on bikes or walking to get across. We sit atop The Tunnel, eight feet off the ground, and watch through a chain-link fence as traffic speeds by. I think we both like it because no one looks up as they're entering The Tunnel.

Sometimes we talk. She tells me about her parents being workaholics. I tell her about all the mean things Cecile did to me when we were growing up. She promises not to say anything to Cecile, but refrains from agreeing that she's a bitch. I soon realize Marity is different from the others. She never says bad things about anyone, ever.

Sometimes we have a lot of fun. We dangle our heads down and estimate how long it will take pedestrians to arrive, and then we drop pebbles on them, tiny bombs. One time I spit on a man cycling through and Marity clutches her belly with glee. He doesn't notice and I watch the drool roll off his helmet before he disappears down the road. Going to bed those nights I smelled the metal from The Tunnel on my hands, resting them under my cheek.

One particular August day we stop at the corner store on the way to The Tunnel and I shove some pixie sticks into my pants pocket while Marity flutters her great, long eyelashes at the guy behind the till. We go to The Tunnel, break open the plastic tubes, and divide the powdered candy into lines on my math textbook, which I forgot to return at the end of grade eight. Marity skillfully rips off both ends of one tube, puts it up her nostril, and snorts. When it's my turn I scream and grab my nose and roll around on my back, like the pain will kill me. Marity cracks up and grabs me. Her delicate hands save me from falling off the top of The Tunnel.

Then we sit and look at one of the little pixie sticks, talking about how cool it is that our 'drugs' resemble our hangout, only they're tiny and pink and not used as a walkway for people. A placebo experiment, the more she pretends she's high, the more I believe I am. She starts the other stuff first, putting one end of a full pixie stick in her mouth and growling. I chomp down on the other end and we both pull like in tug-a-war. I feel the packet grinding between my molars. I bite further up the stick for a better grip. She does the same, challenging me, a wild wolf.

I laugh playfully before the candy stick bursts on my end and the sweet cherry powder fills my mouth. We spit the chewed-up tube onto the ground by the tunnel and push our faces together. I think she's kissing me before I realized she's fighting for her share of candy, fairness being a big priority to thirteen-year-olds. Her tongue cleans my teeth and the roof of my mouth and I fight back, polishing her lips. Our mouths burn with sweetness.

When a bunch of boys come biking through The Tunnel we rip away from each other. I'm instantly terrified they've seen us, but they ride through without looking back. Marity and I climb down to bite our nails and fiddle with our pockets. She checks and re-checks her braid, smoothing it down. I smile, but she stares at her feet.

I'm a chicken, unable to open my mouth. I think one thing, over and over again.

I like that stuff better in my mouth than my nose.

All I pictured when the tattoo gun started up and the buzzing invaded my ears was Texas Chainsaw Massacre. I sat on a black gurney behind one of the curtained rooms, Mario on a wheeled stool before me. He'd drawn the stencil and placed it gingerly on the inside of my left wrist, letting me verify its position before starting. He pulled on a new set of black rubber gloves and poured the ink into little containers.

You ready?

I watched him dip the gun in ink and lower it to my skin, making contact and dragging slowly. My arm felt like it was being cut by paper or scratched by fingernails. I was in more pain when he rubbed excess ink away with a damp tissue than when he touched me with the tattoo gun.

Within forty-five minutes the process was over, the wound puffing up and the skin around it pinker than Barbie's high heels. Mario saran-wrapped it so blood and ink wouldn't get on my clothes.

Wut you think?

You're a great artist. I gazed at my arm, holding it up to the light. It's beautiful.

Sure, tootz.

My saran-wrapped wrist pulsating beneath the sleeve of my sweater, I sent a message to Raizel's phone.

can I come over?

now?

yeah.

I got on the bus before she could respond. I sat and gazed at the screen of my cell phone with headphones jammed down on my ears. I wasn't listening to the music; rather, I was letting it into my ears. I cradled my throbbing wrist like I would a baby chick.

Finally the screen lit up, flashing blue in the dim light coming through the window beside me. Day was fading quickly, silently. I read the message:

ok

Two small letters were better than nothing. I relaxed against the seat while the bus bumbled out of Wainmont, glad to leave before dark took over. Even I, having grown up in Oakwood Terrace, could be afraid of walking on a street at night.

When I got off the bus in her quiet neighborhood, my cell phone told me it was nearly eight o' clock. I shuffled down the sidewalk and paused on the corner to pull up my sleeve and check the tattoo. One glance told me I hadn't made a mistake.

I went up the walkway and rang the doorbell, noticing how they'd strung red and green lights around the doorway.

A short, plump woman with blond hair peeked out the door, eyes framed by thick, old-fashioned glasses, torso hidden under a blue robe. Before I could speak, she yanked the door open and motioned for me to step into the junk-filled sunroom.

It's freezing out, girly. Come in, come in. My name's Susan, by the way. Raizel's downstairs.

I'm Venice. I shook her warm hand and moved forward, closing the door behind me.

Now, what would you like to drink--orange juice, tea, coffee? Beer?

I couldn't tell if she was serious. I grinned.

Juice would be nice.

We'd never talked about her parents; they'd never come up in conversation, but I had imagined all sorts of people. I had imagined a tall, middle-aged couple with polo shirts and white khakis and busy schedules. I had imagined an old man and woman who knitted and read books together and talked about traveling without ever going. I hadn't imagined Raizel had come from someone so regular.

The kitchen smelled of patchouli and sugar. A bright platter of pineapple and strawberries sat in the middle of the table.

Bob, this is Venice, Raizel's new friend.

Hello. The broad-shoulder man at the table nodded at me over the tops of his bifocals. His blond hair was streaked with silver. There was no question as to why their children were so blond.

Sorry. Susan smiled. He's grading papers right now.

Yes. Sorry. Bob smiled distractedly. He looked at the paper on the table before punching something into a calculator.

Bob and Susan, a teacher and something else. Probably a nurse. I smiled.

It's nice to meet you both.

I went down the familiar wood-paneled staircase, careful not to spill my juice. A Kanye West music video was on the television, light from which danced across the empty sofa. I set the orange juice on Raizel's hairdressing vanity table and removed my coat. After noticing a strip of light under the bathroom door, I sat on the rotating stool and fixed bits of my hair that had been lifted in the winter wind.

I heard the bathroom doorknob turn and the latch click open.

Oh my god. I didn't know you were here.

In the mirror I spotted Raizel, in booty-shorts and a white tank top, the least clothing I'd ever seen her wear. She crossed her arms over her chest.

Hey. I twirled around on the stool.

Don't look! She scampered toward her bedroom.

Stunned, I spun back around and looked in the mirror. My cheeks had reddened into two plump tomatoes.

I watched a whole Madonna music video before I heard her wooden door budge open.

Okay. You can come in. She'd pulled on her beige cardigan, polka-dotted tights and a denim miniskirt.

Raizel's floor, desk, and dresser were covered with stuff. Even her bed was covered--books, a stuffed Kangaroo, nail polish, instant coffee packets, a twist-tied bag of miniature marshmallows, bobby pins, the remote for her CD player, clothing, a guitar case.

Here. Sorry. Raizel pushed stuff around, clearing a space for her butt and another beside it for mine.

No, I'm sorry. I mean, out there-- I motioned toward the door.

Don't worry about it.

With one hand I twirled the drawstring of my hooded sweater, with the other I picked up some incense.

Dragon Tail. I sniffed the opening of the bag. Can we light some?

Hmm. . .I don't really like that one. Raizel rested a hand on my knee and reached past me. Something in me fluttered when the tips of her hair brushed my cheek. She still smelled like lilacs.

This is the King of All Incense. She handed me a bag labeled *Nag Champa.*

My mom doesn't let me use incense. I fingered the bag's plastic zipper. She gets headaches. And stomachaches.

Raizel stood up, allowing me to sink comfortably into the old mattress. I pressed my back against the wall and watched as she shoved a t-shirt into the ceiling air vent.

My parents hate it, too.

We sat and watched the stick emit a long, narrow strand of white smoke, floating toward the ceiling before breaking into miniature clouds. The fragrance met my nose a moment later.

That smells really good.

I love it. Raizel nodded. She leaned back against her pillows, head on the wall.

So. . .I came here to talk to you. I heard myself swallow.

Something crawled out from under the desk then, a big pink elephant trampling everything on the floor and the foot of mattress between us, though we couldn't hear it. Silence hung in the air before dropping on everything like iron paper weights. Raizel looked down, seemingly studying her cardigan, the bottom button of which had fallen from its slit. The fair skin on her eyelids shone next to the bedside table lamp. I wished it was appropriate to pull out my camera.

Well? She finally looked up, annoyance creasing her forehead.

I'm not good at this, Raisin. My voice was tiny, an ant edging toward a gaping crack in the sidewalk. I'm sorry.

For. . .?

For accusing you of…things. I don't know what happened the other night. I honestly thought I was dreaming. I fingered the sleeve of my hoody, hearing saran wrap crinkle against my wrist. I got something, though. For you.

What is it? Her face remained calm, though she cocked her head.

This. I edged my sleeve up to my elbow.

What is that? Is that a tattoo?

Can you tell what it is? I can take the wrap off.

Oh my god. Raizel cradled the bottom of my wrist, inching her face closer to it. Is that a raisin?

I grinned.

Oh my *god*! Are you crazy? Her face lit up, the shadow of her eyelashes brightening above her eyes, mouth curving up gracefully. I was instantly reminded of the smile she'd given me on Halloween when she'd seen me dressed as Ellen. I. Can't. Believe. You. Did. That.

48

SLSHHHHHH. The noise of the new latte machine at Team Bean filled the shop's air for three seconds. A disturbingly perfect amount of beige liquid trickled from the nozzle into a large paper coffee cup.

It's so cool. Tiff smile, accepting the drink from the machine.

We'd successfully served, and seated, the usual crowd of seniors. Walter, in an especially good mood, had tipped us twice the price of his coffee. I'd wished he'd secretly slipped me the tip before remembering I'd received four hundred dollars on my latest paycheck.

So, I got my books for school. Tiff leaned over the counter, wiping away non-existent crumbs.

Cool. I stood with my arms crossed, listless after our morning of hard work. How much did they cost?

Eight hundred bucks.

What?! You paid eight hundred dollars for *books?* I shook my finger in her face.

Damn, this is good. Tiff sipped her latte.

Way to change the subject.

Wanna try some? She held the cup out.

No, thanks. Look at all the cream.

So?

So, I'm being careful about that kind of stuff.

I feel like I haven't seen you in a long time. Are you okay? Tiff eyed me for a moment, her eyes darting around my body and face. OH MY GOD. Is that a tattoo?

What? I slapped my right hand over my left wrist.

Let me see it! Tiff tugged on my right arm.

Be careful. I tsked, slowly pulling my hand away. It still hurts.

What... Tiff held my arm delicately, black nails nearly wrapping around my wrist. She brought her face closer. What is it?

What? You need to get your contact lenses checked. It's a raisin.

Oh.

It's still healing. See? I stroked the rough skin. It still needs to flake off.

One question--why a raisin?

I paused, stalling while I sipped my coffee.

Because...it reminds me of my grandma. I stifled a smile. We used to eat raisins together.

Oh. Tiff nodded. She reached up and rubbed my shoulder. Memorial tattoos are so nice.

She didn't remember that I'd never even met my grandmother.

So, I have something kind of awkward to ask you. Tiff's hand played idly with a strand she'd left dangling from her ponytail.

Yes, I got the tattoo for a girl I'm into. I glanced lovingly at the raisin, not giving a shit what she thought.

Sophie said she called you a little while ago, asking about that Raizel chick?

Yeah? I felt my eyebrow rise. And?

She wants to know if you've spoken to Raizel yet. She specifically asked if Raizel is 'taken'.

I giggled at Tiff's discomfort.

I don't know about that. But she's definitely not free.

We were on the road in Liam's car, pebbles and dots of dirty snow gathering on the windshield. Liam was out cold in the back, recovering from the impossible task of waking up at seven-thirty that morning. Raizel had taken the wheel and I was in the passenger seat with the heater aimed at my toes.

Three white hits of daisy I'd picked up from Seed were nestled in my koi fish pill box, which had served me well over the past few months. I'd strategically placed a sticker of Bob Marley's face over the cherry blossoms so Raizel wouldn't have to be reminded again and again of some bitch who had broken her heart.

I would protect her.

I'm so fucking stoked. Raizel shook her head in disbelief, keeping her eyes on the highway.

Me, too! I hope they play *Meet Me Again.*

Oh, man. That's my favorite. Raizel's fingers slipped from the steering wheel to change the song.

The sweet intro lilted through the car. I watched Raizel in my peripheral vision. Her smile was enough to light up the gray sky and the muddy winter highway.

I hadn't left Sloam in at least three years, not having had a purpose or the means. I'd looked up 'sloam' in a dictionary once, subsequently discovering the meaning of the whole city.

Sloam. V. to throw or force something across a room in distaste.

The only time I'd ever seen my mother kiss someone other than Dana or I, I was six years old. One July weekend day, a thin, tall man with crisp Levi's jeans and a ball cap had appeared in our driveway in his car. My mother had slipped into the front seat while my brother and I had climbed into the back. The car was long and shiny and had smelled nicely, like a hair salon waiting room. Dana had firmly told me not to touch anything, because our hands would ruin the car and make it all scratched and rusty like our mother's. I'd kept my hands in the lap of my three-sizes-too-big second-hand skirt and watched the back of the strange man's head.

When we'd left the car, the man had offered me his hand, my mother on his other side. I'd opted to pick up a long stick and drag it on the ground behind me, something to fasten me to the earth.

As we'd strolled through a meadow to Sloam's summer carnival, anyone who'd seen us would have thought we were a perfectly average family--a mother, a son, a daughter, and a man to assume the role of holding the rest of them up. *Father. Dad.* I'd wondered what to call him, as at the time I hadn't known that kids were meant to be born with fathers. I'd once found a two-dollar coin on our front lawn. I'd once found a broken badminton racket at the field near our house. I'd later learned that fathers couldn't just be found.

The man was rich; I'd known because he'd opened his wallet at the entrance gate and I'd seen a whole wad of bills. He'd paid for all of us and my mother had blushed, thanking him profusely. We'd all walked through Kiddy Land to the Daring Dragon rollercoaster, and I'd begged my mother to come on the ride and sit beside me. She'd said she was over the height limit, but she must have forgotten I'd known how to read. The sign hadn't even mentioned a height limit.

Dana and I had been swept up in the line with all the other kids, my stomach flipping with nausea at the caramel popcorn and hot dog fragrances all around us. I'd watched the rollercoaster rise far above my head, up up up. At the last second when I'd wanted to turn around and run into my mother's arms, my brother had grabbed me by the arm and said I wasn't going anywhere.

We'd strapped the flimsy rollercoaster seatbelt across us and I'd squeezed the metal bar like I'd tip out if I didn't, though we remained upright. A bell rang and the whole contraption lurched forward on its magnetic track. When we'd gained enough height to overlook the heads of the crowd, Dana had nudged me and pointed at something below.

There's Mom!

I'd peered fearfully over my brother's lap, spotting my mother by the railing near the ride's entrance. All I'd seen was the back of her dirty brown hair, as she'd stood with the strange man's arms entwined around her waist, their faces together. Extreme embarrassment had washed over me, as I'd only ever seen people kiss on television, and it was far too intimate an act for a public setting.

I'd resumed my position in the seat, having forgotten where I was and what was about to happen. The cart had risen substantially, up a mountainous arrangement of bars and seemingly random pieces of metal. Everything had moved slowly--my brother's words, the carnival music, and the crawling cart we were in. I'd been about to die, without my mother watching. I'd wanted to scream out over the hundreds of heads below.

Goodbye, cruel world.

All at once, my body had pushed back into the seat and my hair had whipped my face; my toes had curled into themselves and I'd watched the world turn below me; I'd forgotten about everything but the sun and the clouds and the humongous teddy bears far in the distance; I'd sucked breath into my lungs and let out a scream, gripping the bar before me harder than ever. My shoulder had rammed into Dana's and I'd caught his eye, laughter and saliva spurting from our mouths.

Twelve years later, I got the exact same feeling when I spotted the sign.

Welcome to Bowville

When we arrived at the motel, one Raizel claimed she'd stayed in millions of times, Liam checked us into the two rooms he'd booked, one for him and one for us girls. He winked and said he might need the privacy later if he met someone at the show. Raizel and I laughed together, glossing over the awkward fact that we'd have to share a bed.

We walked up a metal staircase on the outside of the building, stopping on the second floor. Everything in the motel room was old, from the flowery wallpaper to the wood-paneled television, quite like the one in my own basement. Raizel immediately opened the window in our room, trying to clear out the dust and the smell of Pledge from the staff's recent cleaning attempts.

We dumped our stuff on the desk in the room before running outside, three doors down. Raizel and I sat on the bed in Liam's room and waited while he combed his hair to perfection.

Though the air was cold against our skin, the sun was out and grinning, shining against everything it could. We went to a shopping mall full of old people and ate Mexican food for lunch. Sparkly red and green boas hung from the ceiling, signs outside of every shop advertising Christmas deals. The three of us wandered around the mall before deciding to take off to Value Village. I was shocked that Liam knew exactly where to drive and which turns he could take off the overpass to get to the road we needed.

How many shows have you been to in Bowville? Sitting in the back, I poked my head between the two front seats.

Tons. Liam grinned over his shoulder before turning to face the busy road. The Latch, Caesarline, Fighting the Urge--

I've seen Tegan and Sara here. Raizel turned to smile at me. And Millie Fischer, of course, and The Wine Tigers. So many more. Last year I saw The Bitchy Circus.

The Bitchy Circus? I laughed out loud. What kind of name is that?

I know. Raizel giggled. But they're fabulous.

They're so lesbian, though. Liam shot over his shoulder.

So are The Silly Rainbows. Raizel tsked at Liam. I don't see you complaining about *them.*

I make exceptions for *good* music. Unlike The Bitchy Circus.

Come on, Liam. Who doesn't like a good disco rap love ballad?

The Silly Rainbows were playing at the bar on Bowville's college campus, the roads of which were lined with snow banks and dead winter trees. I imagined summer on campus was beautifully green, verdant and grassy and leafy. Liam and Raizel and I each downed a beer from a six-pack I'd purchased earlier in the day with my newly legal-in-Alberta ID card. We left the car in a massive parking lot and skipped down a path between what I assumed were the college's two main buildings.

That afternoon Liam and Raizel had created a First Concert Ever outfit for me. Unlike in Sloam, Bowville's Value Village had three floors, one of which was dedicated solely to accessories. My friends had dragged items back and forth between the aisles and my change room until a huge pile had formed outside my door. The kid working outside the change rooms ignored us, slumped in a chair with his handheld PSP.

I'd put most of my outfit in my backpack, opting to pay only three dollars--for a belt checkered like a picnic blanket, knife and fork decals scattered randomly about.

That belt is so cool. Raizel had grinned at me as we'd left the store. That's all you wanted?

Embarrassed, I'd patted my backpack. Then it had occurred to me that if Amara had lied about her coke problem, she may have lied about other things, too.

We all shoplift. There aren't any cameras.

With a wince, I remembered my response.

But it's bad karma.

Raizel had dropped the subject quickly, a hot piece of coal.

Treading through the mere inches of snow on the path behind the buildings, I had on an old gray fedora, baggy jeans, the cool belt, and a graffiti-splattered t-shirt. A long, thin chain hung around my neck, a red pendant hanging against my chest. We'd all left our jackets in the car, not wanting to lug them around the concert.

I heard voices as we neared the corner of a building. We happened upon a well-lit area, a line of excited people have gathered outside the doors to another building. The three of us got in line, wishing we'd brought the remaining three beers. Everyone in front of us seemed tipsy already, shouting excitedly to fellow fans of The Silly Rainbows.

Wow. Liam gazed before us. So many chicks.

Long-haired, tall girls teetered on heels, seeming to scan the air above our heads. Short girls with boyish haircuts and ankle-biting jeans giggled together. Big chicks in bandanas and hooded sweaters stood with their arms crossed, checking everyone else out. There were girls in leggings and baby-doll dresses, yellow hair and tanning-bed skin. A few boys with skinny jeans mingled about, arms hugging their own petite frames.

Then there was me.

49

After half an hour of standing in line and listening to drunken chatter, the double doors swung open. Warmth pushed out of the building, enveloped us, and sucked us back in. We threw our tickets in a bucket and headed down a hallway, straight to the bar. We showed our ID cards and received purple bracelets meaning we were of drinking age. Liam immediately bought us each a shot of tequila.

The bar wasn't too big--probably enough for two hundred people packed like sardines. Through the dim lights I made out the center of the room, steps leading down to a stage, the space before which having already begun to fill up with fans.

Bam. Bam. Bam. The drums started seconds after we'd purchased pints of beer, though the room remained dark.

Come on! Raizel exclaimed, grabbing my free hand with hers.

I'm gonna hang out here! Liam called after us.

I took control, stepping ahead of Raizel to pull her through the crowd of girls.

When we were several layers deep and five feet away, the stage came ablaze, spotlights slapping the faces of The Silly Rainbows' six band members. The drummer's arms rose from the depths of darkness, sticks molesting the drums. The guitarists chimed in all at once and then there were words.

bad bad bad
things will never happen, my friend
you'll never have to fight for me
bad things will never happen again

my pack of wolves are at your gate, my owls gathered high
outside your heart, inside your fate, my oh my oh my
bad bad things will never happen, this I can promise

if anything

THIS IS SO AWESOME! I yelled over the music near Raizel's ear.

I KNOW! Raizel screamed back, grinning, keeping her eyes on the singer.

Behind us, the crowd pushed forth. I kicked someone's ankle.

Sorry! I yelled.

She turned around, a girl about my height, dark hair cut short around her heart-shaped face. Dark features morphed into a smile, eyes shining at me through sparkling black eye-shadow.

It's alright! The girl leaned back to yell at me. She came so near, I felt hot breath inside my ear. What's your name?

Venice!

Huh? She squinted and brought her ear toward me. I caught a whiff of the conditioner she'd used.

IT'S VENICE! I put my hand over my mouth, fearing beer breath.

WANNA GO SOMEWHERE QUIETER? The girl nodded back toward the bar, silver hoops shaking in her ears. Her cheeks sparkled with makeup. MAYBE GET A DRINK?

She already has one! Raizel yelled from behind me, putting her hand on my shoulder.

It's true. I smiled, holding up my beer. Sorry.

Have a good night then! The girl smiled and shrugged, turning to ease into another part of the crowd.

Dude! I yelled toward Raizel. Was she hitting on me?

When I turned around I realized Raizel had dodged forward into the spot left vacant by the girl. She probably hadn't even heard my question, which was stupid, anyway. There was no reason for such a pretty girl to be interested in someone like me. I stood behind Raizel and bumped my beer mug against hers. She smiled and sipped her drink, bopping her body to the music.

By the time I finished my drink, I'd moved so much forward that I could almost touch the rough wooden edge of the stage. The crowd pushed so hard against our backs that Raizel and I became separated, a couple of boyish girls dancing raucously between us. I tried twisting around to see the bar and gauge how easy it would be to score a new drink, but if I left I'd surely lose my spot. I stole a glance at Raizel with her hands raised appreciatively, beer mug having been discarded. I touched the outline of my pillbox in my jeans pocket.

Raisin! On my tip toes, I called over the heads between us.

Raizel continued to dance, head down while her arms moved above her.

EXCUSE ME! I slipped my arm between the girls who were jumping together, reaching blindly for Raizel. A red light flew over the crowd just long enough for me to catch the glaring face of a short, tough-looking girl.

Excuse you is right! She yelled, fingering the bits of hair coming out from under her toque.

Sorry! I patted the shoulder of her acid-washed jean vest and pointed at Raizel, thinking I knew how to get what I wanted. I'm just trying to get to my girlfriend!

Oh! The girl's glance followed my finger. She turned back to me and wiggled her eyebrows. *She's* your girlfriend?

Yeah. I smiled as I lied, watching Raizel in her polka-dotted dress and black tights and red shoeboots, resisting jostles from the crowd despite her petite frame. Her hair hung around her bare shoulders, loose white-blond curls. I *know*.

I looked back at the band. I was getting so close that I could see the humidity of human exertion rising around them every time the lights flashed over.

The guitar players looked especially in their element, eyes closed as their hands made magic.

When I looked back toward Raizel, she'd been engulfed by the short girl and her friend; the three jumped and shouted lyrics together like they'd always know each other. I quickly came to notice the clasped hands of Raizel and the girl in the toque, high in the air. In a split second, they shared a smile, one where the strange broad's head tilted slyly and Raizel's lips parted in a full-on blush. Afterwards, I felt the girl's eyes on me as I turned my back to them, concentrating on the band.

Eventually Raizel managed to squeeze into a tiny space beside me. I felt her cool palm on my forearm as she exclaimed that she'd missed me. I nodded her way, pleased to find that the short chick was nowhere in sight. Raizel sang all the words, all the while gazing at the singer, a skinny girl with short hair and tattooed arms and a red skirt that came up to her breasts. As we jumped along with the music, sweat dripped down my lower back, bodies pushing Raizel and I forward and together; we were so close I would probably have felt her heartbeat on my shoulder if not for the bass pounding from the speakers beside us.

I was about to pull out my pillbox when silence and darkness took the stage. The crowd grew louder than ever, chanting for The Silly Rainbows.

Get silly! Get silly! GET SILLY!

A light twirled over the head of the singer, whose catlike eyes pondered the crowd before she plucked the string of a cello. Immediately afterwards, the band chimed in, though they remained somewhere in the dark.

Oh my god! Raizel exclaimed, squeezing my arm. *Meet Me Again!*

I grabbed both of Raizel's hands and we threw them in the air together, fingers braided together. I found myself shouting the lyrics and belting out like I always imagined I would if I had my car. I sang like I was the one on stage and people adored *me.* The music absorbed me and I absorbed it; forgetting about everything but the moment I was so lucky to be a part of.

When we made it back to the second floor at the motel, the air in our room seemed almost colder than outside. Raizel kicked off her wet shoeboots and stalked over to the window.

Sorry. She pulled the window and latched it closed. I forgot I left this open.

Brr. I shivered, scampering to my backpack.

Raizel and I turned our backs to each other to change into our sleepwear.

Did you have a good night? I spoke over my shoulder. I quickly shuffled out of my jeans and yanked my sweats up.

Yeah. Raizel's muffled voice floated over to me, probably mid-removal of her t-shirt. You?

It was awesome. I threw off my fedora and pulled my hoody on over the graffiti t-shirt, running my hand through my hair.

I'm done changing.

I turned to see Raizel in a black hoody and baggy, old sweatpants. We both crawled onto the bed, sitting with our backs against the pillows and heads against the wall.

Actually. Raizel played with her labret piercing, looking down at her own clasped hands. It was probably my favorite show I've ever been to.

Ever? Are you sure?

Definitely. Raizel let her green eyes dash up to meet mine.

Is that because you got that chick's phone number?

Huh? Oh... Raizel lifted the sleeve of her hoody, gazing at her wrist. I read the black ballpoint ink, placed neatly under her tattoo.

Josie
681-2930
:)

Did you know she lives in Sloam?

So, you liked her? I nudged Raizel's ribs.

I was just being nice. Raizel laughed. Don't tell me you're one of those people who thinks lesbians are attracted to every single girl and gay boys are into every single guy.

Fuck no. I said this quickly, defensively.

And anyway, did you see her teeth?

No... I held my hand up over my own gapped front teeth.

She totally didn't have any.

NONE? I pulled my hand away as my mouth dropped open.

I mean, like, no front teeth. I bet she's been in a billion fights.

Pause. We sat for a moment, hearing car wheels crunch on the snow in the motel parking lot. Someone parked and slammed their door. Keys jangled.

Hey. My cheeks felt hot. I've been meaning to ask you something.

Yeah? Raizel, wringing her chilled hands together, looked at me.

Remember when I asked what your tattoo means?

Mm hmm?

I wasn't talking about the one on your wrist.

She paused before speaking.

I got it in honor of my brother.

Why?

How do you know about it?

I snuck a picture of it during that, 'photo shoot' with Amara.

What a silly day. Raizel cracked up laughing. That already seems like so long ago.

So...?

Oh, speaking of which, I really think you need to buy a new camera.

I really want one. But they're so expensive.

That's true, but if you're going to move ahead with your plan, you gotta take the first steps.

I loved how the word rolled out of her mouth. *Plan,* not just pipe dream.

Ready for bed? Raizel rested her hand on the lamp's switch.

Ok. I felt at a loss for words, my questions about her brother having whipped around the motel room's air before cowering under the old TV stand.

Darkness fell upon the room. My eyes begged to adjust to the blue moonlight outside the window. I peeked at Raizel, barely-present light cast upon her face. She smiled at me.

We wiggled our bodies down like a couple of worms.

My pillow smells like dust. I scrunched my nose.

Raizel moved her head over, sniffing my pillow.

Ew. Maybe we should pull our hoods up.

Definitely.

Simultaneously, we slipped the hoods of our sweaters over our heads, pulling the drawstrings. I was reminded of the first night I'd met daisy, how comfortable Raizel had made me feel. Shivering, I pulled the blanket up around both of us.

All night, I'd been waiting for the perfect moment to pull out my pill box and offer something to my friends--in the line outside, something to cheer us up for freezing our asses off. I could've passed them off right after we'd gotten our drinks. I could've made my offer halfway through the show when our limbs were loose and ready to dance. I thought Liam would surely accept, if I'd had the guts to offer, but I didn't know about Raizel. There was so much I didn't know about her. The strange thing was that at times she seemed so laid-back about drugs and at others she became hesitant and worrisome.

I concluded that the night couldn't have gone any better, whether it had included daisy or not. I felt oddly successful.

Night, V. Under the blanket, Raizel poked me in my side.

Night, Raisin.

Raizel's hand crossed back to her side of the bed as though a strict line had been drawn between us. She turned on her side, back to me. Inside my hoody pocket, I locked my own hands together, though they could easily have inched forward and wrapped around her waist. I could have pulled her toward me and nudged her hood off with my nose. I could have put my lips on the bit of skin behind her ear.

Bang bang bang. My heart pounded furiously. I stroked my wrist, feeling slight bumpy scabs where my own tattoo had near-healed.

50

When I got home from Bowville, about which my mother asked no questions, as she'd never fully approved of me going, the Christmas tree had been set up in a corner of the living room not often reached by the light of our touch-lamp. As my extended family--my aunt Blanche her husband--hadn't invited us to spend Christmas with them for nearly a decade, that year it would once again be my mother and Dana and I. Dana said he'd bring Molly over for the big day if her family wasn't so obsessed with her. He always seemed to do that, portraying her as the perfect angel. I wondered if we should shove something up her ass and put her on the tree.

We didn't have a real evergreen, just a faded plastic thing we used every year and stored in the attic, erect, with the decorations still on. It came up to my shoulder. Some of the lights we'd left wrapped around the fake branches had short-circuited throughout the years, but I had to admit that mine and Dana's grade-school decorations were cute. One morning as I sat and watched the Simpsons' Holiday Special, I caught myself reminiscing about childhood Christmases, staring at the miniature wreath picture frames and the macaroni chain wrapped around the plastic tree needles. Their cuteness didn't fail to mask the utter hopelessness surrounding Christmas, a season I'd long since stopped regarding as the best time of year.

Molly ended up ringing our doorbell at ten to three on the afternoon of Christmas Eve.

Get in here! My brother flung the door open, pulling his girlfriend by the forearm onto our front landing. She stumbled over my high-tops.

Wow. He knew exactly how to treat her.

How did you get away from your family? Dana touched his hair, making sure it was matted perfectly on his chubby head. What did they say?

Oh. Molly waved her gloved hand as she stamped the snow off her boots. The real celebration at our place is tomorrow night. They said I could stay here if the snow's too bad.

I think the snow's too bad. Dana wiggled his eyebrows.

Ew. You can't have *my* bed. I tore my eyes off them to glance at the television, seeing a commercial about last-minute gift shopping at Sears.

Oh, hey, Venice. Molly's jacket and boots were off when she finally noticed me. Nice hair.

Thanks. I had on the most festive thing I'd worn in years--Raizel had convinced me to put across the tips of my 'hawk a stripe of temporary red dye, a box of which she'd gotten from work. I moved my legs off the sofa. You can sit here, if you want.

I'm actually gonna see what your mom's up to in the kitchen.

Probably nothing. I made my prediction according to Christmases past, ones where our 'feast' had included KFC buckets or turkey TV dinners.

Hi, Molly! My mother called from the kitchen, as if she was unable to get away from the stove for more than five seconds.

Hi, Kath! Molly's shortened version of my mother's name was enough to make me cringe.

Molly and my mother were in the kitchen for over an hour when I caught a whiff of baking chicken. I finally tore myself off the couch and went to see what they were doing.

As the kitchen was a complete mess, my first thought was that I'd have to spend a long time cleaning later. My second and third thoughts were *That chicken smells amazing* and *Is there really a pumpkin pie on the counter?* I had no idea what to say.

I watched Molly at our kitchen sink, rinsing broccoli, my mother chopping garlic beside her. It seemed she was finally acquiring the daughter she'd always wanted. Only when I had that thought did I know what to say.

Can I. . .help?

Ask the chef. My mother used her thumb to motion at Molly.

Oh, Kath. You're quite the chef yourself. Molly glanced over her shoulder at me. Would you mind making the deviled egg filling, Venice? The recipe's on the fridge.

Okay. I wandered over to the fridge, reading her girly, bubbly writing. I memorized the ingredients so I wouldn't have to check the list a million times over.

By six o' clock we had a good variety on the table--a mixed green salad, boiled vegetables, mashed potatoes, stuffing, a whole small chicken, and my deviled eggs. Dana, who we'd let drink beer and watch hockey all afternoon, whooped when he wandered into the kitchen.

This looks great. He rubbed his round belly, drawing his t-shirt up enough to reveal an expanse of hairy skin.

I stifled the urge to ask when he was due.

Why don't we all get plates and go out to the living room? My mother wrung her hands as she suggested this, undoubtedly craving a cigarette. She hadn't smoked anything all day, probably afraid of what Molly would think.

Okay. Dana opened the refrigerator door. Anyone need a drink?

Is there anyone wine? My mother inquired, continuing to fidget. Preferably red?

We all got plates, piled high with food, and moved out to the living room like we'd done the night I'd had Seed over. We turned the TV off and talked between bites, though none of us had anything important to say. I washed down every bite with a gulp of red wine, having to refill my glass before I'd even finished half of the meal.

Oh! I just remembered something. My mother put her plate on the coffee table and jumped up to look in the front closet. From her purse she withdrew a CD case. I figured, well, it's Christmastime, so--

A minute later, an acoustic version of *Deck the Halls* was souring through our living room. Dana downed the rest of his beer can and let out a belch, over the music. I glanced between him and Molly, wondered what she possibly saw in him. Then my brother bobbed his head joyously, making fun of the music without our mother realizing it.

My family *always* listens to this at Christmas! Molly exclaimed, not knowing how unusual the evening was, for people like us. When she caught sight of Dana's dancing, she began laughing so hard she spit broccoli into my mashed potatoes without noticing. I bent to set my plate on the coffee table and leaned back on the sofa, patting my belly as if I was too full to move.

Geez, these lights really don't do justice. My mother got up and fingers the edge of a branch. As she was on her third glass of wine, I was surprised not everything appealed to her liquor-filled eyes.

I think there's more in the attic. I immediately regretted my words and wanted to chase after them; they were like escaped prisoners of my head.

Day, would you mind? My mother turned to Dana, a worrisome frown on her face. The place will just look so much better.

Dana belched again before patting his stomach like I'd done my own. I sipped my wine and felt the sofa groan as my brother tried to stand up. He finally came flopping back down, resting his head on the arm of the couch.

I think someone's drunk too much. Molly laughed, not realizing more broccoli was stuck between her teeth.

Look in a mirror, I thought, my eyes darting around this strange girl's pink cheeks.

If your father was here maybe he'd do it. My mother turned her back to us.

Without some choir's rendition of *We Three Kings,* the room's silence surely would have shattered everything--the ice-frosted picture window, the television, our dinner plates. Quietly, I gulped my dark wine and set the glass on the squat table.

I'll get them, okay, Mom? I stood up, squatting crumbs off the crotch of my jeans.

Beside me, Dana hiccupped. Molly rubbed his hair, probably coating her hand with dandruff.

With no response from my mother, I moved down the dark hallway with my arms up and ready, hopping a few times to reach the string. I pulled the attic ladder down like I had a thousand times before, putting my hands on the first steps to hoist myself up. I quickly scaled the wooden apparatus toward the dark square above me.

After flicking on the light, I recovered the electric string of Christmas lights from around the wooden railing in the attic, remembering Dana had put them there the last time he'd sorted through things. When I brought them back down Dana snoring and my mother was talking quietly on the couch with Molly.

The devilled eggs are *so* sweet, Venice. My mother laughed heartily, apparently having recovered from her pity party freak-out. What did you do--put sugar instead of salt?

I blushed, realizing I might have done exactly that. I turned away from the couch, bending to plug in the string of lights. Nothing happened.

They're busted. I padded quietly to the front door and bundled up in my shoes and jacket and a couples of scarves.

My mother asked me where I was going, for god's sake, it was Christmas Eve.

I'll be back.

What are you doing here? Raizel spoke up at me through the inch she'd managed to open her basement bedroom window. Her hair was so bright, so white, near the light in her room. I mean, why didn't you come to the door?

I--I don't know. I thought this would be fun. How are you reaching the window?

I'm standing on my dresser, silly. Her cheeks were a charming shade of peach, like she'd drunk something with mere hints of liquor. Probably rum and eggnog. I wondered if she had extended family over. Funny you caught me down here--I was just grabbing Scrabble when I heard your knock.

Look at this. My hand shook as I held something out, something sacred I'd never shared with anyone but my brother.

Oh? Her forefinger and middle finger reached out to pinch the edges of the photo, which she drew into her room.

Do I look like him? I caught a glimpse of rich, crimson bed-sheets. I wished I was nestled warmly beneath them.

You have the same eyes. Raizel's own eyes darted up to meet with mine. She glanced around my face as if she'd never seen it before. And I suppose the same mouth. Who is he?

My father.

He's pretty handsome. Raizel was gazing at the picture again. Where is he?

I don't know. And I don't know if my mother knows. We never talk about him. But I had to come show you, because I think he's my mother's 'one that got away'. I mean, I think my mom didn't get a real chance with him because my brother and me happened.

Raizel's face became the softest I'd ever seen it. I got the sense that she'd give a newborn baby the same sort of look.

Oh, V, I'm sure--

I'm not trying to get your pity, Raisin. That's not why I'm here.

Raizel ducked her head and got down from her dresser. I saw her toss Scrabble onto her bed. I bent my knees and peered into her room as far as I could before the window fogged up.

A moment later Raizel came sailing around the corner of her house, red shoeboots clumsily stamping the walkway, as she hadn't tied them. She threw her arms around my neck and I wrapped mine around her coatless waist, disbelieving I was worth the cold.

I missed you. Raizel's hushed words dared to be caught and carried away in the softly howling December air.

I trembled and squeezed her small body.

She loosened her arms and held me inches away so we could see each other.

Is this okay? Her eyes inquired, dark and deep and daring.

No. My left eye replied. I'm confused--

Of course. My right eye interjected. Definitely. Absolutely.

Like holding a honey bottle upside down, waiting for the first drop to fall, I was allotted time to back out. When her warm lips pressed against mine, I felt myself press back, disbelieving the tenderness. I barely felt the little ball of her lip piercing as it bobbed against me. Our mouths were demulcent together, fresh bread, the inside of tangerine rind, a sheer t-shirt.

After the kiss she leaned her forehead on mine, arms still looped around my neck, eyes lively. I blushed and smiled, instantly as shy as the first time we'd met.

51

We never hang out anymore. Tiff sipped her latte. She'd stopped drinking cappuccinos when Team Bean had upgraded its machinery.

I feel like you're too busy, getting ready for school. I gulped down some of my own coffee.

I know. I feel bad. Let's hang out after work, okay?

Fuck. I really didn't feel like it.

Okay. What do you want to do?

What we do every night, Brain. Try to take over the world.

I laughed. Maybe I could get high and pretend I was drunk. I still had a bit of Special K in my desk drawer at home.

You wanna go to the bush?

Tiff rolled the idea around in her head, swigging some more of her drink.

Not really. I don't feel like partying.

We agreed to go to my basement and watch one of our favorite old DVD's.

Don't invite anyone else, okay? Tiff frowned.

Huh? Like who?

Like...that Amara bitch.

Okay. I scoffed. She had no idea who I even hung out with. As long as you don't bring Meaghan.

It didn't even cross my mind. Tonight is just you and me, okay?

Alright. Hey, check out that lady's jacket. I lowered my voice to change the subject, motioning across the store with my elbow.

She looks like a woolly mammoth. Tiff giggled at the furry gray coat of a customer.

Later that afternoon I looked at my cell phone, hoping Raizel would send me something sweet, something to confirm she didn't regret kissing me on Christmas when she was meant to be inside with her family. When I saw the one text I received, an awful feeling came over my stomach, repulsion at its finest bubbling in all the coffee I'd downed. A text from Seed was in my message inbox.

boo I got sum blue ls u like. going fast. stop by L8r.

I briefly wondered what 'blue ls' meant. Could he possibly mean the blue lemons, the first pills he'd ever sold me? I recalled the playground with Liam, the dreamlike world we'd ran off to for a night, the love my hands had felt when I'd run them over everything in sight. And the conversation--our words had gone on forever, rockets soaring ethereally through the universe. Nothing was more fitting for New Year's Eve.

ok. i got sumthin 2 do but i'll get outta it. save 8.

As I pressed SEND, I looked up at Tiff. She stood at the counter with her long, curly red ponytail hanging down the back of her black polyester Team Bean apron. Her mascara-clad eyes concentrated on separating coffee filters from each other, something we did before rushes so we wouldn't have to do it in a sweaty panic when the line was out the door. Separating them completely was important, because if you used two at a time the coffee wouldn't seep through and would end up a bubbling mess all over the counter. Sometimes it took a whole minute to wedge my finger between two of them, to find the edges of the thin paper filters and separate them and shove them into the coffee makers.

A minute was a long time. People could get married in a minute. A baby could be born in a minute. In the same minute, someone could spin out of control on the highway and crash into a semi and become paralyzed.

I realized Tiff was smiling, something the rest of us tended not to do when we were doing the coffee filters. I concluded that she'd probably still be happy little Tiff if I had to cancel our plans. She would probably enjoy some extra time to sit at her easel and paint a masterpiece.

Hey. I sidled up to her.

Hey. I was just thinking about which flavor of chips I'm gonna bring over tonight. I think dill pickle.

About that...

Don't tell me you're cancelling. She dagger-eyed me; it'd been so long since I'd seen The Look.

I widened my own eyes innocently. Okay, so maybe she would care.

Oh, no! It's funny, I was just going to ask you which chips you wanted to have. I smiled, picked up a stack of the filters, and started tearing them away from each other. Dill pickle's fine with me.

That *is* funny. Her face relaxed. I guess we are still meant to be best friends.

I was inclined to feel awkward and strangely guilty, knowing the truth her words lacked. We stood beside each other, working steadily and only stopping to serve the most sugary of Team Bean's desserts to some kids whom we agreed should've been in school. At some point in time, people had probably said the same things about us. We laughed about how we used to skip math class and hang out at the strip-mall in Oakwood.

In the back of mind and sometimes etching to the front were these little pills the shade of the ocean, far out where boats and litter and oil couldn't reach. I hardly believed how soon I'd be dancing on the clouds. I'd probably get to be with Raizel and share them with her later that night. I couldn't wait to hear her giddy voice tinged with aqua.

If I couldn't cancel on Tiff, I'd make her cancel on me.

A convenience store in the parking lot beside Team Bean sold everything from frozen pizza to travel-sized shampoo. On my ten-minute break I told Tiff I was going over to buy those chips we'd talked about. She grinned widely at my high spirits. Fending off pangs of guilt was no easy feat. Emotions were like cockroaches; after being exterminated they had a tendency to return with a vengeance for having been rejected. But I *had* to do it. I couldn't pass up a chance at another amazing night.

When I got back with my supplies, I smiled at Tiff.

I'm so pumped for tonight.

Me too, Hon.

I was instantly reminded of Rhonda the One-Buck Bitch.

Since when do you call people 'Hon'?

Do you want another latte? I smiled. I'll make it.

Sure. She grinned back. Thanks.

Walter came in then. He was the slowest customer we had, so the plan went smoothly. Tiff took his order while I prepared her beverage, one splash of coffee, four Gravols from the pocket of my dirty black Team Bean jeans, three seconds under the latte machine nozzle, two more pills, another splash of coffee, all the while disbelieving my luck that Team Bean still hadn't installed surveillance cameras. Then again, I had been really careful, giving her just enough to feel sleepy and perhaps a bit loopy.

I stirred the concoction the whole time she talked to Walter, gave him his change, and carried a tray with half-coffee-half-hot-water and a blueberry muffin, hold the butter, to his table. I laughed, knowing her customer service skills would never score her a one-hundred-dollar tip.

Cheers!

I held up my drink like I'd done so many times at Oakwood bush parties. Tiff bumped her own drink against mine and we took delicate sips. I waited for some indication that she knew what I'd done.

Ouch, hot. This tastes different. Tiff licked her lips. I can't quite place it.

Bang bang bang. My heart. I hoped the pills had dissolved.

Oh! I snapped my fingers. I put an extra splash of coffee in there for ya.

Oh, thanks Hon. It's delicious.

When Monica came around the corner mere minutes later, we both feigned hard work, checking the coffee levels and restocking napkins in their flimsy contraption.

Venice, how do you feel about watching the counter? I need Tiffany for a bit.

Sure. No prob.

Okay, yell if you need us.

Deal.

Can I bring my drink? Tiff cradled her drink as though it was a baby.

Sure. Monica nodded enthusiastically, the hair on her mole shaking.

At that point in my tentative career as a coffee bitch, I was a speed demon, typing orders into the till as quickly as people made their demands. I seated people and brought their coffees out, able to remember exactly whom received what.

When I heard a loud bang I jumped up, expecting to see a customer rapping a mug against the counter. Instead I noticed everyone ceasing serene conversation to look around and ponder the noise. The shop door opened and two people stumbled in, a big whoosh of white winter air surrounding them. The man nearest the door pulled his coat collar up around the back of neck, straightened his newspaper, and continued reading. I turned to the coffee machine and waited for the customers to make it to the counter with their undoubtedly cold legs and fingers that would tremble when it came time to muster up coins from their pockets.

Venice! Monica cried out.

I turned around and realization took over--of the two people, one was my manager, and the one leaning against her was a girl with a long curly red ponytail and pale flesh and bent legs. She seemed to be melting onto the floor like the wicked witch of the west, only not so wicked with her eyes fastened shut.

What's wrong? Blood rushed to my head.

Bang bang bang. My heart pounded in my eardrums.

I don't know, I told her to change the sign from two fifty-nine coffee down to one ninety-nine, because of the winter promotion and everything, and I went to shed and came back and she was just lying in the snow.

Is she unconscious? A customer piped up.

The next minute passed on fast-forward slow-motion; I hopped over the counter and ran across the tiled floor to them, wet sneaker bottoms screeching. I caught Tiff under her armpit and we dragged her to some seats near the window, two women there hopping up in shocked obligation. I held the back of my friend's head as she sunk into one of the armchairs, and used a napkin to wipe snow off her hands.

Tiff's eyes opened briefly, thin white slits, before they retreated back into her head. The women were nice, one of them calling 911 and the other slinging her furry gray woolly mammoth coat over my friend.

This strong doctor guy plucked Tiff up from the armchair and for an instant they were newlyweds about to enter the threshold of their new house. Her legs and arms were soupy, swinging involuntarily as he placed her on a stretcher and tucked her shivering body under a white quilt. I wasn't sure the whole thing was real, all the customers crowding around the action, paramedics squeezing our minds like oranges for details.

I stood in silence as the ambulance took off, this huge, screaming white contraption. I pondered the fact that they had chided us for moving her from where she'd fallen. Looking across the eerily peaceful white parking lot at the store sign, I pictured Tiff face-planting the snow bank, and leaving her there because someone in a serious-looking dark blue costume said I should.

My stomach got all queasy when I noticed the ladder and the sign.

$ 99 Cof

Flip flip flip.

Hotness spread up my body; it came up my neck and encased my cheeks and my forehead. The sign was at least ten feet off the ground. Had she fallen off the ladder? If I had known she'd be going up on a ladder, or anywhere besides standing at the front counter, I never would have done what I'd done.

I'd done it. I was a criminal.

52

When I arrived at Seed's he had over the same three kids who'd been there when I'd picked up the Special K. Equally as friendly as they'd been before, everyone sat gazing at the television, eyes glossed over as they watched *Across the Universe*. The girl with her miniskirt didn't even acknowledge me with her usual evil eye.

We were immediate with our exchange; I handed Seed a steaming hot tea and eighty bucks, held open my pretty cherry blossom koi fish container, and in slipped eight beacons, bright blue pills with tiny lemons etched on top. My eyes got lost in their docility and innocence. For them, I'd made Tiff's eyes roll back in her head.

What's wrong? Seed leaned over to peer into the box.

His scent wafted my way, a pleasant mixture of cologne and tea. I liked tea. I noticed the sober version of Seed's eyes, youthful green things with long, dark lashes. I debated dragging him to the couch and having him wrap his arms around me, pat my back, and tell me everything would be okay and that I hadn't done the most messed up thing ever. Too bad the couch was occupied by stoned teenagers.

Nothing's wrong. I closed the container and put it in my pocket. I'll see you later, okay?

For sure, boo.

I called Tiff's house that night, but no one answered. They were probably with her at the hospital. She cancelled her next few shifts at Team Bean, milking her ambulance trip for all it was worth. On New Year's Eve, the third night in a row that Monica called me in to cover for Tiff's three-to-eleven shift, I wanted to scream.

But, she only had Gravol, she's fine, she doesn't have a deadly disease. I zipped my mouth shut when the words dared to fly out. I agreed to work, thinking around nine o' clock I would feign sickness and ask to leave.

Apart from some kids and their parents coming for New Year's Eve coffees, something to keep them up until midnight, Team Bean was completely dead. I texted back and forth with both Raizel and Liam, finding out they were already at a Broadway house party. Raizel sent me the address and *begged* me to come as soon as possible, but neither of them was fit to drive and get me. Having cleaned and putting everything away neatly, I watched out the window and down the snowy road as a group of police pulled every car over in a routine New Year's Eve alcohol checkpoint. I wondered how many of those car trunks were full of liquor waiting for be drunk. I couldn't wait to see Raizel, as I hadn't stopped thinking about her lips.

My wish came true as early as eight o' clock, when Monica shuffled out of her office and down the hall and said we may as well lock up for the night. She thanked me for sticking around as long as I had and offered me a ride home.

I changed into an outfit when I got home, something I had set on my bed before work--tight jeans and a white button-down t-shirt with a black tie. When I looked in the mirror and realized I looked like a Red Lobster server, I tugged the tie off, rolled up my sleeves and undid the top button. I tousled the shirt collar and pulled over my head something I'd scored from Value Village--a crocheted turquoise toque, the color of which was more than shocking against my fake-blond-with-a-festive-red-stripe bangs. I coated my eyes with mascara and tapped my toes to some quiet music in my room.

The taxi I had called upon arriving at home appeared in the road, honking its horn. I told my mom I was going out and wouldn't be home until long after midnight.

There's no point in waiting up for me.

She waved goodbye from the front window, clutching her afghan around her shoulders.

Traffic was dull, as people across the city were probably already pissed and out for the count. Despite the taxi driver thinking I was crazy, I rolled the window down an inch, just to feel the briskness of New Year's Eve on my face. Several times we drove by party houses, the walls of which shook with music, people spilling out front doors without proper shoes on.

I threw money at the taxi driver--more than enough for the fare and a tip, subconsciously making up for recent events in my life. The address we'd arrived at wasn't the biggest house on the street; rather, it was tall thin, quite like Raizel and Abby's. All of the lights were on and I heard the bump-bump-bump of music.

The house's front door opened before I could reach it, and a couple emerged, blowing cigarette smoke everywhere. I dove in, immediately greeted by the warmth of human bodies shoulder-to-shoulder in a front landing. Spotting the mountain of pleather boots and mud-streaked runners, I decided to keep my shoes on. I hopped up the narrow staircase through a sea of unfamiliar faces, hugging my backpack close so I wouldn't bumps drinks. The lights were dim, but someone had taken the effort of hanging sparkly streamers from the ceiling. People around me shrieked drunkenly. Beer breath was everywhere.

Fuck it. I unzipped my backpack, digging around for my cell-phone. *I'm never gonna find them.*

As I was flipping my phone open, someone yelled in my ear.

HEY BABY HOW YOU DOING?

Annoyed, I shrugged away and move toward a wall, to regain composure and decide if I really wanted to be there. The person who had spoken grabbed my wrist, and I thought about how much that would burn if my tattoo hadn't healed. I looked up with a mighty glare on my face.

Raizel smiled.

I smiled.

She seemed to be hiding under a lock of hair that hung at one side of her face, courtesy of a far side-part. She had on a tight black dress, something that would make the fat on my chest bubble over at the top if I dared to try it on. Strapless, the ensemble elongated her neck and outlined her collarbone elegantly.

You look amazing, I said in her ear, catching the lilac scent of her perfume. I didn't know if it was her perfume; it could have just been her natural scent. I grabbed her hand and told her to twirl. The dress hugged the small curves of her hips, stopping short at the tops of her legs, the likes of which she had dressed in floral-print tights.

Oh my god. I pointed at her feet. Where are your shoeboots? I mean…your red boot things. You know.

Raizel glanced down at her simple black flats and clicked her toes together like an Irish dancer.

It's gonna sound silly, but I needed a change…something to match the way I feel inside. A pink, slightly alcoholic hue came over her cheeks. Her shining lips radiated the slightest remnants of a sweet beverage. It's gonna be a new year.

Satisfied with her answer, I asked Raizel to show me around. She took my hand and pulled me through throngs of partiers to the kitchen, where she poured me some champagne from a bottle she'd brought. She instructed me to chug my glass, so I could catch up, and then poured us each a new one. Our shoes made smacking sounds on the sticky floor, over which I assumed a drink or two had already been spilled. A bunch of kids stood smoking in a circle, flicking ash on the kitchen counter or wherever they pleased.

Where's Liam? I have something for all of us.

Flip flip flip. My stomach.

Oh, this way. Raizel flashed me a smile before picking up her glass. She led me up a steep staircase, the champagne already buzzing in my head, and into a dark hallway with several doorways. The party was thinner up there; only a few people lingered around the doors and in the rooms. Raizel twisted the knob of one door. All at once, people were shouting.

HEEEYY!

HEEEEYYYYYY! Raizel yelled back.

What did you bring with you?

Just this one! Raizel laughed and pulled my arm.

I staggered into the room, a master bedroom with a wide mattress on the floor, no bed-frame or box spring. I smile through the lights emitted from the colorful electric disco ball, just like the one in Amara's room.

A bunch of people lay across the mattress on the floor, bottles all around their feet and heads. More people sat cross-legged with their backs against the wall, drumming their hands on their knees along with the beats permeating from a stereo on the floor. Liam, at the center of the mattress pile, was held around the waist by a kid with wild blond hair--I recognized him as the door-boy at Morgan's.

This is the *gay* room. Raizel whispered, gesturing with her elbow at the door. Are you in or out?

I looked around, swallowing heavily. I recognized several people--Queenie, Robby, James. To my surprise, I even recognized Morgan, who I would have thought would be hosting her own wild New Year's party. Several others smiled my way before going back to having epic conversations or sifting through an atrocious pile of CDs.

It's not the *gay* room, Liam spoke up. It's *gay-friendly*.

Back in the hall, a girl complained about the run in her tights and the bad smell in the bathroom.

I'm... My eyes darted back to Raizel, whose face was a question. In, of course. Definitely. Of course I'm gay...friendly. I love gays!

HEEEEEYYYY! Liam hollered. SHE ADMITS DEFEAT!

HEEEYYYY! Someone hollered in response.

I laughed embarrassedly, waving at Liam to get up. He obliged quickly and stumbled off the mattress, leaving in his dust the small, yellow-haired boy.

I got some stuff. I whispered as I pulled my koi fish box out of my backpack.

The three of us shared a secretive smile as I opened the box and revealed eight blue lemons.

They're so pretty. Raizel smiled, disco light passing over her features.

Oh my god. Liam laughed, clapping his hands together. I remember these! We did them on the playground right?

Yup. I laughed. They're fucking awesome.

Yeah? Raizel patted the small purse hanging off her shoulder. How much do you want for them?

I looked between Raizel's face and the box, baffled.

Nothing...? I got them for all of us!

Oh... Raizel chuckled. It's just that--

It's Amara. Liam tsked. She makes *everyone* pay. By the way, can I get one for Jack?

We were crazy by eleven, letting the music pound while we bounced out of our skin. Someone turned on a black-light and kids began taking their shirts off to suck liquor off each other's bare bellies, Liam and little Jack included. Raizel and I spilled out of the exclusively gay-friendly room into the dark hallway, rampaging, talking up a storm with the people in the bathroom line. I added five numbers to my cell phone contacts list within an hour, thinking I'd call them, but knowing I wouldn't.

We smoke a hookah in the living room, cool blueberry smoking smoothness flowing down my throat and back up again. I coughed and sputtered and opened my throat for more. Raizel conned a boy who was hitting on her into giving us a fat joint, but we snuck away through throngs of partiers before he could cop a feel.

Outside, Raizel and I stamped our feet and talking excitedly about the Christmas lights up and down the street. The moon was high that night, matching our mood, casting a pale auburn glow on the sky and the icy road.

Raizel and I borrowed a lighter and passed the joint between us, watching as people emerged from their homes, clutching noisemakers and crystal wine tumblers and each other. All around and behind us, people laughed. I clenched and unclenched my jaw, suddenly feeling the need to cry.

I have to be honest about something. Raizel poked me, holding the joint out.

Huh? I glanced from the street back to Raizel, blinking my tears away. About what?

You know my mock Docs? She looked down and tapped the toes of her flats together. My 'shoeboots'?

Yeah?

I changed them because of *you.*

Me? I pulled the joint away from my mouth. How so?

I got those boots when I was with Amara. Now I'm with you. I mean, not *with* you. But I like you. You like me too, I assume. I mean, the tattoo, and Christmas--

No. I laughed, letting my hand dangle. I clutched Raizel's dainty fingers. You *are* with me.

Ten!

Oh, shit!

Nine!

The countdown!

Eight!

Is it twelve already?

Seven!

I didn't care if we were surrounded by people.

Six!

We pushed our ravenous mouths together before the countdown was over. I bit her bottom lip. Her nails scraped the back of my neck. She stepped on my sneaker-clad toes. I pinched her waist. Fuck, she was beautiful.

ONE!!!!!

fists rich with confetti find the air,
gape open
lips together, and the world's two chests
past and present
bump uglies, embrace

ha pea knew ear
(happy new year)
meaning to scream

Happy
New
You

53

For a few days after New Year's, I lay low in the coffee shop, drinking coffee and staring out the window. I imagined over and over Raizel and Liam slumped over milk-crates at the pharmacy, playing with their cell-phones and smoking a big one. It would be sweet if I could get hired there, but no position was open. I felt so lonely thinking about the two of them laughing together without me that I allowed myself to drink three cappuccinos. My hands buzzed with caffeine, dripping cold sweat.

Five days into January I had a shift that started at nine in the morning. When I arrived, I dragged my feet across the tiled floor so Monica would know I was tired of working. Monica wasn't anywhere to be seen, but Tiff was behind the counter. She didn't look at me, wiping the base of a coffee maker, steam rising from her hissing cloth. She was either ignoring me or trying to make up for all the shifts she'd missed.

Oh my god, you're back. I was baffled to see her. When Tiff didn't respond I waved my hand in front of her face.

She turned and faced me, eyes wide and mouth slightly open, looking genuinely surprised. No makeup on, and wearing her old glasses, she seemed younger than ever.

Hi.

How are you doing? I touched her forearm, desperately wanting to ask what had happened at the hospital. Did she know?

Tiff stopped her incessant wiping and looked from my hand on her arm up to my head, her own face expressionless but for a quizzical knitting of her eyebrows.

I'm good.

Sorry I didn't come over. I was waiting for you to call me. I figured your family was suffocating you enough, with all their red hair.

She didn't laugh the way she should've.

Really though, are you okay?

Sure. Tiff nodded, a smile daring to cross her mouth.

There was no way she knew. No one would smile at someone who had poisoned them. I'd *poisoned* her.

They don't believe me. Tiff's eyes passed over the store like a set of tiny canoes in an ocean.

What? About what?

Sorry, I'm a little out of it.

I choked on a lump in my throat, a lump that told me I wasn't imagining things and that I really had tampered with the health of my oldest companion.

I made my way down the back hallway, listlessly flapping my hand at Monica when she greeted me. She got out of her computer chair and followed me into the crew room.

How are you doing, Venice? Monica spoke softly, dark eyes trained on me.

Fine…why?

I mean, your best friend tried to kill herself. You must be--

What? I felt my face frown tiredly. She didn't try killing herself.

She overdosed, Venice. That's serious. Her mother told me they got her a psychologist. What, she didn't tell you any of this?

Not really. I glanced up at my locker, wishing it wasn't so high. I barely had the energy to unlock it.

Well, it kind of figures…I know when she's not working she *only* wears black. She's on anti-depressants now, though, so I hope she's okay. Anyway, the way you handled that 'episode' the other day was amazing. I mean, you jumped right into action. Monica reached out to shake my hand. Keep up the good work.

Flip flip flip. My stomach. I knew it was there before I dared to steal a glance.

Venice Knight
Honorable Staff Member
of Team Bean Café
January

I knew I had to free Tiff from the apparent friendship she'd been subjected to just because of the order in which a grade ten art teacher had pulled our names from of a paper mache hat. I couldn't eat supper that night, my stomach in a fist of guilt. I put on my burnt Tegan & Sara CD and stared at my closet. I pulled out everything that reminded me of high school--that is, of sitting cross-legged under the bleachers during pep ralleys and eating in the bathroom whenever Tiff was absent, especially the time she'd gone to visit her dad in New York City and had left me alone for a whole week. I remembered telling her I'd had a great time while she was gone, that some of the girls from our math class had invited me to their table in the cafeteria and that we'd laughed together about our dorky teacher. I'd actually managed to make her jealous, though she was the one who had come home with a mind full of ideas and a painting from her father's exhibit in Soho.

In one garbage bag I threw things someone else could use, my backpack, hoody, baggy jeans, Nirvana sweater, black t-shirts, and discman; I stopped for a moment when I happened upon the CD book full of the all of the DVDs I had ever ripped and burnt for Tiff's personal enjoyment. In another bag I threw a photo album, a couple of home-dubbed mix-tapes, and my twelfth grade binder, which I'd never burned in the Abraham family fire pit because the shit Tiff had written on it was too funny to sacrifice.

While getting rid of things, I reflected on the notion that I had come out, to myself and several others, *and* gotten a girlfriend on New Year's Eve. Thoughts of such importance, however, couldn't lift the guilt from my shoulders.

Liam took me for a drive that night, stopping the car in a random alley for me to chuck the bag of garbage into one of the massive trash bins. We took across the city the other bag, the one full of semi-useful stuff, including the hundred-or-so DVDs I had contemplated keeping. Lugging the black plastic bag into Value Village, I knew I couldn't be making a mistake. I breathed in the scent of thousands of peoples' lives coming together.

I dialed an unfamiliar number on my cell phone.

Hello?

Hi, may I speak with Ilene?

Speaking.

This is Venice, Amara's--

Amara's girlfriend?

Not anymore. I mean, I don't think I ever was. I fingered the zipper of my backpack. But anyway, remember when you offered me that job?

Yup.

Are you still hiring?

54

I'd never been to the little bar next to Mars, Broken String, but became curious when bright posters lining the alleyway advertised The Bitchy Circus. I thought about it before remembering where I'd heard of them--Raizel had mentioned seeing them in Bowville once. On the evening of my first shift at Mars, I stopped and read one of the neon posters, the wind threatening to tear it from its staples let it become trampled in the dirty alley snow.

The Bitchy Circus, feat. local rappers The P.M.S. Crew
LIVE at Broken String Bar Wednesday, January 12, 9:00pm
$10, with and a free Bitcher of Beer

The doors didn't open at Mars until eight-thirty pm. When I arrived at seven, Ilene was waiting at the front door. She introduced me to the bouncer, Big Ted, punching him on the shoulder to prove his strength. Big Ted lifted his thick hand and wrapped his whole arm around me, squeezing. His beard tickled my forehead.

Damn, you're short.

I laughed and backed up, playing with the strap of my backpack.

Ilene introduced me to the bartenders, two smiley boys I'd seen working before. She showed me the kitchen staff, who were busily preparing for the evening rush. Ilene gave me a tour of the bar as if I'd never been there before, telling me the names and purposes of different rooms. As she led me upstairs, my new boss told me how, for each shift, everyone was assigned to a specific task--except the cooks, DJs, dancers, and Big Ted.

Oh, shit. Did she still think I was destined to be a dancer?

Speaking of which, Ilene spoke, What do you do best?

Oh. I smiled. I'm so happy you asked. I--

Whoa. Ilene smiled back, stopping at the top of the stairs to lean on the rail overlooking the first floor. You look like you've just seen a ghost. Are you sure you're cut out for this job?

I thought about my high school ID in my bag, how it neatly displayed the fact that I was under-aged. I was appalled by my good fortune that Ilene paid cash and wouldn't need my SIN number, unlike Team Bean.

Definitely. I nodded emphatically. I don't know about the dancing, like you asked me before. But I'm pretty open-minded about everything else.

Awesome. Ilene patted my shoulder, gesturing for me to follow her down the staircase. We'll start you on something easy before you work your way up. How do you feel about doing coat-check tonight?

My shifts Thursday, Friday and Saturday night all went well. An older guy showed me the ropes in the coatroom. Although I was working in the same building as Amara, she was so far away in her birdcage, practically in another dimension. I greeted hundreds of customers happily, taking their jackets and scarves and purses and tucking them safely into the hangers and shelves. By two am on Sunday, I felt like a professional.

Liam didn't want to see The Bitchy Circus, so Raizel and I decided to make it a date. When she arrived at my family's duplex Wednesday night, I left before my mom could ask questions. Raizel drove us downtown to the parking lot beside the Mars and Broken String Bar alleyway. We sat in the car with the heat on and listened to Le Tigre, something to amp us up while we each chugged a can of beer.

We went down a narrow stairway and waited in a short line, frosty air pushing at our backs each time the door opened and someone came in, stamping their feet. We paid the cover charge and left our jackets at the coat check. I smiled at the chick behind the counter--from one coat-check girl to another.

Broken String Bar was like the dark, unfinished basement of a house with its concrete floors and exposed ceiling beams. The walls were covered in concert posters and fliers. Four massive heating lamps stood in the corners of the room, capturing everyone in a net of warmth. The whole place had one small window, up near the ceiling, not unlike my own family's basement.

Wow. I didn't have to turn my head to see the whole room--a makeshift stage at one end, a large rectangle space before it filling with fans. There're no tables?

Nope. Raizel smiled, her made-up eyes shining up at me. She had a black skirt and tights and the beige cardigan she'd worn the day we'd met. Under a floppy purple toque, Raizel's hair was ridiculously bright.

Well, should we get a 'bitcher of beer'? I held up the pink ticket the coat-check girl had given us.

The P.M.S. Crew opened at nine-thirty, hollering into the microphone for everyone to crawl out of their graves and wake the fuck up. Raizel and I passed the beer pitcher back and forth, sipping straight out of the plastic jug, as there were no counters to rest the massive drink upon. We stood among a crowd of tattooed girls with short hair and facial piercings.

I was tattooed, short-haired, and pierced.

As the P.M.S. Crew played drums and recited fast poetry, Raizel and I migrated forth, our limbs loose with beer. The pitcher was still half-full and I couldn't wipe the goofy grin off my face. I held Raizel by the waist and leaned in for the scent of her hair and soft skin. Her mouth smelled of liquor.

There's Queenie! Raizel exclaimed, pointing.

What? I took my head off Raizel's shoulder, looking toward the stage. On tiptoes, I saw over peoples' heads. Queenie stood between the rapper and the drummer, plucking heavily at the strings of a bass guitar. I didn't know she--

She's so awesome! Raizel heaved the pitcher back to me, beer threatening to slosh out the top. She lifted her arms and danced to the beat of Queenie's bass.

Yeah, she's pretty good! I exclaimed, tipping the pitcher back to inhale another mouthful of liquid, which had grown lukewarm between our hands. I nudged Raizel. Drink up!

Right! Raizel accepted the jug from me, denting the drink in three heavy gulps. She kept her eyes on the stage. Just look at her. Imagine how many straight chicks 'turn' for her.

I eyed Queenie, not ever having found her attractive. She seemed to play her instrument with intense passion, the tattoos on her arms popping with contrast under the yellow stage light each time she moved.

I guess so. I looked over at Raizel, who had begun to dance again. I stole the pitcher from her precarious hold, tipping it over my own mouth. I swallowed the thick drink. One more sip, and it would be gone. Bottoms up.

I wiped my mouth and moved to the wall, setting the jug on the floor under a Tegan and Sara poster. When I returned to Raizel, she had moved forth in the crowd, watching the band as if they were among her favorites, though I'd never seen them in the Camaro's book of CDs. The vocalist was talking into the microphone about Murphy's Law I hung around the outside of the crowd with my hands in my jean pockets, watching the white-blond back of Raizel's bobbing head.

Turn around, I willed her. *Wonder where I am.*

The P.M.S. Crew played three more fast-paced songs, telling the crowd The Bitchy Circus would be pissed if we didn't get hyper. The beer had relaxed my muscles and mind, pulling my weight into the floor below me. When the stage went dark, I pressed my back against a wall, feeling the edges of a concert poster through my t-shirt. Raizel would probably not even come to find me. The idea that we were on a romantic date was quickly evaporating.

Hey! Suddenly, Raizel came from the depths of the crowd, her slender thighs preceding her body as she stepped toward me. Where were you?

Too much beer, I replied, hiding a smile. She *had* wondered where I was. I glanced around at groups of laughing friends. I went to the pisser.

I missed you. Raizel bobbed up to meet my lips briefly. We should have another pitcher.

Yeah, totally. I slid of one of my backpack straps off, reaching through the zipper for my wallet.

No, I mean, every person who pays for the show gets their own pitcher. Raizel dabbed at the beads of sweat on her forehead, pulling her front curls back. The sign said so.

Hold on. I reached in the low pocket of my funky new jeans, pulling out a pink ticket. My loose mouth fell into a grin. You're right.

We sipped the second jug of beer throughout the intermission, watching as even more people streamed in from outside. The light from the heating lamps displayed a floor full of muddy boot-prints and long streaks of water, melted snow. At the merchandise table, Raizel bought a P.M.S. Crew sticker for the hair-doing mirror in her basement. I couldn't believe I hadn't even known about Queenie's band.

The Bitchy Circus didn't take long to come on stage, bright pink lights greeting them as a chick with dreads announced that she was The Ringleader. She wore a tight white t-shirt, under which she was blatantly braless. She was stick-thin, anyway. Had I been invited on stage, I would have looked so out of place--a big-boned, tan-skinned chick with no apparent grace or self-awareness.

As Raizel and I gulped down the second pitcher of beer, she became the friendliest person in the bar, talking to passing girls, complimenting their hair or their tattoos. She cheered so loud that The Ringleader yelled into the microphone.

Whoa! We're still setting up! Hold your panties!

Raizel's purse slid off her shoulder and I bent to pick it up, holding the near-full pitcher in my other hand.

You okay, Raisin? I asked, searching Raizel's face.

Yeah. Her liquor-tainted eyes made contact with mine for a moment before slipping away. It's really hot in here.

True. Why don't you take your cardigan off?

K. Raizel pulled her arm out of the sleeve of her cardigan, nearly hitting someone behind her.

Watch out. I set the beer jug on the ground and pulled Raizel toward me by the waist, helping her remove the sweater. As I leaned to pull her delicate wrist from the sleeve, I felt the warmth of her body fuming over me. My face became hot. My eyes traveled, without the rest of me, over her collarbone and bare shoulders in their skintight floral tank top. I coughed and reached up, straightening the purple toque on her head.

We left the rest of the beer in its pitcher on the ground and moved into the crowd. I held Raizel's arm as I led her toward the stage, keeping her purse and cardigan over my shoulder. The five members of The Bitchy Circus had taken their places at their instruments and microphones. I realized I had no idea what to expect, but recalled Liam despising them for something to do with disco rap love ballads--which was why, when the soft drumming and twanging of the acoustic guitar began, I was more than faintly surprised and impressed. One look at Raizel, swaying with a dreamy look on her face, and I felt like we might have a chance to regain the night's romance. I nodded my head along with the gentle jingling of a tambourine.

Hey, guys. I felt a hand on my shoulder.

Queenie appeared between Raizel and I, her arms looped over our shoulders.

Queenie! Raizel exclaimed, pulling her interested away from the stage. She threw her arms around Queenie and squeezed. You were sooo good.

Queenie removed her arm from my shoulder to put her hands around Raizel's small waist. I raised my eyebrows, looking the two of them up and down as they embraced for too long. I shuffled away, listening to the singer of The Bitchy Circus proclaim her fears about relationships and how-ooh-ow-ooh-ow nothing la-ee-ahh-asts. I crossed my arms and let the crowd engulf me until I was more alone than I'd felt in a long time.

Let's go! Raizel demanded, poking my side.

They're not done. I pointed at the band, in the middle of a more-raucous-than-usual number regarding self-esteem.

But I'm wasted.

So you can't drive?

That's something I've been meaning to tell you. Raizel touched her side, looking down. Oh my god! Where's my purse?

Here, silly. I patted the small, girly purse hanging off my shoulder.

Look in the back pocket. She leaned against my side and closed her eyes.

In the dark, my fingers pulled the purse's back zipper open. Someone bumped my elbow. I sighed and flipped my cell phone open, holding it over the purse and peering in.

A tampon? I felt my eyebrow rise, holding up the plastic-wrapped period stick.

Oh no! Raizel turned red, ripping the tampon from my hand. She reached for the purse and let her fingers disappear into the tiny pocket. She pressed a small item into my palm, something cold and hard.

What's this for? I held up a key, its head decorated with rainbows.

It's for my hunk of burnin' love. Are you okay to drive?

55

Oh shit. I reached out for something to hold me up, finding nothing. I pushed my sneakered feet into the snowy lawn and leaned forward, hands on my knees. Bits of ice trailed up the calves of my jeans.

Oh, you drunk little mess. Raizel loosely heaved her arm over me, encasing my thickly coated waist.

Inebriated, I giggled and bumped against her side. At least I'd gotten us safely to her house. We trekked across the lawn.

Walk *straight*, if you can. Raizel's breath tickled my ear.

I let out a loud laugh.

Don't even know why you're laughing. Raizel giggled, nearly tripping on a garden hose hidden under the snow.

Same reason you are. I spoke quickly despite my drunken stupor.

Yeah? Something smug passed over her face. And what's that?

Because we have fun together.

Speak for yourself. She stuck her tongue out.

Whatever. I moved so there were a couple of feet between our walking paths.

Hey. You know I'm kidding.

Maybe. I shrugged, hoping to get her to say more.

Come on. You know I have fun with you. That's why I'm gonna spend the rest of the night with you.

The cold of the breeze fondled my top vertebra and traveled down. When it met my toes I walked quicker; delight was evident, fear was apparent, the sky would close its eyes on us when she opened the front door to her family's tall house and let me tread through the sunroom with my dirty, snowy shoes. At that point my heart became the lead drum in a fifty-person orchestra. Things felt different. Something grand was happening between us and I wanted to confront it at the same time as wanting to run as far away from it as possible.

We abandoned our shoes and she led my drum-heart to her basement quarters, past the hair-cutting chair and sticker-clad mirror. I hung my coat over the back of the couch, a habit she hadn't discouraged. I excused myself to the bathroom and locked the door behind me so I could pee and gaze into the mirror for a moment. I put toothpaste on a wad of toilet paper and scrubbed my teeth. I made a cup with my hand and drank three handfuls of tap water, except it probably wasn't that much because the water was leaking between my fingers.

I opened the bathroom door and turned the light off simultaneously, hesitant to walk out. In the moment my eyes took to adjust to the dark, everything was a black abyss in which anything was possible. Soon I was able to make out the shapes of the couch, the television, the bookshelf, and the displaced medieval pattern of the carpet.

Come to my room. Raizel's arms pulled me from my two-second funk, hands clutching me by the wrists. She didn't turn on her bedroom light; instead she padded quietly across the carpet and flipped on the bedside-table lamp.

Amid Raizel's room of junk, like her family's sunroom upstairs, I felt safer than anywhere. In one swift yank she pulled the top blanket off the bed, sending things flying--a long scarf, a bike lock, a picture frame, an Archie comic, a bottle of vitamins. Everything had a soft landing on the floor's layer of clothing.

I watched Raizel tiptoe on her dresser like she'd done before, pushing a shirt into the ceiling vent. I didn't look away when her skirt rode up at the back. She turned around to press one stick of incense into the mouth of the Buddha figurine on her dresser. Although I was intoxicated, I immediately remembered the smell from the day I'd come to show her my tattoo.

Raizel sat down, the mattress daring to tip me toward her. She pulled a notebook out from under some junk.

You wanna play the Daisy Game?

I bit my lip, looking at the bedside alarm clock. It was already five to one and I was sufficiently intoxicated.

Flip flip flip.

It's a drawing game. She giggled, knowing I'd been wary of her suggestion. First, draw a daisy with lots of petals.

I complied, relieved. I was ninety-eight percent sure I would have said yes if she had offered me a pill.

I get a prize. She shaded one of my drunkenly scrawled petals with the blue Bic pen. Now you color one petal and that means you get a prize.

What's the prize? I colored the petal next to hers.

Just think of something. She skipped across the flower and colored a petal.

I get a prize. I colored another petal.

We continued taking turns, quietly passing the pen back and forth over the paper.

YES! I get the prize! Her voice oozed with triumph as she shaded the last petal. She greedily rubbed her hands together and looked at me, waiting.

I put a pillow on the floor by my feet and told her to get down on it, facing away from me. Sitting on the bed, I put a leg on either side of Raizel. I kneaded her shoulders the way a kitten does a blanket. She leaned back and emitted a noise like I'd given her cherry cheesecake, only she probably never ate that because I felt her bones and muscles through her cardigan. I rubbed her for a while, The King of Incense twirling around our heads, and became afraid that she was sleeping. I coughed, not wanting our night together to end.

What would my prize have been? I wondered aloud.

Raizel looked over her shoulder at me, the lamp glowing on the top of her cheeks and along her eyelashes and one side of her dainty nose. She slipped her purple toque off and turned around to rest her hand on the bit of fat below my belly button and above the waist of my jeans, a smaller version of my brother Dana's spare donut for which he'd been teased throughout our childhood.

I saw my drunken hands grab Raizel's hips and help her up onto the bed. She lay on top of me, our breasts rubbing through our t-shirts and bras. Her face was so close. Our mouths met halfway. I let my head rest against the pillow as our tongues and lips moved together. My arms wrapped around her waist. God, she was small. She didn't stop my hands from slipping under the back of her t-shirt, her own hands crawling up my sides.

Raizel pulled away to smile at me in the dim light.

Do this. She pulled her t-shirt up to just under her breasts.

I did as she said, keeping eye contact with her.

She lowered herself back onto me. When our bare stomachs met, I gasped at the softness of our colliding skin.

Great prize, I commented.

She giggled.

I squeezed her in my arms.

Safe and sound.

I clicked into the folder I'd labeled 'V's Shit' the first time I'd uploaded pictures from my camera. A lot of photos had been taken while I was rolling high--ones that were upside-down, tilted, too-close, overexposed, out-of-focus.

A series of feelings and thoughts began to pass through my head. Before anything, I felt proud. I had several shots of my bedroom, before and after pictures from the last time I'd cleaned. The after pictures told a story--I *saw* me changing as a person. I'd replaced an assortment of high-school doodles with a big poster of Tegan & Sara, one where they stood casually in a pitch-white room, looking all pretty with dark, androgynous haircuts. Surrounding them were my Andy Warhol prints, which would remain faithfully on my walls for as long they'd stay.

I felt welcome. I felt uncharacteristically alive in an exclusive, new world I'd climbed into as awkwardly as possible.

The third feeling I had was hesitant excitement that I could barely admit was happening. I tried to figure it out as I looked at Raizel, standing on a road near my place with streetlamps gracing her angles, unglamorously glamorous. I dared to feel as though I'd found the model who could do anything I asked of her, and more, a girl who could appear to bear any emotion or intellection. I chuckled when I remembered thinking Amara had more modeling potential than Raizel just because of her height.

I had to get a new camera.

56

The morning air was warmer than others, brining me out of my bedroom to my front steps in just my sweats and slippers and a hoody. Raizel and I sent text messages back and forth.

morning, u
morning back, how r u
wonderful
I know u r but what am i
wonderful

Kids walked by me on their way to school. They cracked frozen puddles and streaked the sidewalk with their winter boots. The ones who quarreled over the prize from Cap'n'Crunch were especially charming. For too long I hadn't seen the sky so blue. When I breathed there was the scent of orange pekoe tea warm in my hands.

I went to a different library that day, one on Broadway in the opposite direction of the branch downtown. I popped half pill on the bus ride over, white with a heart on top, something I'd recently picked up from Seed.

I could have stood smelling the pages of the old books forever. Most of the novels had ripped covers and illustrations of big-haired women in leotards and men whose packages popped under tight Levi's jeans. The DVD selection was made up of German indie films and movies with bright labels.

Artistically Brilliant
Visually Stunning

I borrowed a hard-covered book called Magic and put it in my awesome backpack.

I had a fourteen-dollar backpack from Value Village. I'd thought that was too much for a secondhand bag with no apparent brand name, but then I had noticed the pockets. I'd counted them, all fourteen of them. A dollar per pocket. I would have been fine with five. Maybe they would have sold it for five bucks and then I would have had money for a real camera bag, or another memory card. I might have opted for the other backpack they were selling if the price tag hadn't said fifty cents. Fifty cents was another way of saying Broken Zipper.

After the funny little library I walked down Broadway, wondering why I didn't do so more often. The area called out to me, fiercely wonderful with its shale walkways and fat tree trunks. A long brick wall ran alongside the road, upon which I imagined musicians sat in the summer, belting tunes about social standings and sexual alleviation. I walked past boutiques and French cafes, massage parlors and instrument shops, recognizing some of them from the night Liam and Raizel and I had gone to Morgan's. I savored the aimlessness of my day off, grinning hard when I saw my already-grinning reflection in a store window.

I was drawn to the Nepalese store with its bright handbags and sarongs and headscarves in the display window. When I entered I inhaled a warm smell, so familiar I could barely stop myself from snapping my fingers and saying, 'I know it, I know it.' The smell was strong and brought on memories I couldn't quite place. The sense of smell is the easiest way to remember something, but all I could feel was something terrific. The scent wafted over to me innocently from its place by the cash register, incense smoke meandering around my head. Then it clicked.

How much does the King of Incense cost? I looked at the boy at the counter. He was young and skinny and wore glasses. I wasn't rolling too high, but the corners of my mouth twitched up like I'd dealt the most brilliant riddle.

By which I mean Nag Champa.

It's not for sale. He looked me up and down, but not in the way boys are apparently supposed to look girls up and down. This is our last pack.

Hmm. I looked around disappointedly. I examined the glass case of jewelry, all with little symbols I didn't know the meanings of but admired. I asked him to show me something, and when he took out the velvet pad of rings I hardly believed their wooden beauty. I chose one for twelve dollars, the most expensive gift I'd ever bought for someone, beside pills.

He turned his back to me to grab a small paper bag. I swiped the pack of Nag Champa off the counter and put it in my sleeve, despite bad karma. I grinned at him and gave him money and when I got outside I literally patted myself on the back for not breaking a sweat. I was so stealthy that Spiderman would either kill me or kiss me upside-down. Not that I was sure I wanted him to.

Raizel began work at noon that day, which meant I'd have to wait until eight to hang out with her. I took the other half of my pill and went past all the shops to the park by the river. I didn't know my grandparents very well, but imagined they were like the old people who strolled hand-in-hand and wore matching down-filled leisure suits and mittens embroidered with maple leaves. I took Magic out of my backpack and began to read about a Chinese girl who had been adopted by an American family, warming my own hands between my jean-clad thighs.

When the daisy kicked in and my toes had begun to numb, I put the book down and pulled out of one of my backpack's fourteen pockets my new camera. I took pictures of the elegant ripples in sections of unfrozen water in the river and the sun cascading over everything. I walked beside the water for nearly an hour before hiking up the stone bridge to cross the river. I'd never been so high on my own before. I *loved* how I could do whatever I wanted. I gritted my teeth and seduced all the bright colors with the lens of my camera, which was better than any camera I'd ever used, including the ones I'd borrowed in high school photography class. I loved the click of every photo. I had found a completely comfortable hole to crawl into, one where I'd give myself to the shot and I'd breathe evenly and feel entirely sure that I was doing what I was supposed to be doing. There was something amazing about blurring the line between reality and not, directing both real moments and posed fabrications toward believability. As cliché as it was, I knew the reason I had been born was for the world of photography.

Every hour on the hour Raizel sent a message to my phone, a countdown of sorts.

five hours left soo bored
four hours i want to leave
three hours vvv uggh when will it end

I wandered around all afternoon before taking the bus downtown. I was coming down, but didn't want to. I want ten million more white heart pills. I sat in a small restaurant, warming my fingers over a tabletop candle, and ordered a cocktail without being carded. Then another. And another. My stomach growled, but I had to wait for Raizel so we could eat together.

I was right to think she'd be hungry after work. I saw her grin through the glass door of the drug store before she came barreling out. My heart swelled.

How was your day? Raizel linked her arm through mine and pulled me down the sidewalk to her Camaro.

Good. I smiled, spotting the car a block away. I was taking pictures all day.

Of what?

The river, Broadway, you know. Nature.

You've been *outside* all day? She rubbed my arm through my flimsy winter coat. Aren't you cold?

No. I am a little drunk, though.

Really? She laughed, her breath emerging in a whoosh of winter-air whiteness. Maybe that's keeping you warm.

We went to a Mexican restaurant called Serena and sat across from each other in red-cushioned booths. I showed her my new camera and the pictures I'd taken that day while we treated ourselves to nachos and soft-shell tacos and a pitcher of Sangria. The booze helped me come down smoothly. I couldn't stop smiling.

You're being so secretive. Raizel leaned back in the booth and eyed me in her confident, all-knowing way. I hoped other people were looking, seeing that I was with the prettiest girl in the city.

I know. I was unable to keep it in, not being able to wait for her smile. I got you a present.

What! What is it? She came over and sat next to me on my side of the booth.

Okay, first. I twisted around and took something out of my backpack's bigger pocket. I placed the flat box on the table.

Oohh! Raizel clapped her hands together. More nag champa!

There's more. I twisted again, taking the real present out of the smallest of my backpack's fourteen pockets. I held it out to Raizel, afraid she would think it was lame and cheap. I'd chosen the light brown one with a tiny tree etched into the wood.

She seemed hesitant before moving closer to me. Her eyes shone the way they did when she was happy and tipsy. She let me slide the ring onto her finger.

Do you like it?

I love it. She grew quiet. It's a perfect fit for my ring finger. Do you know why the ring finger is the ring finger?

No...Do you?

Because there's a vein in the ring finger that runs to the heart. She smiled shyly.

I smelled the sweet grapefruit drink on her breath and got the sudden urge to lean in and kiss the skin by her ear. I imagined her turning her head quickly, as though she'd heard a gunshot, and pressing her mouth against mine. Nothing came of my thoughts.

We split the bill. I was immediately overcome with guilt. I shouldn't have spent so much on my camera. I should have been able to pay for everything. Raizel didn't seem to care, but I couldn't wait for the day when I'd have all the money in the world.

We went out to the car and each took a pill she had acquired at a discount from Liam's boyfriend of the week, eight bucks a pop when they were normally ten. She said she'd been good and deserved to let loose.

Raizel would surely have thought I was greedy if I had told her about my afternoon high. Her pills were purple, different from any daisy I'd ever seen, with little bow imprints. They were pretty, like something a Hilary Duff fan would wear, but took forever. Raizel drove around, Peaches on the stereo, both of us worried that nothing would happen. I used my bank card to cut another pill on the dash. We swallowed our halves eagerly while skidding over the icy roads.

Finally the air moved around me like the feeling I got when I was little and ran through the sprinklers. My heart grew wings and fluttered busily around the inside of the car. I could tell Raizel was starting to feel it when she gave me her riding-the-clouds smile. She turned up the music and revved the engine at every stoplight. Continuing to drive, she danced in her seat and begged me to shout the lyrics with her.

I sang the wrong words, ones that didn't go together, but rhymed in the end. Raizel followed my lead. Soon my abdomen hurt from laughter. I was delighted by her carefree aura.

The sun had gone down long before our drive. Some houses' leftover Christmas lights brightened the air. We ended up far away from both of our homes, in the richest part of East Bay--near the homes directly backing the lake. Everywhere we looked were Hummers and Porsches and long driveways with gates that only opened for people with electronic keys.

Raizel parked the car in a gravel alleyway between two mansions. When she cut the music I felt like we were on a speedboat slipping out of waves onto cool calmness. We left the Camaro behind and scampered wordlessly toward the water, frozen grass crunching below our feet. Eons had passed since my alone-time at the city river.

We climbed out on the rocks like the signs told us not to. That dainty white railing didn't stop anyone. In the summer, I had seen dogs swimming and kids dipping their ankles, catching minnows with little nets. We settled on the flat top of a huge boulder, snow-swept water solid around its bottom. The rock was cool on my palm.

We talked. I told her about the schemes Tiff and I used to devise to get out of math class; she told me about using her mother's blender to mix mushroom smoothies. I wanted to ask what mushrooms were like. Did they feel like daisy? Like Gravol? Like cocaine? Instead, I asked when she'd started trying drugs and she asked if weed counted and I said no. She said she had tried lots of things in the summer after grad--that was when she'd really felt a need to get high.

I closed my eyes and tried to swallow the starry sky, its little lights gliding around inside of me like ringette players skating on a rink.

We talked about the future. Raizel told me she was saving money so she could move away, eventually. I told her I wanted to be a famous photographer. She said she could already tell I'd make it far. I wanted to ask if we could go away together, one day. I wished she would ask questions that made different parts of my heart feel weird, things I didn't have answers for.

Why don't you have a father?

When did you realize you're a lesbian?

Have you ever been in love?

Finally, the conversation deepened.

Have you ever mourned over someone? She gazed out, the narrow crescent of a moon barely lighting the water's surface.

This is it, I thought to myself. She was finally going to open up about her brother. I didn't know if I was equipped to offer emotional advice.

My grandmother died last year, but I didn't know her very well. As I spoke I watched Raizel's profile, waiting for her to look back at me. She kept facing the water.

I didn't even cry when my brother told me. At the sound of the words leaving my mouth, I squeezed my hands together so tightly the knuckles hardened and drained of blood, ghostly. My mom cried for a long time. Sometimes I still hear her through her bedroom door. She thinks I can't hear anything through the door. It's just wood. She also thinks cigarette smoke doesn't seep out her door and in through mine. What...why do you ask?

I lost someone once. Raizel stared straight ahead. He was one of my best friends. We used to come here together for walks.

Oh, Raisin. I reached out and touched her forearm, wondering if she noticed through her pea-coat. I rubbed the material. I couldn't even imagine how I'd feel if my brother died. We weren't close, but I had a feeling that didn't matter. What...happened?

He was fifteen years old. Nobody even thought he would live that long.

What do you mean? I felt my eyebrow rise. Was he sick?

He just seemed so *old*, for his last few years. I remember a few years ago, when Sloam was super humid, more than any other spring, so the floors in our house were covered in water for, like, a week.

Ours were, too. I smiled gently, disbelieving we had something so menial in common, but hadn't known each other at the time. It was weird, wasn't it? Were your walls wet, too?

A little. And I remember the weather reporter actually advising people about how to deal with it--turn on air conditioners, use fans, don't open the windows, blah blah blah. Raizel finally tore her eyes from the blackness outside, piercing me with them. I remember doing my homework at the kitchen table and him walking by, tracking dirt through the water, making everything muddy. My mom got so pissed off. I have a photographic memory. I can still see his huge paw print glistening on the floor. I hate myself for not tracing it, or taking a picture, or *something*. That would've made a nice tattoo.

Yeah. I watched her eyes, shining with wetness as though they were stuck in that humid spring moment. I suddenly realized what she'd said.

Wait--did you say paw print?

Yeah. I think I've shown you a picture of Tony before. He was a St. Bernard.

I pulled her toward me on the boulder top, and with her face on my neck, felt the water of her memories slip down her cheeks. She left her head resting below mine. She didn't know how the air caught in my throat and forced tears out of my own eyes. Later I'd claim I'd been sweating in my winter layers. I remembered what Raizel had told me the first time I'd met daisy, on orange Buddha pills.

I had a downer once that made me feel like I was sinking into the floor. I cried the whole time.

I wondered what made me so untrustworthy that she couldn't talk about her brother.

We lay there, on a boulder beside the homes of people with organized lives, until the sky lightened to to the foggy violet of January dawn.

57

I'm in the eighth grade and I don't want to be. I want to be a tiny fish in the ocean somewhere, dodging whales' mouths and the sun. I'd like to be blue, or green like my eyes. All I ask for is a little color.

If every girl in the world got to choose how they looked, gravity would be so confused. Everywhere you turned there would be flat bellies and big boobs and tiny asses. The world would be so much lighter. I wonder if it would float away like a balloon from a child's hand.

Everything would balance out if the boys got to choose bulging biceps and humongous things in their pants.

If I got to choose my appearance I would be very, very dark. I'd have black hair and purple toes. When I opened my mouth and smiled, people would be shocked at the contrast between my teeth and my skin. The insides of my ears would be like caves. Black bats would fly out when people fucked with me.

I have never touched my hair. It's the color of evaporated milk and falls in a braid down to my butt crack. I have been regarded as The Albino. The White Witch. Ginger Skin. When those names retired they called me The Ghost. When that name grew old, I *became* a ghost. I still wander into traffic and no one honks. I steal things from the corner store without getting caught. I breathe an inch away from the bathroom mirror without it fogging up.

I'm in homeroom on the first day of grade nine. Homeroom is second period and I haven't said a word to anyone yet. I saw some kids from elementary school in the hall, but I ducked into the girls' bathroom before they could see me. Maybe they wouldn't have seen me. I'm just a ghost.

Kids are talking all around me. They laugh and greet each other. They introduce themselves and try desperately to climb a social ladder.

I live in East Bay.

My father's a CEO.

My boyfriend's in grade twelve.

They make paper airplanes solely because they've seen kids do so on Degrassi. The teacher is clapping her hands and quieting everyone down, but I'm already quiet. I smile if anyone looks at me, but I don't say anything.

Most kids take the bus, including my older sister Abby, but I walk home after school. Forty-five minutes. I don't go outside in the summer because my skin is too fair, but now it's fall. I like the breeze on my cheeks and the leaves at my ankles.

My brother Sullivan is always home before me. He's still in the seventh grade so his school is around the corner, next to the church with the pointy cross. He hangs out in his bedroom upstairs with towels plugging the crack under his door in case his friends want to smoke. They all ride skateboards and have shaggy mops of hair.

How was your first day? My mother asks me when she gets home from work.

Good. Can you take us to East Bay?

Us?

Me and Tony.

Can't you just walk him around the block?

He hates this block. There are too many small dogs. St. Bernards hate small dogs.

My mother sighs and reaches for her car keys.

I hate Golden Street. Too many kids with sneers on their faces and venom in their voices boxes.

Tony and I watch Ellen Degeneres' talkshow in my basement after school every day. Abby and Sullivan have friends, so they don't fight me for the remote. They don't even come downstairs. Ellen is so funny I sometimes crack up laughing. With her, I'm less alone. I watch the corners of her eyes crinkle up and feel my own face morph. I grin and wish I was on the set, in that comfy armchair. Far away from everyone in Sloam, except Tony.

Sometimes I look in the mirror in the basement bathroom and try to make facial expressions like Ellen's. She has short hair. I wonder if I could look like her. We're both girls. We're both blond. I take out my long braid and fold it around my face, imagining myself with short hair.

I look up instructions on the Internet and take these old scissors from the bathroom drawer. I prop a mirror on the towel rod behind my head and begin cutting. Snip. Snip. Suddenly my face is framed by my hair and my mind isn't as heavy. I tilt my head and enjoy my uneven hair flopping over my ghostly complexion. It's not as short as Ellen's. I'm not that brave.

Tony barely recognizes me when I come out of the bathroom. I ask him if he likes it and he licks my hand. I scratch the skin under his collar and ponder the notion that a dog can be the most reliable friend in the world.

The next day at school, a girl from my math class asks me to hang out. I wait ten minutes for her by the bike racks before I walk home alone. Frost has begun pinning leaves to the ground. I used to wish I was a tiny fish in the ocean somewhere, but I realize that's what I have always been.

I thought high school would be different. I thought my sister would have my back and introduce me to cool, older kids. I thought everyone would be mature. I never thought someone would write ALBINO FREAK on my locker with liquid whiteout.

When I see at Abby at school she always looks happy. She jokes and steals everyone's attention and I sit nearby, a cookie too burnt for anyone's appetite. When her friends get licenses they start taking off in cars at noon hour to places like McDonald's and Arby's. They joke about whose wheels slide best in the icy mall parking lot, reliving scenes from Tokyo Drift. Soon Abby will be old enough to get a job and I'll see her even less and we'll differ from each other on a whole other level. I stop hanging onto the fringe of her friend circle.

I want a re-do; I want to start my life over with a soul so hard it can't hear bad things. I want to be born again as someone who knows Ellen Degeneres. I want to be someone else, period. At conception, my siblings went unscathed by my father's lack of pigment--both of them have yellow-ish hair instead of tooth-white. So, if I was Abby, I'd be happy. If I was Sullivan, I'd be ecstatic. The only thing in the world boys aren't allowed to do is wear skirts. They're allowed to be attracted to girls, like I am.

Spring of ninth grade, Sloam has ninety-percent humidity and everyone's freaking out. A woman on the news advises people to leave their windows closed and put cardboard on linoleum to avoid slipping. My parents are pissed off because mold might grow under the carpet. They don't put cardboard down because everyone else in the city has beaten them to the flattened french fry boxes from McDonald's.

I go home after school and study for my English class. I like English because we're sometimes given creative writing assignments. I like writing poems so personal they make my teacher itch. If Mrs. McPhee ever asks why I feel the way I do, I'll tell her the poem is fiction and that I was merely interested in the topic.

Sometimes at night I put up a fight,
I lay in my bed and hope to forget
the way I blend in like a dark silhouette.
I'm sick when it thunders, cold sweat on my shirt;
I hate how it feels, how badly I'm hurt.
Depression is a spider, unfolding its legs and traveling through me to plant all its eggs-
A corner of cobwebs: that's all I am, and life has become one stupid exam.
I could stay here forever and try to explain why I'm so numb
and the source of my pain,
but I'm too busy wondering why I didn't stay on Mars,
especially those nights when I'm carving new scars--
those days when I'm down after seeing a mirror.
Soon you'll be wishing that we had been nearer.
I take time off school to plan my own death
I feel worse with every breath.
I lay here alone and I hear myself say that the amount I matter lessens each day;
I wanted beauty and your kind of soul,

I wanted your help, sweet fucking console.
Sometimes at night I put up a fight,
I lay in my bed and hope to forget
the way I blend in like a dark silhouette.
I'm sick when it thunders, cold sweat on my shirt;
I hate how it feels, how badly I'm hurt.

I'm sitting at the kitchen table and Tony is in the backyard, out the porch doors behind me. The glass doors drip with the sweat of spring. I don't understand why people hate humidity. I finger a happy face in the condensation, a little person who looks like me when I'm thinking about Ellen Degeneres. I turn around and stare at my blank loose-leaf. My parents will be home in half an hour and I have to be out of there before they can read over my shoulder.

I'm not going to spend the rest of my time here on one hopeful remnant
don't want to pretend that I'm getting better
my jacket's not that thick
I can't keep out the ice and preserve any remainders of warmth at the same time

here's the wall I slide down to melt into its corner
fishnets can collapse with my knees
here are the pores that were part of my skin and feelings I could fix
I'm probably lovely, but turning to waste for not grooming my issues,
more simply: my thoughts

Tony scratches at the door behind and I lean back and let him in. I continue my poem.

shoulder of the road, welcoming
that's where I always knew to crash
it's the safest edge, there's nowhere to fall and nothing to hit
yet the coldest expanse when there's dick-all to kiss

gravel etched up my jacket for the last time last night
last thought, last sob
last love,
goodbye.

My parents' car pulls into the driveway as I'm finishing the poem. I close my binder and stand up. That's when I notice the floor.

Raisin, honey! My mother calls as she opens the front door. You home?

Yeah! I call back, staring at Tony's muddy paw-prints all over the kitchen linoleum. He's standing at his water dish, gulping mouthfuls with his massive tongue.

My mother enters the kitchen and gazes at the floor.

Why would you let him do that? She cries out, heading for Tony.

Before she can swat his butt, I grab her wrist.

He's a *dog*. I push her arm away. He doesn't know any better.

The paw-prints are huge and chocolate-brown. They're perfect.

I spend the summer between grades nine and ten in my basement watching Ellen reruns and reading about hair-design on the Internet. Sloam has an esthetician school, but I want to go somewhere cool. I want to be a stylist for models and celebrities before their important photo shoots. Fashion-design would be cool, too. Vancouver has a decent-sounding school. So does Ottawa. I cut all of my Barbies' hair and line them up on my messy dresser.

When I'm surfing the net, I happen upon a link for a lesbian chat forum. I click the link and start talking to a girl called Jill. She says she's sixteen and from Winnipeg and that she hates it there. I say I'm from Sloam and hate it here. She wonders if one day we could meet in a city far cooler than either of our hometowns. I say maybe. I *know* definitely.

My fifteenth birthday is near the end of summer. I eat supper with my family and observe the sun-kissed sheen of their naturally pale skin. My own face remains ivory-white. Sullivan gives me a card he made and Abby gives me a book about different ways to braid hair. My dad makes the potato wedges I loved when I was six and gives me a money-filled card from him and my mom.

I buy a webcam with my money as a surprise for Jill. She has one, too, but hasn't shown her face yet because she's afraid of pedophilic creeps. We turn our cameras on and watch at each other, but can't talk because we don't have microphones. I smile as I watch her look down and type messages to me; she has long brown hair and very pretty, upturned eyes. I ask if she put on makeup for me and she says she wears makeup every day. I ask if she'll do my makeup one day and she says she will if I'll do her hair.

Jill and I have webcam dates every night, showing each other our different personal belongings. I let her meet Tony and I think he thinks she's gorgeous. I cover his eyes when Jill lowers the straps of her tank top and shows me her purple bra. I call her a tease.

One evening when my family is sitting down for supper, the phone rings and I pick it up, prepared to tell whoever it is we'll call them back when we're done supper.

Hello?

Hi. Is Raizel there?

Speaking. Who is this?

It's Jill.

My heart thumps in my chest. I watch my family members set cutlery and plates and a steaming casserole dish on the table. Her voice is so sweet and flirty and girly. I feel hot between my legs. My mother stops moving and looks at me.

I hope you don't mind, Jill says quickly. I looked your number up.

Sorry, we don't want any. I slam the receiver into its holder.

Telemarketer? My mother grins and pulls out a chair for me.

58

Let's just go around back, V. Raizel twisted to look at me, her butt in my lap in the passenger seat of Liam's car. It's easier.

No, man, I insisted.

I don't wanna get kicked out or something. Liam turned the key and pulled it out. The engine became quiet.

Trust me, I'll get you in.

We stumbled out of the vehicle, tossing our beer cans at the bottom of the alleyway's metal disposal bins.

The bouncer, Big Ted with his thick chest and linebacker shoulders, grinned when we took our place in the line, immediate recognition crossing his face.

Hey, Shortstuff. What you doing back there?

He motioned at me with his index finger and pressed the buzzer on the wall beside him. The sound of the door's lock clicking open was better than The Silly Rainbows' best song.

In the sixth grade I'd been good at baseball. My palms had been rocks. The crack of the bat had given me even more of a thrill than the flash of a camera. Later, when I'd started practicing photography, I'd aimed with a keen remembrance of eyeing a baseball until its cherry-red stitches were inches away.

The teachers had chosen team captains when gym class had rolled around, usually kids like Thomas Lars and Felicia Dintz, whose fathers both coached baseball and slow-pitch. We'd stood in the middle of the ball diamond, sand clouds relaxing around our ankles. The captains had taken turns choosing players for their team.

I'll take Mitch.

I'll take Howie.

Marity.

James.

Cecile.

Janet.

Dane.

Phillip.

We have too many girls so I guess we'll take Michael T.

And *we'll* take Michael R.

Shannon.

I'd murmured for them to pick me. I was good and everyone knew it.

Benjamin.

Chad.

Stacey.

Finally:

I guess we'll take *her.*

I'd sauntered over to their group like a bird flocking with the wrong species. I'd watched them chatter excitedly about who would bat first, my feelings thrown under the bleachers with all the gum and empty Slurpee cups.

I'd only tried baseball once after elementary school, in the summer between grades eleven and twelve. The experience wasn't worth thinking about.

The line outside of Mars was made up of ten drunk-as-shit people. Boys stumbled in heels and butch girls' bandanas went askew on their foreheads. We skipped past them like giddy schoolgirls, the beer alive in our blood, hot. Not asking for ID, not asking who my friends were, Big Ted tugged the door open and let us enter.

I got the oddest sensation in my toes, warm and numb. I was becoming somebody.

All over Sloam, the spring sun sparkled through luxurious green leaves on trees sprouting from sidewalks and lawns. When we arrived downtown, hoards of people had already gathered at one end of Main Street. A couple of floats would head the parade, advertising different services and clubs I'd never heard of, with abbreviations and implications I was unsure about.

PFLAG
Sloam College Campus Center for the Queer and the Curious
Sexual Health Committee of Sloam
LGB2T Anonymous--Coming Out Support

Drag queens crowded the backs of trucks in sparkling floor-length gowns, ready to wave at onlookers. Behind the vehicles, a long line of rainbow-clad pedestrians had formed. Liam, Abby, Raizel, and I joined the end of the line, all sporting over our sweaters white muscle shirts we'd drawn rainbows on.

People all around me grinned and waved rainbow flags and talked excitedly about the day's events and hugged old friends and complimented each others' colorful attire. I felt Raizel squeeze my hand. My fingers latched onto hers, knowing I'd never let her go. She smiled up at me and my eyes flitted over her long lashes and the dots of sweat that had emerged at her hairline.

Hey, there's Amara! Liam pointed.

I look through the throngs of people, catching the back of the tall, dark girl's tightly curled hair.

I couldn't remember the last time we'd hung out.

I'll be right back. Liam slipped forward to weave his way through the crowd.

Ten minutes later a group of police began blowing their whistles, motioning at the crowd.

Bang bang bang. My heart.

Don't worry! Raizel laughed, catching my expression. They're not telling us to go away.

Liam reappeared at my side.

Where's Amara? Raizel asked.

I couldn't help but feel the familiar pang I got when I thought Raizel wasn't as into me as I was into her.

She said she's gonna be on a float. Liam shrugged. She'll meet up with us later.

Great.

A car began blasting pop songs and the hoard of reds and purples and blues and yellows began shuffling forward. Liam took my empty hand in his and the three of us sauntered together, laughing at everything going on around us. Several teenagers went by on bikes and skateboards, celebrating the recently-melted snow with rainbow ribbons trailing after them in the wind. A group followed them closely, tugging opposite ends of a poster advertising a high school's gay-straight alliance. I wondered what it would have been like to be out in high school, or to have realized I was gay. I might have smiled more.

To our right, a boy I'd seen at Mars several times skipped by with a megaphone, leading a group of gender-inclusive cheerleaders.

Sexist, racist, anti-gay! Born-again bigots, GO AWAY!

Anti-gay is so passé! We're girls, but we're right! We're woman and we'll fight!

Equal! Diverse! Ignorance is a curse!

We're free! We're here! Look at what we've built! We're free! We're here! Thanks to Harvey Milk!

People walking along the downtown sidewalks stopped in their tracks as we neared them, a shouting, laughing pile of color. I thought a couple of old ladies would oddly pale, probably fearing we'd pour paint thinner on their perms. The police held traffic as we crossed the street, drivers honking excitedly when they realized what they were witnessing. I glanced up at the apartments overlooking Main Street, above the shops. Some people shied behind their curtains while others brought out cameras and waved from their balconies.

Hey! I almost forgot. I slipped my hand out of Liam's to unzip my camera bag, which I'd been lucky enough to find at Value Village. I extracted my camera and darted forward. I turned back to my friends, focusing on their faces, the crowd blurring behind them. I didn't have to tell them to smile.

When the parade was over, everyone congregated in a field near the opposite end of Main Street. As a drag show was beginning, Raizel and Liam and I walked to the line of buildings in which the Main Street Pharmacy was situated. Raizel introduced me to their new coworker, an old guy called Timothy, while Liam rolled a joint in the office. On the way out, we each pinched a bag of Doritos.

We passed the joint back and forth on the walk back to the field, arriving when the afternoon's festivities were well on their way, people of all ages dancing in the field while a local band played on a makeshift stage. A beer garden had been roped off, its entrance guarded by Big Ted. We strolled up to him and gave him Doritos and he pulled the rope aside to let us in.

We were on our first round of drinks when I heard my name.

Hey! Venice!

As I was already with the only people I cared to see, I sipped my beer and continued my conversation with Liam about the cute guy at the drink stand.

Do you know her? Liam looked over my shoulder.

I glanced behind me, seeing a short woman with a dark pixie haircut.

Oh! I exclaimed, laughing. Hi, Ilene.

Hey. Ilene tucked her hands in her jeans pockets, pointing her chestnut eyes at me. Where were you at eleven?

Eleven? I held my beer at my side, trying to focus my stoned gaze on my boss. I was in the parade

Well, duh. Why didn't you come on our float?

Huh? My mouth fell open. You had a float?

Yeah, up near the front. Amara said she told you about it.

Are you fu-- I stopped myself from fuming, boiling over like a pot of vegetables forgotten on the stovetop. Are you serious?

Yeah. Ilene shrugged. It was a blast. Anyway. See you at the bar tonight?

Sure. I forced a smile.

Ilene smiled at Raizel and Liam before turning to go.

I'm gonna go talk to him. Liam patted my shoulder and pointed at the guy we'd been discussing.

That night when Raizel and I arrived at Mars, Big Ted let us skip past the line as usual, wishing us a happy pride dance. For the first time ever, we skipped up the stairs without getting drinks.

Have you ever written something here? I scanned the corridor of glowing words, noticing messages I'd never seen before, probably added that week in the spirit of pride.

No. Raizel glanced around. I've thought about it, though.

You wanna? I unzip my camera bag, pulling out two tiny brushes and a bottle of neon yellow paint.

Raizel clapped her hands and laughed, accepting a brush from me. We sought out two empty spaces separated by a foot of silly messages. I sat cross-legged on the floor, ignoring the reek of beer permeating from the crimson carpet.

Okay, Raizel said, a moment later. Lemme see what you wrote.

We gazed at my canary-yellow message, outlined with the daisies I'd drawn in an effort to get the paint off my brush.

V + R = comrades

I gulped.

Cute. Raizel giggled.

What did you write?

She moved out of the way.

I'd rather be anything
(the back half of a galactic star, parts never seen)
(the grimy underbelly of a public restroom faucet)
I'd rather be that
than in the
quiet
black
closet.

I stared, wide-eyed.

I didn't know you were a poet.

I'm not. Raizel stood in front of the wall, blocking her words of wisdom. Is it stupid?

I put my hand on the back of Raizel's neck and inched her face toward mine, wrapping my other arm around her waist. I entangled my fingers in her loosely curled locks and pecked her soft lips, feeling a sudden hunger in every organ but my stomach. I felt my body press into hers. I stopped myself when I remembered the wet paint on the wall behind her.

We clutched each other's hands and darted out of the hallway, heading for the stairs. Amara was on her way up.

Hey! Amara tugged Raizel's free hand. Where you going?

We're going outside for a bit. Raizel pulled her hand away, letting me tug her down a few steps.

Save me a dance? For the sake of pride? Amara smiled widely, trying to charm Raizel with the gap in her teeth. She was probably already on something, the satchel around her neck heavy with illegality.

Fuck that! I laughed. Let's go, Raisin.

We hurried out the front door of the bar, past the line waiting to get in.

We ran to the Camaro.

We sped to the field at the end of Main Street, beer garden fences still in place although the area was deserted. Raizel popped the wheels over the curb and cut the lights. We didn't get out. We dove between the driver's and passenger's seats into the back, landing with ferocity.

As we only wore the muscle shirts from the parade, we rubbed our hands on each other's bare arms before pushing our bodies together. I thought of all the nights when we'd been fucked up and shared a bed, but had never let things go very far. I felt her smiling. Her happiness floated into my mouth and made me grin back. I enjoyed her hipbones too much as they pressed into mine. I craved her nude body. My own desire finally stood before me, clear-cut.

This is what you want.

We took off our shirts and bras. I didn't want to take my lips off hers, but had to look at her flat stomach and little breasts. I hoped I made her tingle the way my skin did when she kissed my neck. We only stopped so she could crank up the heater. When she came back to me I instantly recalled the night we'd played The Daisy Game--the first time I'd been blessed with the unbelievable smoothness of her bare stomach touching mine. That night, we'd made out a lot, but nothing more, too wasted. Now I was more sober than ever. Through the blazing, pumping music I heard her moan and breathe. I groaned back. The button nearly ripped off my jeans, but I didn't care about anything except Raizel's sweet skin.

She straddled me with my ass on the car seat, her slim legs surrounding my thighs, and I shoved away thoughts that she might dislike my body. Nothing could ruin that day for us. I trembled like I'd had five cappuccinos when she put her hand down and touched me. I touched her too, feeling strange about being a girl and knowing exactly what to do. Our hips gyrated together as we continued to kiss.

Everything heightened inside of me. I stood tiptoed on a balancing beam, teetering left and right. She moved her hand back and forth on my sensitive flesh. I couldn't believe when I suddenly felt the lightheadedness I'd only ever felt alone. I wondered if it was just a wave of pride-parade-induced serotonin floating through my head and soon to disappear.

But Raizel's whole body tightened up on top of me. I tipped off the balancing beam. We shook together. She pressed her ridiculously soft chest against mine and breathed the song of pleasure.

You're so fucking beautiful. She kept her mouth in my hair.

I felt like the luckiest girl in the world.

I'm the luckiest girl in the world.

I stopped myself saying something else, regardless of the truth it bore.

59

By May I had regular hours at Mars, seven to twelve Tuesday to Saturday. I'd moved on from coat-check to bigger and better things--table-clearing duty, manning the first-floor beer-tub, eventually being stationed behind the bar. Big Ted always let Raizel in for free, and sometimes Liam and Abby. I'd watch them dance their way in and I'd serve them drinks, pretending to take their money. I could tell when they'd popped pills because before anything they'd mingle with the short-haired middle-aged women and the guys with goatees who drank cocktails and wore mesh muscle shirts. Then they'd wave at me and disappear somewhere upstairs and I'd pretend I needed to pee. I usually snuck in a dance or two and a drink or three in the glow-star room before coming back down.

Sometimes when I got upstairs, I'd find them dancing near Amara, cheering her on as she popped into her ballet poses in a desperate attempt to seduce the crowd. Other times, Amara would be down from her cage, her skinny arms looped around the neck of any girl dancing near my friends. They were *my* friends, who didn't behave weirdly and make things awkward. Amara's hours coincided with mine more than mine than I would have liked, but she usually worked until two, sometimes three.

I could tell when Raizel and the others hadn't taken anything because they would order fun things like vanilla vodka on the rocks or Malibu, never wine or beer. They would look around while they danced, either trying to score something or trying to catch people checking them out. Their eyes focused.

No matter how they showed up, we'd always reconvene when my shift ended, everyone half-cut. We sometimes crushed pills and snorted them off the toilet paper dispensers in the unisex bathroom. When we couldn't score elsewhere, I'd call Seed and someone would drive me out to Wainmont and wait in the car while I filled my pretty koi fish box with as much daisy as everyone could afford. A couple of times, when everyone was too fucked to drive, we hitch-hiked on Main Street, something that excited my entirety, the thrill of doggy-piling in the back of a stranger's truck without knowing if we'd end up where we wanted to.

I was aware of the dangers surrounding everything we did. It was like getting on the biggest rollercoaster at the summer fair. If things got too sketchy I'd freak out at the top and beg to be let off with little chance of actually being let off. If I wasn't careful my wallet and cell phone and tickets for all other rides would fall from my pockets when I got thrown upside-down.

We tugged each other away from the addicts we met who had shaking hands and darting eyes, the ones we could tell would try to leech on until we found something good.

We did whatever the fuck we pleased.

On a Saturday when I arrived at the bar, Ilene told me she'd scheduled too many people for the night and that I could leave at eight if I wanted to. Due to the brightening weather, people were leaving Sloam on weekends to visit their cottages in other lakes and towns. Thus, we were having slow weekends at the bar.

When Ilene approached me, I fought the urge to jump up and down, as I'd awoken that morning with a scratchy throat and stuffed nose. I left at eight, as proposed, checking my cell phone on my way out the door. I found a message from Liam.

can u get shrooms?

I stopped in the alleyway and pressed DIAL.

Riiiiiiing. Rays of sunlight lingered in the sky amid the approaching navy of nighttime.

Hey, girlfriend! Liam chuckled, knowing I'd found his message.

Hey, what's going on? I let out a laugh.

Raizel and me thought it would be fun to do them tonight.

Aren't you working?

Yeah, but we can do them later. *If* we can get them. I'm off at nine. Raizel's at her mom's birthday dinner, but she'll be free later.

Well…I've never asked my buddy, but… I'll call you back in a minute, okay?

Sure thing.

Riiiiiiing. Riiiiiiiing.

Hey, boo.

What's up?

Nothin'. Just surfing the 'net. I'm looking at different colleges in Canada.

Colleges? Are you kidding?

And universities. I almost have enough for a year at Concordia. I like the sounds of their creative writing program.

Writing? I'd never peg you as a writer. But wow. So your current 'job' is really paying off.

Yeah. Seed half-chuckled. So what you up to?

I was just wondering if I could drop by.

Sure. I'm leaving at nine, though.

Okay. I'll be there soon.

Later, boo.

Venice! Someone called down the alley when I was turning the corner onto the street. I stopped and poked my head back around the corner.

Amara was running after me, despite having already changed from her ballet slippers in to her heels. She was more giraffe-like than ever with her gaunt limbs emerging from a white miniskirt. I hadn't paid her heed in so long that I'd forgotten how thin she was; either that, or she'd lost weight. Her hair created a puffy, circular silhouette against the sunset.

Hi. I watched her approach, feeling an eyebrow rise on my forehead.

Ilene let me go early. Amara's chest puffed in and out rapidly. There's--puff--gonna be--wheeze--no one in there tonight.

Probably. I nodded, placing my hands on my hips, missing the pockets of my winter coat. I shivered as a breeze at my back pushed through the thin material of my long-sleeved shirt.

Aren't you cold? Amara wrapped her boney arms around her stomach, gazing down at me. Her eyes and mouth bore a skeletal beauty that still surprised me.

Fucking cold. My teeth chattered. Everyone kind of jump-starts summer, you know? With t-shirts and shit.

Yeah. Amara nodded, her hair shaking around her ears. A familiar curl fell across her dark forehead. I got a car.

Huh? For real?

Yeah. You wanna see it?

Is it here? I looked around at the streets, bare but for a few post-rush-hour stragglers.

We walked down Main Street, passing the One-Buck Store and the esthetician school. Main Street was so long that I couldn't see as far as the pharmacy.

Here she is! Amara exclaimed, pulling her keys out of her same old knock-off Chanel purse.

I stopped on the sidewalk and stared at the car, the boxiness of which resembled Sloam's ancient taxi-cabs. But it was *orange,* like a pumpkin. *Orange,* like the Camaro. I watched through the passenger window as Amara's long fingers pulled up the lock and she waved me in.

I slipped into the passenger seat, enjoying the soft material under me and how much the windows blocked the cool May breeze. Amara turned the key in the ignition, inviting the radio to come blasting out of the dusty dashboard speakers.

This is pretty sweet. I nodded politely, looking around. She had hung a rainbow ribbon from the rearview mirror.

Thanks. I'm gonna get a CD player, eventually. So, where do you want me to take you? Home? Or to Raizel's?

Huh? Oh, no, thanks. Neither. I can take--

What are you doing tonight, then? Amara cocked her head, turning to look at me.

Well…I'm picking up from Seed. Er--Edward. Remember that guy--I was…dating?

Yup. Amara nodded, pretending to believe a lie that had long since fallen into its grave. She eased the car out of the parking spot. I can take you there.

He lives in Wainmont. I can just take the bus if it's too far.

Though…it would be nice to get a ride. I could make it there before he goes out.

No prob. So what are you picking up?

Um. Shrooms. I relaxed, pulling the seatbelt across my chest. Have you ever done them?

Yeah. Amara laughed, baring her pitch-white teeth as she turned down the radio. It was *awesome.* I did them at Johnson Lake last summer. Who are you doing them with?

You went to Johnson Lake? I ignored her question.

Yeah. It was sweet. I saw DJ Lily.

I've always wanted to go there. But I never had a car.

Well. I can take us this year, if you want.

Why the fuck are you being so nice to me?

Hey, I've been meaning to apologize. Amara steered the car through the empty streets, darkness having fallen over everything.

What? Why?

For the pride parade. Ilene told me to tell you about the float, but by the time I saw you, it was already starting. Sorry.

It's okay. I shrugged. She could have phoned me. I was over it, though, having acknowledged that I was more than satisfied to have spent my first pride parade ever holding hands with the prettiest girl on the street.

Amara was a better driver than I would have expected, paying attention to her mirrors and the speed limit. I wondered if my fingers looked so elegant when I drove the Camaro. Her hands were so confident and feminine. I looked down at my short fingernails at the ends of stubby appendages.

As I was looking down, my eyes traveled across the car. They landed on Amara's slender thighs. Her skirt had ridden up. I watched her leg alternate between the gas and brake pedals, the caramel skin becoming taut around her flexed muscles. In remembrance of how she had once regarded me, I couldn't help feeling that she had hidden motives.

Should I turn left or right?

Left. Feeling a sudden warmth in my cheeks, my eyes flitted from her legs to the windshield. I mean right.

When we knocked on Seed's sixteenth-floor apartment door, he opened it immediately.

Hey, boo. Seed looked through his fat wallet, counting hundred-dollar bills. I was just putting my shoes on.

Hi. I moved into the apartment. The familiar combination of Febreze and pot smoke tickled my nose. *Ah-choo!*

Bless you.

Thanks. You remember Amara, right?

Huh? Seed looked away from his wallet, eyes traveling up Amara's bare, mile-long legs. Hi. How's it going?

Good. Amara nodded, her plump lips closing in a tight smile. How are you?

Just...doing business. Seed sat on the floor, rolling one of his jean legs up. How is everyone?

They're good.

I cocked my head, watching Seed press his wallet against his inner ankle. His hand reached blindly through a cupboard below the massive fish tank. When he found what he was looking for, he peered back up at Amara, his green eyes shining from under his gangster cap.

Are you and Raizel still together?

Oh, no. Amara laughed. But we're still friends.

I rolled my eyes.

That's cool. Seed began wrapping duct tape around his wallet and leg, one, two, three layers so it would stay put. So, what were you ladies interested in purchasing?

As I hadn't been able to specify over the phone that I wanted mushrooms, Seed was caught off guard with my order. He said he hadn't had shrooms for a while, but that he'd call me if he found some. When I sighed with blatant disappointment that I wouldn't be able to fulfill Raizel and Liam's dreams, Seed offered some daisy, pulling from the knitting trunk a bag of yellow pills, familiar kiss imprints glowing before me. Amara spoke first.

We'll take eight.

I'm bored of daisy, I replied. I'd rather spend my money on booze.

Are you sure? Seed adjusted his hat.

I'll buy them. Amara looked toward her armpit, fiddling with the zipper on the small purse hanging from her shoulder. My treat.

Are you serious? Why would you do that?

Because. Her dark eyes glanced at me before retreating to her purse. She extracted her pink wallet and smiled sweetly. We haven't hung out in a long time. I miss ya.

When I was stumbling up the front walk of my duplex at five a.m. after Raizel and I had kissed and made tattoo plans for later that week and she had driven off, I looked up. A rosy sweater of clouds was wrapped around the sky's shoulders, first flirtings of the spring sun. I reflected on the particularly nostalgic night I'd had--one that included orange juice and disco balls and my bare feet pawing the rug in Amara's hot living room while I danced my heart out.

60

The next day I awoke with a headache that moved around under the surface of my scalp. Waking up after nights of daisy fun, I didn't usually feel anything but tired--especially when I hadn't had a drop of liquor. I arose from my pillow and touched my temples, wincing. My headache was definitely on the road to a full-blown migraine.

I dragged myself down the hall and into the kitchen. As I was pouring a glass of tapwater, my nose let out a barrage of wet sneezes. I darted toward the bathroom with my hand over my nose, wiping the stringy snot with a wad of toilet paper. Meanwhile, a rhinoceros stomped around inside my brain.

Fuck. One glimpse in the mirror of a puffy-eyed, red-nose girl was enough to send me back to bed.

When my mother got home from work and found me in bed with a tissue stuffed in my nostrils, she let out a sigh.

You're sick?

Yeah. I kept my eyes closed, breathing heavily through my mouth.

Do you think it's bad?

I unno yed. Probably jusd as bad as every year

Oh, my peach. Have you eaten today? I'll make you some soup.

Before I could tell her I wasn't hungry, her silhouette in the doorway was gone. With the blockage in my nose, I doubted I'd be lured to the living room by the tantalizing aroma of no-name chicken noodle soup.

I crawled out of bed at four a.m., having awoken to my body painted on the sheets with sweat. I turned the shower on cold and dove into the tub without removing my underwear. That was the moment in which I accepted the arrival of my Yearly Cold.

A sleepy blur took over my body. For the next week, I called Ilene and told her that yes, I was still sick. My mother ordered me to stay in bed, unless I was getting up to eat. Because she knew this part of me better than anyone, I listened to her. She was sorry she couldn't stay home with me all day, but she was still busy with work. She stocked the cupboards with all different kinds of soups and crackers and tea.

Raizel came to visit, carting with her books and Curve magazines. She sat on my bed with her back to the wall and her legs over my sprawled-out body. She read me articles about coming out and making it big in the world and I closed my eyes and listened to her cinnamon voice. She didn't get angry when I fell asleep and left her talking to the air in the room.

My mother warned Raizel on three occasions to stay away from me, unless she wanted to get sick. When my mother was home, Raizel didn't read Curve. I was afraid of things being heard through my bedroom door. She painted my toenails with fuchsia polish threw out my tissues and massaged my neck.

I hate you seeing me like this, I claimed. Secretly, I adored her attention and her soft hands checking the temperature of my forehead.

When Raizel was working or had plans, I listened to my library CDs and tried to sing along with my plugged-nose voice. I was looking at Veruca Salt lyrics book when I came across the library receipt. The CDs were a month overdue. Fuck--who knew what they charged for that? I tossed the CD on the carpet and rolled over, facing the wall and staring up at a bunch of bananas and wishing Raizel was with me. I knew how selfish I was being, expecting her to drive across the city to me every day, but I couldn't help it. When Friday arrived and she hadn't been over since Tuesday, I sent her a text message.

whats up baby?

She replied half an hour later.

just hanging with amara.
r u serious?
ya. y? u jealous? ;)
no I just thot u were annoyed of her

Half an hour later, my phone beeped and I dove toward it.

no shes being really cool lately.
sure she is

No reply.

I *wasn't* jealous, no way. Amara was nasty. She had toilet breath and skanky clothing and gangly arms. It just would have been nice of Raizel to ask how I was feeling. Maybe she was getting sick of taking care of me. My stomach flipped. As I was telling myself I *had* to get better, I moved onto stage three of my Yearly Cold, my chest and throat convulsing with a round of bronchial coughs.

The next day, again, Raizel couldn't come over, saying she had to work. Good. Amara was probably sleeping, saving energy for Mars, as her shifts usually bore from night into the wee hours of the morning.

Suddenly, an awful thought occurred to me. What if they'd done daisy together? Just the two of them? I knew how ecstasy could force the mind into liking everything. I had never felt anything for anyone but Raizel, even on daisy, but I had no idea if I affected her the way she did me. I trusted that she wouldn't cheat on me, but what if she wanted to? I would much rather have her kiss and not feel than feel and not kiss. I let out a bed-shaking cough.

Peach? My mother knocked on my bedroom door, inching it open.

I'd forgotten it was Saturday.

Hi.

Are you okay? I heard you coughing. Do you want some syrup?

I'm *not* hungry. My stomach muscles were wound in thick knot from my non-jealousy over Raizel and Amara.

What? My mother laughed. I mean cough syrup. Why would I offer you maple syrup? Don't you think I'd offer you pancakes, too?

I didn't respond.

Wow, this cold is really taking its toll on you. My mother moved into the room so I could see her legs, clad in businesswoman slacks. Listen, I was gonna try to get some work done, but...well, screw it. I haven't had a Saturday off in a long time. What if we go do something?

Like what? My eyes moved up from her legs to her face with its hardened eyebrows.

Anything you want. Ice cream?

I told you I'm not hungry.

You have to eat *something*. You're starting to wear thin. I can see your hipbones.

I drew the sheet up, up, up, over my body. Over my face. Over my thoughts.

We could go to the pharmacy and get you some Buckley's.

Main Street Pharmacy? I asked, inching the sheet back down so as to reveal one eye.

Downtown? Why would we go there when--

Because I have to return my library stuff.

Oh, I see. Well, I suppose so. We could pick up some new reading material, too. I'm sure you're running low.

Yeah. My eyes darted to the pile of magazines Raizel had left near my closet door. Definitely.

When we arrived at the pharmacy, Raizel and Liam's boss was at the till counter. I'd left my mother in the car outside, saying I'd run in and get the Buckley's.

Hi. I approached the man with the gray hair and robust belly. Is Raizel here? Or on her break?

Raizel? He shook his head, jowls jiggling slightly. She's not in today or tomorrow.

Huh? I slit my eyes. Are you sure?

Well, yes. I am the one who made the schedule.

Oh. I lifted my arm to place the Buckley's cough syrup on the counter.

When we were driving home from the library, a million thoughts racing through my mind and rapidly beating heart, my mother opened her mouth.

Did you notice anything...? She stared at the busy Elmview road before us, following a black truck. At the library?

Hmm? I stared out the window as we passed Team Bean, suddenly yearning for a glimpse of Walter. The coffee shop came and went as we sped through a green light.

That woman working there--the older one--did she look familiar to you?

In my head, I retraced the way we'd split up at the library, my mother heading to the Danielle Steele shelf while I'd gone down to the CDs. I'd cursed under my breath on three occasions--when I had dropped my library card, when a surprise round of coughs had come barreling from my mouth, and when I'd reflected how hard I was falling for a girl who lied to me and hung out with her ex-girlfriend. When time had come for us to check stuff out, the old woman I'd seen at the library every time had met us at the counter. Her pink old-lady lips had scolded me for returning the CDs late and I had blushed and my mother had paid the six-dollar fee.

The lady at the counter? I turned to my mother. Yeah, I guess. She looks like every old lady, though. What about her?

She looks the way my mother did.

Oh. I watched her blink.

Do you remember your grandmother at all? My mother's voice became hoarse as she steered the car out of Elmview and through Oakwood Heights.

Sometimes, I responded, quieter than the trees outside the car. Sometimes I smell something and I think about a yellow kitchen floor. Sometimes dresses remind me of her. But I don't remember how she was, at all.

Well, she liked things her way. She admonished you sometimes, just like that lady at the library.

She was mean to me?

No, no. My mother laughed. She was just responsible. When I was growing up, she always made me tell her exactly where I was going, and who with, and what we were doing.

Kind of like you?

Venice Anne! My mother's mouth fell open. You think I'm like that?

Well...you used to be. I suddenly felt my fever rise.

I'm just being a mother. She sighed and turned down Oakwood Terrace. I *barely* know what you're doing anymore.

The conversation having turned from sweetness into words laced with implications, I was quiet until we reached our driveway, at which point I began hacking up a lung.

Jesus! My mother turned off the car ignition. Sounds like a smoker's cough.

I don't smoke. I shook my head.

Well, not tobacco.

I suddenly realized I hadn't seen my mother smoke all day. Wow--she really was being kind, not smoking in my presence. She knew that would send me into a coughing fit more than anything. I thanked her and dodged into the duplex with my bag of CDs. I closed my bedroom door and fell across my bed. My diaphragm convulsed with a cough and I reached for the Buckley's. I took a heavy swig of the blasphemous liquid. My mouth and throat squeezed together and I let out a smaller cough.

I dug my phone out of my pocket and began typing a message.

I know you lied to me. Where the fuck are you?

I stared at my phone, quickly erasing what I'd written.

If you want her, I understand. Just say the word and I'll fuck off.

Reminiscent of the first time I'd dialed her number, I pressed END before the message could get anywhere. I began typing a third potential break-up message.

You are breaking my he--

Knock, knock! My wooden bedroom door sounded.

Fuck off! I shouted at my mother, through the door. *Just fuck off!*

The door opened and a full head of white-blond waves came peeking through.

Whoa. What's wrong?

Nothing. I tossed my phone at my closet door, watching as it fell limp on the carpet. I put my face in the pillow and muffle-spoke. What do you want?

Are you still sick? I heard the door close and her feet pad toward the bed.

Obviously. Where were you today?

I was getting a tattoo. Raizel reached for my shoulder, trying to push me onto my side.

With Amara? I retched my shoulder away from her.

Yeah, she came with me. Wanna see?

That's awesome. So you lied to me about being at work, and got tattoos with your ex, even though we *just* made a plan to get some together. Tears poured out of my eyes and my chest threatened to implode. What did you get--matching ink on your ring fing--

You know those ugly scars on my thigh? Raizel interrupted, her own voice quavering. I got something to--

Sure. You can leave no--

JUST *LOOK AT ME!* Raizel shouted in my ear with her loud, cheering-at-concerts voice.

My head ringing, I turned my snotty, spitty face toward Raizel. She stood in the middle of my bedroom in her white panties, her skirt and tights around her ankles. I scanned her slender, pale legs, something so foreign to me that my face and neck got hot, despite my rage. My eyes burned through the tattoo, placed on her upper right thigh so its top barely touched the band of her panties. I had only noticed her pink scars one time, and hadn't thought of them as a big deal, but now they were a thing of the past, completely hidden.

A tiny man stood at one end of a long, skinny boat, rowing through the water under an old, intricately detailed archway between a set of buildings. The water was turquoise and the sky was ablaze with a five p.m. palette and the man wore a striped shirt and a funny hat and a smile he'd never felt more at peace.

Bang bang bang. My heart.

61

I lay with my back on the carpet, half covered by a navy blue blanket. My midriff was bare, my shirt all twisted up and avoiding my jeans as if in cahoots with them. My fingers pinched bits of my skin and I rubbed my jeaned legs together. I hardly felt them, but I saw them propped on the wall. The blanket was whipped cream. My head was honey. I rolled it to my left and saw dark linoleum, unlit kitchen. I rolled the other way and saw Liam's body beneath another blanket.

We're the Blanket Bitches. Liam threw a hand over his eyes and faced the ceiling again. That night, he wore black nail polish and safety-pin earrings and those tight purple jeans. He was beautiful, funny, honest, funny, friendly, and funny. I'd always admired that kind of person--the one about whom such conclusions were to be made so quickly. I also loved how his black hair shook and his blue eyes widened when something was humorous. His deep laughter meandered through the room, smoke from a glossy red mouth. I was forced to giggle and writhe with joy. My eyes ran, the salty water sliding into my hair.

Liam, I said.

V, he said back.

I miss our talks.

What?

Remember how you used to call me every night?

Yeah, but…we're together, like, every night.

Oh, yeah. I laughed, my mind floating in a cloudless sky.

I was in a big, me-sized bubble. Before eating the mushrooms I'd told myself I wouldn't do anything scary, like looking in the mirror, but when I dragged myself to the bathroom I caught a reflection of my eyes. My pupils were big and my irises had turned from gray stones to beams of silver, sweet little snow globes. I wanted to shake them. The luminescence of my face made me shiver. I heard everything going on outside of me, but I was on my own in a world where I looked and sounded amazing.

I heard a little voice mention Easter and I wondered aloud,

Why is Amara in the basement?

What the fuck? Liam laughed. She isn't.

I'm right here!

I couldn't lift my head to see her. The pictures behind my eyelids would shoot into the sky and become too bright to bear. I laughed. We were suddenly on speaking terms with each other. I found myself caring less and less that she had been invited.

I wish I had a puppy. I petted my blanket.

Oh god, me too. Raizel rolled in my direction and did the impossible; she broke into my world and put her hand on mine. My skin shivered away from hers as though afraid of a feeling too grand.

I'm so glad you got better, V.

Me, too.

I looked at Raizel's eyes, which had absorbed the darkness of night, deep and wet and flickering. During my heavy blink I imagined fourteen girls skinny-dipping in a mansion's backyard pool. I bounced twice on the diving board before putting my hands together like a praying child and gliding into the water. The water became Raizel's mind and soon I was surrounded by her knowledge and her feelings and the reigning thought that she enjoyed me immensely and we were getting past anything bad that had ever threatened to consume us. We were looking through a telescope toward the future.

Same. I re-opened my eyes to see her dreamy smile.

Light suddenly inundated the room. We all sat up, alert. Liam and Amara got to their feet, peeking out the living room window. I tried to reverse the polarity of the magnets that were my body and the floor, tried to tear myself from the blanket.

What's going on? Raizel squinted at the others.

Fuck, fuck, fuck. Liam turned to us, wide-eyed and open-mouthed, like a ghost costume made from a bed sheet. My parents are home.

Oh, shit. Raizel jumped to action. She rested her hand beneath the coffee table ledge and scooped the rest of the mushrooms into the pocket of her shorts.

Duuude, I heard my voice say lazily. Why can't you tell them we're just hanging out?

Have you *seen* yourself? Liam scrambled to put the cushions back in the sofa, and fold their blankets.

Venice, get up! Raizel pulled my hand. Get the fuck up.

In my peripheral, the others scrambled toward the doorway leading to the kitchen. I wondered how they were able to function and why they weren't as fucked as me and if the mushrooms had gone wrong in my system the way DVDs sometimes did in the computer when I tried to burn copies. Maybe they had tricked me into eating the magic ones while they had eaten regular grocery store mushrooms, just so they could laugh at my expense.

I stood up and leaned all of my weight on the TV stand, straightening my shirt. I combed my hair with my perspiring fingers. My heart raced like a fifty-horse stampede. My armpits were moist.

Let's go.

Liam led us through the house. Amara was right behind him, then Raizel, who linked her arm through mine and pulled me along. We all piled into the kitchen and then to the back landing where it was so dark no one could possibly notice our gigantic pupils. We heard keys in a door in another dimension, and managed to exit out the side door as Liam's parents entered through the front.

We darted across the lawn and stalked down the street as though we owned it. The air calmed my heart, magnificent on my cheeks and flowing through my hair. We wore only jeans and hoodies; spring had burst from winter's tail-end like an overdue baby, fighting off snowfalls of vengeance. We moved slowly and triumphantly, talking about what would have happened if we'd been caught all super high.

Well… Liam squinted at his watch. It's only ten. What should we do?

Let's have an adventure. Amara grinned.

I didn't think of my life as anything *but* adventuresome, and I couldn't agree more about our dire need to do things. The stars were alive, daring us to light up and dance down the street like fireflies on lily pads across some great body of water.

When I closed my eyes Raizel and I were practically there, watching the sun sparkle through the branches of trees lining the side of a pond in a valley between enormous mountains with flat sides for people to scale and then jump off of, as faultlessly as dolphins diving and then lying stretched in turquoise ocean, serenity's roar when whitecaps crashed on a green patch comprised of emotion. I found a place where liberty burst from our swollen hearts, minds thought what they pleased, and my kisses swept her skin more sweetly than a blue night's breeze.

The wondrous vision disappeared as soon as I opened my eyes. I had to catch my balance.

Shit. Liam raised his eyebrows. How fucked up *are* you?

Don't worry. Raizel smiled at me, comforting my high. I am, too.

We need some cheap entertainment. Amara sighed. Then she emitted a chuckle that rippled through the rest of us. We were all connected, the same wave length. We stopped walking and formed a circle, a team huddle looking down over a concoction of sandals and dirty spring sneakers.

I feel like vandalizing something. Amara tousled her afro with one of bangle-filled arms, twinkling in my ears.

I thought you believed in karma…? I wondered aloud, baffled. I was pretty sure I was the only one who'd grown up in a neighborhood where cars were keyed and lawn ornaments were smashed on a daily basis. My own bedroom window had been egged more times than I could count.

But what if we get revenge on someone? Amara's eyes were glossy.

Part of me wanted to listen to her. Part of me wanted to cower in my bed with a blanket drawn around me, my back to the wall so nothing could sneak up.

Revenge is *almost* acceptable if someone has done something to tamper with your feelings. Raizel looked down.

I watched her face, not understanding how someone had messed with her so hard. *Years* had passed and she was obviously still hurt. I wanted to get my hands on that Hannah bitch. I was a tough girl. If Raizel was talking about the feelings most commonly found in a vault at the bottom of the human heart, I could muster up some understanding.

Only that year, I'd realized I was capable of incubating such emotions.

Think about it. Amara's eyes flitted between the rest of us. What's the worst thing anyone's ever done to you?

I didn't want to think about it.

It's a long list. Liam scoffed, staring at the pavement. Mostly to do with my family.

Mine's easy. Mostly to do with someone here. Amara smiled the smile I'd come to regard as The Doll Smile. Dolls wore the same smile their whole lives, whether being cuddled or squished under the laundry hamper in the closet. Dolls' smiles didn't represent happiness.

The *worst* thing? I finally spoke.

We all held hands and made our way to the busiest road to catch a ride. Finding a driver didn't take long. A truck pulled over and Amara told him to take us to Oakwood Heights, said we wanted to check out the Christmas decorations. They shared a laugh, his surely out of confusion, as it was March, and hers from another realm. I thought the plan was great; I could easily walk home when the mushrooms passed and the fun had been spent. I shivered at the thought of being alone in my current state of mind.

We hopped in the back after he'd checked us out and we'd checked him out, this middle-aged man with a graying mustache. I'd often imagined that my dad was like that, wherever he existed, some broad-shouldered guy who was kind enough to give intoxicated kids a ride if they needed one. I hoped he would open the tiny window between his seat and the back of the truck and give us a lecture about the dangers of hitch-hiking. I hoped he would look at me as he said it. Maybe his eyes were gray.

The May wind was harsher than we'd expected. We lay low on the metal floor between some spare tires, trying not to acknowledge our chattering teeth and jumping legs. I kept my eyes shut, seeing turquoise stars and patterns of fuchsia every time we sped by a streetlight. The man drove for fifteen minutes, nearly bringing us to my neck of the woods. He stopped in Oakwood Heights near St. Timothy's Catholic High School.

The man waved at us. As quickly as he'd come into our lives he disappeared. Something deep in me simmered, the revenge our plan, or lack-of-plan, apparently called for. I told the others I had a little idea, some unfinished business in one of the houses. If we could just get in I could make peace with my past. My words piqued their interested, but they didn't take it as heavily as I made it sound. They laughed.

I'm down.

Let's do it.

Let's get the show on the road.

First we stopped at the 7-11 on the corner of Good and Bad. While the others were getting Slurpees I crept down the aisles, looking for items we could put to use. Everything shone brightly at me from the shelves. Fish-shaped candies reminded me of grade eleven biology class when I would stare at the goldfish tank and plot how to set them free. The security guard didn't mind us because we had

Liam's charming smile and Raizel's perky tits and Amara's long-as-fuck legs. He didn't even glance my way as I slipped everything in my backpack. On the way out we grinned and he said something through severely buck teeth.

Be careful out there, kids.

Warning me to be careful in my own hood.

My memory didn't fail me as I led them down the streets I'd hailed with my ratty bike at one point in time. Barely anything could penetrate the intent I felt, walking swiftly despite my tripping. The houses loomed over us more than ever, trying to intimidate us into leaving. Liam and Amara joked about the richies, not realizing that, to me, even they were rich. Of course, I was rich to someone else in the world. It was a never-ending chain of You Have More Money Than Me. Raizel's fingers trailed lazily up my arm to my elbow. I kept quiet, serenely freaked out about what was going to happen. All I wanted was to play a prank, to scare someone into considering peoples' feelings.

Okay, here we go. I led them down a short catwalk lined with dogwoods and tall, gray fences. I dug into my backpack, loving my friends' faces as they gave me their undivided attention, all of their eyes shining with something I dared to mistake as admiration. I handed Liam a purple can of spray paint. I gave Raizel blue, and Amara pink.

Ohh, I love art. Amara laughed and shook her can. Her giggles rang in the night and disturbed my fluttering tummy muscles.

I thought of something I'd learned in a high school English class--in tragic plays and movies, moments of comedy are the best way to provide temporary comfort to the audience. We snuck along, entering the streets as though on a mission.

What are we doing? Raizel looped her arm through mine, slowing my pace.

I looked at her and her calm hair, wavy like the ocean and white like sand. I wanted to tell her everything about my past that didn't make sense, everything that had probably altered the person I was supposed to have become after graduating from high school. I wanted to tell her about grades eight and nine and ten and eleven and especially grade twelve and the summers in between when other stupid shit had happened. I wanted to tell her about when I was seven and I'd lied to Dana that I remembered some things about our father, and how he'd told me that was weird since he was older and couldn't remember a thing.

Mushrooms were different from ecstasy. I thought everything while looking at Raizel, yet found myself unable to spill my deepest secrets. I must have been thinking for a long time, because she just gave me a quick hug and turned me toward our destination. My nose clung to the scent of her neck and I momentarily considered turning back and bringing her to the railroad field nearby where we could drop our nervously beating hearts onto each other and catch them at the last second like in every stupid action film Tiff had ever made me watch. My chest ached.

Then, there it was. The scene of the crime: a flat cement driveway in the shadow of one of the bigger houses. Chills took over my spine.

62

April in grade nine brings breezy days. One day at school my friends and I decide to plan a party for Marity's birthday. The Tunnel is a distant memory, something that may or may not have actually happened. My diary says it did. Marity and I now resort to only seeing each other when other people expect us to. It's been over half a year and I haven't forgotten about the feeling of her mouth on mine. I write in my diary that she's only keeping me around so she won't have to tell the others what happened between us and why she hates me.

I haven't been to any of their houses yet, except Cecile's, when I was little. The night of the party, when I walk up the front steps to Marity's house, the wraparound porch looms over my head and dares me to ring the doorbell.

Happy birthday, Mare.

She puts the present I've wrapped in her favorite shade of purple on a table by the door. She welcomes me, immediately taking me up the spiral staircase to show me around. Everything smells like potpourri. She leads me to a bathroom with a Jacuzzi, a study with two computers, her parents' room, and a gallery with paintings by people I've only dared to hear of.

When I ask Marity about her parents' jobs she shrugs and avoids looking me in the eye.

I dunno, boring stuff. My dad's a surgeon and my mom has some marketing business.

We go to the kitchen on the main level. She leans on the open refrigerator door in the enormous kitchen, black eyes finally piercing me as she graces my name with her tongue.

What do you like drinking, Venice?

Coke's fine. I'm dazed, unable to look away.

She snorts in disbelief.

No. What do you like *drinking*?

Oh! The word bounces around between my ears and I have to stop my eyes from following it like a cat watching a string. Um, it's a little early.

When she had invited me over to get ready for the party, I'd thought everyone would be there--Janet and Cecile and possibly Marity's family--to relax my knotted stomach. I'd thought getting ready meant putting chips in bowls and making dip out of onion soup mix and sour cream.

You're right. She laughs. It's only five.

We go downstairs and she shows me another bathroom, a lounge with a pool table and a massive television, and her room with a queen-sized bed, a fish tank built into the wall, and a mirror covering another wall, by which lay a section of hardwood floor solely for her to practice ballet.

I imagine her, not in a pirouette, but motionless, arms above her head and caramel thigh pointed effortlessly at the ceiling.

I sit on the floor in the basement family room, watching Friends while Marity sits behind me on the leather couch. She demands that I take out my rat's nest ponytail holder. Then she brushes out the knots, and curls my brown hair into ringlets. I'm sure it will be like a granny perm. I'm afraid to see it in the bathroom mirror.

My hair turns out okay. Great, even. My bangs have been pulled up, drawing attention to my eyes, which Marity convinces me will be perfect under a blanket of gray shadow. The smoky look, she informs me, leaning forward as though she's going to kiss me, but instead concentrating on the art of making up my face. Afterwards she doesn't let me move until the black liquid liner dries and the spray in my hair hardens. I flip through the channels while she stands in the basement bathroom and sculpts her wavy black hair into a messy bun at the crown of her head, leaving chunks around her dark face.

She sighs at my baggy cargo pants and plain blue t-shirt from Walmart. She shares her expensive clothes with me, a Roxy denim miniskirt and a lime green tank top that I don't like until I look in the mirror and seen how big my tits look, something rendered important at the time. She puts on the same shirt, in orange, but it hangs differently off her skinny figure. We both slip on the seashell bracelets she got in Cuba during the February break, and drops of her mother's Chanel perfume on our collarbones.

Liam, Amara, Raizel, and I crept around the side of the house, finding an open window at the back, not far off the ground. Liam pushed the screen in easily and set it on the lawn outside. All of the mansion's lights were off, hinting that either no one was home or they'd gone to bed early. Maybe they were at their second mansion, beside a lake somewhere, like most fortunate families apparently did.

I rubbed my nose, wondering if the mushrooms were wearing off. I felt an undeniable carelessness deep within me. I touched the side of the house, enjoying the cold, flat feeling on my tingling fingertips.

Liam hoisted me up to the window first, as it had all been my idea. I was starting to wonder what, exactly, had been my idea. I landed feet-first on linoleum in a small laundry room, the scent of fabric softener all around me. I turned and glanced out the window at my three friends lingering in the dark on a stranger's lawn.

Stay here, I whispered. I'll see if anyone's home.

My body alive with adrenaline, I crept forward in the dimly light room, through a doorway and into a hall. I began recognizing details of the house--black-and-white checkered kitchen floor, a long breakfast bar, grand banister leading up the stairs, a set of French doors leading to the basement.

At seven p.m. Marity pours our drinks. Her excitement about the party shows in her kindness, first pouring two fingers' width of something from a pearly silver bottle called the Russian Prince and then asking me exactly how much 7-Up and exactly how much orange juice I want.

Cheers.

I pretend it's not the first alcoholic drink I've ever had and that my stomach isn't flipping insanely.

Flip flip flip.

I don't know when she started drinking.

The game begins there--concealing the fear that I'll cringe at the liquor and Marity will know I'm a rookie. We clink glasses and grin at each other with our matching Lipsmackers smiles. We sip the concoctions and all I taste is soda sugar and tangy juice. I've evaded the law and the Naivety Police.

We sit in the living room and read aloud the quizzes from her pile of Seventeen magazines. I expect to be loopy by the time I get through my drink, but nothing happens. When Marity finishes hers I offer to make the next ones. I follow her lead, but pour myself an extra Russian Prince finger. I rationalize that, as a bigger girl, I'll need more to make things tilt like they do in those commercials about drunk driving. It's unexplainable as to why I want such a thing to happen.

The doorbell rings and Marity snatches up her drink before answering it, leaning on the frame like a supermodel in a photo shoot. Cecile and Janet enter and gush about my hair and Marity tells them she crafted it.

You look like a girl. Cecile seems surprised.

I gaze at their made-up faces and slender legs protruding from skirts, rolled up at the waistband because they weren't been quite short enough. I sip my drink and they raise their eyebrows.

I didn't know you like drinking.

Yup.

They smile coyly and ask me to open their bottles of Mike's Hard Lemonade, reminding of Dole Mountain when I used to get apples for them off the trees.

Thanks, pretty girl. Marity smiles and my cheeks get warm. The Russian Prince tells me to follow her to the couch and sit beside her.

The boys arrive after eight, by which time I finish my second drink. Four of them have come, to make it even. We all sit in the living room and play Truth or Dare. Cecile dances with a boy and the rest of us egg them on. Marity does four consecutive shots of something hard, winking at everyone the way adults do when they're being witty. Janet is dared to French kiss one of the boys, but she conveniently spills her drink on the carpet and runs away to fetch a rag and stain remover.

In the middle of my sixth drink, or fifth, or possibly seventh, they dare me to play Seven Minutes in Heaven. They tell me to go upstairs and say one of them will come up after me, but they don't tell me who it'll be.

I crept up the stairs as silently as possible, not letting my sweating hands squeak along the banister. But when I got to the top, the house was ever-quiet, no sound of computers or televisions or voices or snores. I moved down the hallway, noticing that the door to the master bedroom was open.

I gave my eyes a moment to adjust before I realized the covers on the king-sized bed were pulled across the mattress, taut enough to play basketball on. I glanced behind me before entering the room, and snuck toward a bedside-table lamp. I turned it on the lowest setting.

As dull orange light cascaded over the room, my eyes darted over the floor and the bed. I had been so stupid. I quickly turned away and began opening dresser drawers, searching.

As hard as I try to keep my head still, it tips to the side and spins with the rest of Marity's parents' room. I feel like I'm clinging to the neck of a pony on a very fast Merry-Go-Round. I sashay to the bed, press my butt into the mattress, and lean my elbows on my knees. Someone knocks on the door.

You may enter! I feel like a royal descendent.

A boy enters the room, the shortest of the bunch--named either Nick or Neil. We've never spoken, but he smiles.

I found the sexy one!

I accept a beer from him and pat the bed as an invitation to sit. He grins mischievously, locking the door, beside me on the bed a moment later. We french kiss like long lost lovers, as if he's the one I've been waiting for.

You can go down my pants if you want. Nick or Neil speaks quietly, putting on the illusion of romance.

He unbuttons his jeans with one hand, placing the other on my back and lowering me until I'm lying on the bed. He stands up and shrugs his jeans off and I try to look at everything--the paintings on the wall, the mahogany headboard, the window and the dark night outside, everything but his skinny legs and the lump beneath his underwear.

He takes my hand and puts it in through the slit at the front and then I feel everything. I push him down on the carpet and his hand rubs my thighs in my borrowed miniskirt, warming the skin at the top of my legs. The Russian Prince stops me from caring if the skirt rides up. I straddle him and grind back and forth with nothing between us but Calvin Klein briefs, probably from an actual Calvin Klein store, and Fruit of the Loom boy-cut panties from Walmart.

I'm fourteen and clueless and don't know what I want.

The mistake comes not from my actions, but my mouth.

I want you.

As easily as making toast he watches me rocking around, a boat in the ocean, like I'm not in pain. His face is serious and concentrated as he tears into me, deep and unorganized.

Soon he groans and writhes, pulling my hips down hard.

I excuse myself to the bathroom and sit on the toilet and lean my head on the wall, a handful of toilet paper between my legs to gather blood and other stuff.

My bag heavy with a stranger's underwear-drawer riches, I made my way back down the stairs. Raizel and the others passed through my head, but I needed one more thing. Hopefully they'd stayed in the backyard, exactly where I'd left them. Maybe the stars and damp grass would be enough amusement. As I passed from room to room, I let my hands trail against the walls and furniture.

I stood in the dark in her basement bedroom. The ballet corner was filled with boxes and big Tupperware containers, the golden rod and floor-to-ceiling mirrors no longer serving a purpose. The aquarium was devoid of fish and fake coral reef. The bed was made neatly and nothing was scattered on the ground, unlike Raizel's room. I chuckled. Although I would have liked to see where things would have gone with Marity, I knew she never would have compared with Raizel. No one could.

I breathed in, and let air come crawling back out, letting go.

We're upstairs for a short time. When we walk back into the living room everyone protests.

What do you think this is, Five Minutes in Heaven?

Oblivious, they make us stand together in the front closet amid Marity's mother's fur coats, no lights on. I can barely breathe. When we come out we both swear that nothing happened. One boy tells Nick or Neil to go back upstairs.

Maybe you'll get lucky this time, second base at least.

Nick or Neil rubs his hands together, a greedy child, and obeys their orders. They send Marity eagerly up the stairs after him and I feel like screaming. Instead I touch my chin. I've heard several times that when I kiss a boy his stubble will scratch me, but I hadn't felt anything.

They go upstairs for nine minutes; I watch the lemon-shaped kitchen clock like a babysitter watching an infant. I'm not the only pissed one when it comes time for opening gifts; the others are whooping, strewn about carelessly, limbs tangled on the sofa and the living room carpet.

I silently watch Marity's eyes when she gets back downstairs, trying to figure out if her and that boy did it or not. I hug my knees on the floor near the kitchen for easy booze access. I've lost track of how many drinks I've had, but feel numb to anything of a physical or emotional nature. Then Marity picks up my gift.

I feign disinterest as she tugs the dainty purple ribbons at the top of the gift bag. I've teased them with sharp scissors edges for a good five minutes each, striving for the perfect amount of curl. When she looks in I hide my red face behind my drink, tilting my head back and gulping.

Stand up. Marity appears before me. She may or may not be smiling.

I get up and begin to lift my arms for a hug, but she puts them down and pushes me toward the front door. I drag my feet across the carpet.

On her driveway, I stumble as though on a steep hill. Later I'll realize its utter flatness.

What's wrong Mare? The booze has deflated any fears regarding our most recent occurrence at the Tunnel.

This is wrong! She shrieks, grabbing the gift bag's contents and throwing them at my feet. You're *so* sick.

The front door ajar, the others watch us from the living room picture window, probably eavesdropping. I shiver in a gust of April night wind. I've never seen such anger in Marity's dark, pretty face, but in that moment I strive upon provoking her emotions. I *have* to know how she feels.

I thought you liked them.

Well, not anymore.

I'm fourteen and clueless and don't have boundaries. I don't know when to stop or how to apologize or if that's the right thing to do. She asks for her Cuban bracelet back before retreating into the house and slamming the front door so hard that a warm draft comes out and tousles my curly hair, despite extra-hold hairspray. I consider bending to pick up the birthday gift, fifty pixie sticks I bought instead of stealing. I leave them there, a hot pink mess.

I trek on teetering legs through her fancy neighborhood back to my family's grungy abode. I stop a few times to imagine she's following me, looking back and seeing nothing but a dark road lined in shrubs and cars. Any witness would think I'm afraid of vampires or rapists or other nightly terrors.

I don't believe in those things. I barely believe in anything.

63

We took off running, summer stars around us falling like bombs. Looking back was useless as fuck with the red and blue police lights shining fiercely all around, though they refrained from using their sirens. I couldn't tell how close they were. I couldn't tell if I still had feet or if they were on the ground. I couldn't tell if I still had a heart or if I'd left it in the house when I'd scampered out the front door after a text from Raizel.

cops

We're fucked! Liam shrieked. Drop the shit somewhere!

What the fuck were you guys thinking? I shrieked back, images of the mansion's garage doors flashing through my head, long zigzags of blue and pink and purple spray paint.

You're the one who fucking gave us the paint! Raizel hissed over her shoulder at me, running what seemed like miles ahead.

Bang bang bang bang bang bang. My heart. My heart.

Take this. Liam shoved the bag of shrooms into the pocket of my jeans.

It looks like I have a fucking cock! I forced my legs to go, keeping my eyes on the back of Raizel's glowing hair. I wanted to scream apologies.

We darted down a catwalk and tossed the spray cans over a fence into a backyard. We ran and ran. I wanted desperately to know if everyone was as fucked as me, but talking used my precious energy. I choked the night air down. I didn't know how we'd possibly evaded the cop car for so long, but I wanted out. I imagined myself in prison, lying flat on my back staring straight up at a cement ceiling, no one around but a cockroach and a cellmate who'd stabbed her boyfriend. I didn't want the shit in my pocket, but I couldn't ditch it and let everyone down. I would rather have had my body lying on the dented red couch in my basement while my mind had a rancid nightmare. I wanted to be sick again, to wake up with a migraine and a fever that made me so delirious I could imagine such filth.

We were three blocks from mine when I realized we'd lost the cops. I couldn't believe it. I wondered if they'd ever been there to begin with, but thought it impossible. I'd seen the lights. I'd heard shouting. I'd recognized the fear plastered on my friends' faces. I wanted to stop and cling to Raizel, and Amara, and Liam, who was crying a weird, heaving boy cry, but we trudged along until we made it to my yard and crept in through the side door. On the way into the basement I took the shrooms from my pocket and shoved them into the hole in the wall where my favorite Barbie doll still resided, where they couldn't convince us to do bad things.

We were quiet for the rest of the night, which I was pretty sure had nothing to do with my mother or the fact that it was two in the morning and that was when people were supposed to be quiet. Liam stopped sobbing, though I swore I still heard him when he excused himself to our ugly bathroom. I put on an old copied DVD and gave everyone big mugs of blueberry tea made with tap water instead of a kettle. We lay in a line on the couch, the four us leaning in one direction like a pile of dominos, all of the spare quilts in the house covering our bodies.

I dozed between thought and slumber, waking occasionally to reconvene with the hum of the TV and the images behind my eyelids.

Where would I be if I had never wandered into the Main Street Pharmacy that random day in October? Maybe it wasn't a question of where I'd be, but whom. I wouldn't have met the most amazing girl in the world and figured out that I was a raging lesbian in what may have been the pleasantest way possible. I wouldn't have tried all the new things, the daisy and the music and the clothing. The stabbing feeling I used to get when I thought of Tiff had faded; I'd successfully gotten over what happened, except for a dull pang in my chest when I accidentally reminisced. If I'd never met Raizel, Tiff still would have gone running toward her future like someone chasing their homework in the wind. Or money. She had never cared what my plans were. Maybe I would have gotten back with Mr. Shepherd, all the while remaining a lowly coffee bitch with a big ass and a supposed interest in photography.

The next day I awoke to Raizel stirring beside me, trying to find comfort on our flat sofa. I hardly believed the old contraption hadn't collapsed under the weight of four stoned people. Daylight tried to peek through the fabric hanging over the small window above the computer. I lifted my head from Liam's shoulder and rubbed my fists in my sleep-burned eyes.

My friends slumped off the couch quietly, stretching and gathering their wallets and bags. I offered breakfast, adding that my mom was at work and we could do whatever we wanted. No one was hungry.

Last night was a trip. Liam knelt to finger-comb his hair in the reflection of the TV.

Raizel didn't respond, looking down as she adjusted her skirt. Her new tattoo peeked out from the bottom hem; she hadn't worn tights since getting the ink.

It was weird. Amara led the way upstairs, as if she owned the place.

When everyone's shoes were on, Amara skipped out the front door, saying she'd bring them to the bus stop. Liam followed her, but I grabbed Raizel's hand and tugged her toward me. The last thing I wanted was to be alone.

Don't go.

V. Raizel sighed, turning her head toward me, a stray strand falling across her forehead. My car's not here.

So? Maybe my mom can drive you later.

I *want* to go home.

Oh. I dropped her hand, searching the pair of verdant eyes that lit up my front steps.

Don't worry. On tiptoes, she leaned into the front landing and pecked my lips. I'm just tired.

I closed the screen door and clicked the second door shut behind it. Inhaling heavily, I swore I smelled the pile of dishes in the kitchen along with hints of my mother's smoke hole of a room. I looked down at my jeans, ripped at the knees and frayed at the bottom, and my high-tops and backpack in a dirty pile in the corner. I picked up my bag, feeling my wallet in a side pocket. I tugged the zipper of the biggest pocket and reached in, pulling out a fistful of coins and bills. In my palm lay an old lady's gold chain, a ring of jade hanging in the middle, probably a gift from a lover. My eyes passed over the living room's crumb-speckled carpet and faded wallpaper.

I wouldn't have stayed, either.

Surreal images of the night before flashed through my mind, over and over again, making it difficult to forget that I was a thief and a vandal. I stayed in bed all day, ignoring the sound of my mother struggling with her key in the front lock when she came home from work. Outside my bedroom door, she pleaded for me to help her clean up. I remembered a time when I would have jumped to help her, but Dana, my suck-up competition, was no longer around. Plus I was fucking tired.

I couldn't remember the last time my mother and I had laughed together, but I recalled the last time we had sat down together for supper. Mid-April, the house had been so silent that I had begged for my mother to turn on the television while we'd munched our spaghetti-and-meatballs. No longer having anything of interest to tell each other, she had asked about Tiff.

Where's little Tiffany these days, Venice?

Busy. I'd snorted.

Why don't you invite her over sometime?

I told you, she's busy. She has school and Oliver and stuff.

Is she okay? Do you still see her at work?

No. . .why would--

She still thought I worked at Team Bean.

Yeah. I see her at work still. She's just busy, is all. Put the TV on.

Please?

Please.

And?

Fuck. Just do it.

Language! She had eyed me, searching my face for the girl I'd once been. What's gotten into you these days?

I'd brought my dishes to the kitchen, leaving the lukewarm noodles and meatballs to fester on the counter.

After that, I'd taken to eating at Mars, washing down salad with Diet Coke. Jenny, the cook, constantly complimented my figure and offered me free morsels of snacks from her 'healthy menu'--veggies and dip, tofu sticks, wheat thins.

The day after the mushroom-mushrooms was warmer than end-of-May days tended to get in Sloam. I pulled from my messy closet the camouflage shorts I had found in Dana's room the fall before. When I pulled them up my legs, I was able to pull the fastened waist several inches away from my abdomen. I searched through my piles of clothing for a belt, coming up with nothing. Finding my winter coat, I yanked the drawstring out of the hood and slipped it through the belt-loops on the shorts.

I looked in the mirror, admiring my most recent of Raizel's specialty haircuts. I always let her do what she wanted with my hair, practicing. The strip of hair going down the middle of my head had grown out, while Raizel had trimmed the rest to a mere inch of length, and it was all brown--so brown, it tricked me into believing my naturally tanned skin tone was sort-of nice. My bedroom mirror looked smaller than it ever had.

I picked up my camera and flipped it around in my hands. I missed making my heart soar.

64

I think it's this way. Raizel's cinnamon voice wove through the darkness.

The scent of fabric softener wove through the dark room's air. I breathed through my mouth, remembering too easily the room of a house I'd recently broken into.

She didn't turn the lights on, just quietly led me to one end of the apartment building's laundry room to a solid, gray door. Her hair had grown to hang around her shoulders and she had on her favorite old black tights, the ones with a quarter-sized run at the back of her calf. Bouncing against her back was my army-green fourteen-pocket backpack, which we'd come to share. She had decorated it with pins declaring her different opinions about the world.

We skipped up the two flights of stairs, pushing eagerly through a second gray door at the top. Deep orange floodlights overlooked the flat apartment roof.

I can't believe that door's not locked. How'd you know that?

I came up here once. She turned away from me and twirled, hands in her hoody pockets.

Oh. I slung my camera bag off, setting it on the ground. With Amara?

Nope. Raizel looked down as she twirled, loosely curled hair a river flowing around her face. She stayed downstairs.

Alone?

Yeah.

Why?

Reasons I don't like thinking about. She stopped twirling and tried to stand still, but swayed like she was on something good.

Oh. Sorry.

Hey, come with me. Raizel looked up, offering her hand to me.

We moved to the edge of the roof and touched the cool metal railing, looking down over the apartment parking lot. We were only seven stories up, but I felt a million years ahead of the streetlights and the freeway in the distance. Sloam was bigger than I'd always pictured--from there, I couldn't see my home or downtown, and especially not anything in East Bay. I didn't get vertigo; I forgot to feel like I was going to fall and die. I looked over the Dr. Seuss house roofs and the cars parked along Golden Street, quickly spotting the narrow peak of the Kleins' home. My eyes moved on to the elementary schools and their playgrounds and the church with the tall cross--I never thought I could be higher than such a thing. I became so enthralled by the advantages of being above my surroundings that when I looked beside me, Raizel was gone.

I walked a few feet along the perimeter of the roof before lying down in the middle of the roof with my head next to Raizel's, our arms and legs splayed like in a chain of paper people, hands connected by more than mutual admiration.

Raizel? I looked straight up at the plum sky.

Mm hmm?

Are you mad at me?

For what?

For what happened...the other night...with the poli--

Yes.

How mad? On a scale of two to thirteen?

She didn't laugh.

I'm just afraid.

Of what?

I'm afraid of doing bad things, and getting in trouble for it, like me and Amara used to. I don't *like* doing drugs.

Everyone liked drugs. Drugs were drugs because of how good they made people feel.

Why do them, then? Above me, the stars were blurred dots on a palette of purple.

It's mostly just something to pass time until I get out of here.

What do you mean, get out of here?

I wanna leave Sloam. I *have* to leave everything behind, go to a big city where I can *do* things--

Oh. I felt my hand go limp over hers. And am *I* just something to pass time?

V-- Raizel sighed, letting her hand lay flaccid on the ground. That's *why* I'm afraid. You're becoming way more to me than I thought--

So you wanna break up? I pulled my arm away, crossing it with the other over my stomach.

Flip flip flip. My stomach.

Bang bang bang. My heart.

NO! Raizel exclaimed into the dark sky. I want you to come with me.

Oh. My heart began pumping blood through my veins again. Seriously?

Duh. Raizel grabbed my hand off of my stomach. I thought I could study hairstyling for *real,* and it would be good for you to take that camera to a big city. *Imagine* the inspiration you'd have.

A big, fat smile rode across the roof on a motorcycle, stopping on my face.

I rolled over to glance at my camera bag, packed tightly with my wallet and camera and a new lens. I'd used the money from the big house in Oakwood Heights, but had put the jade necklace in an envelope with full intentions of returning it.

I swore to myself that I would never wrong anyone again.

I'm sorry. I whispered to the air, hoping my words would fall upon Raizel and anyone else I had hurt with my carelessness.

Say you'll come with me.

Of course I will. I hoisted myself off the ground and moved toward my bag. I extracted the camera and took a few shots of Raizel, so vulnerable and open, on that apartment roof.

Why are you named Venice? Raizel cocked her head, staring up at me. Are you Italian?

I dunno. I shrugged, holding the viewfinder up to my face. I put my feet on either side of her hips, pointing the camera straight down at her. I think people name their kids according to what *they* want in life. But as far as I know, my mom doesn't even know where Venice is. She's not Italian. I don't know about my dad. I think he was Native. Where did your name come from?

It means rose, in Hebrew. I'm not Hebrew, though. My family is super German. I've always thought Aurora would be a nice name, if I ever have a daughter.

Oh. I like it. Borealis? I joked, smiling behind the camera. I wanted to capture every movement.

Yes.

Raizel lifted her hand off the ground, pointing at the sky. I looked up at the stars and the expanse of darkness, the barely-there moon and the dim colors fading together like a painting with too much water on the first day of a high school art class. The purple moved over as if making room for the pastel blue and the hint of lavender. The colors swirled together as if on a tire swing, friends who would catch each other if they fell and reeled toward Earth or some other planet. Mars. The colors went to one side all at once, replaced by new hues of navy and beige and heather-gray. I caught my breath.

What are you waiting for? Raizel squirmed out from between my ankles.

I pointed my eyes and my camera and my heart at the sky.

65

Mars gradually became, in my mind, a place decorated with dollar signs. As Ilene paid her staff in cash, taxes weren't deducted from my salary like they had been at Team Bean. I was sure something illegal was going on, but I wasn't about to correct it--I enjoyed stashing hundreds of dollars every second Friday.

Although Liam often showed up with his flavor of the week, Raizel usually stayed away, claiming she shouldn't distract me from my work anymore. She spent her Friday and Saturday nights working at the pharmacy or practicing haircuts on a stolen mannequin head and a stack of wigs from Value Village. I didn't mind Raizel's absence from the bar if it meant she wouldn't be dancing and drinking and being otherwise lured by her tall ex-girlfriend in the room directly above me.

Ilene hired two pretty girls with short hair and Australian accent. I knew I would struggle to keep my spot behind the bar--which I only wanted because tips were few and far between in the coat-check and other positions. On a good night I could make two-hundred dollars. On a slow night I made at least sixty, enough for a date with Raizel, though she never requested more than my presence, good music, and a few beers.

I no longer drank beer or wine, careful that my figure didn't become bulky like it had been before, or shapely, or just plain fat. When I noticed customers flocking around the Aussie sensations, I stopped wearing a bra, just like The Ringleader of The Bitchy Circus. Marijuana helped calm my suspicions that I bore less value than anyone else; the magical plant made me the funniest, kindest person in the place, thus my reason for smoking joints before work and during breaks, exhaling out the back door near Ilene's office. After taking a joint-rolling lesson from Seed, I became the master-roller. Ilene didn't care about the weed, sometimes joining me with a cancer stick. Those, I would still never smoke.

When I was off work at midnight, Raizel usually picked me up, the Camaro's stereo blasting a good CD. We had both long-since weeded through the CD section at the downtown library, resorting, instead, to the collection of indie artists at the smaller library on Broadway. Sometimes when I slid into the Camaro passenger seat, Raizel would be wearing the masterpiece wig she had created that evening, catching me off guard. I'd beg her to remove the wig and I'd revel in the softness of her real hair as I weaved my hands through every strand and we would stare at each other and ponder the tardiness of our camaraderie.

When she picked me up we would drive around, laughing and listening to music and using my camera to take pictures in places we never visited in daylight. We usually ended up in a field somewhere, or a dark residential road, fooling around in the backseat, after which we would hold each other and talk until the wee hours of the morning, unless Raizel was working early the next day. I felt like an elated, romanced teenager, sneaking around. As Raizel once stated--we didn't have to worry that we'd get pregnant.

We sometimes slept together at Raizel's Dr. Seuss house, slipping in through the sunroom door after her parents had gone to sleep, though Susan often regarded us both in countertop notes in the morning.

Raisin & Abs (and Venice), check out the new cereal in the pantry.
Mom

Though we were both working so hard that we rarely had spare time to spend with Raizel's parents, I felt my toes get warm when I saw such notes. Besides the night of the mushrooms, Raizel and I only slept at my house twice, finding in the morning that the cupboards were empty of breakfast treats and our throats had gathered smoke-induced phlegm. I'd become embarrassed after that, only retreating to the duplex if Raizel dropped me off without coming in.

We avoided talking about the past on our late-night dates--that is, anything from our respective pasts that made either of us sad to think about. I didn't talk about Kale Shepherd and my failure. She didn't talk about Hannah, even when I found a school picture of her while I was helping clean Raizel's bedroom. As much as I had wanted to, I hadn't looked at what she'd written on the back.

I didn't talk about what I'd done to Tiff at Team Bean.

She didn't talk about anything bad she may have done, though I disbelieved the possibility of such notions.

I didn't talk about my non-existent father.

She didn't talk about her brother's death.

We spoke, instead, about the future and where we saw ourselves going in life, which neither of us could ever predict. I didn't tell her how she was present in every vision of my future-self. She sometimes popped into my head wearing a wedding dress in a bed, hair splayed across the pillow. She built herself a hair studio next door to my black-room and photography shop. We went shopping together for maternity clothes and snuck into fitting-rooms to fool around together, shop assistants none-the-wiser. We sipped lemonade on a balcony overlooking a backyard in which a young girl named Aurora played with her friends.

But we didn't talk that far ahead--we spoke of where to go when we had enough money to leave Sloam, what to do and how important it was to both of us to learn things about the world. We spoke of tricking our dreams into becoming plans.

One night when I slipped into the Camaro's passenger seat after work, Raizel waved an array of colorful papers in my face, spread like a handheld fan. Thankfully, she wasn't wearing a wig; her bright hair curled around her neck. I pushed her wrist out of my face, sputtering.

What is that?

Lottery tickets! Raizel laughed, dropping the tickets in my lap. She steered out of the alleyway onto Main Street. I just visited Liam at work and he gave them to me.

He *gave* them to you? I counted the seven stiff, rectangular papers. Wouldn't it be kind of wrong to win on a free ticket?

I have a good feeling about it. Raizel shoulder-checked, pulling the car over on the street in front of the big, old, magnificent downtown library. I've been meaning to ask you something--what do you think of Toronto?

I've never been there. Why?

Me, neither. But does it interest you?

It's so far away. I guess I never thought about it. It sounds expensive.

Well, think about it now. The reason I'm interested is because Abby got into the Academy of Design in Toronto. It's a fashion school.

What?! Really?

Yeah. She's leaving in the fall.

Good for her!

What if we went *there?*

I breathed in quickly, wheels in my head spinning. Raizel continued.

We could share an apartment with Abby, a two-bedroom. We could get jobs we both liked, and go to shows, like, every night. Just imagine the music scene there.

It sounds...really cool. I gave her a slow, small smile.

Yeah. Raizel smiled back, holding up her bundle of tickets. Do you have a penny?

No. I felt the pocket of my jeans. But I have a bunch of toonies and loonies. Good tips tonight.

Even better! Raizel accepted a one-dollar coin from me, poising over the ticket resting on her knee. She instructed me to start scratching.

I remembered the fall when Tiff and I had scratched tickets. I had truly needed the money and hadn't won anything, so there was no reason for me to win when I was actually in the process of building a savings for myself. Good people won--people like Pam Abraham, Tiff's mom, and probably little old Walter from the lobby of Team Bean Café.

His hands had been so soft. His smile had been so kind.

Did you win anything? Raizel glanced at me while she rubbed gray debris off her lap.

I looked down at the unscratched ticket in my hand.

You're a better person.

Huh? Raizel turned to look at me. What are you talking about?

I think you have better karma. I gazed at my ticket. You should scratch it.

Aw. That makes no sense, V. Watch, now you're gonna win. Raizel pressed her cool loony into my palm.

I scratched the dollar against the gray bar, finding a strip of numbers.

Five. Three. Four. Three. Seven. Zero, I read aloud. How do I know if I won?

If the numbers add up to eight, you win a thousand bucks. And if they add up to one less than eight or one more than eight, you win fifty bucks. Let's see…five plus three plus…okay, your numbers add up to twenty-two, right? Add the digits together until you get a one-digit number.

Four?

Yeah.

So I didn't win?

It doesn't matter. Raizel shrugged, balling up the ticket. She tossed it into the backseat and reached for a new one for each of us.

I began scratching the fresh gray bar.

7+9+1+0+6+2=25

2+5=7

Oh my god! Raizel gasped, holding her ticket up. Yay!

What? I peered at the paper in the moonlight.

6+1+1+6+2+5

2+1=3

I won fifty bucks! Raizel exclaimed.

How? Doesn't it have to add up to eight or one more than eight or--

No, just for that ticket. Look. Raizel pointed at a paragraph of small print at the top of the ticket.

For this ticket only: Scratch all numbers and add 'em up. If your result is a two-digit number, add the digits until you have a one-digit number. If your result is 4, please claim your prize of $1000 CAD from a participating lottery venue. If your result is one less than 4 or one more than 4, please claim your prize of $50 from a participating lottery venue. Check for varying rules on all other tickets from the Add 'Em Up Lottery Series.

I looked down at the ticket in my lap. I held it close to my face and squinted.

For this ticket only: Scratch all numbers and add 'em up. If your result is a two-digit number, add the digits until you have a one-digit number. If your result is 7…

66

In July we organized a camping trip. Johnson Lake was Amara's idea. After the mushrooms we had all continued hanging out as normal, though a tension existed between all involved. Such tension had fizzled after an alcohol-and-weed-only party at Amara's, during which we'd been able to joke about our ridiculously high magic mushroom minds and the horrible things that could have happened. After Raizel had implanted in my mind images of bustling downtown Toronto, and the lottery money we had put toward our future together, I had stopped caring about Amara's blazing orange car paint and how she tended to stand too close to my girlfriend.

I was more than willing to go on the trip--I'd never even been camping with my family. Throughout high school I'd heard the legend of Johnson Lake--annually, for two weeks in July, there was a stage for local and not-so-local bands and a celebration for independent artists at a lake a few hours from Sloam. Punks and the young at heart and the hippest of hippies came from all over the province to drink copious amount of liquor, take an abundance of drugs, and rock out. From what I'd heard, it was a dangerous, wild, terrific place to be. Tiff and I had never gone because our moms wouldn't allow it. Besides, we didn't know anyone who could drive us out there. Surely Tiff would say one of two things now if she knew I was finally going.

I can't believe you're going without me.

or

I can't believe you're still into that.

The five of us--Liam, Amara, Abby, Raizel, and I went shopping on a Friday morning, filling a huge camping cooler with fruit and hot-dogs and condiments. We filled a second cooler with beer and vodka. Into Liam's car trunk we lugged all of the camping stuff we'd been able to muster up--two tents and a tarp and five sleeping bags, none of which Amara or I had contributed. My family had never gone camping and hers lived in who-knew-where. We took Liam's car, because it was bigger than anyone else's and sturdier on the highway, a fact proven during our Bowville road-trips throughout the past year.

People kept adding shit to the communal bonfire, logs and paper and eventually a broken tent. We were sitting on one of the best spots on the beach, high up where the water couldn't tame the fire. Flames blazed in the night and made the air orange and warmed our toes three feet away on the black blanket from the bottom of Liam's trunk. A kilometer away from the stage and its well-lit dance-floor of sand, a reggae band belted their hearts out. People scampered through the sand around us with torches and backpacks of beer, shouting across the beach at their friends. A grassy parking lot behind us was quickly filling with newcomers, people who scrambled to fetch their tents and food coolers from their vehicles and trek into the forest to set up for the two-week festival that was Johnson Lake. I was relishing the warm breeze and the lake's faint glimmer when Amara spoke.

This is lame. I wish I had something better. Amara held her beer out and scowled.

I wondered what could be better.

We could probably find something. Liam nodded.

Yeah. Amara jumped up and brushed the sand off her shorts. I'll ask around.

Should we come with you? I planted my hands in the sand, ready to stand up.

I don't care.

What's wrong with you? I settled back down on the blanket.

If you had called your buddy, we wouldn't be in this predicament.

Seed? I fucking told you, he's out of town, getting B.C. weed. This is hardly a 'predicament'.

The others didn't say anything, drinking their beers, eyes skimming the beach. Did they feel the same way as *her?* I eyed Raizel's side profile.

Amara stalked off, tossing bits of sand back with her bare heels.

Ten minutes later she returned with ten hits of daisy and a clear bag of something white. I wanted to ask if it was coke, but was afraid I'd look stupid.

Coke? Abby looked up suspiciously.

Nope. Amara smiled down at her and shook her head. I haven't touched that stuff in forever.

Remember when-- I started.

This is Special K. Amara interrupted me, waving the baggie. By the way, you each owe me fifty bucks.

Fifty bucks? My mouth dropped open. Are you charging interest?

What's Special K? Liam piped up.

Ketamine. I answered quickly, showing Amara I wasn't so naïve. I poked Liam. We did it in your car that one time.

Amara glared my way.

What's it like? Raizel wanted to know, watching Amara.

Lazy, but magical. Something bugged me about the way Amara smiled at Raizel, how she slit her eyes and puckered her lips.

I turned my face away.

Amara asked the dreadlocked kids on the blanket beside us if we could borrow their acoustic guitar. She laid the instrument across her lap and used a bank card to sculpt four lines on the back. When she began the fifth I spoke up.

I don't want any.

Whatever. Amara divided my share up between the other lines.

Why not? Abby nudged my side with her elbow. We're at *Johnson Lake.*

Yeah, V. Liam nodded emphatically. You can do anything you want at Johnson Lake. It's like Vegas.

He's right. But you don't have to do anything you don't want to. Raizel held my hand and kissed my palm. The light flew through her irises, tiny mugs of hot chocolate with mint leaves floating on top.

Okay. Just a little.

Fuck. I just made four lines. Someone else can cut her a fifth. Amara hoisted the guitar over to Abby and stood up to brush the sand of her corner of our blanket.

How do you know what to do? Raizel peered at her sister.

I've done coke before. It's pretty much the same thing. Abby shrugged, slicing the powder with the credit card. Does someone have a fiver?

Raizel retreated, closing her mouth. The flames softly opened the amber in her usually-green eyes.

Yeah. Liam pulled his wallet out of his back pocket.

After taking the pills and snorting the K, we joined a circle of people around one of the smaller fires. My nostril burned with familiarity. I sniffled, afraid of a tell-tale white nose, though I suspected it would have been overlooked in such a setting. I sat as far away from Amara as possible.

Everyone took turns telling about their First Time, laughing about awkwardness and the thrill of getting caught. The K was strange, pulling me into my head and my memories. I was slowly inverting, imploding, shrinking. I wished I had those other peoples' memories, wished I had lost my virginity in the Lloyd St. Burger King parking lot or quietly in my basement while my mother smoked upstairs. I wanted to suggest telling about our Last Times instead, about how Raizel and I had already christened Johnson Lake and we'd only been there half a day, how we had both purposely worn sweatpants for elastic waistband access, setting our tent up faster than the others so we'd have time inside before anyone could suspect a thing. I wanted to talk about her pulsating flesh and her breath on my neck and her heart pounding out of her lace tank top from Stitches.

Raizel told the story of the girl she was with in high school. I hated Hannah for taking beautiful, lovely Raizel for granted, for treating my girlfriend like a piece of shit. My girlfriend. Raizel had never been with a man, or a boy, something I wanted so badly to truthfully say about myself.

When I was rolling hard, I snuck down the forestry path to the clearing of tents and small fire pits. Liam, Abby, and Amara were staying in the tent next to mine and Raizel's. I opened the zipper door and slipped through the canvas flap. I threw on a hooded sweater, leggings, and a pair of burgundy moccasins Raizel had gotten for me from Value Village weeks earlier. I missed you, I said aloud to the shoes. I recoiled with laughter at my own silliness, but liked my voice in the woods next to the sounds of restless birds and groups of campers disturbing nature.

I went back down the path to reconvene with my friends. Hand-in-hand, we trekked through the sand to the stage, from which we gradually heard bustling guitars and banging drums. Tons of vendors lining the area were selling pipes, hemp jewelry, and piercings.

I realized I didn't need all my clothes. I didn't need anything, really. I flung the moccasins off and dug my soles into the pit before the stage along with all of the other bare feet.

Everything dreams are made of. The band's slowly beating drum resonated with my innards. I wanted to hug the world. Five-year-old girls twirled beside their hippy mothers, from whom I hoped they would derive open spirits, free-loving attitudes, peace of mind, and self acceptance. I grinned up at Liam before squeezing his hand and holding it up in the air, inviting him to dance. The daisy and Special K became one in my mind, not battling as a depressant and a stimulant respectively, but linking arms and swaying. KE. EK. Collective.

Hey. A cinnamon voice, in my ear.

A smile fluttered through Raizel's deeply regal eyes when I looked over my shoulder. We swapped bemused remembrance of our most recent kisses. I pondered the existence of such sweetness. She slipped her fingers into my empty hand. I didn't ask where Amara or Abby were. Raizel and Liam and I danced, arms in the air. Nothing else mattered.

The dream fingers she touched when she left me her hand were softer than water and sifting the sand. When the dreams would tilt and turn into my nightmares, she'd appear and put an end to my fears. The punches she'd give when dream buggies drove by, they never hurt, and I suddenly knew why.

Mornings at Johnson Lake, Raizel crawled out of her sleeping bag and into mine, putting her face in the nook between my chin and my chest. She was so warm. I didn't care that other peoples' laughter and car stereos woke us up at the crack of dawn each day. I didn't care about the tree roots digging into my hip all night. We'd listen to the wind whisper against the blue canvas walls around us, warmed in morning sunshine. We'd pull our hoods tight like our first night on daisy together and pass a joint between us until its last ash fell on the sandy tent floor. Only when our stomachs groaned with emptiness would we emerge from our cocoon and scramble for the door's zipper.

During the day we hung out on the beach at Johnson Lake itself, a dark mass of water surrounded by hills used for skiing in the winter. A doc situated in the middle of the lake was a meeting point for ambitious swimmers and people who hadn't started their daily inebriation. I swam there once, when Raizel and the others were dozing on the hot beach. The icy water seared my kicking legs, my head under the surface cutting out all beachfront noise. I sucked air into my lungs and dove off the doc without aim, letting my body float gaily on the surface of the lake.

When I skipped out of the water onto the beach I plopped down near Raizel, watching her sun-bronzed sleeping form. She was darker than I'd ever seen her, but her porcelain skin remained fairer than mine had ever faded to in winter months. The sun had also somehow further lightened her hair, a cream-white mass of curls she let frolic in the sand. I loved shaking my head like a dog and watching her squirm under stray drops of lake-water.

After supper, and the three times it rained, we cowered under a tarp someone had tied high up between the trees around our fire-pit. We socialized with nearby campers and I envied the high school kids whose parents allowed them to come to this unguarded place where they could do whatever they wanted. We roasted peanuts and drank toe-warming shots of Heather Cream liqueur and made up lyrics to go with the soulful drum circle happening one campsite over. We shouted at anyone walking by with drenched hair, desperate to share our makeshift roof. We played Truth or Dare and Never Have I Ever and What Would You Do If and Would You Rather.

We had started our trip with our coolers chalk full of food and beverages, but by the fourth day everything had either been eaten or gone bad. We resorted to the stage-side snack stands or other campers' supplies--for which we bartered with our surplus of beer and flashlight batteries. I felt like I was traveling through Oregon Trail.

Every evening, when we were sufficiently hammered, our growing group of companions stalked down a path in the forest. Tacked to the outside wall of a decrepit outhouse was a festival schedule, displaying which band or DJ or inspirational speaker would take the stage for the night. A few of the spots were secretive, reading Special Guest or Open Mic. Regardless of the information on the poster, I put on my moccasins and we filled our pockets with beer and moved like a school of fish to the party on the beach. We did the polka and the tango and the Macarena. We moshed to folk tunes and slow-danced to a trance set by none other than Morgan the Samantha-Ronson-look-alike DJ. We re-programmed our hearts to match the thumping drums.

67

A week into Johnson Lake, a large crowd had already formed around the stage by the time our group sauntered up. The day's sun no longer blazed, having dimmed to a chandelier-like lightness touching the mass of heads and freckled shoulders. As usual, I flung off my moccasins, wiggling my liberated toes in the crunchy sand.

'Special Guest', the outhouse poster had read that day, which people had obviously noticed. Older people and couples with young children had set up lawn chairs surrounding the stage's sandpit, ready with blankets for their laps when night fell. Raizel spoke excitedly of the year before when Feist had appeared onstage, taking everybody by surprise.

What if… Raizel whispered in my ear. Wouldn't it be cool if it was Ani?

Hell yeah. I smiled, knowing that, even if it wasn't Ani, I would make *sure* Raizel would see her at some point in time.

A techno beat suddenly bumped out of the massive subwoofers. A thin girl ran onstage. She jumped and clapped her hands together, urging the crowd to follow suit. Intoxicated, we lifted our hands and clapped excitedly, inviting the main act out.

Do you recognize her? Raizel glanced at me and pointed at the girl, who had picked up an electric guitar and was plucking softly at the strings.

Kind of...Who is she?

Nicole Meens. The singer from The Bitchy Circus.

Ohh. So they're the special guest?

I dunno, maybe she's in a different band now.

My friends and I bobbed our heads while the volume of the chick's guitar grew. She kept her face down, shielding her eyes and mouth with her black hair as she concentrated on the creation of a thoughtful tune. The last of the sun gleamed off the metal of her guitar, going down over the hills surrounding the lake.

All at once, the bass beat stopped and three other girls ran onstage, taking places at a drum-set, a microphone, and a violin.

Oh my god! Raizel shrieked, jumping up and down, her heels barely missing my toes.

I squinted at the stage, not recognizing the drummer or violinist.

It's Queenie! Liam nudged my side, laughing. He clapped his hands and threw his long arms in the air, shouting. Queeeeenie!

Queenie stood in the center of the stage in a muscle shirt like the one she had worn for her construction-worker costume the first time we'd seen each other. She had on the least clothing I'd ever seen in her in, patchwork short shorts baring her intricate thigh tattoos. She looked like she had lost weight. She looked damn good.

The P.M.S. Crew? I wondered aloud.

I was talking to her at work. Amara leaned to talk to me, placing her hand unnecessarily on Raizel's shoulder. This is her band, The Calling Alls.

What's up, Johnson Lake? Queenie croaked into the microphone, the volume of 'her band' having been lowered in the speakers. The drums emitted slow rolling sounds that carried the other instruments softly.

Wooo! Someone behind us hollered.

You're hot! A guy yelled.

Whoa. Settle down out there. Queenie joked.

They must have made a mistake on the poster, I commented to Raizel. It should have said 'Open Mic'.

No, man. Amara said quickly, as if I'd been talking to her. Special guest. They're getting pretty good.

I'll say. Raizel clapped her hands and hooted. Aww. Queenie's so cute!

Woooooo!! The crowd yelled in unison, jumping as the volume was raised.

Along with the crowd, Raizel was magnetized toward Queenie like she had been at Broken String Bar, ignoring my hands around her waist and my kisses on the back of her neck. Abby joined her little sister, helping her push through people for a better view. When I looked around, Liam was talking to some guys near the back of the crowd, and Amara was swaying with her eyes closed.

I slipped out of the dance pit and toed my way to a clearing on the beach. I plopped down in my jean-shorts, the entirety of which had gathered a week's worth of grime and grit. People mingled along the water, but I was far enough from the both the stage and the bonfires that a blue darkness surrounded my figure. I opened the beer can from my pocket and swigged the cold liquid, shivering as a gust of wind swept up the back of my t-shirt. Before me, the lake opened into a mysterious expanse of blackness, sometimes shimmering under the stars. I wished I had something better.

When I returned to the stage area, I couldn't find any of my friends in the crowd; I didn't recognize in the excited faces any of the kids staying in the same camping area as us. I circled the dance pit three times before spotting a dark, curly afro bobbing near the front edge of the stage.

Fuck. I examined the denseness of the crowd, eyeing a pathway to the front. I ducked slightly and put my arms forward as though diving, shoving through a group of girls with back-combed hair. I continued doing so until I was almost at the front, liquid courage stopping me from caring about bitchy sneers and cries of defense. Who the fuck back-combed when they were camping?

Hey! I grabbed the first thing I could reach, which was Abby's elbow.

Abby glared at the girls resisting from letting me through. She pulled my hand and I became suctioned to the stage, my belly bent in half over the harsh wooden edge of the structure.

Thanks, Abby. I smiled.

What can I say? Abby grinned back, showing her white teeth. You're like another little sister to me.

My toes felt gingerbread-in-the-oven warm.

I looked down the line of stage-front fans, hoping to catch Raizel's eye. A few people away from me, she kept facing the stage, her white-blond hair a beacon between unfriendly faces.

I need a volunteer for my next song. Queenie paced the stage with a cordless microphone, eyeing her fans. It can't be just anyone. I need one special chick…

Yeah! Amara cried out, waving her hands as high as she could.

I wish I was tall, like you! I heard Raizel exclaim to Amara. From the side, I saw the smile Raizel was supposed to be giving me.

Hey, Rais--

As the words were leaving my mouth, Raizel was suddenly moving up up up, Queenie yanking her forearm and Abby pushing her butt. On the stage, Raizel scooted from her knees into a standing position. She grinned at the gathering of people and stamped her foot on the stage as the beat for the next song began.

Okay! Queenie hollered into her microphone, her voice ricocheting from the speakers off the nearby light-poles. I'm gonna freestyle for this girl right here!

The crowd cheered.

Queenie put her arm around Raizel's waist and began rapping like she was back in The P.M.S. Crew.

Grrl when I saw your face I knew my place in this LIFE, knew the reason I was put here was to make you my WIFE, someone to do the COOKIN with a infomercial KNIFE 'cause you're so good-LOOKIN!

Grrl, then I saw your HAIR and was like damn that's FAIR is it blond or WHAT, I don't know but it kicks Blondie's BUTT!

Her rap was stupid and embarrassing and her hands were all over my girlfriend. My cheeks felt hot and any hints of wind had stopped for the night. I pushed my way out of the crowd I'd fought so hard to get into, stumbling toward the beer gardens. I needed something to tell me everything would be fine and that at the end of the stupid camping trip I would still have a future with my girl.

The bouncer at the beer gardens asked for my ID before I was within ten feet of the makeshift doorway. I scowled and swept my heels through the sand, refusing to look up at the stage and the story of my life.

I made my way down the dark beach, the waves lapping at the wet shoreline. I went down the leafy path and moved past the first tents of the forest, people with their cozy, flickering fires and laughter emerging from their lips. I found my campsite, the pit of which bore glowing coals, and budged open the tent zipper, ripping it down. I ducked my head into the arch of the flimsy doorway.

When I reached for the canvas tent roof and flicked on the flashlight, I saw three sleeping bags, one of which had Liam's colorful hoody strewn across it. I glanced around, not seeing my backpack.

Oops. I was definitely in the wrong tent.

As I turned back around, something caught my eye. I squinted and knelt, pulling the item out of Amara's neon duffel-bag. I smiled and flicked off the tent flashlight, skittering out before I was caught. I took a fresh beer can from our cooler and sunk into a lawn chair by the barely-there fire.

The next morning I left the tent with Raizel asleep inside. I zipped the door closed quietly, shivering in my black leggings, bare feet, and the old red plaid shirt from the floor of my closet, once upon a time--the item I had reclaimed from Amara's bag. With the shirt, I had found the belt I'd been missing, something to hold up those camo shorts once I got home. The flannel hung on me like never before, nearly to my knees. I felt smaller than the mosquitoes flitting around my face. As I walked I crossed my arms over my front, comforted by feeling my hip bones protrude and retreat with every step.

I noticed I wasn't hungry. I had eaten supper and crashed around one a.m., when I'd finally heard my friends' excited voices in the woods and had scampered to my tent to feign slumber. Raizel had poked me and asked where I'd disappeared to and I had said the beer had made me sick. She had told me about her stint on the stage and I had clenched my fists in my sleeping bag and she had kissed my cheek with liquor-stained lips before rolling over and snoring her kitten snore.

I was wide awake and it was only five, or six, or possibly seven. All I knew was the sunrise drawing me across the field of cars and rich kids' family campers. All would have been quiet if not for the techno beats from a nearby low-rider, its owner out cold in the backseat with a hat over his eyes. I stalked across the grass, meeting the edge of the small forest where a path interrupted the trees. Inviting me in were friendly pieces of cardboard on which periods and exclamation marks and i's were dotted with peace signs. Dragonflies and small birds sent drops of dew array while bouncing on midsummer-green trampoline leaves.

When I came to the clearing I reflected. Everything I'd heard about Johnson Lake revolved around getting stoned, fucked up, plastered, tanked, messed, blazed, smashed, obliterated, wasted, hammered, high, low, or plain old tipsy drunk. Some people even got 'zombied'. Such conversations had no room for talk of nature and beauty, but it appeared before me as suddenly as a glass of spilled milk on the kitchen floor. I wanted to punch myself in the face for not bringing my camera, for not being able to catch the sun barging through the evergreens and pines and their steep descent into the hundred-foot wide river valley. Even mud was beautiful, glistening like melted chocolate at the edges of navy-blue water. My tears crept up, sprouting from my eyes like carrots up through garden dirt. I hung my head when I thought of how my jealousy had enraged me the night before.

I wandered out of the clearing and through makeshift buildings to the pit before the stage. Red plastic drink cups lay about, having wandered discreetly out of the designated beer gardens. The sand was littered with cigarette butts and balloons someone had passed out to all of the children. I lilted through the sand and checked under the skirt lining the wooden stage. My moccasins were nowhere to be found.

Feet bare, I lay face-up in the sand pit. I opened my eyes, but I didn't watch the sky; I let it pass over me. The kingdom of blue.

Bluedom.

68

Our second-to-last day at Johnson Lake, when we were packing up our beach stuff and the sun was a setting sheath across the lake and its distant canoes, a boy approached Raizel, speaking lowly. I'd noticed him several times throughout the past two weeks, a boy with long beads around his neck and flowy green pants and eyes that seared everything, faces included, as if he was looking for something. I pretended to dust off my towel while I perked my ears and listened to their conversation.

Hey. Out of my peripheral, I watched the boy stand with his hands behind him, wrapping around his backpack.

Hi. Raizel picked up her own towel, shaking it. What's up?

I was just wondering if you guys want anything. The guy patted his backpack with its elaborate paisley pattern. I got…

Do you think he's gay? Liam whispered beside me, honing in like a bee to a flower.

Shh! I'm trying to listen.

…And I'm trying to get rid of everything.

Well. Raizel looked around between us, speaking as softly as the boy. What do you have?

Amara, lying on a towel next to Abby, stirred. My eyes passed quickly over her jutting ribs and concave torso, disbelieving for the millionth time that another girl's body could differ so greatly from mine.

Pot, shrooms, and E.

Shrooms? Amara lifted her head and hoisted herself up on her elbows, the skin around her clavicle shining from suntan oil.

Yeah. The boy smirked, his watchful eyes stripping Amara of her puny bikini.

Definitely not gay. I whispered at Liam.

Fuck. Liam wandered to his bag, reaching for his t-shirt.

We'll take some. Amara nodded, gesturing at the rest of us.

I don't want any. Raizel shook her head.

Me neither. I agreed, looping my towel around my shoulders.

Come on. Amara groaned. Are you kidding?

No. Raizel and I shook our heads.

What about daisy? Amara's eyebrow rise.

I don't even know if I want *that.* Raizel crossed her arms over her flat, pale stomach.

It's good. The boy with the beads and funny pants spoke up, slinging his bag off his back. He bent to unzip it. I have green sushi and pink apples.

It's the last night here, Amara persisted. DJ Knock Knock Ginger is on tonight. Do you *know* what that means?

Raizel shrugged.

I shrugged.

Liam ignored us, picking up his bag.

Abby, out-cold on her towel, had a snore like Raizel's.

Around midnight, Raizel and I were a couple of daisies plucked from the picket fence edge and strewn across the lawn. We found ourselves in the kids' area, far away from the stage, destined for silence as there were no little ones in sight. We crept up to the playground and I thought, Fuck it, not caring if I sat in the dirt or got something under my fingernails. I lay on the ground and touched the sand with my tingling fingertips.

My cheek flat on the boards lining the playground's edge, I watched a perfect profile that was Raizel's face. Every inhalation was a mix of incense and cigarettes. Her head rolled on the ground to face me. Sparkling seaweed eyes with gigantic, dark pupils bore through the dark at me. I was instantly reminded of the first time I had seen her. Parts of the breeze moved past my nose, down my esophagus, and somehow into my heart. I couldn't discern a feeling I had never felt before.

Hi. Raizel smiled the smile I would climb to the sky and catch the billion stars overhead for. The next words floated to me. How you feeling?

Really good. I nodded. Those green sushi's, y'know.

Yeah. I like that they're green. Like wasabi.

I ran my palm over all the miniscule pebbles and stopped where I could clutch Raizel's hip like it was the edge of a cliff and I'd fall without her. Her hand mirrored mine and moved to my side, fingernails playing music on my skin. She giggled a giggle I had come to know, inviting my own grin to come out and play.

Remember the first time we got together? I didn't know it was on my mind until I said it. After the Greek restaurant?

Pause.

Raisin? Do you have any idea what happened?

Pause.

I don't know.

I've gone over it in my head a thousand times, but can't figure it out.

I have, too. But…I'm pretty sure we were drugged.

Bang bang bang. My heart.

Who would *do* that?

Me and Sullivan used to share the Camaro. I think he used to keep his acid tabs in there in a Listerine strip container.

At the mention of her passed brother, my blood rang with sympathy. I didn't know what I could say about him that wouldn't ruin the mood. Realizing what Raizel had just implied, I suddenly hoisted myself up on my elbows.

Oh my god! We did *acid*?!

Yeah. Raizel looked at me, apologies streaming through her eyes. I mean, probably.

Oh my GOD!

Raizel's looked at me, remaining quiet.

We drugged *ourselves!* I slapped my forehead, letting my cool wrist stay on the side of my head.

We opened our mouths. Our laughter echoed and bounced like balls off metal parts of the jungle gym. The crickets hummed, obscenely loud.

How do you feel? I spoke, my temple lightly bobbing against Raizel's shoulder. My fingers grasped Raizel's.

Really good. I'm just glad to get away from Amara.

Oh, *god.* Me, too. She's being so-- I paused. I never say this, but *slutty.*

She went crazy last year, too. It's actually why we broke up.

You mean she made-out with everything in sight? I pictured the way I'd seen her minutes earlier, slobber-kissing the guy who had sold us the pills. A *guy.* With an adam's apple. And hairy nipples.

No, I mean, the drugs thing. It's *exactly* like last year. And so many other times. *There's a DJ, so let's get fucked up.* She always has a pressing need to get so high she can't even see. There was *no* way I was sticking with that shit. I went through it enough before...well, just before. In high school.

Oh. That's lame.

Super lame. And she stopped eating and--oh I feel like shit, telling you all of this.

No, I softly insisted. Go on.

She has eating problems. I asked her about it when I heard her puking once, and she brushed it off like it was no big deal. Have you ever smelled her breath? It's because she's always...'bringing' things back up again.

Oh my god. You caught her?

Yeah. And she has an obvious lying problem. I still don't know where her family really lives. So how am I supposed to tell them to come get her and care about her?

I kept quiet, listening as Raizel continued.

I did the shittiest thing ever, last year. I broke up with Amara and she got all upset and I was afraid she'd get even more fucked up, so I lied to her.

How? I breathed the word.

I told her--and everyone else--that this tattoo on my wrist was for her. Raizel waved her arm in the air over our heads. I told you that, too. But it's not. It's for *me.* It's so *I* remember to be strong and happy.

I silently wondered why she needed such reminders--she was my happy, little Raizel--a girl born beautiful and into a nice family. *Oh.* She was probably referring to thoughts about her brother.

Anyway. You're so different from her, V. You're so normal. But at the same time, you're not. You're just...special.

You are, too. I grinned, my face stretching wide apart.

Hey, I have an idea! Raizel snapped her fingers. Let's get matching piercings tomorrow, before we have to go back to Stinky Sloam.

We have some! Our eyebrows.

That's not enough for me. Hey, V? Do you regret getting that tattoo? For my forgiveness?

God, no. And it was for more than your forgiveness, Silly.

What was it for? The way her voice peeled out of her mouth, I knew she knew the answer without me having to say it.

How about our ears--up top? I brushed off her question, pinching her ear's top cartilage. For the piercing, I mean.

Okay. And one more thing…let's grow old together. Raizel chuckled at her cliché. Everything is so perfect with you.

I shivered, wanting to swallow her vulnerability. Her words lined my spine, the truth inside of them chilling me one vertebra at a time.

I know. My throat constricted without warning, catching my words on the verge of a sob. I feel it too. When I look at you I know nothing else will ever matter as much as you. I want you to always be this close, within reach. I need you, Raizel.

I need you, too. I always will. Venice Knight. *My* knight.

Forever? I'm a mess. Sorry I'm crying.

Me, too.

Forever, though?

Yeah.

I wouldn't blame my tears or my smile on seeing something beautiful, though I certainly saw beauty. I blamed my reaction on the something inside me that allotted for complete freedom when I was around this other being; perhaps the something which told me so was grooving to her heartbeat and the sound of her thoughts in the same way I grooved to my favorite music. We hadn't taken bum pills or anything; it wasn't like that. I longed with all I was to capture in her lingering gaze something that would do all it could to be near me and listen to my blood pumping around and to enjoy me with all its existence. I knew, in that moment, that she wouldn't be leaving me for Queenie anytime soon.

69

When I entered Seed's sixteenth-floor apartment, the first thing I saw, as usual, was the fish tank. Something was off about the water. I stepped forward without removing my shoes, peering at the murky brown-gray clouds of liquid behind the glass. A putrid odor filled my nose, not unlike, I imagined, the scent in a toilet when a family would return from vacation and realize their four-year-old son had forgotten to flush his shit two weeks earlier. I caught a glimpse of orange near the top of the tank and, scanning the water's surface, saw that all of the fish, with their exotic blue fins and funky black stripes, were floating. Life had been sucked straight out of their gaping mouths.

Hello? I entered the kitchen with its dish-covered counters, a bundle of ants having gathered around a jam jar. *The cleaning lady must be coming today.* I held my fingers over my nostrils in a desperate attempt to fend off the collective odors of fish and moldy bread. I'd come there directly from Johnson Lake to pick up party favors for Raizel's approaching birthday--we'd all agreed to end the summer with a bang. Raizel and I had secretly decided we wouldn't touch daisy again, focusing only on our plan. One last time was all we needed.

I rounded the bend into the living room, squinting through the dark, as the heavy curtains had been drawn closed, unyielding to the light outside. Everything was quiet but for the sound of bubbles in the fish tank. Even the ever-present static of the television was gone; I soon came to realize the whole massive contraption itself was missing. Across from the empty wall, three people sat on a sofa. A boy and a girl lounged with their half-closed heads tipped against the back of the sofa. The quilt trunk lay ajar, its contents scattered about inside like the whole thing had been flipped upside-down.

A third boy, lounging in an armchair, completely ignored my presence, playing with his cell phone.

My voice sounded far-away, like Tiff's in grade ten the first time we'd met. Where's Seed?

Out. One boy brought his head off the sofa for a moment before it went crashing back. The pain didn't seem to register on his face.

Cool bag. The girl's hand, resting on the sofa, pointed at my side. On only three of her fingers she had long, white gel nails people tended to associate with wealth and popularity. I recognized her as the girl who had glared at me with her legs spread at Seed the same day I'd spiked Tiff's drink.

What I wouldn't give now, I thought, flexing my fist, *to get some of those yellow pills and be on my merry way.*

Thanks. I patted my camera bag, feeling the extra lens through the padding. So, do you know when he'll be back?

Maybe he went to get a new TV. The boy who'd spoken before laughed, drawing attention to his unshaven chin.

You got a camera in there? The girl pointed again with her long fingernail. Take some pictures of us, would ya?

Um. I touched the bag. I--

She *was* being friendly, an upgrade from the last time I'd seen her.

Sure. I began to unzip the bag hanging off my shoulder.

The boy in the armchair closed his eyes, not caring at all about the world around him. The boy on the sofa put his arm around the girl, their heads still swept back lazily. Smiles crept across their faces and I snapped a picture.

Let me see it! the girl exclaimed, patting the spot beside her. I felt my jaw tense up as I plunked down beside her, pretending I wasn't perturbed. What was with the dead fish? At least the living room didn't smell as bad as the entranceway.

We look so hot! The girl cracked up, her laugh oddly resembling that of a witch. One of her nail-less fingers stroked the camera delicately. Wow. This must be--what? Five-hundred bucks?

Around that, yeah. I inched away from her, pulling the camera with me. *Try a thousand bucks.* I pressed OFF and nestled it safely into my bag, taking my cell phone out.

The girl started rolling a joint, plucking buds from a massive bag of weed. I messaged Seed.

where r u? im at your house

The girl was licking the joint tightly closed when Seed replied. My heart jumped at the faint bell chime my cell phone emitted.

jus gettin something. c u soon

I sighed with relief, my flipping stomach coming to a stop.

The girl rolled her thumb across a lighter and held her joint in it for a moment before passing it to me.

Ladies' joint. Her chin jutted toward the guys. Not for these fuckers.

Whatever, dude. The guy on the sofa smirked. Mr. Cell Phone paid no heed, over-involved with a game on his phone.

I took a heavy puff of the funny cigarette. The taste of tar filled my mouth immediately, coating my tongue. I stopped myself from gagging and passed the joint back to the girl's three-nailed hand.

What's wrong? She sucked the joint as if she'd been underwater her whole life and had finally found the surface. I watched her breasts swell as she filled her lungs.

That tastes weird. My jaw came down from my face and I licked the insides of my mouth.

It's new shit. Mr. Cell Phone finally piped up. It's from B.C.

Ohh--this is it? I accepted the joint back from the girl, holding it up as an offer to the boy who'd spoken.

Oh, no thanks, Birdy. He held up a tall, red bong. This is for us guys.

Birdy? I laughed something fierce, feeling my mind loosening up. This isn't badminton.

My head felt silly; I wanted to roll it around on my neck like I'd slept poorly and was trying to work out a kink. I puffed the joint one more time before my wrist went limp and I passed it back. The girl and I started giggling together and my limbs became butter. A bright blue jelly-fish-like light began floating before me, so I reached out for it, grabbed hold, and it purred like a cat.

Suddenly I felt angry. Something wasn't right. My mind told me to ask out loud what the fuck was going on.

Was the fuck goin' on. I slurred, glancing at the others.

They shrugged, as nonchalant as when I'd first walked in. If they had slipped me something, drugged me, then the girl beside me was experiencing the exact same thing. In fact, I'd watched her roll the joint. Unless...unless when we were smoking she had secretly been alternating between two joints--a clean one for her and a dirty one for me. How carefully had I really been watching? I felt robbed of my memories. I began sweating. When I looked over, everyone was doing exactly what they'd been doing the whole time I'd been there. I told myself to breathe.

Liam was waiting in the car outside. I suddenly became afraid that he had come up and opened the apartment door and left because of the fishy odor inside. I imagined he had walked away, leaving the door open. The cops would surely be there any minute, judging by the smoky sheath of air around us. I got anxious thinking they'd walk in and arrest me for possession; though I didn't have anything in my pockets, I seemed to hold a lot in my mind. A whole portal of drugs. But no, it couldn't happen. Liam didn't even know which apartment was Seed's. Amara was the only one who had ever come up with me. I hoisted my back away from the sofa and wrung my hands together, briefly acknowledging their clamminess.

I remembered what Tiff had said, long ago, when I'd suggested we try weed together.

Olly smokes weed sometimes, and he said people can freak out if they're not in the right state of mind.

Remembering these words calmed me a little. *Breathe. Just breeeeeeaathe.*

But my mind was relentless; a moment later my heart was racing again. I'd noticed the difference of that joint and others, the bitter tar-like taste in my mouth, but I'd been distracted in my wait for Seed. I opened my eyes as wide as I could and then squeezed them shut, where white and black stripes began swirling like they'd been flushed in a toilet. I needed to talk to Seed, to ask him what kind of effect B.C. pot was meant to have on people. Where was he, anyway? Had I simply imagined the text he'd sent me, saying he'd be there soon? Beside me, the girl lay with her eyes closed, a gigantic clown smile stretched across her face.

I drew my cell-phone from my pocket and pressed a button, making the screen light up. I fumbled to find Seed's name in the contact list.

Who you calling? The girl asked, displaying the first sign of intelligence since we'd smoke up.

I ignored her, holding my phone up to my ear.

Riiiing. Riiiiiing. Riiiiiing.

I heard music, some Eminem song Seed had recently been into. I remembered making fun of him for just *how* into it he was, rapping alongside his phone every time it rang. Funnily enough, he and Mr. Cell Phone had the same ring-tone. Mr. Cell Phone snatched his phone off the table, silencing it.

In my ear, the call was lost. I frowned at my phone and pressed REDIAL. It didn't even connect.

The phone you are trying to dial is currently busy, a robotic lady told me. Please--

What the fuck. I turned to look at Mr. Cell Phone, whose deadpan eyes daggered me.

I shoved my phone into my camera bag. With tremendous effort, I pushed myself off the sofa and raised my arms high, pretending to stretch.

Well, I'm gonna get going. I reached for my bag.

Wait a sec. The girl pulled the bag toward her, wrapping the strap around her wrist.

My eyes flitted to Mr. Cell Phone. He was still watching me.

Come on. I tugged on the bag as hard as I could, making the girl's arm fly up. Give it to me.

No, *you* come on! She kicked my knee and yanked the bag back toward her.

Kerri! One of the boys said harshly. You're so heat.

With my liquid, uncooperative limbs, I gathered all the power I could. I threw a punch at the girl's jaw, my first unwrapping before I reached her face. Unsteady on my feet, my knuckles landed on her nose with half of my weight behind them. She winced and her hand flew to her face, her grip loosening on the bag. I snatched it into my safety and didn't look back as I darted out of the living room.

Half a second later, I was facedown on the carpet with my arms locked behind my back. A knee dug into my spine and I heard the distinct snip of scissors as the strap of my bag was cut, my belongings freed from my arms. I shrieked, my tongue coming out and touching the carpet upon which Seed had let everyone walk with their dirty shoes.

Don't bother with your shoes. My cleaning lady's coming tomorrow.

If that murky fish tank hadn't been there, I would have gotten out and screamed bloody murder in the hallway. If that fish tank hadn't been there, I wouldn't be sprawled out in the dim apartment hallway, pinned by someone whose strength I'd underestimated. Mr. Cell Phone. Mr. Head Honcho. Mr. Impress-Your-Friends.

Lemme go! I cried out, desperate to pull my arms away, to get my camera back. My weak muscles dipped toward defeat. I felt more spaced out than ever, unable to focus on bits of carpet lint and even the metal grate of the hallway furnace vent.

Holding my wrists with one hand, the boy dug through my pockets. He pulled out my house-key and the Camaro key Raizel had gotten cut for me, passing them to his friend.

Here. Check on Kerri. Is she alright?

I'm fine! The girl shrieked, though her voice was muffled.

She has other shit in here. The other guy's voice came from another dimension, one where my belongings were dumped out on the rug, making thudding sounds.

Wallet, forty bucks. iPod. Fuck yeah. It's one-twenty gigs.

I heard my house-keys jangle, purple rape whistle and all.

Who has time to pull out a whistle and reef on it when they're being attacked? Raizel's voice floated through my head.

Mr. Cell Phone held my wrists so tightly I was sure my hands would have to be amputated. He sat his ass down right on top of mine, posed like a monkey, barbaric. He instructed the other kid to fill the big red bong and bring it over, let him toke so he'd calm down. For god's sake, his girlfriend had just been punched by 'a beastly dyke'.

I allowed my body to relax, to slump under his hold as if I'd given up. But I wasn't a regular girl. He didn't know the fire in me. I listened while he lit up and sucked the bong, water in its base bubbling heartily. He exhaled and the pot fumes fell all around us, coating my already-stoned brain.

Jackpot. This camera's fucking dope.

Suddenly I writhed and bucked like a horse, throwing Mr. Cell Phone off with all of my muscles going crazy. I scampered toward the end bedroom and twisted the doorknob.

CRACK.

Just that.

CRACK.

Red was everywhere--glass and lights and blood, dripping down my face. The bong lay open on the floor, rigid edges where the contraption had been broken across my head. I gagged at the putrid, used bong water splayed across the rug in the end bedroom. I'd never smelled anything that bad, even worse than a tank full of fish oozing with death. My mind reeled, ethereal stars shooting everything around me. I closed my eyes in fear of stray glass shards and shut my mouth to keep out dots of tangy blood.

I cringed when I felt a hand undo the fly of my jeans and a gathering of strong fingers pinched me hard, down there. My arms and legs lay around me, useless parts of a young woman. Old girl. His other hand hit my cheek where the water of my metallic eyes had surfaced.

70

Grade ten isn't any better than grade nine. Jill and I have stopped altogether, so I concentrate on my studies. Mrs. McPhee isn't my English teacher anymore; Mr. Geoffrey is. He has a gruff voice and a beer belly and I will never submit a poem of emotional substance to him.

I have a few acquaintances in Art 10, other kids who are different from anyone else in the school. I'm not good at art, but I am good at being different. They don't ask me to hang out after school; in a way we aren't even friends. We are just lonely people who are less alone when we sit beside each other.

Abby gets both her license and a clothing-store job in October. Soon after, my parents help her buy a ratty used car, provided she'll give me rides. Because I'm small, she makes me lay across her friends' laps in the backseat on the way to school. When I'm on top of Shelly I plug my nose because she wears so much J. Lo perfume. When I'm on top of Kristal I close my eyes because she's very beautiful and talkative and I'm afraid I can't conceal the funny feeling in my groin. I finally find a reason to be thankful I'm a girl.

I walk home when Abby works after school. I still enjoy fall leaves and think they would make a nice tattoo.

One November day when I get home I pour myself an orange juice. Something feels different. Wrong. I hear Sullivan in his bedroom with his obnoxious friends, or his little girlfriend. I shudder when I imagine what they're doing in there. I lug my juice and backpack downstairs, flicking on the light and the TV. When Tony hears Ellen's voice he will surely come running. I listen for the jingle of his collar tags.

Tony? I look in the laundry room. Not there. I check the bathroom. I push open my bedroom door and turn on the light.

Tony's large body is sprawled across my bed, back to me. He's lying on my candles and Barbies and loose pages of poetry. What a sleepyhead. I moved forward and run my hand down his spine. He has liver-spots under his aged amber fur. His skin is cool.

I lie so my body curls around his, my hand on his unmoving side. I look at the tearstained fur around his closed eyes, tar-black jowls sagging around his mouth. I squeezed my eyes shut and tried to follow him into the darkness.

My grades start slipping and my mom gets pissed off. I hear her wonder to my dad if I have an eating problem. I don't. I just walk a lot. I get an iPod for Christmas and I fill it up with all of the badass chick singers I can find on the Internet. Ani Difranco is my favorite because she's not afraid of filtering her emotions through her voice.

Ellen doesn't do it for me anymore. She's still beautiful, but I stop laughing at everything she says. And I no longer feel funny around Abby's friend Kristal.

One night in January I lie in bed and try desperately to revive my groin. I move my fingers around in my pants and think about Jill, who hasn't replied to my e-mail about Tony's death. She probably has a new online girlfriend, someone her age, with big boobs. I gaze around my room for other encouragement. My eyes land on my haircutting scissors. Hair-design--what a dying dream. My parents would never let me be a hairdresser. They think I have the brain of a doctor. I laugh. I could never nurture anything.

I take my hand out of my cold panties and reach for the scissors. I open them. I pull my jean leg up and my sock down. I drag the blade along my inner ankle, but nothing happens. I press harder, in a straight line. Drops of red liquid bubble and surface. I press even harder for the next line, creating a T. This one's for Tony.

I make sure my bedroom door is locked and I return to my bed. I expose my other ankle and carve a J on the inside. This one's for Jill. My ankles aren't sensitive. It doesn't hurt. Experimentally, I press the open scissor blade against my upper right thigh, toward my hip. I push. Hard. Harder. I do it again, in the same place.

The blood moves in lines down my thigh, cherry-red birds desperate to fly. I close the scissors and sneak to the bathroom for a cloth.

My nightly ritual becomes smile at the supper table, pretend to do homework, retreat to my room to listen to music and play with scissors. I don't bother with anywhere but my upper thigh, a hidden place I can scrape away at without anyone knowing. When scissors aren't sharp enough, I graduate to other things--a purposely broken compact makeup mirror, a beer bottle cap, a steak knife. Whenever I make a deep cut I gasp and push a cloth against it and lie in my bed and watch the ceiling spin and wonder how I'm the only kid in the world who doesn't have friends.

Art 10 is over and my acquaintances have come and gone. Now I stare out the window during fourth-period History 10 and wonder what happen if I got out of my chair and pushed the window open and fell out. I sometimes catch myself rubbing my upper right thigh through my jeans or pressing freshly sharpened pencils into my palm. They always break.

I float through the halls like the ghost I've always been, iPod blasting inside my head.

In the spring when other girls whip miniskirts and short shorts out of their closets, I continue wearing jeans. Because I'm trying to prove I'm not anorexic or bulimic or otherwise mentally unstable, I let my mother take me to Winners. She stands outside the change-room while I try on jean skirts with embroidered daisies around the pockets. My freshest scars show below the skirt hems. I don't let my mother in.

I wear the new skirts and shorts to school, but only with tights underneath. Kids make fun of me because tights are not meant to be worn under shorts. I notice a couple of ninth-graders following my trend, and soon the whole school catches on. They don't credit me, but I wear all sorts of patterned tights--polka-dots, roses, buttons. Distractions.

When I bring my report card home at the end of grade ten my mother takes it to her room and cries. My dad stares at me and asks who I've become. I don't understand. I've passed everything by at least a few percent.

I go downstairs and lock my door and breathe heavily. I take out the serrated steak knife and watch it lurch across my inner wrist over and over again. I rip the skin into poppy-red oblivion. I feel a whoosh of heat come up my neck. My head is light. I fall across my bed with my arm hanging over the edge. I am Raizel Klein, but you can call me Razor.

When I stand up an hour later, I am still alive. I strip my bed, thankful my sheets are already crimson. I stand in the shower and let the water run over my already crusting wound. Soap gets inside and burns like fingertips on a stovetop. I fetch a tensor bandage from the first-aid kit upstairs and tell my parents I sprained my wrist in gym class.

The next day I shop for a leather cuff bracelet.

My parents hoax me into summer school by saying they'll help me with a car, like they helped Abby. I consider this and, after deciding it's a good idea, I hit the books. I also begin a driving education course for my learner's license.

A car is a good idea because it will be very helpful in my eventual fate. If things don't get better soon I can drive off the city river bridge between downtown and Broadway, make it look like an accident. Or I can run a hose between the exhaust pipe and the driver's seat window.

My parents buy the car for my sixteenth birthday--a large sports-car called a Camaro. It's orange, like a sunset. Abby is angry until my dad tells her the car has no transmission, whatever that means. My parents buy her a set of fuzzy blue seat-covers for her own pile of junk.

By the time grade eleven hits I have been practicing driving with my parents for two-and-a-half months, but will have to wait three-and-a-half more to get my actual license. I touch the car on my way up our driveway every day. The metal is cold. I peek inside at the low seats and a stereo system perfect for Ani's voice.

Sullivan starts grade nine the day I start grade eleven. He already has friends, the group of kids he's gone to school with forever. I see them following him around the cafeteria like ducklings. Niners aren't allowed in the smoke lounge so he and his friends crowd around the student parking lot. I don't tell him smoking's bad because he's already heard it a bunch from our parents.

An international students' program has started at our school this year. Abby talks about volunteering, to beef up her resume. She wants to get into college with the best reputation possible. She's always been ambitious. When my parents suggest Sullivan and I getting involved, my brother laughs and makes fun of an East Indian accent. I shake my head and say I'm too busy with my studies. If I have any job, it's going to be a paying one.

I edit my resume and claim I've volunteered with animals at the ASPCA. I take the lie to every place I can think that hires under-qualified sixteen-year-olds. If I'm going to run a hose into the Camaro's front window I'm going to need money for gas. When I think about my plan I get jumpy and excited.

At school, I'm so over the friend thing. I go to class, eat lunch with my back against my locker, and write poetry in the library. Teachers mistake my quiet demeanor as studious and attentive. They call on me in class, but my voice is low and they can't understand me. Their information becomes garbled in my mind. I pass from class to class like a penny whose sole purpose is to meet tax costs.

71

I heard the apartment door open and shoes scuffling through the kitchen and front landing. The door clicked shut softly and then there was no noise but a car outside honking.

Liam.

I pushed my head up off the floor, pressing my palms against the carpet. I leaned forward and grabbed the wooden door frame, clinging on with my fingertips to pull myself into a standing position. My head pounded thickly, everything inside my skull muggier than the fish tank. I was able to lean my hip on the wall in the hallway and stumble toward the living room.

My camera bag lay open on the ground, empty but for my house keys, cell phone, and wallet. I picked up my wallet, finding my cards intact, but my forty-some dollars were missing.

An old woman in the elevator glanced uneasily at me. I saw her frightened eyes in the mirror, but she didn't say anything. We were in Wainmont, for god's sake. She probably saw stoned, beaten-up people all the time.

My head was in such a tornado of pain that I couldn't tell if I was high anymore. I hugged my body and pushed open the glass front door of the building. Liam jumped out to help me into the backseat, asking me repeatedly what the fuck had happened. I didn't respond as he placed his old trunk quilt under my head. Tears poured from my eyes as Liam sped us across town, whispering over and over that he'd fucking kill whoever had done that to me.

I kept my eyes closed, nausea striking my belly every time we turned a corner and my head was jostled. I heard Liam on the phone with Raizel, or Abby, warning them that I'd been hurt and we were coming over.

I don't know, he kept saying. I don't know.

Liam parked the car and I felt the back door open, hearing Raizel shriek as she and Abby helped me to my feet.

What the fuck happened?

Is she coherent? Should we take her to the hospital?

She was talking, before.

Venice, sweetie?

I shook my head, leaning on the outside of the front door. I wrapped my arm around my stomach and bent forward, gagging into the hibiscus plant on the front step. Small, ruby-red circles appeared on the cement around the plant's pot.

No hospital, I croaked. I have a headache.

No shit, Abby croaked back.

They brought me to the basement sofa in a room encased by darkness, covering my body with a blanket. Someone pressed a warm, damp cloth against my forehead, dabbing gently at different spots.

Does she need stitches?

I can't tell. Does it look deep?

There's a lot of bl--

Shh!

I don't think she needs stitches. Should we call her mom?

No, I whispered.

Should we--

Shut up! She's trying to say something.

Can I have-- I breathed heavily, feeling the tears start up again. I closed my eyes without squeezing so as not to disturb my forehead. A pill?

Fuck. She's right, that'll probably help with the pain. Does anyone have something?

No, man. That was the whole point of going over there.

Who does he fucking think--did you *see* him, Liam?

No.

Someone call Amara. She probably has something.

I didn't have the energy to tell them I wanted Tylenol, not daisy.

I awoke tucked under the covers of Raizel's bed, lamp light displaying her randomly scattered belongings. Raizel was perched at the edge of the bed, lightly plucking the strings of a guitar, her back to me.

Hi, I whispered, my throat dryer than the desert.

Oh. Raizel slid the guitar to her clothing-clad carpet. Sorry. Did I wake you up?

No. It's nice. Like a lullaby.

Raizel smile, her mouth opening slightly. She rose and moved to the bedside table, appearing before my face with a tall cup of water. I lifted my lips quickly, sipping from the glass before my head could begin to pound again. Too late, I fell exhausted against the pillow.

Come here. I lifted my arm out from under the covers.

Raizel crawled onto the bed, carefully avoiding the lumps my limbs made under the quilt. She slipped beneath the blankets and lay under my open arm, carefully placing her hand on my stomach. I caught a whiff of her lilac-infused hair.

Where did Liam go? I sounded like a frog.

Home. Abby's upstairs, though. And my parents.

Did they…see me?

Really? You don't remember? My mom put that gigantic bandage on your head.

They probably think I'm so fucked up. I felt my chin tremble.

Oh my god, no. They were really worried. Abby told them you got lynched and tried sticking up for yourself.

Oh.

V? Her soft stroked my stomach softly, under my shirt.

Yeah? I sounded like a frog.

Liam called Amara earlier and told her what happened. He said she said she wants to get revenge.

Why?

Well...she's always been like that, especially about her friends.

We're not really friends.

Not that I blame her, Raizel continued. When I saw you in Liam's car I was terrified...I didn't know what to do...no one knew what happened. There was so much blood. I think your shirt's wrecked. But when I saw you--so helpless--and your jeans were undone. Why were your jeans undone? What the fuck did he *do* to you?

I reached up, my arm sore from having been pulled back. Above my ears, wrapping around my head like a headband, my fingers felt layers of soft gauze, sealed with tape like a love-letter.

Oh, don't worry. Raizel grabbed my hand, pulling it back down. Your cut's not very big. It just bled a lot.

I reached under the covers and felt my hips. My jeans were off, but I wore panties. I moved my hand over my groin, wincing. Raizel got on her knees on the mattress and tugged the quilt away from my body. She pulled the top elastic of my underwear down to my thighs until I was fully exposed.

Oh my god.

My gaze came to rest on Raizel, sitting back on her heels with her hand over her mouth.

You're bruised. I mean, *really* bruised. She kept her hand over her mouth and sobbed, making the bed tremble against the wall. You're purple and fucking black.

I closed my eyes and shivered. She pulled my underwear back up. I wrapped my arms around my stomach and turned onto my side. Raizel lay behind me, curving her body around mine. She pulled the covers up tighter than ever, demanding they consume us and make everything go back to normal--whatever normal was.

I didn't know you played guitar.

There's lots we don't know about each other yet. I felt her wet face on the back of my neck.

Yet.

For the next few days I stayed in Raizel's bed, confined by her strict demand that I needed to recuperate. Though I'd already taken off two weeks for Johnson Lake, I called Ilene at Mars and told her I'd been jumped. She guffawed at my misfortune and told me to call her when I felt better. More than anything, I felt like shit about my camera. My iPod was gone, too, but I could get a new one. I *couldn't* get back the pictures I'd taken of Aurora Borealis and Johnson Lake and Raizel's winning lottery ticket.

Everyone said things like *at least you still have your wallet* and *you're lucky you don't have any broken bones,* but I cried three times solely for the loss of my second-most prized possession.

Raizel carted her family's TV into her room and we watched all six seasons of The L Word, including the special features disc. I had seen a few episodes before, but never the whole thing. I couldn't believe a TV show could be so good--it wasn't like ER or hockey or any other suppertime show with my family, wasn't like the hundreds of DVDs Tiff and I had watched together. It was different because, over and over again, I saw myself in the characters and their relationships.

Susan made soup and Bob made potato wedges from scratch and Abby gave me a copy of Curve magazine and Liam phoned me to gossip, like the old times. I reflected on the idea that Amara lived down the road and didn't show her face once.

One day, Raizel worked up the courage to play for me the only song she'd ever written on guitar, the lyrics of which had come from her own poem. She said she would only do it because Abby and her parents were at work and wouldn't hear anything. She turned her back to me on the bed and strummed delicately, pausing to cough and swallow and get her fingers in the right places on the strings. Her bright locks shook as her voice came from her mouth like soft white flour powder from a sifter.

Take me to the North Saskatchewan River with a couple of victory cigars, grape flavored will do

One year decent, one year decent is coming fast

I cannot wait for this to do

Stand in my arms and sing of the holiday when one year decent began

Play your tambourine

Basic songs are pretty, too

My fingers on these frets would freeze without one mitten new, purple for strumming and yellow for you--

The house phone rang and the ethereal music came to an abrupt halt. My head remaining against the pillows, I blinked the wetness from my eyes as Raizel dove for the cordless.

72

Where the fuck have you been? My mother emitted the most emotion I'd ever seen, even more than when I'd failed photography class at the end of grade twelve.

I closed my eyes, lightheaded. I felt myself sway, wishing I was anywhere but in our dingy living room. When I opened my eyes she was still there, hands on hips. I thought of the painting on the wall behind her head and how elated she'd been when I'd found it for three dollars at a garage sale. The image was just a bowl of fruit, but I knew she was proud that I followed in her footsteps at just ten years old. Bargain-hunters, that's what we were. Eight years later the painting still hung, dusty and limp, the peace it had brought to our home long forgotten.

Well? She squeaked, nearing hysterics. Her eyes flickered.

I didn't like people focusing on one of my eyes and the other, and back again; it made me feel like a jigsaw puzzle, to be figured out. My mother's brow furrowed and she had the sudden audacity to care about my wellbeing.

I wished Raizel hadn't received that strange phone call from her mother, the one requesting her immediate presence at her workplace. She had thrown the cordless at my feet on the bed and said she'd have to bring me home.

I don't wanna, I had protested, holding Raizel's hand. My heart had begun pounding. I really don't wanna.

It's okay, V. Raizel had pulled her purse over her shoulder. You can get your stuff. A change of clothes and things.

And then what?

And I'll come get you later. She had started for the door before I could pull my unwashed post-Johnson Lake, post-mugging limbs out from under her covers.

I was out. I hissed, hoping spit droplets would land on my mother's royal blue banker blazer.

For three weeks? You smell horrible. Where were you?

Johnson Lake.

Johnson Lake? What are you on, then? Do you have it on you now?

What the fuck? Is it 'cause I'm dirty? I touched my hair protectively. I was *camping.* I just need to shower and--

THIS HAS NOTHING TO DO WITH THAT. What happened to your head?

I couldn't speak to her anymore, her highness with fiercely flickering eyes and a mouth blatantly on the verge of overflowing with rage and, though she would never admit it, fear. I was finally growing up, into my own person--a person who might be different from her virtuous self. I scavenged my mind for something to say to convince her that I was fine, tried to will myself to say anything.

Everything. I thought it perverse that I'd never been able to defend myself with articulation.

No... Involuntarily, I glanced at a snag in the carpet.

When I dragged my eyes up from the floor, they met hers for the instant. She looked so ferocious that my legs froze, starting with my thighs and ending at my toes digging trenches in the carpet.

You disgust me! Her arm retreated as though gearing up to hit me, which I knew she'd never do.

Nonetheless, I couldn't move.

My mother's palm was strong and flat and unforgiving when it struck my ear, forcing my head to the side. A faint snap widened my eyes. She was destroying my eardrum. When she pulled her hand back again it was bloody. She looked at it and recoiled.

Oh my god. She stepped toward me. What am I doing? Are you okay?

I touched my ear. Blood trickled down my fingers. A small piece of metal landed in my palm.

My new piercing. Me and Raizel's new piercing. The earring was broken and the skin around the wound throbbed, torn. I felt like vomiting, not because of the physical pain, but because my mother was an intruder trying to reach the most important thing that had ever happened to me. Something entered my head then, a thought I'd had the last night at Johnson Lake. I distinctly remembered feeling like Raizel and I had been living on a ship for the past year, a humongous yacht with a rainbow flag flapping in the breeze. We had no worries except the sharks in the sea. My mother was a big shark, but we could avoid her merely by staying away from the edge of the boat and refraining from looking at the water.

On daisy it was a beautiful thought, but the image was twisting in my head. My mother was no longer a shark, but a thief on the enemy ship, the one with a skull flag on its mast, approaching with unfathomable speed and agility. When close enough she shot arrows until our flag crumpled into an ugly polyester mess by our feet. She jumped over the edge of her boat onto ours and pointed the bow at us. We raised a white flag in her honor. She took us down with disturbing ease.

I'm so sorry, Venice. *So* so sorry. Let's go to the bathroom and clean it up. Oh god, I'm sorry.

Everything flashed through my head in an instant. I couldn't bear it anymore.

Homophobic bitch. I didn't run to my room. Something bubbled and erupted at my mouth, volcanic. You don't understand anything. You made my father, whoever the fuck he is, go away, and I'm gonna leave, too.

Thinking and screaming, screaming without thinking--like a volcano, I was unable to control my words as I spewed them, unable to care if they scalded her like lava.

Wild confusion struck her face.

What, pray tell, makes you think *you* know what happened between your father and I?

You know what I think? *You're* the one on drugs.

Later I'd wish my last contribution to the discussion had held more dignity. I spun on my heels and darted to my room, escaping. I quickly locked the door and threw my body against it as if she might try to beat her way through, though she definitely wouldn't. I heard running water and dishes dropping into the sink. I'd come to learn that she only cleaned when she was really happy or when she didn't want to think about anything. I shivered and slid to the floor, grabbing my short locks and squeezing my eyes shut.

My stomach churned as a billion thoughts fought for room in my head. I'd felt that way time and time again. I wanted Raizel more than anything. Where the fuck was she, anyway? Wasn't it an unspoken rule that we'd *always* be there for each other? I wished when I opened my eyes her hands would be there, reaching for me, offering to yank me to my feet and make everything better again. The hands I had played fortune-teller with, following the lines with my index finger and talking about the brightness of her future.

You'll reach all of your goals. You know how people set high goals and then reach them and feel like they have to set higher goals? You'll reach all of your goals and be *so* satisfied. You'll be Gwen Stefani's hairdresser, and Lady Gaga's, and Taylor Swift's, if you want.

Wow, so many blondies. Can I do Ellen Degeneres, too?

Um. Definitely.

She had giggled more at her tickled palm than my words, believing me. And then I'll just kick back and chill, hopefully with my lady friend, she'd responded before smiling coyly and slipping her fingers between mine. She had kissed me where my mouth met my cheek. I wanted the hands that had cut my hair, the hands that had run smoothly over my skin more times than I thought possible. Her hands had made love to my entire body, even when I was a big mess, the parts I had deemed unlovable, the extra inch on my thighs and the folds in my belly when I sat with no shirt on. I was friends with her hands, eternally connected.

During the car ride home, I had wondered over and over why Raizel's mother would need her so urgently. Each time I opened my mouth, a cottony feeling had took over my tongue and gums. Raizel went above the speed limit, her green eyes frequently flitting to the rearview in case there were cops. I pondered the thought that her birthday was the next week and I hadn't gotten her anything yet, but now that I knew she liked guitars, maybe I could get her a cool strap. No, she deserved more than that. Being dropped off was a blessing--a chance to think of something really special for my girl. Her mother was probably pretending there was an emergency so she could give her an early birthday surprise.

When I looked up, Raizel's hands definitely weren't in front of me. I shivered again and curled into an inconceivably small pile, my head coming to rest on the carpet. A penny lay three inches from my eyes. Under the bed, partly concealed by a hanging corner of my duvet, was a near-empty bottle of white wine with half a cigarette in it, all that remained from my desperation to prove a lie to Amara--a big, fat lie.

My belly gave way to queasiness and I gagged. If my heart rose it wouldn't splatter on the floor or my Andy Warhol guns or bananas pictures, wouldn't roll around screaming confusedly and collecting lint. My heart would pop out of my bosom and sit on the carpet, flimsy and gray, a used bomb whose purpose has come and gone; an organ ready to become ashes without the rest of me, me and my hair and piercings and overly sentimental tattoo of a dried grape. I ignored the noises in the hallway.

73

When I finally got up, my hair stuck to my face like I had rubbed it on a balloon, my lips smacking together dryly. My ear pounded as I lifted it from the floor. Everything was dark; no light came in from the hall outside. I rose and hit the light-switch, squinting at the brightness. I drank the half-cup of water from my bedside table even though the liquid had gathered dust and resisted going down. My mother was right about one thing, I smelled bad with my armpits and oily scalp and dirty feet.

I twisted my door handle and pushed. In the summer the wood swelled and the door became stubborn in its frame. I rammed my shoulder into it like a log into the door of a castle. I thought of all the times when I was seven and Dana was ten and he wouldn't let me through until I guessed the magic word.

Someone had locked my door from the other side, somehow. I got down and looked under, but was unable to see anything through the dark.

I slid my fingers under the door. They came to a solid stop. Something big blocked my door, a dresser or a bookshelf full of encyclopedias.

Bang bang bang. My heart.

Let me out! I hollered, hitting the door with the tripod I'd bought with my lottery winnings, right before Johnson Lake. The door wouldn't budge. When I stopped there was nothing but silence and a boomerang-shaped dent.

I screamed for someone to come save me. I screamed for my older brother to come out of the room he'd left empty, to push the bookshelf aside and say he was just kidding around. I screamed so hard my tonsils shuddered in the back of my throat.

When nothing happened I pulled my window aside and tore through the mesh screen behind it. I put my face out and relished the air, cold in my nostrils and hot in my lungs. I pushed the whole screen to the ground below and jumped, landing barefoot on gravel.

My cell-phone was dead, so I took off running to the strip mall off Oakwood Terrace. Chester's Pizza Parlor. The Pet Den. Finally, the trusty old 7-11. Outside, I shoved a quarter into the payphone, trying all the while not to step on the glass from years of broken bottles and probably a few broken car windows. I held the receiver away from my ear in remembrance of all the times I'd seen condoms wrapped around the thing. How funny such things had once seemed.

Rapid Taxi, how may I help you?

Hello? I coughed, my voice hoarse from all the screaming I'd done. Can I get a cab to the Sev in Oakwood?

That's the seven-eleven at one-eighteen Oakwood Terrace?

Yeah.

A yellow and red taxi picked me up minutes later. The driver said he'd been in the neighborhood, anyway. I didn't have time for his small talk.

I seen you somewhere before. The man's eyes passed over my body.

Oh? I glanced away, gazing out the window at the darkness surrounding us. *Shut up, Creep.*

Yeah, a while ago. In winter, maybe.

I looked back at the driver. His jowls sagged under his goggle-like glasses.

I dunno. Sorry. I shrugged, unrolling the window slightly. I was suffocating.

I know! He slapped the wheel. You did that, with the window. It was New Year's Eve and you put the window down. I thought you were crazy.

I'm not crazy. I shut the window.

Alright, sorry. I caught his swift glance at my shoeless feet. Don't mean no offense or anything.

Can you let me out here?

Here? He slowed the car a little. Got about three blocks 'til your destination.

I know. I tapped the meter. I only have twelve bucks.

'S alright. As I remember, you left me a good tip. On New Year's, I mean. What goes around comes around, right?

Hello, karma.

I thanked the driver, waiting for him to speed off before I walked up the driveway to Raizel and Abby's home. I banged on the sunroom door, watching my hand. Inside my fist, sweat collected, daring to drip.

No one answered. I let myself in and knocked on the second door, the one leading to kitchen. *Come on in.* I peered in through the small diamond-shaped windows at the top.

Hello? I called out, my voice like a kitten's. HELLO? Is anyone home?

The lights were off. The knob was locked.

Blood pounded in my head. I caught my breath on the bench by the door. I suddenly felt like sucking my thumb, an act of childishness I hadn't ever craved, in conscious memory. What the hell was I supposed to do? I didn't know where to go. I had no money. I tried entering through the side door and all of the windows before leaving Raizel's house behind.

I headed toward a main road, looking over my shoulders every few seconds, though I couldn't specify what I was afraid of. I'd already been pummeled and torn. It actually probably would have been funny if someone was to mug me. They'd surface with a dead cell-phone and an empty wallet.

I made sure no cops were coming, and displayed my thumb to traffic passing by. Show and tell. Cars honked, their headlights dancing to the beat of a summer's Friday night.

A maroon station wagon finally pulled over on the other side of the road. The car spun around and lurched to a stop beside me. The windows opened. Some college-aged guys hooted and hollered.

Hop in, sexy!

Yeah, baby!

Hurry up!

Their cologne was overpowering, but I moved toward the back door, anyway. They had nothing on me and my fists. When I touched the handle, the car started moving and my hand bounced off. I watched them speed away. I bit both sides of my cheeks so I wouldn't cry and worsen my headache.

Five minutes later, a middle-aged woman pulled over. She was awfully brave, stopping in the dark like that, though she kept the door locked and only unrolled the window two inches. I got all choked up when I saw her kind face, short curls around her head just like Patty's, Patty Gavinsford, Honorable Staff Member of Team Bean Cafe, the woman of a million words.

Hi, sweetheart, you need a lift?

Yeah. I took my thumb down and put my hand on my warm cheek. I need to go somewhere.

Are you going home, dear? She squinted out at me. Are you hurt? I think I should take you home.

I--tonight--I kind of left home-- I started bawling, raucous sobs that shook my core. I don't know--

Okay, just calm down. I can help you.

The woman unlocked the passenger door of her car and let me in, providing me with tissues and a mint candy from the restaurant she'd just been to with her boyfriend, Bill. She said they'd gone to that new Indian restaurant in East Bay, and had I tried it yet? The nervous talk subsided when she realized there was nothing she could say that wouldn't make me weep. The next minutes were a blur of tears and a tell-all, to a complete stranger, of the things that had recently happened to me. When she asked if my mother had kicked me out because I'd come out to her, I realized I hadn't come out to my mother at all, which began a whole new round of sobs. If we were being honest, I hadn't even been kicked out. I had simply left.

The woman said she knew someone I could call in the morning, a free counselor for gay kids. Her friend from work was a member of a group for parents of lesbians and gays. Her work friend had had a hell of a time getting over her son coming out, but she was finally coming to accept the boy, whose name was Liam.

Not understanding why I would cry my eyes out over the mention of Liam, the woman asked if I had someone to call, a friend or a relative? If so, would said friend or relative mind putting me up for the night?

She ended up driving me over to Broadway and parking the car and walking me up the steps at Phantom Cinema, carefully because I still didn't have shoes. People stared at my feet. The woman with the curly hair slipped out of her own beige old-lady flats and told me to wear them, even though they weren't my 'style'. She took my forearm in her hand and repeated over and over

Everything's going to be fine.

At the ticket counter, I requested to see Dana Knight. A robust man with a short haircut and a black suit came out of a set of swinging doors, stopping in his tracks when he saw me, the girl with dirty legs and a beaten face.

Venice?

Dana? I looked him up and down, choking back the waterfall of tears.

Oh my god.

My brother stepped toward me with his arms out, fingertips touching my shoulders. He scanned my face, pausing over the purple-red wound on my forehead.

He was treating me too delicately. I wanted to cringe. I stepped forward in a brief embrace, showing him I was okay. The crispness of his suit's material startled me. The last time I'd visited Dana at work, he'd worn a visor and had stood behind the concession stand. He'd had pimples from all the popcorn butter in the air.

When I took my face away from Dana's chest, the woman was gone. She had left me there, in a pair of shoes I didn't want and a brother I didn't know how to talk to. I wondered, for a moment, if she had actually existed and I hadn't just stolen the shoes to pretend good things could happen.

Dana hesitated when I asked to stay with him, saying he didn't know what Molly would think. But when he saw my wet eyes and quivering lip, he looked at me the way he had when we were kids, the only siblings at daycare who didn't fight.

The theater closed at eleven and Dana was supposed to have one more hour of paperwork, but he said he'd let it slide. I wanted to thank him, but couldn't get the words out without choking up. He took me in his nice-smelling car to his place, which was only a couple of blocks down. We passed Morgan's on the way and I strained my neck trying to see in, though all of the lights were off.

Whatever happened to *walking* to work? I settled back into my chair, trying to break the thick ice. Wasn't that why you moved over here in the first place?

I guess I got lazy. Dana shrugged, glancing at me. Sometimes things don't go the way we plan.

Dana's place was a nice, a suite in the basement of a blue bungalow. He set me up in his office, a tiny room with a futon and computer. The rest of the place bore the simplicity we'd grown up with, a three-quarter bathroom and a combined kitchen/living room. It was weird to see all of my brother's old furniture picked up and plunked straight into his new life--his emergence into society as an adult.

Dana informed me that he and Molly had gotten serious and that she would be coming over the next day, which I took as a warning. He told me she liked the place to be clean.

So don't leave your shit lying around.

I just got here, dude.

Dana ran his hand over his head, an old habit from when his hair was all shaggy and greasy. He started opening all of his cupboards.

You hungry or something?

No...why do you have SlimFast? I asked him not out of a curiosity, but to tease him. Chip chip chip at the ice between us.

It's Molly's. Dana quickly shut the cupboard. So, you wanna watch a movie?

I guess so. But can I use your phone? I cursed myself for having forgotten my phone's battery charger.

Alright. Dana handed me his phone before squatting near the TV. He shuffled through a stack of DVDs.

I dialed Raizel's cell number.

The phone you are calling is currently power off.

I dialed Liam's cell.

Riiiiing. Riiiiiiiing. Riiiing. Riiiiiing. Riiiiing. Riiing.

I hung up and started dialing Amara's number, quickly realizing I didn't know it off by heart. Was there a zero at the end? A three at the start? Every combination I tried led me further from the truth, until all of the digits became mixed in my head.

Dana and I were halfway through Roadtrip when he fell asleep on the sofa, his big feet facing me. I turned the DVD player off, silencing the hum of the TV, and went to the futon in the tiny room he was letting me stay in. There wasn't even a window. I sighed and rolled around on the futon.

If only I had something better. Special K would have done the trick, knocked me out good.

I got up and sat in front of the computer. No new e-mails. I opened a new message and began typing.

raisin,

I don't know where you are, and it's freaking me out. why haven't you answered your phone? I kind of had a fight with my mom, my cell is dead and I'm staying at my brother's. the number here is 432-0916, so if it pops up on caller ID, now you know it's me. get back to me asap, baby.

V

After clicking SEND I went to the bathroom and leaned my hands on the counter, looking in the mirror at a skull with skin on it, purple in places and brown in others, blondish brown hair fried like a corn dog, sticking up in different directions. I was so fucking dirty.

74

One day when I come home from school, Abby is at the kitchen table. A girl from school is in my usual homework spot, books spread before them.

Raizel, this is Hannah, from International Club.

I look at Hannah. Her coarse black hair is cut short into a style I would have liked to learn, back when I was an aspiring hairdresser. She nods, training her black eyes at me, squinty and pulled up at the corners. They remind me of Jill's eyes. My heart stings.

Hi. Nice to meet you. I turn around to get some orange juice from the fridge. I don't shake her hand because she's probably already heard I'm a loser.

Hannah's from Japan, Abby says to my back. She's helping me with math and she's only in grade eleven. Maybe she could help you.

I don't need--

You don't need math help? Abby pries. Since when?

I upgraded in summer school. I'm all over Math 20.

All over? Hannah asks, her eyebrows knit.

I mean… My cheeks are warm. I search for a paraphrase. I'm doing well. Fine. Good. *Excellent.*

You should help *us.* Hannah stares at me. Her finger jabs her text book. This question?

I shrug and walk to the table, my heart thumping quickly. I pull a chair closer and plop down beside Hannah. Abby gets up to retrieve herself a drink.

Easy, I say, picking a pencil up off the table. My hand shakes as I scribble the solution.

Very good. Her face finally breaks into a smile. You're 'all over' it. Thanks.

Hannah has the smoothest complexion I've ever seen, light olive skin lain complacently on her small nose and rosy mouth. She reaches for her pencil and her pinky sparks the back of my hand.

I haven't felt this kind of spark in so long that I've forgotten about it. The best thing is that she's being friendly and clearly hasn't heard about me yet.

So, do you like Sloam? I ignore my sister hovering over the text books on Hannah's other side.

It's okay. Hannah nods. But people are not very fashion.

I know, *right?* Abby agrees. They're not fashion*able.*

I like your fashion. I look down at Hannah's bright orange sweater. It matches the car that is soon to be mine.

I like your fashion, too. Hannah nods. Your trousers look good.

Trousers? I looked down at my legs. Oh, you mean my *tights.*

You are funny. Hannah leans back in the chair, a smirk on her face. Her eyes pass between Abby and I. You have the same…

Hair? Abby asks.

No way. I shake my head. Mine's way lighter.

No! Hannah points at her throat. The same...

Neck? Abby suggests.

No, idiot. The same voice, Hannah. I shake my head again. And no we don't.

Thanks, Abby mutters.

Can we study now? Hannah asks my sister. My mother arrives here five o' clock.

The warmth leaves my cheeks. My toes freeze. Just like that, she's done talking to me. I get up from my chair. Of *course* she doesn't feel as excited about me as I do about her. Not every pretty girl is gay. Hardly any are.

I go out the front door of my family's house and let my hand pass over the Camaro. My time in high school has crawled so slowly that I feel like I've aged forty years. I move away from the house in the way of the setting sun. I've barely noticed the approach of my favorite season, autumn.

I enter an apartment building at the end of the block, one I used to trick-or-treat in when it was snowy outside. The outside door never locked properly. I got so much candy and warmth from those people. I go to the top floor and look in the stairwells for a door or a mysterious square. Finally, in the laundry room, I find a gray door, unlocked, leading to another steep stairwell.

I climb the stairs onto the square, flat roof of the building. The sky is mandarin-orange and lilac-purple and fuzzy car-seat blue. I walk to the edge and sit on the foot-high ledge, my lower legs dangling over.

I feel a recent cut on my upper right thigh chafe against my tights. I want to take them off and throw them over the edge and be done with my cutting days. At the same time, I want to hurl my whole body over the edge and splatter on the apartment parking lot and be done with *everything.* I can't stand the thought that I might fall for girl after girl without ever getting anywhere.

But the spark--it was so clear. She must have felt it, too, running up to her elbow. She looked at me funny after that. I'm sure she did. I never thought this yearning thing would happen again. If I let myself fall off this roof, I'll never know.

When I look down I'm so far from the ground that I gasp. The yellow parking lines on the pavement are blurry. I pivot my butt and swing my legs back onto the solid roof.

A few stores and restaurants call me back about my resume, but the interview at a pharmacy downtown goes the best. The manager is an old guy with a beer belly like most of the teachers at my school. He says he doesn't mind employees doing homework or reading when the store's not busy. He doesn't ask about my volunteer work at the ASPCA, but he says the job is mine if I still want it.

During my first shift I learn everything, including the till. The only other employees are a woman with frilly shirt collars and an even older man with a gray mustache. They work during the day and sometimes at night, but I can have all of the weekend hours I want. A bag lady wanders in from the bus terminal and the manager says it's okay to kick people out of the store if they're not buying anything. He also says it's okay to eat chips for free if I get hungry. He *also* says I can wear whatever I want under my Main Street Pharmacy smock.

Exactly six months after getting my learner's license, I try out for my actual driver's license. My dad has replaced the Camaro's transmission, but I use my mother's car because it's automatic. The test woman is stern and her face gets all narrow toward her chin. It's mid-December and I am direly worried about slipping on the ice. After I ace my parallel park the woman shakes my hand and tells me I've passed. I ask if she's joking and then I do a victory dance in my seat.

The funny thing is I no longer want my license for the reasons I used to. I laugh when I think of my plan to put a hose in the exhaust pipe; what would I use--my family's central vacuuming tube? I haven't cut myself in a while, either, not since the day I was hired at the pharmacy. I just haven't felt the urge. I've had other things on my mind.

Abby has Hannah over twice a week. She helps her with English and gets help with math. I linger around the table and poke fun at both of their mistakes. I brush Hannah's hand every chance I get and squirm when she pokes me with her pencil eraser. During study breaks, Abby checks her cell-phone while I ask Hannah about the music scene in Japan.

75

By the next night, a sizable rock had grown in my stomach, for I still hadn't been able to reach Raizel. She hadn't replied to my e-mail. I was forced to push her out of my mind, as I had a shift that night.

In my shorts and trusty old high-tops I sauntered up to Mars, my bag bouncing against my back. I'd drunk two beers at Dana's, one of which I'd had during supper and one of which I'd taken into the shower with me, loving the coldness in my throat while the warm water cascaded over my skin. I'd crushed the can and left it floating in the drain, a present for Molly.

A few people were in line at Mars, some I didn't recognize and some I did. I moved past them with my usual VIP attitude.

Hey! Someone grabbed my wrist. Venice!

Huh? I turned, seeing a girl with tattoos flowing up her arms and around her neck. Hi, Queenie. What's up?

Nothin' much. Is Raizel with you? She scanned the doorway, the pictures on her skin moving around as she twisted in line.

Bang bang bang. My heart. What did she want from *my* girlfriend?

No. She's at work.

Too bad. Tell her I said hi, okay?

Okay. I nodded, chewing my gum. I glanced at Big Ted. I will.

Dance with me later? Queenie grinned.

Deal. I forced my mouth to smile back while the rest of me sank to the floor, a puddle of person.

Keeping my smile plastered on, I turned to Big Ted and nodded. I rested my hand on the knob of the heavy-duty door.

Can I see your ID? Big Ted dabbed his forehead, mouth twitching as he spoke.

I pushed a laugh out of my throat.

Come on, Teddy Bear, I'm gonna be late. I looked at my cell phone--ten twenty-eight. Two minutes was hardly enough time to throw my stuff in a locker, chug a beer, and get behind the bar, opening my ears to the demands of sweating customers. Oh, and I also had to ask around for a spare tampon, go the bathroom, and shove it up my twat.

Be honest with me. Big Ted crossed his bulging arms over his chest. How old are you?

I felt the customers', and Queenie's, eyes on the back of my neck.

Nineteen. You?

THIS IS THE LAST TIME--SHOW ME YOUR ID.

Not knowing what to do, or say, I dug into my wallet and pulled out my high school student card, keeping my thumb over the birth date. I cringed at the picture.

I used to have long hair.

Big Ted tore the white plastic card from my fingers, holding it high above my head, where I'd never reach it. He squinted for a moment.

You're eighteen?

I'm *sorry*. It's not like drink while I'm working.

You know what kind of shit I could get in? I could lose my job. I could be charged thousands of bucks. Hold on a second. Big Ted pressed the button, buzzing a few people in.

I pretended not to notice Queenie's hardened eyebrows as she slipped into the club.

The door slammed heavily, metal ringing in Mars' dim entranceway. Big Ted dug an iPhone out of the pocket of his slacks, pressing a few buttons with his thick forefinger.

Ilene? Venice is here. Oh, okay. Sure. No problem. He slipped the phone back into his pocket.

I tugged at my own pockets, eyes trained on his face, refusing to look at the floor. I wasn't a dog. My cheeks burned. I didn't have the courage to ask if we could still be friends.

Finally, his face softened.

I'm just doing my job. It's important. He looked up as a group of thin, made-up boys approached, digging in their tight jean pockets for ID.

My legs, my knees, my fingertips--everything jolted. I would probably never be let into Mars again.

Ilene says go around to the back door.

I shuffled off, not looking back, kicking stones as I went through the alleyway. I felt every pebble under my feet, my walk of shame. I wondered *why* I should 'go around to the back door', instead of just turning around and running home.

Home.

Hey, Venice. Ilene poked her head out the back door of the building, the red metal sheet I'd snuck in through once upon a time. Music darted out as she wedged a flattened box in the doorframe to keep it from closing. She held a lighter up to her face, sucking the end of her cancer stick.

Smoking's bad for you, I retorted automatically.

So is fraud. She leaned against the brick wall.

Do you mean tax fraud?

Ex*cuse* me? Her tongue chased the smoke out of her mouth. She wasn't afraid of me. How is that any of your business?

Ilene, I'm *sorry*. When my voice caught, I nearly flipped on myself. I wasn't a crybaby. I wasn't a crybaby. I coughed.

You should probably be saying that to Amara.

Huh? What do you mean?

I mean you should apologize to Amara. You must have done *something* to make her rat you out.

I let my jaw drop, hot air filling my lungs. I breathed in quickly, heavily.

Are you kidding? Is she in there? I lunged for the door and yanked it open. I tugged the cardboard box inside and let the metal door slam, creating a deafening thud behind me.

Holy fuck, what did I just do? I pushed the door experimentally, though I knew it needed to be opened with keys.

I once heard something--people couldn't be sort-of in love just like they couldn't be sort-of pregnant. You probably also couldn't be sort-of in trouble.

I ran down the hall, jumping over boxes like an Olympian over hurdles. I pushed through the swinging doors and ignored the eyes of the mesh muscle-shirt-wearing, martini-sipping men on the first floor. I grabbed the wood railing of the spiral staircase and darted up through customers, following the light of the bathroom. For a moment, I considered diving in and hiding behind a flimsy stall door.

I'd have been discovered in an instant, through the huge cracks.

The glow-paint hallway was a one-second blur in my peripheral. I tumbled into the starry room with an exuberance I'd never felt--not even on the best of substances. I ran around the still-sparse crowd of dancers, pushing through them when I reached the DJ stand. Above me, Amara's form flowed in her white under-dress, untouchable behind the silver bars of her birdcage.

I fumed, willing her to look down.

Behind me, people laughed over the beats of the music. I felt their sweat press into the air around me. A red disco light passed over Amara's face, displaying her severe jaw bone and closed eyes, in complete bliss.

Amara! I grabbed two bars and tried to shake the cage, not feeling it budge. AMARA!

I hoisted myself onto the black platform beside her, my hand hitting the tall stage curtain. A wave rippled up the black fabric, up up up. I yank open the door at the back of the cage and found myself face-to-face with with her.

AMARA! Do you know where the fuck Raizel is?

Stunned, her eyes popped open, demonic black pupils training on my face. In her eyes I saw a dreamy mixture of booze and MDMA, not daisies or anything like them. Of what else rattled through her skull, no could be sure. Her arms fell from their lazy swaying above her head. She stepped forward and to the left, trying to push past me out of the apparatus.

What? I stood in front of the door, my hands at my sides guarding the metal rungs. You're not even gonna talk to me?

I'll say one thing. Amara leaned forward, near my ear. Serves you right.

I suddenly felt the door give out behind me. I grasped desperately for a metal bar, a baby bird towards the worm in its mother's mouth. I fell backwards into the sweaty arms of Big Ted. He clutched my wrists behind my back, a similar pose to how I'd been manhandled at Seed's, and pulled me toward the edge of the stage.

As the cage's metal door banged shut, I caught a flash of Amara's grinning face.

My wrist had been bent so far back that it swelled minutes after I scampered down the alley from Mars and into dark downtown roads. I was just like a rat discovered in a kitchen.

I went the few blocks down to Main Street, peering at the pharmacy. In a moment of hope, I thought the lights were on, but as I approached, I knew they had already closed for the night. Fuck. They would have given me free stuff, for sure, tampons and icepacks and tensor bandages. Especially when they heard what Amara had done to me. I was *jobless.* I felt my heart sink into the dirty, cracked sidewalk.

A 7-11 in the bus terminal boasted that they were open all night. I stalked into the bright store, cradling my wrist around the bone, where it hurt the most. In the first-aid section I found a small icepack. In a daze, I picked up a box of tampons, a can of Diet Coke, and a chocolate bar.

Hi. The girl behind the counter began ringing my items in. Beep. Beep. How are you tonight?

Not bad. I nodded, distracted by the pain shooting up my forearm.

That'll be twenty-one even. Weird.

What's weird?

It's just weird when it lands on a number perfectly. I mean, no extra cents.

Yeah. I handed her my debit card. But it's not the weirdest thing that can happen.

She smiled and let me enter my PIN number. A man got in line behind me, tapping his foot. He was probably a bus driver; they always seemed to tap one foot or the other. I wondered what it was like to be restricted to such a tight schedule.

Sorry. The girl pulled a long, white receipt out of her debit machine. It says 'incomplete'.

She swiped my card again and had me reenter the PIN. She got the man his pack of cigarettes and rang him through on the other till.

Sorry, it's still not working. The girl pulled another receipt out of the machine. Our machine might be down. Sooo sorry. Do you have another card? Or cash?

I held my wrist as I slumped away from the till and into the dark.

I went back to Dana's and shoved a wad of tissues in my panties, accepting that I wouldn't be getting any tampons for the night. First thing in the morning, I'd go to the bank and get a new card. I'd probably accidentally put it through the wash, though I couldn't remember when I had last done laundry. I curled up on the futon with the lights off. That became my neediest moment ever-

-the most appropriate moment, over mere insomnia, to have a case of beer and a fat bag of Special K. I was whimpering out loud when I heard a knock on the door.

What? I turned over to see Dana, his cell phone dangling at his side.

Hi. My brother crouched, perched on the end of my bed, which wasn't really my bed.

What's up? I'm trying to sleep.

Yeah, um...Mom just called. Dana threw his phone in the air, caught it. The device reflected the computer screen's faint light. She said you haven't called her yet.

So?

I think you should call her. Did you hear anything about Oakwood?

What? What about Oakwood? I'll call Mom when I feel like it. I'm sleepy now, and my wrist fucking hurts.

What's wrong, now? Did you get in another fight?

I was quiet. Dana dove off the futon to flick on the light.

Fuck. I squinted through the blaring brightness.

So you *didn't* hear what happened? He came back, sitting on the floor.

What happened?

That little forest thing burnt down--you know, in the field.

I stared at him.

...*Our* field? At Oakwood Terrace?

Apparently.

Are you kidding? How could they just burn down?

I dunno. But there's police tape everywhere. They're saying...I mean, Mom thinks she heard that someone *died.* In the bushes. In the fire.

What? I lifted my head off the pillow. With my good wrist, I pushed myself into a sitting position. Who?

Some kid. Dana shivered. Will you just come with me to Mom's tomorrow? She needs to talk to both of us. She's worried. I mean...that could have been one of us, you know?

The words floated around the air between us. I nodded, swallowing heavily. I couldn't fend off a sour taste on my tongue.

That looks swollen. Dana nodded at my arm. Lemme get you some ice.

76

The next night, I dared to show my face in the alley behind Mars. Thankfully, Big Ted wasn't at his post yet, being a good little doggy. I didn't know what I would have said or done if I'd seen him, though I had some idea. I'd probably have shown him the tensor bandage on my wrist and asked him what kind of man would treat chicks that way.

Just before Mars, at Broken String, I ducked and went down the dark stairs quickly, paying at the entrance with a toony from Dana's change jar. A brass-rock band was playing. As always, the fragrance of beer infected the air. I breathed in, yearning for a tall bottle to suck on, something to soothe my bloodstream and give companionship to my soul, which seemed stuck in perpetual limbo.

Raizel still hadn't called me, or e-mailed me back. Every time thoughts of her popped into my head, a nervous tirade broke out in my stomach.

I spotted Tiff leaning against the far wall with a bunch of artsy-looking types, probably from school. The boy next to her wore a beret and a flowered shirt. Meaghan from Team Bean was there, too, but I avoided making eye contact with her. I didn't want anyone to know who I was if they didn't yet have a clue. Who would I be known as, anyway--the real question being: Who was I to Tiff? The girl who had ditched her for drugs? The sad little mess? The late-bloomer of a lesbian? I'd have to come out to her and tell her about my relationship with Raizel and how I was so in love I thought my heart would burst, like the things I'd heard her say about Oliver. I imagined what would pass through her head, things she might not hesitate to say.

You're a dyke? But I let you rub my feet. I know I said I loved you, but not in that way. What about when we squatted in the bushes together? Were you looking at me?

Come over here.

I watched as Tiff mouthed the words, but I was paralyzed. Maybe if I had something good, a strong pill that locked my jaw and made my shoulders jump around to whatever music was playing, I'd go over and say hi. I'd reminiscence about the good ol' times with Meaghan and I'd wave at all of their other friends as if I'd met them before. I would squeeze between Tiff and Mr. Beret and we'd make fun of other people like we used to.

I turned away, heading to the row of ATM machines near the bar. I hadn't made it to the bank that morning, as I had awoken with menstrual cramps and a splitting headache. I crossed the fingers on my good hand while I slipped my card into the first machine.

Funds unavailable. Remove card now or complete other transaction.

I tried the next machine.

Unauthorized transaction. Remove card now or try new transaction.

Hey, Venice.

I turned around, face to face with a pixie fairy that was Tiffany Abraham.

Hi.

How's it going? She bobbed a little on her heels. Can I buy you a drink?

I glanced at the ATM machine and took my rejected card.

Sure. Better anyway, as Tiff had just turned nineteen and I was still underaged. I opened my mouth to wish her a happy birthday, but couldn't muster up the words.

We got two beers and sat on stools at the bar, idle hands playing with our shirt hems and the soggy coasters. I mumbled something about not believing she was drinking beer and she mumbled something about being a starving student and beer being the cheapest thing. Not that she wasn't happy to buy me one.

So, what's new? Tiff's eyes darted from my bandaged wrist up to my face.

Too much, since we last talked. I felt my eyes move away before coming back again.

Oh. Like what?

Just stuff. Hey, Tiff? I have to ask you something.

Yeah? I figured you didn't just come here to shoot the shit. Her eyes were moist. Why *would* you?

I just looked at her, out of excuses. That part of my brain had been completely used up.

I miss you so much, Venice. She choked on her words, coughing a little.

What was I supposed to do? I felt my back tense up on the stool. You're *so* judgmental of everyone I befriend.

You're so fucking blind. She shook her head and drew her eyes away from me to scan the crowd without aim. I was just jealous.

Oh god. I stared at her, hard. Why?

Not, like, in love jealousy. Her eyes still swam in tears.

Phew. Relieved, I pretended to blot my forehead sweat.

I knew you were gay a long time ago, and it dawned on me that you'd get a girlfriend at some point, or a partner or whatever you wanna call it, and I wouldn't get to be your best friend. She used her sleeve to dab the edge of her eye.

What do you *mean,* you *knew*? Like, how long ago?

I probably knew a few weeks after we met, even when you dated Gus and that stuff happened with Mr. S. and every time you told me you'd made-out with some guy. But I didn't care because I fucking loved you. You were the *only* friend I ever had before Oliver.

Past tense. Oh my god, why was she speaking in past tense? Memories flooded in as though a dam had suppressed them. She'd been so standoffish the first time we met that it hadn't occurred to me that she'd been lonely and miserable and not just a bitch. I thought of pint-sized fourteen-year-old Tiff in her huge black sweater and big red mane.

Why didn't you just tell me?

I guess I didn't...it wasn't in my 'conscious mind'. Selene helped me realize all of this.

Celine Dion?

Selene, my psychologist. I started seeing her after...well, you know...

Tiff put her arms around me and squeezed. Through my t-shirt I felt her face scrunch up against my shoulder. Her repressed sobs dove into my collarbone.

Oliver saw you with that Seed guy. Just promise me you'll stay away from him. I got a bad feeling about him.

I clenched my fists and hated my entire existence. I pulled away from her.

Tiff, do... I hugged myself and gulped. Did you hear what happened at the bushes?

Um, kind of. She crossed her arms over her own chest, our touching moment having come and gone. Oliver was there, though. He called me when he got home that night, real upset. He said it was like a gang fight or something, a bunch of people in bandanas running around with gas and lighters--

Oh my god. *Gas?*

Yeah, he said everyone was screaming and going crazy. I think--I think someone died, Venice. In our neighborhood. Right by our houses.

The air became stale. Not even the bashing of the band's drum could have come in through the ringing in my ears. I felt my blood grow cold, like a bowl of Alphagettis when a kid's too infatuated with her Barbies to come to the dinner table.

Did he see who it was? I swallowed, my throat a dry, dirt road. A girl or boy?

He said it wasn't anyone we knew. I was so shocked that I just kind of sat there and listened and then told him I'd call him later.

Huh. I touched the condensation gathering around the outside of my beer mug. I would be shocked, too.

I mean, not only from that. I was stunned, hearing from Oliver so randomly.

What? Why would you be 'stunned' to hear from him?

We broke up *ages* ago.

I stared at her, disbelieving that two people so in love could separate so nonchalantly. He was 'the one'. They were supposed to get *married.*

What happened? My voice was so small, an ant on the ground.

We're just not right for each other.

Oh. *Snap out of it, V.* I pulled my brain back to my money dilemma. I gotta go, Tiff. But first...do you have a spare tampon?

Yeah, sure.

And, sorry, one more thing. Could you--possibly--can you tell Walter I say hi?

Who's Walter?

Um, 'Old Man Winter'.

Ohh, yeah. Sure. Tiff cocked her head. Venice, are you okay? I mean, is your arm okay? And...it sounds weird, but you look small. Or something.

I'm fine. I touched the tensor bandage. I just fell.

Oh...be careful, okay? And come back soon, we're here a lot. Tiff gestured to the whole crowd as if to say they were all her friends. For all I knew, it might have been true. Bring Raizel, if you want.

The tips of my toes curled up, cold.

I wished I had a crowd of friends to whom I could gesture.

77

I was lying on the futon, staring at the computer and my empty e-mail inbox, when Dana waked straight in without knocking. I didn't move, apart from my eyes traveling up his chubby body.

We're going to Mom's. He held up his car keys. Come on.

Nah. I think I'll stay here. I patted the futon. I'm tired.

Do you want your money?

What?

I mean, do you want access to your account?

How do you know about that? I felt my face frown.

Who do you know who works at a bank and who co-signed for your account?

Mom fucking--she--how could she? Is that legal?

Doubt it. He shrugged. But she said if you'll come home she'll set it back to normal.

We drove across Sloam, parking on the road outside our Oakwood duplex. Number eleven was the farthest one could go without entering the great, dry field, the perimeter of which had been blocked by strands of yellow and black investigation tape. Squinting as hard as I could, I barely made out some dark shapes in the middle of the field.

My mother wore a green sundress and a French braid in her brown hair, something I'd never imagined I would see, not with her busy job and subsequent inability to care about anything. I smiled politely, refraining from begging for my money. She hugged Dana and patted my shoulder and asked us to sit in the living room, which smelled like lemons.

I skittered off to my room and retrieved my phone charger. I plugged in my cell-phone, anticipating it to buzz a million times with messages I hadn't been able to receive. When nothing happened, I figured it would probably take a minute. I went back to the living room.

What's going on? Dana asked, sitting on the sofa with his shoulders hunched and elbows resting on his knees.

Well, I've called you both here today--She spoke like we were members of her book club--because I have some news.

Good or bad? I put my elbow on the couch arm and leaned over.

Good. She smiled.

Just tell us, Mom. Dana was twisting his fingers together, his knuckles going white.

Okay. My mother crossed her legs under the skirt of her dress, setting her hands obediently in her lap. About a year ago, I received a promotion at work. I am the general manager of the SCPB in East Bay.

What? Dana clapped his hands and whooped. That's great!

I stared at my mother.

I know you're wondering why I didn't tell you earlier. When I got promoted I started a plan...one where I would save up money, enough to dig me out of my credit card debt and finally move on.

You see, when you two were born, there was a different plan. Each month, your father and I would contribute to savings accounts. I only gave a little, because at the time I had a part-time job with developing, fiddling around with photography. But we were doing well, saving college funds for both of you. Fun things, too. I wanted to take pictures of the world and make a big, fat photo album of everything I thought was beautiful. Which, back then, meant everything. My mother glanced my way. Her eyes were wet. We were supposed to go to Europe together, all of us. We were supposed to see Venice.

I thought you said this was good news. Dana continued wringing his hands together.

I left my head on the armrest.

I--where was I? My mother stared at something that didn't exist between my brother's shoulder and mine. Ah, of course, you know how life goes. Or--you *don't* know how life goes. When Todd left, *I* was the one with a minimum-wage job and countless bills and two babies. I had to move back in with my mother and my brother Doug...do you remember him? He has some problems. Autism. OCD.

I had to sign up for school and find a real job. So I quit photography and took accounting. Meanwhile, I had my mother harping at me for screwing things up with Todd. She said things to my sister, like, 'If only Katherine could be more like you', 'If only Katherine wasn't such a hippy'. My mother's voice became a whiney snarl here. 'If only you'd have married him, he wouldn't have gotten away'. I think...truthfully...that she was taking out her anger on me. She was a very angry woman. Her husband--my father--died from a heart-attack nearly twenty years before she passed.

Anyway, I was lucky my mother agreed to care for you two while I went to school. At first I thought I would take out a bank loan, but they wouldn't allow it when I had still had money in those savings accounts. I had a very big decision to make, then. I told myself I would take the money out, but put it back as soon as things were stable again.

Two years later I graduated and searched and searched and searched for a job in Vancouver, but there was nothing. It wasn't easy, without the Internet. I couldn't just go online and choose a job from anywhere in the country.

Finally, I received a phone call from someone in Sloam. A bank in B.C. had faxed them my resume. I packed up all of our stuff and said goodbye to my mother. Do you remember Vancouver, at all? Do you remember leaving?

I don't think so. I whispered, keeping my head down, watching patiently as my mother's mouth formed the words I thought I'd never hear.

Yes. Beside me, Dana poked at a thread coming from the knee of his jeans. I remember Grandma. I remember the pancakes she made...and the raspberries with evaporated milk. But I don't remember her being an angry person. And I don't remember saying goodbye, or the airplane.

Oh, we didn't fly. I didn't have *any* money, and the savings were all gone. My sister, your aunt Blanche, used her husband's car to drive us from Vancouver to Sloam. I started at the bank immediately while Blanche cared for you. And finally, I was able to afford the duplex. Then my sister went home to Alberta.

But the bills started piling up again. The car, the house payments, electricity bills. I tried as hard as I could to manage everything and do well at work. When Blanche found out I'd slipped into my old debt, she took pity and started giving me money for food and clothing. Do you remember that Christmas when she gave us so much money? She said it was for your college funds, but she just didn't understand that there are more important things in the world. She didn't understand. Her husband is a surgeon. She got *so* angry when she found out how we spent the money.

Last year, when I proved my strengths at work, with all of that overtime, I was finally promoted. When it happened, I didn't tell you guys because I didn't want to put all of my eggs in one basket. I couldn't stand the thought of another huge failure.

Now for the good news. My mother smiled, shuffling in her chair. The thing is, this promotion was better than I ever thought. East Bay has given me benefits, a huge new office, and a big salary. I mean big. So big, that I've decided to finance a house.

A house? Dana nodded. He'd successfully pulled the thread off his jeans. Where? Like, in Oakwood?

Well, no. I've actually been looking at one in East Bay. It's a modest size, and the basement's unfinished, but there are two bedrooms upstairs. My mother glanced at me, an implied invitation. I figure I'll start with a house I can walk to work from, and then get a better car if things go well.

I swallowed. A house? In East Bay? I opened my mouth, my words like those of a squeaking mouse.

What's wrong with here?

We can't stay here, Venice. Her eyes flitted to the picture window, from which one could see the edge of the field and hints of blaring investigation ribbon. I don't want to.

Well, good for you, Mom. Dana stood up, stretching his arms tall.

Now, first thing's first. There's an open house here tomorrow, and I need help cleaning. I've tidied the first floor, but I really wanna go through stuff.

This might be a problem. I held up my bandaged wrist, metal clips gleaming.

Oh my god. What happened?

I was given the duty of going through old, unused things in the smallest room in the basement, down the hall with the Mexican bead drapery. With my good hand, I lifted things off the shelves into boxes labeled 'Keep' and 'Give

Away'. Nearly everything went in the 'Give Away' box--all of the VHS movies, as we no longer had a VCR, cassette tapes, children's books, a Cabbage Patch Kids doll. The shelves were looking scarce by the time I reached the closet.

I fingered the lace collar of a long, flowery dress, remembering the day my mother had come home from Vancouver, from her mother's funeral. She had retreated to that tiny room for over an hour with the door closed. I'd thought she was doing laundry, but when I'd snuck in there later, a dozen salmon-pink and sky-blue dresses hung from the rod in the closet.

I decided to leave everything hanging and let my mother do what she wanted with them. I touched the sleeve of a lavender number and wondered if my mother sometimes smelled them; that was the only room in the house in which she forbade smoking.

When I thought of it, the rest of the house no longer reeked of smoke. I ran through my mind, trying to remember the last time I'd seen my mother with a cigarette. Perhaps she had finally quit, and I'd been too absorbed in myself to notice.

I left the boxes in the basement and was heading up the stairs when something in the wall caught my eye--the hole that had served as a black pit throughout my childhood. I knelt onto the wooden steps and peeked in, though it was too dark to see anything. I stuck my fingers in, realizing how much bigger the hole had seemed when I was young. My finger caught hold of something and pulled out Hollywood Hair Barbie by her rubbery legs. I smiled and set her on the step beside me, peering back in. The next thing I pulled out was a plastic baggie of broken mushroom caps and stems.

Flip flip flip.

I had to get ahold of Raizel.

I hid the shrooms in my pocket and went upstairs. Dana was on a chair, dusting above the cupboards. I went down the hall to my room and flipped open my phone. No messages appeared. What the fuck? I got the sinking feeling that, when my phone was powered off, it simply rejected messages instead of saving them until the phone was on again. I dialed Raizel's number.

Riiiing. Riiiiiiing. Riiiiiing.

The same response I'd been getting for the past few days. I pressed END.

Venice, peach? My mother called from her room.

What?

Is your arm okay?

Yeah. And I'm done the basement. I looked at the naked doll, which I'd placed facedown on my pillow. I envied Barbie for not having a mother to clean up after. I was about to ask my mother about my bank account when she called out again.

Would you mind going in the attic? There are just a few boxes to go through up there.

Sure. I responded, staring at my bedroom carpet. I wondered briefly what my room would look like in East Bay, if I chose to live there.

Here's a bunch of newspaper. I heard a thump somewhere outside my door. You can use it to pack fragile things.

I pulled the attic stairs down and clung to the sides as I hoisted myself up, putting pressure on both hands. I winced and made my way up the stairs.

Light came in from the seashell-shaped window at the far end of the attic, eliminating the dust-covered boxes and the knots in the wooden floor. I shuffled to the old desk and pulled open the drawers, searching. I suddenly remembered how I'd taken the photo on Christmas and scampered like a madman to Raizel, showing off a father I didn't actually have. I couldn't even remember where I had put the picture.

I put my hand on the window and peeked out at the world. The window's glass was thick and made everything seem underwater, the streetlamps and the roofs of other houses. I opened the latch and pushed on the window. I lifted my leg and rested my barefoot on the rough shingles outside before pulling the rest of my body out.

I cradled my wounded arm against my chest and let the warm air circulate through my lungs, the sun greeting my skin. I saw wind rifle the leaves of the neighbors' fat oak tree, the gentle fluttering a song I hadn't listened to in years.

I carefully leaned back against the slant of the roof and stared at the field, past the blazing yellow crime tape. My eyes scanned the dry, yellow grass and stopped where pieces of black trees lingered. They were probably confused about how their parts had been burnt and torn. I thought trees were like human in the way things could just happen to them, out of their control. They couldn't run from lighters or boys with cans of hairspray, or engulfing flames. The frame of an old sofa remained amid the trees, but there were no other clues.

Realizing I'd left my cell phone inside, I inched back through the attic window.

Still no messages.

I closed the window and knelt on the floor near a box and the stack of newspapers my mother had left me. I rolled the ancient figurines and jewelry and a porcelain tea set in different pieces of newspaper, wondering about the purpose of keeping such items. My fingertips gathered ink quickly, sweaty gray smudges like a priest's hand on Ash Wednesday. I lifted a ceramic jewelry box, admiring the tiny red flowers scattered around its sides, and set it on the next piece of paper. I rolled the paper around the object and placed in the pile I had created.

His eyes bore up at me, deep, frozen in time.

Oh my fucking god.

I picked up the small package I'd just created, quickly unfolding the sheet of newspaper. The lid of the box slid out and cracked against the floorboards, abrasive noise resonating in my ears.

It is with deep sorrow that we announce the passing of Sullivan Edward Klein on July 18th, 2010 at the age of sixteen, in Sloam, SK. Sullivan will forever be remembered by his parents Susan (Wolfe) and Robert Klein; older sisters Raizel and Abigail; on his mother's side Aunt Frieda (Dean), Aunt Rita (William), Uncle Michael (Colleen); and on his father's side Uncle Fredrick (Winnie), Aunt Donna (Stephen); he will also be missed by dozens of cousins and the hundreds of people who were blessed to have met him during his short life. Sullivan is predeceased by his grandparents Abraham and Meritza Wolfe; grandparents Miles and Ula Klein; and lifelong pet, Tony the St. Bernard. Sullivan was born in the small city of Sloam, SK on March 19, 1994, after which he almost immediately gained the title of Family Rebel. Sullivan will always be remembered as generous, intelligent, and thoughtful, a strong young man and aspiring writer who would have met and surpassed his ambitions had his life not come to a startling halt. A memorial service will be held at 2:00pm on July 25nd, 2010, at Golden Paths United Church, 343 Golden Street East, Sloam, SK, with Reverend Norman Schultz officiating, after which we welcome you to join us at a reception in the lower floor of Golden Paths United Church. In lieu of flowers, food, and monetary tributes, donations may be made to Stable Shoulders Drug Rehabilitation Center for Youth, 9019 Betty Avenue North, Sloam, SK. Sullivan Edward Klein will live on in our hearts.

We miss you, Sullivan, the way you were at five and ten,
And suddenly sixteen,
We miss the laughter in your eyes,
Your eyes--they were so green.
We miss your smile, a strength you always had,
We miss your mind, your thoughtful thoughts,
Through the good times and the bad.
Time will pass and we will grow,
And many things will change,
Though we continue living here on earth,
In our minds you will remain.

78

In February, Sullivan offers me twenty bucks a month to give him rides to and from school. He says he's sick of the cold and the bus. I don't have to think about it; afterall, I don't have friends to fill the passenger seats. When I ask where he'll get the money from he says he's starting his own business and I laugh because it's probably a lemonade stand on our driveway.

We're on our way home one day when Sullivan asks me to take a detour. He pulls a cell phone out of his pocket and I ask him where he got it. I can't even afford a cell phone yet. I should charge him more for gas money. He tells me to stop the car and runs up to the front door of a house a few blocks away from ours. A minute later he comes back with his wallet out.

What was that about? I ask Sullivan.

Promise not to tell? He asks, looking sideways at me. I know he means Mom and Dad.

Of course.

I'm just sold an ounce to that guy.

An ounce? I stare at him.

Of weed.

Oh.

Are you gonna tell?

No. I pull the car away from the house and move through the dirty snow towards our own home.

Why not?

I dunno.

Over the next few weeks, I watch Sullivan become more popular than ever at school. People wait by his locker and outside his classes. He calls girls 'boo' because he heard it in a stupid song on the radio. He keeps his phone on vibrate in his pocket so no one else will hear it at home. My parents beam at how close my brother and I are becoming. I know why I won't tell them what's going on. Kids start recognizing me as Sullivan's sister; even though they all eventually ask about him, people *talk* to me. The more houses and apartments we pull up to in my beast of a car, the more people notice me and say hi in the hallways. They smile and ask where I got my cute tights. In class, they clue me in on jokes about the teachers.

In the spring Hannah starts bringing little gifts to our house, flowers from her mother's store, cookies, a big jug of orange juice because she knows I like it. I notice her watching me in her peripheral when she should be studying.

One day I lead Hannah away from the table for a 'study break'. Abby calls her friend Kristal, who I've long-since gotten over. My heart is bumping around in my chest and I'm not entirely sure what I'm doing. All I know is I want to be alone with Hannah. She follows me downstairs and looks around my room with wide eyes.

My parents tell me 'clean up!' if my room is like this.

Ohh, trust me. I smile. My parents say that, too.

You have music, right? Hannah points at the CD player.

Yeah. I cross the room and turn on the player. Ani pumps out of the speakers.

Who is she? Hannah nods her head with the beat of the guitar. I like it.

It's Ani Difranco. She's bisexual, I blurt before I can stop myself.

Pardon me?

She's bisexual. My cheeks are warm. She likes boys *and* girls.

Oh. Hannah continues nodding. I don't.

Don't want? I turn to the CD player and skip to the next song, my favorite.

I don't like boys. I forgot that word--lesbian, I think?

Huh? I turn my back to the CD player, eyeing Hannah. Are you joking?

No. She shrugs, smiling.

Our eyes lock while we dream of pinning each other.

A minute later we push our warm bodies together. I pull Hannah's t-shirt over her head. She's sixteen and doesn't wear a bra. She sucks on my neck and undoes my denim skirt and slides her palm down my stomach and into my tights and panties. I remove my own shirt as she paws at me, a sensation I haven't felt in too long building between my legs.

When we finally kiss on the lips, all of the sparks I've been afraid of imagining come flying out of my mouth and into hers. I wonder if she's done this before. I've never touched anyone but myself, but I want to do to her all of the things I've done in my dreams. I slip my hand into her plain white underwear and follow her lead. Our tongues swirl together frantically.

Hannah steps away and whips the blanket off my bed. She pulls my hand and forces me down, climbing over me. She has definitely done this before. I whimper when her knee rubs up my skirt between my legs and her hand pinches my breast. She moves down the bed and kisses the outside of my groin through my clothing, hot breath that comes inside of me and shoots up my torso into my brain. She tugs my tights and panties down and kisses me before she can notice my upper-thigh scars. I shudder and writhe and sigh, the sheets damp under my sweating lower back.

When we get back upstairs, Abby's not on the phone anymore. She's swearing and erasing part of her college application. I offer Hannah a glass of water and the sides of my mouth twitch upward. We sit at the table and I watch her write something on the outside of her binder.

Hana + Razil

She doesn't know how to spell my name, but until now, I haven't known how to spell hers.

Hana and I start hanging out every day that I'm not working; she tells her parents she's studying for finals. My own parents are just happy I've made a friend other than my little brother. Abby meets a new student at International Club, someone she won't bring home and let me 'steal' from her. She's still concerned about maintaining high standards for herself.

I start hearing about parties at school and being asked if I'm going. Because I'm Sullivan's sister, kids assume I'm dealing *with* him. I'm not. I'm still just the driver. I tell them I have nothing but that I'll get Sullivan to come to the party with his stash. Naturally, Hana wants to come with us.

On a Friday night I finish work at eight. I swing by my house to get Sullivan and his stuff before we go to Hana's family's East Bay mansion. She tells her parents we're having an all-night Canadian-style study session, whatever that means. I meet her mother at the door and she smiles and says my hair color is beautiful. I say I'll drive safely and bring Hana home the next morning.

I glance toward the bay in honor of Tony. Then we speed off to Duhill Crest, the area surrounding our school. I park the car and we saunter up to the house. The way everyone stares out the windows, I feel like I'm on that TV show, America's Most Wanted. A girl from my chemistry class swings the door open and smiles at the three of us.

Get your asses in here!

We enter the warm house. The miniskirts and short shorts are back, but I haven't taken mine off all year, nor my tights. Some of my scars are still too noticeable. A few kids accost Sullivan straight off, so I let the party host lead Hana and I to the kitchen. She says there's beer and liquor, if we want. She compliments my hair and asks how I made it curl like that.

Hana steps between us, her back to the girl. The girl shrugs and wanders away to enjoy her party. I laugh at Hana's smirk.

Have you ever been drunk? I stroke the vodka bottle on the counter.

Yes. Do you know Meili, from International Club?

No.

She is from China, has short hair?

Oh, yeah? I vaguely know who she's talking about.

On a Friday, we have soo many sake bombs.

What's a sake bomb?

Japanese wine and beer together. We can try with vodka.

That doesn't sound good. I laugh.

Definitely not good. But you get drunk.

She pours us two beer-and-vodka bombs. We scrunch our faces before we've even tried the drinks.

Two hours later we're part of a lounging circle in a bedroom upstairs, smoking joints I'm sure were made from my brother's stash. I start coughing when I smoke, but Hana takes it coolly. The more I drink, the more I talk to strangers. The less I care what they think. Almost. Hana grabs my hand and holds it in her lap. I feel my spine stiffen. Maybe that's cool in Japan, but not here. All of a sudden a girl on the bed pipes up.

What's it like, being gay?

I rip my hand from Hana's lap, putting it in my pocket. I don't look at anyone's eyes.

Sorry, I'm not trying to be rude, the girl says. I really mean it. What's it like?

Yeah? A guy joins in. When did you know?

I pull my eyes off the carpet and look up at them. Five others in the room sit quietly, awaiting my answer. In the hallway outside, music pounds and kids holler drunkenly.

I was nine, Hana says.

I was eleven. I glance at Hana, moving my hand back toward her.

When did you know you were straight? Hana shoots back. Her hand accepts mine, squeezing my fingers.

Everyone laughs. A flood of questions comes pouring out of them. The pot spreads my mind wide open and I loosen up, answering them.

How long have you been together? Did you tell your parents? What did they say? Are you going to have kids? How? Have you ever been with a guy? Would you ever be with a guy again? Is it hard to come out of the closet? Do you want to get married? Is it legal for gay people to get married in Canada? What about Japan? What's Japan like? Are there lots of gay people? What's the music like? What's the fashion like? What's school like, in Japan? Hey, have you guys ever been to a pride parade? Have you ever been to a gay bar? Have you ever seen a drag queen? Would you ever have a threesome with a guy? What about another couple? Has anyone ever said something homophobic to you? Did you tell them to shove it?

Sullivan appears in the bedroom doorway and I throw my arms around him, yelling, Little brotherrrrr! The other kids look raise they eyebrows.

Hey, Raisin. Sullivan smiles, hugging me back. He reeks of pot, but so do I.

Hana gets off the carpet. We wave goodbye and everyone says things like,

Nice meeting you!

See you at school!

Have a good weekend!

Partiers look on as Hana and I hold hands and follow Sullivan. I don't care if Sullivan notices--in fact, I *want* him to know. I'll keep his secret if he'll keep mine.

After a whiff of my liquor-stained breath Sullivan takes the Camaro's keys from me, urging me into the backseat with my 'little girlfriend'. We laugh the whole ride home and I scold him when he presses the breaks too hard. I don't ask how he already knows how to drive a standard. I spray our hair and clothing with Hawaiian Ginger perfume from my job at the pharmacy, in case Mom and Dad are still up.

Inside, Hana and I skip down to my basement bathroom and strip out of our clothes. I just expose myself and the scars on my inner ankles and my thigh and a particularly pink one on my wrist under my leather cuff bracelet. We sit in the tub and turn on the shower and hold our nude bodies together under the warm water. This is all I've ever wanted.

79

Kids at school don't treat Hana or me poorly after the weekend, even though we're the only students officially out of the closet. A couple of girls from the party smoke circle smile at me and ask what's up and how Hana's doing. They say if we ever want to go shopping together to just say the word. I keep a straight face so they don't know about the vivid pink lotus flowers blooming all over my insides.

I start noticing these little plastic boxes at school, brightly-colored cubes in lockers and purses and under the benches in the gymnasium change room. I have no idea what they're for. They're only big enough to fit a gumball or a jawbreaker.

One day when Sullivan's dropping something off for a usual customer, he leaves his bag in the car. I never look through his stuff--we've grown to respect each other--but I notice he has one of the little boxes, which I pick up. It's covered in animated cherries.

I open the box, but it's empty. I glance at the still-closed front door of the customer's house before picking up my brother's bag, hearing things clunk around inside. I peek in. A hundred or more of the tiny boxes inside surround Sullivan's ninth grade math book, their sides and tops decorated with little images. They're all empty.

Hana and I become so attached at the hip that when she's not with me I feel like half of my body is missing. She comes to the pharmacy when I'm working. My boss doesn't care if she sits on a stack of milk crates at the back of the store and does her homework. Hana's parents don't care, either, because she still gets her studying done.

We go to parties every weekend, helping Sullivan out with his business. He doesn't give us money but he hooks us up with beer and pot. I still don't see the harm in pot or how my brother earns his cash. I understand why people protest against the illegality of marijuana.

Hana and I are like an icon at school now. People think she's hilarious and I've heard them saying we're one of Duhill Collegiate's hottest couples. I wonder if we'll get in the yearbook. Since people found out about us, three boys and another girl have come out of the closet. I feel bad for the boys because people are not as accepting about their gayness. I feel guilty when a see 'fag' on a boy's locker because of the stuff people used to write on mine. But by now I know everyone goes through some rough times in high school. If I was never depressed, I wouldn't appreciate life half as much as I do now.

I think I'm in love.

When school lets out for the summer, my grades are the best they've ever been. So are Hana's, but her parents force her to join the East Bay Eagles, a girls' summer baseball team. She groans and complains and swears in Japanese, even though I've taught her the foulest words in the English language. During the first game I get so aroused watching her run around in her uniform that I jump on her as soon as we return to my house later. After that, she doesn't complain. She says she's happy I was looking at her and not the other girls' legs.

We have a pretty tight social circle going, parties still happening every weekend. I soon realize that the purpose of the mysterious little boxes is to store pills or other small drugs. At a party when people whip out their little boxes Sullivan admits he is selling E as a side business, just to make extra cash. He also has a little bit of cocaine. And some acid. He's going to stop when he has enough for a laptop. I tell him he doesn't need one and I'll share the family computer with him. He disagrees and says he needs his own computer because he wants to write a novel. I don't say anything after that. I just listen to my little brother tell kids that when they're asking about E over the phone they should refer to it as daisy. I think it's the stupidest code on the planet.

I'll have six purple daisies, please.

I'm coming over. Can you hook me up with five daisies?

How many daisies can I get for a hundred bucks?

Do you have any blue daisies?

I think the students at Duhill Collegiate are some of the stupidest high school kids who ever existed--that, or in the most need of displacing their minds. They get high off anything they can get their hands on, including over-the-counter medicines, like Gravol. I don't even want to know how many have tried snorting Ritalin or smoking oregano.

Halfway through the summer, the East Bay Eagles are in a ball tournament against three other teams. I joke to Hana that I'll love her no matter how good she plays. She jokes back that if she rubs her bat between my legs maybe it'll be good luck. I slap her forearm and sit behind the diamond, watching intently as her team squares off with the Wainmont Warriors. I cross my fingers because everyone knows Wainmont has the toughest chicks.

The Warriors suck at batting. The Eagles pull out of the game on top. Hana stalks toward me on the grass with her shoulders bunched up, a grin on her face, slanted eyes glimmering. She says she's pumped to pummel the other teams. I congratulate her and we wait while the Duhill Devils begin a game against Sloam Community Team.

Sloam Community Team is made up of girls who weren't accepted on area teams during tryouts, who signed up too late, who simply want exercise and don't care about winning, and girls whose parents have forced them to *do* something with their summer vacation. Hana never would have ended up on Sloam Community Team; she's too fast. I, however, would have automatically been placed on this team as soon as they found out I don't like sunshine and haven't taken my tights off yet since the snow melted.

I pity them because they don't have a name, Hana says, dropping onto the grass beside me.

I guess so. But you shouldn't pity them. I look through the spaces in the metal ball diamond. Their team is full of hotties.

What?! Hana turns and looks at the team, lining up on the bench. The Duhill Devils have taken their stance in the field and on the bases. Which girls are hot?

Um…I was just saying in general.

What's that?

'In general'. I'm so stupid. Her English isn't *that* good yet.

Okay, how about that one? I pointed at a blond girl with long, tanned legs sticking out from her shorts.

Her? Hana's eyebrows go up. Her cheeks redden. She looks like Barbie dolls.

True. I laugh. I point at a girl on the bench with square shoulders and brown hair, her back to us. What about her?

I can't see her face. Hana sits up straight, her face have darkened drastically.

I'm just choosing one, I say. I don't really care.

Okay.

The Duhill Devils need to polish their pitching skills. One after another, Sloam Community Team gets home-runs. The brown-haired girl is the last to come running around to home base, her bronzed skin glowing under the sun. She wears a big, white smile. Her face is *gorgeous.*

You like that girl, right? Hana nudges me.

Huh?

You think she is hot?

I think *everyone* likes her, I respond, watching the girls' teammates give her high fives.

The brown-haired girl takes the pitcher's mound and gets a look on her face like she wants to slice the ball through each batter's forehead. We watch as Sloam Community Team blows the Devils out of the water with their pitching and catching skills. I clap when they win, happy that a nameless team has something good going for them.

The Wainmont Warriors and Duhill Devils pack up their stuff and head to another ball diamond across the field. They're going to play each other while The East Bay Eagles go up against Sloam Community Team.

I kiss Hana's cheek before she gets up and goes to linger around the diamond wall. Some of her teammates pat her shoulder and get her to check that their facial sunscreen is rubbed in. The straight ones treat her like they would a cute boy. I don't mind. At the end of the day, she's coming home with me. She glances at me and I flash the peace sign, my index and middle fingers spread wide.

Sloam Community Team fills the bench while the Eagles take their places in the field. Hana's on second base. The first three girls strike out from the Eagles' hot pitches.

The gorgeous girl takes the plate, shiny amber locks flowing down her back. I think of what I want to do with her hair, all of the different braids and styles I could create. The girl bends her knees and holds up the bat. From behind, her legs look nice, darker than mine will ever get. She probably lies in the sun most afternoons; if not, she's damn lucky to have such a deep complexion.

The pitcher throws the ball, her arm wobbling at the last second. CRACK! The bat meets the ball, which soars into the air. I strain my neck and clap my hands, willing the girl to run. She takes off like an agile panther toward first base.

I glance at Hana. She's watching me watching another girl. The girl makes it to first base, sailing past. Someone in outfield retrieves the ball.

GO HANA GO! I yell. I'm still on her side.

Hana turns away from me and open her mitt to accept the ball from her teammate just as the bronzed beauty is sliding into second. A cloud of dust gathers around them as the girl's feet meet Hana's ankles. Hana falls. I jump up and move toward them. Through the dust, I can barely see more than a pile of girls' limbs. The Eagles' coach sprints toward them.

A long wail soars out of someone's mouth. This wail ends in shrieks. I can't understand what they're saying. Is Hana yelling something in Japanese?

I'm ten feet away when the dust clears. Hana's fists fly in the air and come down repeatedly, pummeling the girl's shoulder. The girl holds her hands over her face.

I pull the back of Hana's shirt collar. She gets to her feet. The coach helps up the crying victim by her unscathed arm. Hana's face is beet red. We gather our stuff and run to my car before anyone can phone the cops. Whatever. Fights like these always happen, in sports. They were probably fighting over whether or not the girl made it to second before Hana caught the ball.

Deep inside of me, I know what happened. I'm so afraid of losing Hana that I keep my mouth shut.

80

I slipped out the front door, ignoring my mother as she called after me, desperate to know where I was going.

I hopped on the number 84 bus, Old Faithful, paying with money I'd borrowed from my mother's purse. I immediately pined for my iPod or something to distract me from my nerves. As we traveled out of Oakwood and through Elmview, my shaking hands unfolded the rest of the paper from the attic. I skimmed the article under the four-inch-by-four-inch photo of a dry-grass field in a rundown neighborhood at the edge of Sloam.

> *One Deceased After Oakwood Fire*
>
> *...an unsupervised teens' pit party, resulting in one fatality...was discovered with his wrists under rope restraint, face scorched and a lungful of smoke...wallet taped to leg lead police to suspect an involvement with drugs...DOA at Sacred Heart Hospital...three possible gangmember suspects have gone unrecognized by witnesses...no comment from family...*

I rested my forehead against the cool metal back of the seat in front of me, putting my hand to my chest. Everything past my mouth felt squeezed, like a lemon--my throat, my lungs, my chest.

I stayed that way through the downtown bus terminal, all the way down Main Street and beyond. I arose from my seat and got off the bus near the elementary school and the little church with its brassy sign grazing the sky.

Golden Paths United Church

I entered the building just as people were streaming from the first floor pews into a stairwell to a basement room. I was shocked by the realness behind the tiny words printed in a piece of newspaper.

In the stairwell, I stood with my back in a corner, watching grieving people as they clicked and clacked down the stairs in their fancy funeral shoes. I didn't recognize anyone. Few of them glanced my way. When the crowd thinned and there was yet no sign of Raizel, I slinked down the last set of stairs and peered into the big basement room. A long table was against one wall, its surface a smattering of desert squares and tiny, triangular sandwiches. A line had formed before a coffee machine, and some people lingered around an arrangement of sofas. It wasn't like TV. No one wore black birdcage veils.

When I saw Raizel's parents, I shrunk into my cardigan and hid in the shadow cast by the door. Susan leaned her on Bob's shoulder, listening as someone I assumed was their friend gave deepest consolations.

I watched Bob carefully, standing like a brick wall in a storm. One day, maybe I'd provide a strong shoulder like his for his daughter. His jaw was firm, but he kept blinking with eyes as luminescent and green as both of his daughters'. I shivered, realizing those eyes resembled Seed's more than anyone else's.

When Bob's eyes landed on me and stayed, I couldn't handle how they gaped, blank. I swiveled and darted up the stairs, clinging to the railing. I ran out into the beating sunshine. I rounded the side of the church, under the shade of the building's overhanging roof.

I spotted them, then--a group of teenagers and kids my age in the alley between the church and the elementary school. There were dozens, *dozens*, possible a hundred of them. They all wore black, paying respects as if they had really known Seed. He probably would have preferred for everyone to stay in their baggy jeans and diamond-encrusted gangsta caps.

Amara's afro poked out from somewhere in the group; she had probably made sure it was voluminous and funeral-sexy. As I moved forth, I made out Liam's hanging black curtain of hair, beside him Abby's long, blond locks. Still, no Raizel.

I skimmed the others' heads, finally stopping on a girl in a long black dress and Doc Marten boots redder than blood. Her hair was black and shorter than mine, sticking out like the feathers of a chick. I imagined she had on one of her practice wigs and that I could slip it off her head and reveal my white-blond angel, the girl in all of my best photos, my tittering muse.

What the fuck are *you* doing here?

I froze. Several kids turned and looked. I didn't know most of them by name, but recognized their faces. Customers, they'd been. Boy, if I had spotted Mr. Cell Phone or his fucking accomplice in that crowd...

I need to talk to you, Raisin. I spoke like a cobra had wrapped around my neck, squeezing, choking. I don't know what's going on.

She looked so different. Dark and small, a windowless closet, like my room at Dana's. I wanted to dart forth and scoop her up. I wanted to get her out of there and bring her across the world, where the past didn't exist. Behind her, Liam and Abby were quiet. Amara smirked.

There's nothing you can say. Raizel's voice sounded different without her hair curling complacently around her neck and shoulders.

I didn't know. I didn't know. My face dared to crumple far sooner than I allowed. I didn't know he was your brother.

Who the fuck invited you here?

I saw the obituary. I didn't even *know*. Didn't know why you were ignoring my calls. I *had* to see you.

Okay. Do you have anything else to say? As Raizel spoke, Amara's arms snaked around her waist, from behind.

Stop fucking touching her, I warned, daggering Amara with my eyes as hard as I could. At my sides, my fists got hard.

Or what? Amara's face was unearthly calm. Or you'll fight me? Hurt even more of Raizel's loved ones?

I glanced at Liam, who stood as useless as fuck, not saying anything. Some friend.

I love you. I know you love me, too. I softened my eyes at Raizel and put my hand on my chest. It's practically tangible. You can't just throw me away.

Raizel shook her head, holding her hand up.

I didn't know, I swear. I swear on everything we are. And besides, I was buying from him for *all* of us--

It's not that, Venice. Raizel barked, voice sharper than a new razor. She nodded at Amara. Show her.

I heard a familiar electronic chiming sound. In Amara's hand I spotted my old camera, the one I'd found in a pile of unwanted belongings.

You stole my camera? You fucking thief! FUCKING KLEPTOMANIAC! I stepped forward.

I had to protect her, Amara said innocently, holding my camera out of reach, high in the air like yarn for a cat. She began flipping through the pictures on the memory card.

When she turned the device toward me, the image displayed curdled my blood and made my stomach clench up. Panic struck all the organs inside of me. There I was, my hair all messy, darkness surrounding me. I was on a sofa near a gathering of trees and I was sucking face with Seed.

That's not what it looks like! I recoiled in horror, jutting my chin at Amara. I was trying to get her off my back.

Wow. Raizel scoffed, poking her head out of the crowd. She looked me up and down. Who are you? I don't know you. But I must say, you did good at getting her off your back. And my little fucking brother.

Her eyes cracked like antique vases, the water falling onto her deserted meadow of a face. She crossed her arms over her chest, saving her heart from further destruction. I was supposed to be the protector, the one who made her feel better after her war with Hannah. After all of my good intentions and aspirations, I'd caused Raizel more pain than she would probably *ever* feel.

Go on. Abby finally croaked, grabbing her sister's hand. Under their eyes were identical lines of fatigue. Get out of here. You're not welcome.

I threw the bag of mushrooms on the ground, along with the Barbie doll. The sun shone sadly on her mangled, ratty, Hollywood Hair.

I hated myself for saying the words too late, just like Kale had, Mr. Shepherd, teacher of high school photography classes, weak-hearted statutory rapist. I couldn't take my eyes off Raizel.

I love you.

81

When grade twelve starts I have automatic friends, the kids we partied with throughout the summer. Without knowing some of their last names, I've held back girls' hair while they puked up Hot 100 and Mike's Hard Lemonade. Times like those are enough to form deep, meaningful bonds. I catch these girls' eyes in class and we giggle with secrecy.

Sullivan's business is going just as strong as last year. Abby has graduated and attends random classes at a random college, something to study while she waits to get into a fashion school in Toronto.

Fall goes smoothly, my grades staying high. Hana and I have a routine of studying as fast as possible and then getting up to no good in my bed. We still never hang out at her house, but her mom and I are on a first-name basis. My own parents think Hana is the funniest person in the world. They can't believe we've fallen in love so young. I silently honor them for being so cool with our relationship.

Shortly before Christmas, everyone at school starts talking about the winter formal dance. I've never thought much of school dances, but a plan is brewing. Everyone's still carting around their pillboxes and whispering loudly about sneaking some E into the dance. They want to turn it into an all-night rave, something that'll confuse the fuck out of the chaperones. I can't help but notice the primitive widening of their eyes as they discuss such matters.

I think it's a bad idea, but I don't say anything. I don't want to look frigid. Sullivan has a new supply of what he describes as 'the craziest daisy ever'. They look like tiny blue lemons. He says it makes you feel like running a marathon. I can't believe he has tried it. I lie in my bed and fear that he'll become an addict. Hana doesn't understand the funk I'm getting into. She wonders what daisy is like and I cringe. Pot is one thing, but E is another.

I buy a black dress and thick Wonderbra tights with some of the money I've saved from my job at the pharmacy. Hana wears a black vest and a silky red button-down shirt, Christmassy. Her family doesn't celebrate Christmas. The girl at the ticket booth blushes at Hana's handsome attire and witty smile. I squeeze Hana's forearm. We still haven't talked about the ball game in July and the blindingly obvious double-standard prevailing in our relationship.

Everyone pops their tiny blue lemon pills early in the night; we know, because word buzzes quickly in our circle of friends. Soon it's obvious, the drug buzzing in their blood. Hana and I are both sober. We sit at a table and watch as girls' bra straps begin to fall and their feet stomp the gymnasium floor.

When I look at Hana's face, I see something I never thought I'd see. Her black pupils are huge and she can't stop smiling like she's floating along the ceiling with the homemade snowflake decorations. She laughs at being caught and I just stare at her, wondering how she could go ahead and do such a thing without talking to me. She says she can't stop moving her legs and biting her mouth and that she wants to dance. I let her lead me to the dance floor and I sway quietly while Eminem blares around us.

I haven't felt so alone since the tenth grade.

Hey, everyone's going outside for a smoke, a girl tells us. I recognize her as a host of one of the summer's best parties.

Sweet! Hana cries out.

I follow her out of the gym, down the hall, and out the school's front door. A huge group of kids stands around, chatting and leaning their heads on the brick wall. There must be at least forty kids outside, all jacketless. I shiver. They don't realize it's twenty-below. A couple of girls lie down on the pavement and laugh about something together. Sullivan is off to the side with a girl he likes, called Kerri. They pass a cigarette back and forth. As I look around, I notice how skeletal some kids' faces have become over the past year, their skin sunken in under their cheekbones. These are the kids who need more than one pill to have a good high.

Back inside! A man's voice suddenly booms over the group.

My head snaps to the front door. Mr. Schewer, our principal, stands with half of his body outside.

We're smoking! An anonymous girl's voice yells back.

Yeah!

Where are your jackets? We don't want anyone to get sick. Mr. Schewer frowns and opens the door wider, hallway light spilling out.

My heart beats quickly. We are going to get caught. *I* haven't even done anything.

Fuck that! Another anonymous voice yells.

EXCUSE ME? Mr. Schewer booms. Now, get inside, kids. You have five seconds. Five...four...three...two...one.

No one moves. I watch everyone stand with their arms around people they wouldn't normally stand with. Mr. Schewer huffs and goes back inside. The group explodes with chatter about authority having no authority. Some kids slink back inside, but the rest of stay and let our teeth chatter. I plea with Hana to come back in and dance with me, but she refuses.

When a cop car pulls up to curb outside Duhill Collegiate, the crowd stiffens. Kids quiet down and watch two officers in navy blue uniforms get out of their cruiser. The lights aren't flashing and the siren's not on, but their presence is clear. I hear a few kids shuffle to the door and yank it open.

Hana and I dodge into the school after a few other kids. Sullivan's not with us. I want to wait for him inside the door, but Mr. Schewer ushers us back into the gymnasium. I wring my hands.

Minutes after questioning a few kids, the police find what they're looking for. My little brother's body is up against a bulletin board in the hallway, hands behind his back. His face is turned away from me; I only see his hair, as white-blond as my own. A big officer cuff's Sullivan wrists. Along with hundreds of other kids, I stand and stare, wide-eyed. I feel like I'm stuck in one of those dreams where something horrible is happening, but I can't find the power to scream. If my voice box worked, I don't know what I would say.

I follow them outside and watch the police car speed off into the night, and *then* I am more alone than I've ever been.

I go home that night and lie in my bed and cry. Hana says her blood is still happy and she needs to go partying with the others. I wonder how she can be so carefree. I think about Sullivan constantly--about where, exactly they've taken him. I wonder if he'll rat me out for being his driving accomplice. I wonder what kind of punishment he'll get. He'll probably have to pay a lot of money. Or my parents will. They're going to kill him.

When the phone rings I run to the bathroom next to my room, lock the door, and turn on the shower. Someone bangs on the door and I huddle between the toilet and the tub until they go away. The house is empty when I emerge.

The next morning when I wake up I'm surprised to find Sullivan sitting at the kitchen table. He suddenly reminds me of small Sullivan, the brother who would guilt me into walking him to the corner store for candy. My parents are across from him, my mother's hair tangled and her eyes red and my dad's forehead more wrinkled than it has ever looked.

I skitter out of the kitchen and to the Camaro before anyone can say anything. I drive and drive and drive, but I don't go to Hana's. I end up outside of Sloam, surrounded by flat Saskatchewan prairies. Snow on the highway is so thin I can see mud and gravel through its white façade. All at once, it rushes over me--the deepest craving I've ever had, far stronger than any craving for orange juice or potato wedges. I want to smash my rearview mirror into a million sharp pieces and slink into a nearby field and roll down the top of my tights and relive my lonely tenth-grade nights.

Deep inside of me, I find the strength to pulverize my thoughts before they can control me.

The next few days are a blur of avoiding my parents and giving the silent treatment to everyone involved in the winter formal daisy fest, including Hana. She brings me gifts like she used to, slipping them into my locker because she knows the code. Chocolate, thong panties, a teddy bear.

I'm walking down the hall at school when I see police officers lining the halls, opening lockers. Mr. Schewer stands with them, giving out combinations and the names of kids. My locker is nearby, but I don't know what they're looking for. I walk slowly and stop at a water fountain, listening.

...found another one, a policewoman says. It's empty.

This one's not, a male cop replied. Out of my peripheral, I see him lean and show her the insides of something--a tiny, plastic box.

Over the next week, kids all over the school are charged with possession of ecstasy. They haven't checked lockers at other schools, but I'm sure they would find more. Each time I hear of another student being caught, a rock in my stomach grows harder. I'm afraid Hana will be caught and sent back to Japan. I'm afraid Sullivan's charges will grow because of his customer base, even if they can't prove it all came from him.

Hana doesn't get caught because she doesn't have a pillbox in her locker. On the twenty-second of December, my little brother Sullivan is sentenced to six months at Baits Juvenile Disciplinary Hall, after which his case will be revised. I don't understand the police and their technical terms as they sit down with my family. Everything just passes over my head as the boulder inside of me threatens to roll over. Abby and my parents sag against each other like three wilting flowers. I hug myself.

Kids at school don't ask about Sullivan, but they want to know where they can get daisy, now that he's gone. I say I have no idea. They start shooting me glances and saying things I can't hear. One girl asks me if Sullivan told on everyone or if the police did a polygraph test. I tell her the police were checking lockers and it wasn't my brother's fault.

Besides, I say, Who the fuck told the cops it was Sullivan?

She nods in agreement. Later I hear, through the grapevine, that this girl thinks I am 'such a bitch'.

Hana and I stop having sleepovers and hanging out after school. She makes excuses every day, saying she has to do Christmas baking with her mom or go out of town to visit relatives. They don't have relatives in Canada. She doesn't put presents in my locker or wait outside my classes. In the cafeteria, I watch her laugh with our party-crowd, unaffected by anything. I go home and cry every night and leave my homework in a pile on my bedroom desk. I'm not surprised when Hana phones me and says things are just not working out anymore.

A newspaper in Sloam interviews my parents and their quote appears under a close-up of lime green unicorn-stamped ecstasy.

We didn't raise our son to deal drugs. We sent him to a nice school in a nice neighborhood. We just want to know what we did wrong.

Numbing grief takes over my body.

82

Abby and my parents and I attend family counseling on Saturdays for two solid months. They want Sullivan to be involved, but he's not allowed to leave Baits for any reason, except medical emergencies. Abby starts saying she's too busy with college to continue counseling, and my parents say they've learned enough about 'good family communication'. They're surprised when I want to continue alone, but my dad says if I feel I need it, I can go. I get Selene, the counselor, alone on Saturdays at three. I don't care that it's in the middle of the day and I have to pass up on some of the best shifts at the pharmacy.

Selene is beautiful and young, not how I always imagined a counselor would be. She listens to me and laughs when appropriate and I feel like I could talk with her about anything. She has dark hair and a dazzling smile and she gives me apple-scented tissues when tough subjects arise. Which they do. Every week.

One Saturday in April, Selene says she wants an overview of how I've dealt with everything. She asks me if I feel like I've moved on from my breakup with Hana.

I'm…things are definitely weird, at school. Hana walks by me and pretends she doesn't see me.

How does this make you feel?

It used to bother me a lot. I hid in the bathroom whenever I saw her coming. I didn't want to give her the chance to snub me.

Do you still hide?

No. Now I just pretend I don't see her. We just don't look at each other.

Okay. Do you feel hurt by this behavior?

I feel lonely, more than anything. She hangs out with all of our old 'friends', and I don't have anyone. I *have* had more study time, though.

What are you studying?

Everything. I'm trying to pick up my grades.

So you can graduate?

Yes.

How important is it to you that you graduate on time?

Extremely important. I don't want to disappoint my parents like my…like Sullivan.

Do you think they would be disappointed despite everything you've been through?

No…I don't know. I think they want me to be happy, but I couldn't stand the look on my mother's face when Sullivan was sent to juvy.

What was the look?

Like…she looked like someone was kidnapping her baby. He *was* her baby.

And how have you dealt with Sullivan's absence from your home?

What do you mean? I go to school and study and try not to think about it. About him.

So you haven't gone back to visit him?

Not since Abby and I went in. . .February, I think? It was just. . .awkward. He didn't look happy, but he didn't look sad. It wasn't like the movies.

The movies?

You know, when people visit their family member in jail and something dramatic *always* happens. We just sat and looked at each other. There was nothing to say. Can I show you something, though?

Sure.

Promise not to tell my parents?

Depends what it is.

Despite her conditional promise, I stand up and lift the bottom edge of my t-shirt, revealing my hip. I pull the top hem of my tights down and stand, letting Selene look.

A tattoo! Selene exclaims, peering closer. 'Like waves relying on beach I'll be waiting for you.' Tattoos can be very significant outward expressions of one's soul. What does this mean, to you?

It's about Sullivan. About him getting out of juvy.

That's a very thoughtful tattoo. Do you miss him?

Yes.

Does Abby miss him?

I don't know.

Do you and Abby ever talk about how you feel?

Only when we were coming to you together. My family is kind of like a plant when they're talking to you. It sounds cheesy, but they're like one of those plants that blooms for a little while and then closes again.

I see. Raizel, I want you to do something for me.

Sure.

I want you to spend some time with Abby, just you two. I think you will be pleasantly surprised by your support for each other.

I see. Um. I guess I could do that. I just don't think we have much in common.

Remember, I have spent hours with your sister. I think I know her, a little. Selene bats her dark lashes. Try, for me?

I melt.

Okay.

Now, onto other topics. What have you been doing for *you?*

For *me?* What do you mean?

Well, what are you interested in?

I'm. . . I glanced out the window. I used to be interested in hair-design. *Really* interested. And writing poetry. And listening to music.

Have you been engaging in these things?

Not really.

Not really?

Not at all.

Then I need you to do one more thing for me.

Okay.

Close your eyes--in a figurative sense, of course--that is, stop thinking so much about everyone around you. Try to do what's best for yourself. Learn about hair. Write your poetry. Write about anything. When you expel sad thoughts, you will be able to move on. Listen to the music that inspires you. *Make* music, if that's what helps. I want this girl, inside of here, Selene reaches out and sweeps my long bangs aside, tapping my temple. I want her to be happy.

Hotness comes up my neck and invades my face. I nod, the numbness I've carried since December lifting from within me.

And one more thing.

One more thing? I think. *What more could she want an 'overview' on?*

Promise me you won't hurt yourself again. I'm not talking about tattoos. She looks me up and down, slowly choosing her words. Please don't hurt my dear friend.

I glance down at myself, my cardigan and my tights and denim miniskirt. When I look back up, wetness hits the corners of my eyes.

Selene smiles and reaches toward me, an apple-scented tissue dangling from her fingers.

Counseling with Selene ends shortly after our overview session. I miss her, but I enjoy Saturdays immensely. I start going to concerts on weekends, even to bands I've never heard of. A few times, I drive to an Albertan city called Bowville to see more well-known bands, like Tegan and Sara. I don't tell my parents I'm taking the 'junky old Camaro' out of town. I've grown so fond of my ridiculous orange car that I don't believe it'll ever fail me on the highway--especially since the warmth of spring is well on its way. I hope with all my might that Ani Difranco will have a show in Bowville.

At shows, I hate that I have to stand outside the beer gardens and watch the partying from the outside--I haven't had a beer in so long. Instead, I squeeze in near the front of the crowd and let the music intoxicate me.

In March one of the employees at the pharmacy goes on maternity leave. The person hired to take her place is a tall boy with box-dyed black hair and a lot of jewelry. His name is Liam and I feel overly comforted by his paleness. We come out to each other within an hour of working together. My heart sings as he hands me a joint. The manager isn't around so we slink to the back of the store and light up.

Liam and I have some of the most interesting conversations I've ever had. He says he goes to St. Theresa's High School and they have a gay-straight alliance. I say I go to Duhill Collegiate and maybe I'll try to start something like that, before I graduate. He tells me when he came out to his parents they told him to pretend he's straight. I tell him I didn't have to come out to my family and that we all just kind of knew. He tells me about the college guy he's into and I tell him about Hana. Talking poorly about her feels great. When Liam and I are busy with customers, I thirst for more conversation with him.

Have you ever been to the gay bar in Sloam? Mars, I mean? Liam asks me one day while we're sitting at the back of the pharmacy. The store is dead and we're munching out on Doritos.

No. I lean my back against the wall and look down at my cell phone, which is actually my dad's old phone.

Never?

Well, I've stood outside of it, when I was waiting in line at Broken String Bar.

Oh, yeah? Down that alley?

Yeah. Isn't it weird how Mars is tucked into an alley? Like a shameful secret?

That's what it is--isn't it?

What?! I swat his skinny arm. I'm proud to be gay.

Sure you are. But sexuality is meant to be one thing, and when it's not that one thing, it's pushed under the rug. Or back into the closet. Or in an alley.

Don't you think the world is coming around?

Of course. Liam shrugs and his bangs fall over his eyes. But when Mars first opened in the eighties, and by the way, at the time it wasn't called Mars, it was strategically placed in an abandoned theater, where straight people didn't have to notice it.

What was it called before?

Freedom Bar. Liam looks up at the pharmacy's blaring fluorescent lights as though they're the past.

Oh, right. I nod. I remember reading that on the sign.

Do you have any idea *why* the name changed?

Nope. I shake my head and crumple the empty chip bag.

The original owner was a gay man named Kelly Hansel. A *very* gay man. He opened the bar because he knew what it was like to want to meet others like...well, like us. He called it 'Freedom Bar' because he wanted to make a place where anyone could come and be accepted for who they were. I read all of this online, the articles and stuff.

The bar was a big hit and attracted all kinds of people. A lot of gay men they interviewed at the time, anonymously of course, said they never felt more accepted than at Freedom Bar.

But something *horrible* happened one night. A crowd of men came into the bar, which is what happened every night, but no one realized they were an anti-gay organization until they were protesting with signs and calling everyone in the bar 'queer' and 'wrong' and 'blasphemous'. When people refused to leave, some of the members of the anti-gay group cornered Kelly Hansel and forced him outside with them to their car. No one saw him after that.

I'm stunned. I've just finished a fat joint and my lips are salty from the Doritos. I don't know if I should believe Liam, but he always seems to know a lot.

Anyway, Liam continues. This feminist gay woman, Ilene Warner, reopened the bar as 'Mars' in the nineties. She paid tribute to Freedom Bar on the sign outside and got a front door that only unlocks when you press a buzzer from the inside, like in an apartment building. And she hired big bouncers to watch out for hate crimes and stuff. Oh, there's a customer. You want me to get it?

Would you?

Liam gets up and I pick blazing orange crumbs from the Doritos off my fingers. I've heard of hate crimes and homophobia, but I didn't think those things happened in gay bars. That's gay *territory.* It could be my territory, too. I shiver.

When Liam returns I ask if we can go to Mars sometime. He says he went there with his last boyfriend, and he wants to go again, but doesn't have any legal friends. I tell him I'm definitely not of age, yet. He says he has a fake ID and asks if I know someone whose driver's license I can use to get in. I say no and then I jump from my milk crate and shout that I have an older sister with hair just slightly less blond than my own. Liam asks if he can touch my hair while I call Abby with my semi-new cell phone and ask to borrow her ID for a very important reason. She's so surprised to hear from me that she agrees warmly and offers to lend me the shirt she wore in the picture. When I hang up, my hair is utterly tousled from Liam's man-hand. He tells me he has never touched a girl's hair before and that it felt better than petting a kitten. I am warm inside my chest.

83

I was body-broken, not heartbroken. I used to read fortune cookies when I didn't know what to do.

I returned to my mother's home and fell asleep with my head and all of my limbs under the covers. I lay that way for days. I awoke at odd hours--four in the morning or two p.m.--to cry in a fetal position, my mouth coughing and my chest heaving like a bomb had gone off and my own family had blown up. I cried like a baby who'd been left in his crib for too many hours. I cried like a man with a gun in his mouth.

On more than several occasions, I popped a few Gravol just so I could fall back asleep and not have to think. I had weird dreams, but mostly, I didn't think.

On August 20th, my mother and I moved from a crumbling duplex at 11 Oakwood Terrace to a modern house at 592 Anchor Road. I retreated to my new second-floor room without paying heed to anything. I didn't eat what my mother left in a bowl outside my new bedroom door, one with no dents in its bright brown wood. I stopped trying to hear her words, instead letting their tone surround me and float out my open window. Something about the walls being bone-white. Something about the sky-light in the kitchen. Nothing about getting my girlfriend back.

I was only eighteen and I knew I'd never love again.

If I still had Tiff, even she probably wouldn't have known what to do with me. She'd sit beside my bed and pull at the covers and say whatever came to her mind.

Life goes on.
Let's go get coffee.
It's not the end of the world.
Let's go to the library.
Maybe you should stick with boys.
Just kidding!
Let's leave your house.
Come on, Venice.
Let's leave your room.
You'll find someone else.
Are you even listening to me?

And I wouldn't reply.

Two days and thirty-three minutes and one half of a Starbucks' blueberry muffin later, I stopped crying. I looked in the mirror at the sallow girl with eyes pepper-red at the corners. I poked at my swollen cheeks like answers would pop out.

I couldn't listen to music, because it reminded me of her--even Alexisonfire, who we'd never listened to together, but who I'd probably had in my Discman the day we'd met.

Everything came back to her. My clothing. My posters, rolled up and piled in one of my new bedroom's corners. My own mouth.

The sun outside my window.

I turned the radio on to get away from our old tunes; I craved something new. I'd never been one for the radio, even at Team Bean, even on the bus. Ever since I'd taken an interest in music in the seventh grade, I'd listened to 'teenage angst crap', as Dana had referred to it when I put a CD on too loudly. He didn't know that I had found in his music folder on the computer some of my exact same *favorite* bands.

I'd found his porn too, when I was fifteen. Cum fuck cocktails. Squirting girls titty bitch. The kind of videos I'd later claim were 'sooo fake' while blushing about the curious moisture south of my belt.

I was lying there, with the radio on, when I almost starting tapping my limp hand against the side of my wooden bed frame. Some stupid song was on--one about boys and girls and partying all night with some fabricated DJ. Amara would love it. I reached over and turned the circular dial until static fuzz cleared out. A woman sang with a long, lilting voice, bird-like.

The tune caught me off guard, so familiar that I hoisted myself on my elbows and stared at the speakers of my little, old CD player.

Meet me again…

This woman was covering The Silly Rainbows' best tune. She had stripped the song down slow and cool, jazz-like. I let my heart soar through the whole two minutes remaining of the track, gripping my bed-sheets so hard my knuckles ached afterwards. When the song was over a radio announcer came on.

Alright, that was 'Meet Me Again', an original by Midge Selleck. I'm Shaun Burns, this is seventy-point-two FM and you're listening to the Oldies.

I fell back on my bed, deflated, the side of my face against the pillow, which had begun to smell like scalp. Heartbroken scalp.

For moments I'd been like a bleak, gray sky after a rainstorm. When that song stopped, my blood followed suit. Fucking Midge Selleck. The black clouds reappeared and broke, stinging the raw, pink skin around my eyes. I cried not for what I'd lost, but what I'd probably never had.

84

After I meet Liam, the gay boy at the pharmacy, school gossip barely registers in my ears. I'm able to walk with my head held high even when I see Hana and Meili, the Chinese girl from International Club, holding hands near the water fountain. I conclude I will never be able to start a gay-straight alliance club at the school my ex first-love and her new girlfriend attend. They probably drink sake-bombs between classes.

When I'm not working, I go straight home after school and study for a bit. Then I practice cutting my remaining Barbie dolls' hair. I have the pixie cut down pat.

Liam drives over one evening and I introduce him to my parents. They're happy I have a finally have a new friend. Liam sits at an old vanity table outside my basement bedroom and I stand behind him with a pair of scissors. Abby is doing her homework in front of the basement television, but she keeps looking at us, probably trying to figure out our relationship. She sits on the back of the couch and watches me snip Liam's bangs, which have been bugging the hell out of me.

Can you do mine? My older sister asks quietly, hands folded in front of her.

Seriously? I pause with my scissors mid-air. Your bangs?

Yeah. Abby lifts her locks off their place on her shoulder. And maybe my split-ends? Unless you're busy--

Surethatwouldbefun, I breathe toward her.

Hold on a sec. Abby turns and runs up the stairs.

You should decorate the frame of this mirror, Liam suggests.

Good idea. I snip a lock of his hair, blacker than my Camaro's tires.

You can have this. Abby says when she returns, breathing heavily from her jaunt. She thrusts a white shirt toward me.

Really? I smile and open the t-shirt, the front of which bears a picture of black scissors. This'll come down to my knees.

You can wear it as a dress or something. Make it your hair-doing shirt.

Thanks. I smile again and wave Liam out of the chair, making room for my big sister.

Liam and I go to Mars for the first time in May, when all of the snow has melted. I still wear tights every day because I still have scars on my upper right thigh, no matter how faint they've become. For Mars, I specifically pick out black tights with tiny rainbows all over them. Liam brushes his black hair and we parked in the parking lot near the alley. My dinner flips around inside my stomach.

Hey, Liam? I ask as we walk down the alley toward the door. I heard music through the brick walls.

Yeah?

If I don't meet a girl before June, will you be my grad escort?

Um, hellooo. Totally. And you'll be mine?

Of course.

We walk to the door and the big bouncer smiles and glances at our ID. A buzzer sounds and we pull open the door. So far, everything Liam has told me about the bar is true. We go inside and are immediately swept into a line of people waiting to get drinks. I lick my lips at the prospect of finally letting loose with a little alcohol. Liam buys the first round of slushy cocktails and he leads me up the stairs and through a hallway of glowing words to a dark, magical room. The ceiling is covered in stars. The dance floor is covered with people. The air is covered with pounding music.

We dance and gulp our drinks quickly, handing them to a shirtless male server. In the dark, I catch Liam blushing. Too lazy to go to the first floor, I buy a round of coolers from the beer tub in the starry room. As we dance, I try to inconspicuously scope the crowd for a hot girl who will sweep me off my feet.

Suddenly the DJ interrupts her set to make an announcement, and a spotlight illuminates a dancing cage to the right of her stage. A tall black girl in a ballerina outfit twirls inside the cage and smiles at the crowd. Her legs are so long, they go on forever in the dark. I move forward to watch the girl as closely as possible. The skin on her angles catches the light. I take the last sip of my cooler and set the bottle on the floor near the stage.

Minutes later, when the girl comes down I rush to follow her down the stairs. Liam nods at me, his arms around another shirtless boy. The girl slips behind the bar on the first floor and pours beer into a water bottle, ignoring the crowd demanding her to pour them drinks. I want to tell them she's better than that, she's a dancer upstairs. When she comes out from behind the bar she moves toward the bottom of the staircase and leans against a wall. When I stand beside her, I realize she's a full foot taller than me.

Hi! I call up at the girl. I move onto the bottom step of the staircase so we nearly see eye-to-eye.

Hi. The girl smiles. Her teeth are very white and her black girl hair is very big. She sips her beer-in-a-water-bottle.

You're a very good dancer! I tell her, stretching my voice over the music.

Thanks, sweetie. What's your name?

I'm Raizel. You?

I'm Amara. Nice to meet you!

I'm startled by her friendly attitude toward regular old me. She is, quite possibly, the hottest girl I have ever talked to, including Selene the counselor and Abby's old friend Kristy. I'm so tipsy that I barely blush when Amara catches my eyes traveling down her body and up again. She laughs and says I'm cute.

Liam and I have a lot of shifts together at the pharmacy, because we're the only ones willing to work during the evening and on the weekend. We gossip about Saturday nights at Mars and all of the cute guys he's met. I've hung out with Amara three times at Mars and we've already utilized what she refers to as 'the make-out couch' at the bottom of the stairs. We've only kissed, but I touched her bare thigh once. Her skin is softer than Hana's, and smells like coconut body lotion. I wonder if I will ever stop comparing girls to Hana.

My graduation ceremony is on June sixteenth, a week before Sullivan's scheduled release from Baits. I haven't gone back to visit him, but he's called a few times. We never have anything to tell each other.

Abby offers to take me shopping for grad stuff. We have never gone shopping together like a pair of normal sisters. *Two* shop assistants in a row ask if we are twins. I catch a boy at Cheap Shoes, where I buy a pair of knockoff fire-engine red Doc Marten boots, blushing at Abby. For the first time in my life, I think she might be pretty. She smiles and doesn't say anything about my non-grad purchase. I have saved up so much money from the pharmacy that I don't care what I spent today--today is the day I honor my promise to Selene and spend some time with my sister.

When I have new tights and my shiny blue gown and my strappy black heels and a shimmery clip for my hair, I announce that I'm all set for grad.

But what are you going to wear *under* all that? Abby counteracts, eyes wide.

A bra and underwear? I dunno.

No special plans? Like in that American Pie movie?

But I already lost my virginity. I feel my cheeks get warm.

So? You can still make it a special night. I know *I* did.

Really? On your grad night? Who were you dating?

Well. We weren't *dating,* but Mike was my date.

Mike? Like, Mike Barthem? I crack up laughing. *Ewww.*

Hey! Abby slaps my arm, laughing back. At least I wasn't with *Hana.*

Yeah... I feel my smile fade.

Oh, sorry. Is the wound too fresh?

All at once, the smiles come flipping onto my face.

She *was* a dud, wasn't she?

We go into a lingerie store and get change rooms beside each other, trying on a billion bras each. We say we're shopping for grad night and the shop assistants leave us alone, nostalgic smiles crossing their faces. Over my tights, I put on the tightest black corset I can find and invite Abby over.

What do you think?

Abby slinks through the pink fitting room drapes and stands beside me in the full-length mirror. We're wearing the exact same thing.

Oh my god! I giggle.

Samesies! Abby exclaims in a singsong voice. We look hot.

Yeah, but... I point at the tag hanging off the back of her corset. They're, like, a hundred bucks each.

So? Abby raises her eyebrow. I have an idea.

I watch her switch the tags between my corset and a sports bra, puncturing the tags with her fingernail. She uses her fingertip to smooth over the old holes so they're barely noticeable. Now my corset is only thirteen dollars. In the mirror, I grin at the girl by whom I have been pleasantly surprised--though I'm not sure how I feel about her morals.

85

Liam's barely disappointed by my un-invitation to my grad ceremony, as he has a new boyfriend named Scotty. Amara, who I've found out lives in an apartment building down the street from my house, shows up on the morning of my grad with a bouquet of roses. I laugh at the startled expression on my parents' faces when Amara sets the flowers on the kitchen table and reveals herself. She has on a tight, ribbed blue dress a few shades lighter than mine; her torso is so long that the material only reaches a few inches down her thighs. She has on shimmering makeup and has sprayed her tight curls with a honey-like fragrance.

The grad ceremony is in the afternoon. In the evening, Amara and my parents and I head to an auditorium on Broadway for the dinner. Another family of four is seated at our circular table, but I don't know the boy very well. I'm overly relieved that he was never one of Sullivan's customers, nor an avid partygoer.

My parents strike up a conversation with the boy's parents. Amara and I chat quietly about other girls' dresses and which boys we think will come out of the closet in five years. She says the boy at our table is definitely flaming. His escort, a girl I've never seen before, blushes when she hears this, and her eyes flick around behind thick glasses. I feel bad, but I shouldn't apologize for things someone else says.

I spot Hana and her parents at a table across the room, alongside the family of another International Club student. I squint and hold my breath until I realize the other family isn't Meili's, but that of a Japanese boy whom everyone calls Honda. Hana's back is to me, but she's definitely wearing the same vest she wore at the winter formal.

After dinner, people start clearing away the tables and chairs to create a dance floor. Amara and I head to the bathroom, which is absolutely teeming with bras and hairspray and tubes of mascara. When girls see me standing with Amara, they don't say the snotty things I've imagined they will. Their eyes just flick up, up, up at Amara's perfect complexion and heiress-like movements. We take our place in a long line of gowns and sparkly high heels.

When a stall becomes free, Amara follows me in. I smirk at the thoughts surely going through other girls' heads. Amara helps me hold up the skirt of my gown while I pull my panties down and sit on the can, laughing.

I wish we had some beer, I whisper up at Amara.

I know, she whispers back. She's nice, looking at my face instead of between my legs. I could get us some.

How? Are you old enough?

I'm twenty-three.

What?! Cool. So you really *can* get us some…

Or we could do something better, Amara suggests. She starts digging through her purse. Girls outside the stall whine about their bra straps showing.

I pull up my tights and underwear and stand up, flushing quickly. I wait while she withdraws from her bag a tiny satchel. Her dark fingers force the drawstring open and she reaches in for two thick orange pills with dollar signs stamped on top. The blood leaves my veins in half a second.

Is that...E?

Yeah. You want some?

What have you been doing for you? Selene's words fall all around me, in the toilet and on the straps of my dress and down to the bathroom linoleum. *Close your eyes--in a figurative sense, of course--that is, stop thinking so much about everyone around you.*

Yes, I say. I want some.

Later in the evening when families of students are filtering out of the building, Amara and I say goodbye to my parents and rush back to the dance floor. The music is worse than wedding reception dance music, the DJ insisting on numbers like *The Macarena.* Regardless, the E soars through my limbs and has me dancing like a madman. Boys keep asking Amara to dance, and their grad escorts keep getting mad, and Amara keeps her eyes on me. She holds me tightly around the waist. We put our forearms together and laugh about the difference in our skin tones. I assume no one's calling us dykes because they don't want to ruin their chances to get with us. I feel as though *nothing* could ruin my evening.

We're dancing near the DJ's speakers when I feel a hand brush my lower back. My spine stiffens and I turn to look through the dark.

Hi. Hana's eyes flit over my face. Are you okay?

Huh? Yeah. I step back, forcing her hand to fall off my back. Where's your *girlfriend?*

There. Hana points at a row of chairs near the wall. Meili has stretched her body across three, eyes closed with her hands under her cheek. Honda's beside her, playing with his cell phone.

I laugh.

Amara scans the sea of heads, ignoring Hana's intrusion on our dance.

You are happy? Hana whispers in my ear. She slits her dark almond eyes at Amara.

For a moment, I desperately want her back. I want the girl who giggles over math assignments and makes me writhe with pleasure. I *don't* want the girl who beats up beautiful strangers and stands in front of me like a weapon. I don't want the girl who follows me to popularity and leaves me in her dust.

Who's to say? I ask, a loopy grin all over my face. What *is* happy?

She doesn't understand.

I take Amara's hand. We swim through the crowd and escape from the building, laughing.

Amara and I go back to her place and I make her wait in the living room while I put on my illegally marked-down undergarments. When I look in the mirror I can't believe how beautiful I seem, my white hair glowing in the bathroom light. The corset encases my tight torso, pulls my chest up and makes me look like I actually have breasts.

I bustle out of the bathroom and stand before Amara in her living room, hands on my hips. The ecstasy is still jostling around under my skin. Amara clenches her jaw and jumps from the couch, pulling me toward her. We land on the rough carpet in a pile of long limbs and hastily-fastened lingerie. This is the weirdest thing I've ever done. I can't stop kissing her dark skin, so different from mine. We moved together on the rug for over an hour, hands tugging and finding and frantically groping.

Afterwards, Amara has a cigarette out the living room window. She says she only smokes when she's high. I ask how often she does E and she says this is her first time. It was her grad present to me, but if I like it, we can do it again sometime. I say I don't know if I like it.

I love it.

Throughout everything--the dance, the arousing ride home in the backseat of a cab, the rough carpet sex, I've had a prevailing thought--*How can one teeny tiny little orange pill with a dollar sign on it make me feel this way?* I feel like I'm on a dancing on a cloud in a Mario game. This is the feeling I've been looking for my whole life, utter satisfaction. This is the feeling I needed when I was standing on the roof of this *very same apartment building.* I'm suddenly in the shoes of all of the kids who ever gave my brother business. They didn't want their perfect worlds, like the one I'm in, to come crashing down. When I think of how the drug won't last forever, I shudder.

On the twenty-second of June, Sullivan is released from Baits, his future to be determined on a court date set in July. I bite my fingernails the whole ride to pick him up, and my dad changes the radio channel halfway through every song. He finally chooses the fuzzy one, pure static roaming the car. My mother is flipping through a magazine and Abby is beside me in the backseat, gazing out the window.

As we pull up to the curb outside of Baits, I watch a boy with a backpack through the tinted window of my parents' van. His yellow-blond hair is knotted into dreads and he's thin, arms hanging slack out the sleeves of his t-shirt. He turns and swaggers toward the car like this is a regular occurrence. The skin under his eyes is the color of eggplants.

Hi. Sullivan opens the back door of the van. He throws his backpack on the floor and crawls onto the seat.

Hi, Abby responds.

My parents are quiet.

I am suddenly the angriest I've ever felt in my life. He is as skeletal as those kids the night of the winter formal, the ones everyone called 'e-tarded', the ones who told the principal to fuck off. *I want to make some extra cash. I'm going to stop after I have enough for a laptop.* Red spasms come up the skin on my face.

Steam shoots from my ears. I clench my fist and put it under my thigh. I close my eyes and put my face near the air-conditioning vent.

Hi, I squeak out at my little brother, who I'm not sure anymore is really my little brother.

We go home and spend the night avoiding looking at each other, retreating to separate rooms of the house. My parents try talking to Sullivan about his experience at Baits and he leaves the house. When he comes back at five a.m., I am the one to wake up. The front entrance is over my bedroom. I hear him stomp around and laugh. I understand, but I don't. My parents quickly realize my brother is using. One look at his scabby complexion and gangly arms and saucer pupils, and anyone would know.

We all get in the van and take a quiet ride to a building in Elmview, sort-of near the edge of Sloam. Stable Shoulders Drug Rehabilitation Center for Youth, the sign reads. Sullivan's asleep next to me, Abby on my other side. My father opens the van's back door and nudges my brother's skinny knee and soon they are trudging up the facility's gray walkway. I squeeze my eyes closed and wish it was winter so I could wear earmuffs and silence my mother's soft gasps for air. She stays in the car and re-uses a crumpled tissue from her purse.

I pick up extra shifts at the pharmacy because I can't deal with the gaping black hole everyone's dodging at home. Even Selene couldn't give us proper directions. Abby comes down to my bedroom and doesn't ask to come in. She just sits on the bed and reads. I know she's afraid of the destroyed world above us.

Liam and I continue going to Mars, and soon Abby gets curious. She states clearly that she's not gay but she loves gay people. Liam and I, in reference to one of our most political conversations, agree that generalizing all gay people is similar to racism. Abby doesn't give a shit what we think. She buys us a case of pre-drink beer, puts on a rainbow wristband, and we all show up at Mars with our limbs loose. Because I've been using my sister's ID, Amara, who is working, opens the bar's back door and sneaks Abby in.

When Amara offers us E one night, Abby says she has never done anything but drink and that she wouldn't mind letting her hair down a little. I laugh because she has always been the studious one in the family. I follow in her footsteps and accept one of the pills, which are blue tonight.

After that night, the four of us are inseparable. Abby has the summer off from college, Liam and I have just graduated, and Amara has no apparent direction in life. She and I make out most nights and sneak into bathroom stalls together. We go home together a lot, too, to her apartment. When I'm on E, which I've taken to calling 'daisy' as extremely passive-aggressive revenge on Sullivan, I favor lying in Amara's king-sized bed with her colorful disco ball flashing around my head.

The weird thing about Amara's apartment is that she keeps the heat on full blast at all times, even in the summer. I usually end up so sweaty in my tights that I nearly take them off, but I can't. I'm not ready for the glances and the questions. One time, when I ask Amara to turn the heat down, she jokes that her landlord pays for it, so why not make him? I insist that I'm hot and she snaps that she's fucking cold. One look at her nearly-transparent limbs, and I surrender.

Amara has a beautiful face, something that constantly captures peoples' eyes when we're out. I'm not very attracted to her body. She has no girth. I'm afraid that her apartment heat is turned up so high because her body can't generate its own warmth. When we lie in bed together I'm always the big spoon. I wrap my short arms all the way around her waist.

But sex with her is interesting, and happens every time we're intoxicated. We have sex in the shower and on the bathroom floor. We do it in the kitchen and on the living room sofas and even on the mat by the front door, when we can't make it far into the apartment without exploding out of our clothing. The way she wants me, and the *amount,* is what drives me toward her.

When my anger toward Sullivan fades a little, I ask my parents if I can go visit him at Stable Shoulders. My mother openly explains that they're afraid he'll get back into his old ways and he'll drag me down with him, because they know we like partying together. Instilling extra sarcasm in my voice, I ask how they know so much about their children.

Before long, Sullivan appears at Mars. He says he only lasted one day at rehab, and laughs. I'm so shocked to see him that I don't say anything. He knows that people who aren't even gay flock to Mars because of the good DJs. People just want to have a good time. He offers me a dip in his stash. When he talks, his eyelids flutter and his tongue gets caught between his teeth. I turn away from him and keep my head down and get lost in the crowd, my own brain fuzzy with someone else's chemicals.

When Liam, Amara, and I go to Bowville in Liam's car, Amara strikes up a conversation about cocaine and how she's going to try scoring some for the evening. Liam says he has tried coke and it's not really his thing.

It's like daisy, he says, glancing away from the highway. But it only lasts, like, twenty minutes.

That's the good thing, Amara urges. You can do just a little and keep the bag in the pocket for when the effects wear off.

I don't get the purpose. I shrug. Why not just do daisy?

Here. Amara reaches into her knockoff Chanel purse. She pulls out a baggie packed tightly with a flour-like substance.

Are you serious? I frown. You've had that in your bag the whole time?

And...? Amara plucks a CD case off Liam's car floor. I don't see you supplying substance on this little trip.

'Supplying'? I cry out. You just lied and said you wanted to score some. You're crazy.

Amara moves so she's hidden behind my passenger seat. I twist around and watch her put a straw in her nose. She inhales the jagged line on the CD case, her hand shaking. She slams back against the seat with her eyes closed, a flaccid smile taking over her mouth and her white-rimmed nostril.

The summer goes by with dozens of road-trips to Bowville. Amara always takes to the backseat with a baggie of coke and the nearest CD case. We stop having sex, the fire beneath her skin smothered with powder. She still hangs off my arm and calls me her girlfriend, and I like the looks of longing other people give her. I like having something other people want.

Weekend nights when Amara's working, Liam and Abby and I either go to Mars or Bowville or to house parties. These wild house parties start happening at a house on Broadway, where they charge entrance fees and sells drinks and provide entertainment. Morgan's an aspiring DJ and I sometimes wonder what it would be like to lie in her arms at night. Then I remember the mess that is Amara and how much she needs the rock that is my shoulder.

86

Let's go to the bay.

My mother made the over-cheery suggestion two weeks after we'd moved into the new place.

But I'm unpacking. I lay on my bed amid piles of clothing, unopened cardboard boxes denting the plush carpet around me. I'd been paralyzed for thirty days, my bones becoming part of the mattress. The ceiling was whiter than any ceiling I'd ever lain under.

Just come with me. Fresh air will do you good.

Minutes later I was at the front door in my dusty old Converse shoes, hands shoved in my jean pockets while I waited for my mother. I hadn't stood up in so long that I felt queasy and had to lean on the doorframe. In my right pocket, I felt something small and hard, like cardboard. I pulled out a business card.

Eliza Bukawitz
Property Owning and Leasing
(phone) 301-4029
E-mail: eliza_bukz83@gatewaymail.com

In the top right corner was a centimeter-by-centimeter picture of a woman with short, curly hair and a smile to save the world. Or maybe she was a rotten person with a ten-minute urge of generosity. I wonder if she missed her beige old-lady shoes.

My mother appeared on the stairs with a coffee can tucked under her arm--her own mother's ashes. I'd brought something of my own, hanging against my body in my backpack.

She didn't say anything, just slipped into her flats. We walked down Anchor Road. Every front yard had a camper and every backyard had a tree-house. I wondered what it was like growing up where there were no bushes to party in, though I knew kids would party wherever they could. They probably got fucked up in those campers and tree-houses without their parents ever knowing, or in the basement of the kid whose parents took long trips to resorts in South America.

I caught glimpse of a tree losing a leaf. September had just begun.

Flip flip flip.

In the moments before meeting Raizel, I'd been storming along downtown pavement, the beauty of autumn lost under my shoes. I'd rapidly grown to love the chill that made me walk faster to stay warm. When I closed my eyes and smelled fall, I gathered remnants of things that had once been. Fall was more romantic than St. Valentine himself.

Still, everything came back to her.

The leaf was scarlet and golden, sashaying before the seduction of gravity.

87

This morning I watched an episode of Ellen's talkshow. Watching her doesn't remind me of my bad years or my self-hating tendencies. She reminds me of hoping for something. For *someone*. Ellen Degeneres inspires me to love. The next time I see Sullivan, I'm going to tell him I love him. I haven't seen him since June, and he hasn't apologized, but I've forgiven him.

My shift at the pharmacy has just begun. I'm stocking shelves and Liam's at the counter, picking stuff out from under his black nails. I love Liam. Liam makes me love my job. I'm stomping around in my blazing red fake Doc Marten boots because a leaf is stuck to the bottom of each one. I only walked five meters from my car to the pharmacy, but leaves are everywhere these days. I should write a poem about the prominence of fall.

I turned eighteen in the summer, after we got home from Johnson Lake. After I broke up with Amara. So, now that I can legally accept lottery winnings, I'm considering buying a ticket. I don't like thinking about winning enough money for hair school and everything else I've ever needed because when I snap back to reality and fluorescent pharmacy lights I feel almost as depressed as I did in high school. But I *have* saved a good chunk of money from the pharmacy. I have enough for a plane ticket to somewhere cool. Whisper-thinking is what I do when I'm afraid of something too good. I whisper-think about big cities like Montreal and Toronto and New York.

The pharmacy door opens and a gust of cool air comes in and moves the bottom hem of my skirt. I don't mind. My calves are getting sweaty. I bend over and pick up an armful of pill bottles from a plastic shopping basket on the floor. I'm almost done placing them on the shelf when I hear the soft squeak of a sneaker.

I look to my left and see a girl studying a box of medicine. She's oblivious to me, intent on reading anti-nausea pill instructions. I watch her shining brown and the slightly upward curve of her nose. Her tan has lasted since summer, somehow. I like how she stands with her hand on the hip.

Suddenly, I realize who she is--the last time I saw her, she was crying. She was holding her arm and being escorted away from a baseball diamond by her coach. She's as gorgeous now as she was then. Her jeans are baggy and she has on stupid shoes, but I don't think she cares. I have never felt so drawn toward a stranger. I should only regard her in the quietest of whisper-thinks, but I *have* to talk to her.

I hop over my basket of pills and land with a thud beside the girl. Her eyes move up, wide transparent thunder-cloud-colored orbs twinkling before me. I point at her hand, in which she holds a box of Gravol. I blurt out the first thing that comes to mind.

Did you know you can get high off those?

88

My mother and I traipsed down the squat, hilly road to the water's edge, stopping at the walkway running alongside the bay.

I'm gonna go down that way. My mother held the coffee-can urn in one hand, using her other to point down the path. The wind moved the straight ends of her hair. Do you wanna come?

Um. I glanced at the coffee can. I'd never known my grandmother. That's alright. I'll stay here.

Okay. She patted my shoulder before turning to go.

After my mother had confessed to Dana and I, I'd realized she hadn't just been keeping the urn of ashes because she wasn't ready to let go--she was waiting until she was ready to forgive her mother for judgment and for protecting her too closely. As I watched her move away down the path, I got the eerie sense that a grand moment of forgiveness hadn't come for her alone.

I slipped out of my shoes and socks and moseyed over the railing, lowering myself onto the flat boulder I'd met only once before. I extracted from my backpack a small, smooth box decorated with koi fish and cherry blossoms and half of a Bob Marley sticker, the other half of which had peeled off. When I closed my eyes my white-blond gypsy unicorn angel was nearby, smelling of lilacs and sounding like cinnamon.

I reopened my eyes. My hand lingered on the spot beside me, empty stone. I turned my hand over and gazed at my purple-brown piece-of-shit wrist tattoo.

I was near the boulder's hard edge. I could fall in the water and people would think it had been an accident. My mother, with her back to me, became smaller. By the time someone had unlocked the keypad of their iPhone to call for an ambulance, I'd have sunk, my bare toes unknowingly dancing in the mud at the bottom of the bay.

I knew what being a sort-of good person felt like.

I knew how being a horrible person felt.

I inched my butt toward the edge. My legs swayed along the rounded front of the boulder, a foot above the sloshing waves. I held my arm out and opened my fist, letting the empty pill box drop in the water, preceding my fall. I knew what baby dolphins felt the first time they hopped the divide between sea and sky, hot sunshine skimming their backs. I knew how they felt the first time they dove nose-first back into a freezing sheath of water. That feeling was love, coming and going.

Dolphins jumped again and again.

I turned around and grasped the white railing, sliding my body back across the massive rock. My stomach growled. Maybe I'd ask my mother for some saltines and tomato soup with a slice of cheese at the bottom.

My shoes were waiting for me where I'd left them.